07|20

Please return/renew this item by the last
date shown. Books may also be renewed
by phone or internet.

www3.rbwm.gov.uk/libraries

☎ 01628 796969 (library hours)

☎ 0303 123 0035 (24 hours)

www.rbwm.gov.uk

Royal Borough
of Windsor &
Maidenhead

2005, and the Premio Grinzane Cavour from Italy in 2007. His
works have been translated into thirty-six languages, and he
was recently named by the London *Times* as one of the fifty best
authors to have been translated into English over the past fifty
years. He was a distinguished writer in residence and visiting
professor of literature at Bard College in 2017, and was most
recently a visiting professor at Dartmouth College in the spring
of 201

RUSSELL HARRIS is an editor at the Institute of Ismaili Studies, in London. He has previously translated works by Naguib Mahfouz and Alaa Al Aswany. His latest work, *A Journal of Three Months' Walk in Persia in 1884*, was published in 2017.

WILLIAM MAYNARD HUTCHINS, a professor of religious studies at Appalachian State University, was awarded National Endowment for the Arts grants for literary translation in 2005–2006 and 2011–2012. He was a co-winner of the 2013 Saif Ghobash Banipal Prize for Arabic translation and won the American Literary Translators Association National Translation Award in 2015. He is best known for translating *Palace Walk*, *Palace of Desire*, *Sugar Street*, and *Cairo Modern*, all by the Nobel Laureate Naguib Mahfouz. In addition to *Return of the Spirit*, Hutchins edited and translated *In the Tavern of Life*, a selection of short stories by Tawfiq al-Hakim, and a two-volume collection of al-Hakim's plays. His one critical study is *Tawfiq al-Hakim: A Reader's Guide*.

TAWFIQ AL-HAKIM

Return of the Spirit

Foreword by
ALAA AL ASWANY

Foreword Translated by
RUSSELL HARRIS

Translated with an Introduction and Notes by
WILLIAM MAYNARD HUTCHINS

PENGUIN BOOKS

PENGUIN BOOKS

An imprint of Penguin Random House LLC
penguinrandomhouse.com

This translation first published in the United States of America by
Lynne Rienner Publishers, Inc., 2012
Published in Penguin Books 2019

Foreword by Alaa Al Aswany translated into English by Russell Harris.

LIBRARY OF CONGRESS CATALOGING-IN-PUBLICATION DATA
Names: òHakâim, Tawfâiq, author. | Hutchins, William M., translator.
Title: Return of the spirit / Tawfiq Al-Hakim ; foreword by
Alaa Al Aswany ; foreword translated by Russell Harris; translated
with an introduction and notes by William Maynard Hutchins.
Other titles: °Awdat al-râuòh. English
Description: New York : Penguin Books, 2019. | Includes bibliographical references.
Identifiers: LCCN 2018060081 (print) | LCCN 2019005406 (ebook) |
ISBN 9780525505754 (ebook) | ISBN 9780143133971 (paperback)
Classification: LCC PJ7828.K52 (ebook) | LCC PJ7828.K52 A913
2019 (print) | DDC 892/.735—dc23
LC record available at https://lccn.loc.gov/2018060081

Printed in the United States of America
1 3 5 7 9 10 8 6 4 2

Set in Sabon LT Pro

Contents

Foreword

If you want to understand Egypt, you have to read this novel.

Tawfiq al-Hakim wrote *Return of the Spirit* in 1927 when he was studying in Paris, and the moment it was published in Cairo in 1933 it took its place as a classic of Arabic literature.

The author was more than just a talented novelist or playwright; he was one of the pioneers (such as Taha Hussein* and Muhammad Husayn Haykal†) who studied in Europe and then returned to Egypt and took it upon themselves to develop Arabic literature into something that could hold its own on the world literary stage. Tawfiq al-Hakim was born in Alexandria in 1898 and lived until he was eighty-nine, during which time he never stopped producing literary works and engaging in literary disputes over his oeuvre, defending the values of freedom and democracy to the very end. In his youth he suffered from the clash between his headstrong artistic tendencies and the stable professional life his aristocratic family wanted him to live.

His father was a judge and one of the great Egyptian landowners. His mother was a Turkish lady, proud of her origins, who considered herself a cut above Egyptians and who never allowed the little Tawfiq to play with the local peasant boys. When he was old enough, he was sent by his father to Cairo, where he lived with his uncles and went to the Mohammed Ali

---

* Taha Hussein (1889–1973) was an Egyptian author, literary critic, and university professor, and figurehead of Arabic literature.

† Muhammad Husayn Haykal (1888–1956) was an Egyptian author, poet, and politician.

Secondary School. This distance from the pressures of his immediate family gave him a golden opportunity to submerge himself in the artistic life of Cairo, and when the revolution of 1919 broke out, al-Hakim, along with his uncles, took part in it with the result that they were all arrested and thrown into prison for a few months. He was accepted at the College of Law, but his obsession with the arts did not diminish and he would skip lectures to attend musical and theatrical performances wherever they were taking place. A profession in the arts was considered beyond the pale at the time by refined members of society, and this led him to write his first works under a pseudonym. After al-Hakim received his degree from Cairo University, his father sent him to Paris to study for a doctorate in law at the Sorbonne. However, the spirit of the arts took hold of him in Paris and he neglected his law studies, throwing himself into the cultural life of the city and devoting his time to theater-going and studying the latest literary trends. It was three years until his father discovered that he had abandoned his studies and brought him back to Cairo, where he joined the judiciary. His work as an attorney to the public prosecutor provided him with rich human experience, which he drew upon for his brilliant book *Diary of a Country Prosecutor.* This was followed by a stream of novels and plays that made him, justifiably, such a great name in Arabic literature that the Egyptian writer Naguib Mahfouz, upon being awarded the Nobel Prize in Literature in 1988, stated: "If Tawfiq al-Hakim were alive, he would have won it!"

Al-Hakim's works for the stage played a role in establishing the "New Arabic Theater," and he created the "theater of the intellect," a term applied to theater as a literary form that incorporates the protagonists, plot, and dialogue into its dramatic elements. However, his stage works are not particularly performance-friendly, as they speak more to the educated literary reader than to the ordinary theater-goer. In this regard, al-Hakim himself stated: "Today I am attempting to establish the theater of the mind. I turn the actors into free-flying ideas clad in symbolism. That is why a gulf has opened up between me and the theatrical stage. I have not been able to find a conduit to make these works reach the people other than through the printing press."

At the same time, the works of al-Hakim generally incorporate many theatrical devices. He, like the great Russian writer Fyodor Dostoyevsky before him, proved that it is the artistic content that defines the shape of a work and not vice versa, and that the creative energy borne by the literary text is more important than any academic strictures, because life precedes theory, and art is a living work whose creation comes before any hypothetical categorization of its supposed genre.

Although *Return of the Spirit* brought al-Hakim literary glory, it caused him no end of trouble. Gamal Abdel Nasser, the second president of Egypt, was greatly impressed by the novel when he was young and considered it an inspiration for the revolution of July 23, 1952. We have much evidence pointing to the fact that Nasser was not a regular reader and that he preferred watching films (particularly American) to reading novels, and when he took power in Egypt, he ordered a projector and screen for his residence and used to watch at least one film a day. Moreover, in 1966 Field Marshal Abdel Hakim Amer (the deputy supreme commander) took a strong dislike to Naguib Mahfouz's novel *Chitchat on the Nile* due to its criticism of the Nasserite regime. Abdel Nasser had not read the book himself, but he asked his minister of culture, Tharwat Okasha, to read it and then accepted his opinion and authorized its publication.

Why did Nasser particularly like *Return of the Spirit*? I believe it was because of an opinion uttered by one of the protagonists (a French archaeologist), who stated that the Egyptian people were a storehouse of enormous cultural energy built up over long centuries and that they were just waiting for a leader to adore. At that point they would as one fall under the leadership of a strong man who would bring about their cultural renaissance. This idealized relationship between the people and their leader was the benchmark for Nasser during his years in power, and in practice he silenced all opposing voices and relied upon massive popular support to cement his rule over Egypt.

After reading *Return of the Spirit*, Nasser developed a great fondness for Tawfiq al-Hakim, awarding him the country's greatest honor and dedicating to him his own book, *The Philosophy of the Revolution*. For his part, Tawfiq al-Hakim liked Nasser on a personal level, but he never let himself become too close to him; he was perhaps the only Egyptian writer who offered his excuses when Nasser invited him to dinner. As al-Hakim wrote: "Any ruler wants loyal, not honest, opinions from his intellectuals. He wants to hear words of support, not opposition, but it is truth and freedom that constitute the essential message of an intellectual who might make mistakes, mislead or lose consciousness, but who will never consciously betray his message. I always worry that too close friendship or affection for someone, or even hatred or resentment, can stop one being able to see things as they really are."

The nature of Tawfiq al-Hakim's relationship with Nasser was paradoxical. He had an incontrovertible fondness for him and would never have questioned Nasser's devotion, but at the same time al-Hakim resented his heavy-handed methods of rule and his ruthlessness toward any opposition. He expressed criticism of the Nasserite regime in two plays: *The Confused Sultan*, in which the sultan cannot decide whether to wield the sword or the law, but ends up choosing the law; and *Anxiety Bank*, in which al-Hakim expresses the nervousness afflicting large segments of society as a consequence of oppressive military rule. When Nasser died in 1970, al-Hakim was greatly saddened and mourned him, but the writer's conscience soon came back to the fore and he published *The Return of Consciousness* in 1972. In this work he directs stinging and objective criticism at the dictatorship of Abdel Nasser, stating that the great leader had plundered the people's consciousness and that they had lost the ability to make decisions for themselves. He explained:

"[Abdel Nasser] somehow managed to cast a spell over all of us without our knowing it. Perhaps it was his so-called special magic, or perhaps it was the dream he had us living in with all those hopes and promises . . . not to mention that romantic image of the achievements of the Revolution which he had brought about for us—an image reinforced by a constant diet of films and songs in the state media. We thought we were living in a great industrialised nation, a leader of the developing world in agricultural development and production and the strongest fighting force in the Middle East. The face of the adored leader used to fill our television screens. He would peer down to us from temporary pavilions and conference centres. He used to tell us these tales for hours on end, going on about how we used to be and what we have now become—and no one could get ever a word in, correct a fact he stated or make a comment! All we could do was accept it as the truth then applaud until our hands were raw."

The book elicited a ferocious attack on al-Hakim by some close supporters of Abdel Nasser. However, the writer, who was by then over seventy, was in the habit not only of salving his conscience regardless of the consequences but also, despite his age, of making statements that aroused the ire of both the political and the religious authorities. In this vein, al-Hakim himself collected signatures from intellectuals to add support to a statement he issued announcing his solidarity with Egyptian university students demonstrating against the president, Anwar el-Sadat, and demanding democracy. This particularly irritated Sadat, who then described al-Hakim as "that old windbag." Shortly before his death, al-Hakim wrote a series of pieces for *Al-Ahram*, Egypt's largest newspaper, under the title "A Question from and to God," in which he imagined that he was conversing with God. This incensed the sheikhs and clergy, who launched vicious attacks on him, accusing him of insulting God. This had no effect on al-Hakim and he went on writing. He died in 1987. The question remains as to why *Return of the Spirit* gained such significance.

The Italian publisher Giangiacomo Feltrinelli stated, "I only know two types of novels—live or dead ones. My job is always to publish the live ones." *Return of the Spirit* is a live novel in the sense that it depicts the life of a middle-class Egyptian family in 1918, and not only do we follow the protagonists almost obsessively throughout the novel as they shout and scream but we also feel their every breath and whisper. In addition, as with all great novelists, al-Hakim is not judgmental. The novel is not populated by the standard good and evil characters of superficial melodrama; rather, al-Hakim presents his protagonists as people of flesh and blood who all have evil and virtue within them, who all experience moments of weakness that push them into evil or whose better sides see them defending human values.

Al-Hakim's expressive power turned the novel into a historical documentation of Egyptian society a hundred years ago. Since 1882, when Egypt fell under British occupation, Egyptians had never stopped fighting for independence, but resistance to the occupation did not all fall under one banner. Some people held that Egypt was an Ottoman principality and consequently their resistance was that of Muslims and not of Egyptians. They wanted to see the British leave so that Egypt could return to the fold of the Ottoman caliphate. On the other hand were Egyptian nationalists who were fighting not to replace the British with the Ottomans, but for the establishment of an independent democratic state for all its citizens regardless of religion. The 1919 revolution aimed to resolve the conflict in favor of a secular state, and for the first time demonstrators held up banners reading "Egypt for the Egyptians" and "May the Crescent live with the Cross."

After the revolution's victory, Egypt drafted the first constitution in her history in 1923, and notwithstanding the British occupation and attempts by the palace to seize power, from the 1919 revolution on, Egypt lived through a highly liberal period in all aspects of her culture—until the military coup of 1952. Since that time, Egypt has remained trapped between two fascist powers: the military fascism represented by army rule, and the religious fascism represented by the Muslim Brotherhood, who consider Islam not merely a religion but an ideal for a state, and they are fighting for the restoration of the Islamic caliphate.

This political Islam gained much strength with the rise in oil prices in the 1970s, with millions of dollars from governments and various groups in the Persian Gulf states being spent to spread the Wahhabi version of Islam all around the world. In addition, millions of Egyptians went off to work in the Gulf and then returned imbued with the Wahhabi outlook, which was so alien to the culture of Egypt. The extreme and aggressive Wahhabi form of Islam is the ideological root of terrorism; the Egyptian society described in the novel would perhaps be astonished by the new generations of Egyptians, as they now live in a completely different society.

In medicine, we can understand a disease only after we compare healthy body tissue with tissue that has been infected by the disease, and this novel offers an eloquent description of Egyptian society when it was healthy, before it became afflicted with the distortions brought about by military dictatorship and religious extremism. In the novel we read how Egyptian society was liberal and culturally diverse in the then-prevailing spirit of tolerance and coexistence. Al-Hakim does not focus on the religion of his protagonists, and we see that religion in society at that time was a completely personal issue and never in the foreground. When it is time for prayer, the only individual in the family who goes off to pray is Mabruk the servant. We see just how cosmopolitan Cairo was a hundred years ago, with places of entertainment everywhere and foreign dancers performing and mingling with the clients. That was how Egypt respected diversity, privacy, and the right of individual choice. There were bars and nightclubs along with mosques, churches, and synagogues, and each and every Egyptian could decide where to go, with society accepting whatever choice he might make. Over the centuries, this sophisticated notion of personal behavior has set Egypt apart from some other Arab countries, such as Saudi Arabia, where strict moral behavior is imposed on the population by the vice police. In the novel we read about a young middle-class man and woman who pass their talents on to each other, with him teaching her to sing and her teaching him to play the piano. Sixty years later we find the Wahhabis promoting the idea that singing, music, and acting are activities forbidden by Islam, and this attitude has struck a chord with many Egyptians. The religious tolerance we see in

the novel no longer exists in Egypt. In 1918 there was no con-
fessional violence of any sort, and Egyptians lived together in
harmony and respect whether they were Muslim, Coptic, Jewish, or even atheist. In the novel a dancer from a Jewish Egyptian family has to deal with a strange incident at her son's
wedding reception, but the writing is such that we do not feel
any derision or lack of respect for the Jewish religion.

Dear reader, you now have in your hands one of the greatest
works of twentieth-century Arabic literature, and I hope you
enjoy reading it.

ALAA AL ASWANY

Translator's Note

This translation has been thoroughly revised, with multiple changes on every page to improve its accuracy and flow. I have benefited from two decades of translation practice and especially from the line-by-line editing by Jacqueline Kennedy Onassis of each of the volumes of the Cairo Trilogy; from the 1986 publication of *A Dictionary of Egyptian Arabic: Arabic-English*, by Martin Hinds and El-Said Badawi; and from sections of the M.A. thesis by Amira Salah El-Deen Askar for the Department of English Language and Literature of the Faculty of Arts of Zagazig University: "Text Migration: A Study of William M. Hutchins' Translation into English of Tawfiq al-Hakim's *Awdat Ar-Ruh* as *Return of the Spirit*."

—W. M. H.

Introduction

Return of the Spirit is a gloriously Romantic tribute to the solidarity of the Egyptian people of all classes and religions and to their good taste and excellent sense of humor. It begins with the flu pandemic of 1918 and ends with the Egyptian Revolution of 1919. Admiration for the novel by the military entrepreneurs who replaced the monarchy in Egypt's 1952 revolution may have dampened enthusiasm for it, but the 2011 Egyptian revolution has brought new life to the work, making it seem like today's news, all fresh and glowing again.

Novels celebrating the 2011 revolution will appear in due time, but Alaa Al Aswany, author of the immensely successful novel *The Yacoubian Building*, is already in print with remarks that echo *Return of the Spirit*: "The revolution makes much better people. When you participate in it, you regain your ability to say 'no.' . . . Egypt regained its identity. . . . And I believe that the personality now of Egyptians is very different. I think we regained what we lost in the [past] thirty years."[1]

Egyptian critic and journalist Ghali Shukri, in his book-length study of Tawfiq al-Hakim, responded to criticism that the 1919 revolution was merely used by the author as a deus ex machina to end the novel: "The truth is that al-Hakim intended it to be that way. . . . He wished to affirm that the Revolution was latent in the Egyptian Spirit so that it was hidden from the naked eye," in such fashion that at the right moment, given the right catalyst, "the Revolution would explode."[2]

Return of the Spirit is a comic novel with a serious, nationalist theme that is as relevant today as it was when it was published more than eighty years ago. The plot has the snowballing inevitability of a tragedy as the character flaws of Muhsin's relatives accelerate the romance between their love interest, Saniya, and their rival, Mustafa Bey, for whose sake Muhsin's aunt, Zanuba, invests scant family resources on love charms. Their failures in love strengthen the young men and motivate them to join the 1919 revolution against the British, who throw them in prison. Through his suffering, Muhsin finds his calling as an artist who aspires to become the eloquent tongue of his nation.

Return of the Spirit is, then, at once a portrait of an Egyptian as a young artist and therefore an apprenticeship novel; the narrative of a failed romance that transforms everything; a political novel that celebrates the 1919 revolution in Egypt and calls for national solidarity; a work of Arab Muslim literature; and a novel that presents its blended family as a model for Egyptian society and its characters as symbols for tendencies and ideas.

The novel is also simply enjoyable reading. Because it was a first novel and subject to little if any editing, not surprisingly it retains certain infelicities: the digressions, the political ambiguities, the possible symbolic overload, and the ending that perhaps arrives too abruptly. All the same, there are more than enough felicities to make up for these.

AN APPRENTICESHIP NOVEL

Return of the Spirit is comparable in certain respects to James Joyce's *A Portrait of the Artist as a Young Man*. Both novels were written in the early twentieth century; have positive, upbeat endings as the young protagonists find their callings as artists; are rich in dialogue and colloquialisms; celebrate significant details of daily life; and have a political agenda, namely, liberation from British rule and recovery of their nation's authentic culture and consciousness.

Both heroes appeal to a feminine religious intercessor: Stephen Dedalus to Mary and Muhsin al-Atifi to Sayyidah Zaynab bint Ali, a female descendant of the Prophet Muhammad and the de facto patron saint of the Cairo neighborhood where Muhsin's extended family lives. Both heroes, who are approximately the same age, struggle with lust or love; and both are haunted by language. Irish Stephen is of course fluent in English, but finds that this language, "so familiar and so foreign," causes him "unrest of spirit."[3] The one characteristic that most significantly ties Stephen to Muhsin is belief in his vocation as an artist. Stephen's desire "to forge . . . the uncreated conscience of my race"[4] is the Egyptian Muhsin's dedication to become the eloquent tongue of the Egyptian people.

A NARRATIVE OF FAILED ROMANCE

Like Goethe's *The Sorrows of Young Werther*, *Return of the Spirit* recounts a failed romance, and each work caught the imagination of its contemporaries by capturing the spirit of its generation. Muhsin, who is only just past puberty, falls madly in love with his talented teenage neighbor, Saniya, when he is grudgingly allowed to exchange music lessons with her. After flirting with Muhsin, Saniya breaks his heart and also the hearts of his adult relatives Hanafi and Salim. When Charlotte and her fiancé, Albert, present Werther with the pink ribbon she wore the first time he saw her, he kisses it repeatedly, like Muhsin with Saniya's handkerchief.[5] Werther consoles himself for his lost love and for the falsity of contemporary society by pairing simple, rural life with Homer.[6] Muhsin rebels against his parents' snobbery and seeks out the company of farm laborers, thinking not of Homer but of ancient Egypt. For Muhsin (and for al-Hakim at the time he wrote the novel), the Egyptian farm worker was a link to what is ancient and authentic in Egypt. Both Werther and Muhsin tend toward nature pantheism, with Muhsin's revealed by his vision in the cowshed. As his despair increases, Werther's earlier cheerful pantheism takes on a terrifying, malevolent form.[7]

Goethe's book was said to have been carried by Napoleon on his campaigns and to have caused countless suicides,[8] and al-Hakim's book is said to have influenced Gamal Abdel

Nasser in a significant way and to have contributed to an acceptance of totalitarian rule by Egyptian intellectuals.[9]

A POLITICAL NOVEL

Al-Hakim's response to European colonialism was less a call to arms than a call to spiritual rebirth through pride in Egypt's heritage. Although tension between modern, urban Cairo and ancient, rural Egypt is a vital element of the novel, for Muhsin the choice is not exclusive. Muhsin is as positive about streetcars as he is about waterwheels powered by oxen. What he opposes is the suppression of human dignity. The waterwheel, in fact, guarantees that Egypt will have streetcars (and astronauts). The tip of the pyramid points, metaphorically, to the Aswan High Dam and beyond.

From *Return of the Spirit* to later works such as *The Thorns of Peace* and *Voyage to Tomorrow*, solidarity has been an important theme for al-Hakim. M. M. Badawi says of al-Hakim's 1956 folk play *al-Safqa* [The Deal]: "In their desire to possess the land they have been tilling with such toil and dedication, the peasants present a remarkable spectacle of solidarity and self-denial."[10] He adds: "The peasants are not devoid of foibles. . . . They are a noisy, but good-humoured crowd, who with a few bold strokes are brought to life as distinct individuals."[11]

Joseph Conrad placed comparable emphasis on solidarity, as for example in a famous preface in which he said that the artist speaks to the "conviction of solidarity . . . which binds men together."[12] Al-Hakim, like Conrad, understood that art has political implications and that the artist has a duty to champion human solidarity. In *Return of the Spirit*, al-Hakim focused on an Egyptian nationalist solidarity that cut across class lines; in later works the human solidarity stressed was international, as in his play *Poet on the Moon*.

In a newspaper column dated November 13, 1948, Tawfiq al-Hakim compared the events of the Egyptian uprising of 1919, celebrated in *Return of the Spirit*, with later strikes and demonstrations in Egypt and concluded that the difference between these diverse moments of civil unrest was the unanimity of heart in 1919—a solidarity as much spiritual or religious as political.[13] Critic Ali B. Jad has observed: "The author is determined to see manifestations of the special unity of the Egyptian people in almost any ordinary social phenomenon, be it the gregariousness of passengers on Egyptian trains or the crowdedness of some Egyptian houses."[14]

In *Return of the Spirit*, instead of angry denunciations of British imperialism, there are happy expressions of the solidarity of adverse circumstances. Even as a child, Muhsin insists on eating with the members of the musical troupe instead of with the guests. In the digression about the Sudan, the story about the monkeys down the well celebrates their primate solidarity, which holds up even under attack. If an artist is to become the eloquent tongue of his people, the solidarity of a nation's citizens (as in *Return of the Spirit*) or of all earthlings (as in al-Hakim's *Voyage to Tomorrow*) must be assumed.

In Egyptian literature, *Return of the Spirit* was a pioneer political novel that tied an individual's awakening to the political awakening of the nation. It clearly served as a precedent for the Cairo Trilogy of Naguib Mahfouz and for Latifa al-Zayyat's *The Open Door*. Hilary Kilpatrick, in *The Modern Egyptian Novel*, characterized *Return of the Spirit* as "a wonderfully romantic expression of that nationalist philosophy of rebirth which inspired the revolution of 1919" and observed that the book has won "the admiration of successive generations of Egyptian readers."[15] Bayly Winder, who called *Return of the Spirit* "al-Hakim's most important and famous novel," explained, "This story of middle-class Cairo life plays on the Egyptian myth of Isis and Osiris to set al-Hakim's theme that the revolution of 1919 . . . constituted the return of national spirit to Egypt."[16] The Egyptian critic Ghali Shukri wrote that the Cairo Trilogy is a natural outgrowth of *Return of the Spirit*, pointing out that both works end with the revolutionaries in prison—as part of a social revolution in the Mahfouz trilogy and of a nationalist one in *Return of the Spirit*.[17]

Toward the end of his life, Naguib Mahfouz, in an interview he granted Mohamed Salmawy for *Al-Ahram Weekly*,

said that al-Hakim's "works were truly landmarks in the evo-
lution of Arab novel-writing. In the truest sense they represented and helped shape a new age. . . . My direct mentor was
El-Hakim. *Return of the Spirit*, I believe, marked the true
birth of the Arab novel. It was written using what were then
cutting-edge narrative devices." In fact, it was so unlike previous Arab attempts at writing novels that it "was a bomb-
shell."[18] Mahfouz also told me in a private conversation (circa
1991) that until he wrote the trilogy, al-Hakim's *Return of the
Spirit* was the best Arabic novel.

Mahfouz's hero Kamal in *Palace of Desire*, the middle volume of the Cairo Trilogy, is comparable to al-Hakim's hero
Muhsin. The important scene in which Kamal's father con-
fronts him about his future and the choice of a branch of education (law school versus teachers college), although dissimilar
in details, is directly parallel to the scene in volume one, chapter seven of *Return of the Spirit*, in which Muhsin insists that
he and his friend Abbas must enter a secondary school for the
arts. In each scene, the young hero takes his stand and voices
his aspiration to become an artist—a responsible, authentic
Egyptian artist.

AN ARAB AND ISLAMIC NOVEL

If *Return of the Spirit* resembles several Western types of novel—
whether portraits of a young artist, stories of an unsatisfied and
transforming love, or political novels—it is also an Arab and Islamic work. Denis Hoppe, while criticizing al-Hakim for being
an author who "more than any other Arab writer, sees the Arab
world through the rose-colored glasses of the West," also mentioned that one of his "most striking characteristics" was "his
sensitivity to the Arab past."[19] Perhaps Hoppe did not contradict
himself. A Muslim author who looks at Goethe's *The Sorrows of
Young Werther* can find there the story of Majnun, the hero of
numerous works of Islamic literature, such as Nizami's *The
Story of Layla and Majnun*,[20] a story of self-sacrificing, Udhri

love. Majnun goes insane when his love for the beautiful Layla is thwarted by her family. Layla's life too is transformed by her love for Majnun. At a deeper level, the story relates Majnun's quest for God, whose earthly reflection—Layla—he pursues. *Return of the Spirit* differs from Nizami's tale of unconsummated but all-consuming love, because it is a realistic story of modern, urban life and because it substitutes the artist's calling for the mind-ravished spiritual quest of the desert wanderer. Majnun, however, was also an artist, a poet. At the end of *Return of the Spirit*, Muhsin delights in his physical contact with the other prisoners in his prison cell. Recognition of this physical, human solidarity signals a spiritual rebirth. From a Sufi perspective, Majnun is not a failure or a tragic hero, because he progresses by leaps and bounds in his quest for the divine. Of the three—Muhsin, Majnun, and Werther—only Goethe's Werther seems suicidal and despairing.

It is more difficult to find premodern Islamic apprenticeship novels. A study called *Interpreting the Self*, edited by Dwight F. Reynolds, includes translations of autobiographical selections by thirteen authors, ranging from the ninth-century Hunayn ibn Ishaq to the nineteenth-century Ali Mubarak.[21] *The Book of Contemplation*, by Usama ibn Munqidh (d. AD 1188), although a book of edifying reflections on God's creation, contains elements of an apprenticeship novel like the author's account of his youthful adventures combating serpents, lions, and Franks.[22] *Deliverance from Error*, by al-Ghazali (d. AD 1111), is another example of religious discourse decorated with autobiographical details, as the author recounts the stages of the intellectual and spiritual apprenticeship that led him to embrace Sufism.[23] *Hayy ibn Yaqzan*, by Ibn Tufayl (d. AD 1185), although a work of philosophy, is also an apprenticeship novel that relates the story of a wild child who grows to manhood nurtured by a kindly doe and who gains, by his use of reason alone, complete knowledge of the Aristotelian universe surrounding him on his desert island—although he does need to travel to a nearby inhabited island to discover how many times to pray each day.[24]

In *Return of the Spirit*, the main religious, symbolic framework is admittedly not Shariah-based, act-right Islam. Throughout much of the novel Saniya is portrayed as Isis. A hint of earth goddess symbolism comes when a green field reminds Abduh of Saniya in her green dress. In his later novel *The Sacred Bond*, al-Hakim also has his hero recognize that he had transfigured a young woman into "more than a living being; she was lofty and abstract and no longer real. She was a poem and a legend."[25] No matter how beautiful and talented she is, Saniya is not the twentieth-century Isis. She is at best a representative of Isis. The Prophet Muhammad's granddaughter Sayyidah Zaynab bint Ali has a better claim to being the novel's Isis. Although not a character, she is invoked throughout, and the novel takes place on her turf.

Muhsin has trouble realizing that the Saniya to whom he is speaking is not the Saniya of his dreams, not the new Isis. Ali Jad has claimed that disappointment with an overly idealized woman is a recurrent theme in al-Hakim's fiction, whether here, in *The Sacred Bond*, in *Bird of the East*, in *Shahrazad*, or, arguably, in *Maze of Justice*.[26] The tension between dream and reality is an important theme in al-Hakim's works; even Muhsin's adolescent wet dream, after he discovers the true nature of Saniya's feelings toward him, is treated by al-Hakim as an example of this tension.

When a traditional Muslim implies in *Return of the Spirit* that there is only one choice—Islam or nothing—a fellow traveler gently corrects him and says that the question is rather of having a heart or not having one. Egypt in 1918 was still, the modern gentleman held, traditional enough to have a heart, whereas Europe was so modern that, like the Tin Woodman, it lacked one. In other words, Egyptian Christians and Egyptian Muslims are brothers; they all have hearts, even the same heart. This is the true meaning of Islam. For al-Hakim this was not secular humanism. It was important to be religious, but not in a one-dimensional way. He did not see Islam as having had a single pure and perfect era that needed to be revived. The issue was to reawaken the Egyptian spirit. This nation-building task was spiritual and therefore religious. In the discussion between the French archaeologist and the English irrigation inspector, the Frenchman argues that whereas the uneducated Egyptian farm laborer is heir to the wisdom of ancient Egypt, the typical European has no inherited culture. These ideas turn up again in al-Hakim's *Bird of the East*,[27] in which the title refers to the hero, who is an Egyptian student in France and therefore an heir of the spiritual East, defined to include Egypt. On the other hand, al-Hakim in the preface to *King Oedipus* credits the French with a literary inheritance that goes back to the ancient Greeks, and he contrasts the rich French inheritance with a gaping theatrical void faced by a twentieth-century Egyptian author like himself.

One key religious section in *Return of the Spirit* is Muhsin's vision in the cowshed, which seems almost a parody of Martin Luther's revelation in the tower. In this cowshed, which is also the residence of a farm family, Muhsin comes to know the unity of existence and the unified duality of the emotions and logic. When his rival, Mustafa, succumbs to love and tries to decide whether to put his feelings into a letter to his beloved, he becomes a prime example of this notion of al-Hakim (and of others) that the heart and the mind actually reason in different ways. Both are trustworthy guides, no matter how much they appear to contradict each other on the surface. In his vision, Muhsin, by having a feeling of the unity of existence, has had a "feeling of God." This could be another example of latent Sufism in al-Hakim's writings, of a secular spiritualism, or of a secular Islamic pantheism, except that al-Hakim cites Dostoyevsky here, taking the passage from a book by Mérejkovsky.

THE FAMILY AS A MICROCOSM OF EGYPT

The novel's characters, well developed in themselves, also stand for things that form part of the book's meaning.

Zanuba is criticized for shaving the food budget to spend money instead on magic and charlatans. The Islamic modernist message conveyed through this example is that uneducated women are not the fruit of Islam but a danger to it. Society, and particularly Islamic society, must protect itself by educating women thoroughly in every field.

The scenes contrasting Saniya with her mother show generational change in the outlook of women in Egypt during that period. Saniya is even more strongly contrasted with Zanuba when Zanuba makes a determined effort to attract the attention of Mustafa, the man who will fall in love with Saniya. (Of course, everyone who encounters Saniya falls in love with her.) Saniya is not only beautiful; she is also the representative new woman. She is the second Prisca, the modern Prisca, in al-Hakim's landmark play, *The People of the Cave*—which was published the same year as *Return of the Spirit*—because she is an educated woman. Both Saniya and her mother successfully manipulate the men in their lives, but Saniya has a turn of mind that is the fruit of her education and that allows her to debate with her mother and to guide her intended mate in an appropriate direction. The marriages of the mother and daughter are instructively different. Saniya's father waited to marry until he had virtually completed his career—until he had made enough money to retire. Saniya marries, for love, a young man she has encountered by chance. Fortunately, money is not in short supply here either.

Of all the characters, Saniya is the most heavily burdened by symbolism, although she is slow to understand her plight. She would be justified in protesting, as King Oedipus did in al-Hakim's play of the same name, that what happened was the fault of other people casting their fantasies upon her. Saniya is Isis, or a representative of Isis. She is therefore a symbol for woman and for the Egyptian woman as goddess, or vice versa. She is also a symbol for the reawakened spirit of Egypt. Critics have complained that Saniya is not a strong enough character to bear the weight of all this symbolism.[28] Without meeting her, without losing our hearts to her, can we believe in her? The symbol gap is, however, an important theme of al-Hakim's works. In his play that is named for her, for example, Shahrazad pulls out all the stops in an attempt to save not herself but her husband from his obsession with her weighty symbolic baggage. Even Muhsin, in time, realizes that Saniya is less important as a person than as a symbol. Saniya at least has the courage to follow her own course. In this respect she resembles the heroine of E. M. Forster's *Howards End*, who expressed her satisfaction with her spiritual compromises.[29]

Mustafa Bey's blond mustache and chestnut hair are not accidental details in *Return of the Spirit*. They suggest that he is partly of Turkish heritage—like Muhsin's mother (and of course Muhsin too, thanks to his mother). Furthermore, his status is specified by his servant: "He's one of the gentry." Blond or not, Mustafa turns out to be a hero parallel to Muhsin. In fact, *Return of the Spirit* is full of heroes: the entire Egyptian population. Mustafa's dilemma—whether to sell out to a foreign concern—looks forward to the industrialist-technocrat hero of al-Hakim's play *Tender Hands*. In other words, Mustafa is the son of a true Egyptian businessman and has a duty to develop his father's company and engage in nation building. He needs only Saniya's encouragement to make this decision. Like Muhsin and his uncles, Mustafa is a sleeping beau awakened by the charming princess Saniya.

Muhsin is a callow artist who aspires to become the voice of the people and thus a reformer. He shares in the popular revolution and suffers the consequences. In al-Hakim's later works, such as the play *Princess Sunshine*, the artist's role is limited to reforming the nation's leaders, even, at times, from an ivory tower. Muhsin's attitudes contrast strongly with those of his parents, who even comment on this. Muhsin shows us the right way. As our role model, he teaches us to shun narrow ethnic prejudice and snobbery and to throw our lot in with the masses. Muhsin is aware of the difference of status separating him from the farm laborers who work his parents' estate, but the opulence of his parents' house revolts him. Muhsin of course represents Tawfiq al-Hakim in this novel. Al-Hakim's autobiography, *The Prison of Life*, portrays the child's mother in a more flattering way.[30] The novel's account is, possibly, the franker version.

The drowsiness of Hanafi, the honorary head of the household, reaches a climax at the end of the first volume when Muhsin misses his train because Hanafi was napping on a bench at the station. This personality trait, which helps define Hanafi's character, is also symbolic, for this novel is all about awakening Egypt.

Two of the weaker characters—the French archaeologist and the British irrigation inspector—are also two of the more transparent symbols. Their identification by nationality and specialization is hardly accidental. That an Anglo-French team should be entertained at the beginning of the twentieth century in a Turkish/Ottoman fashion on an Egyptian farm is historically accurate. The division of labor speaks to a paradox of the early twentieth century in Egypt: Great Britain exercised a commanding political and military presence, but France was important culturally. Al-Hakim himself went to France to further his legal studies. Although a digression, the scene between the Englishman and the Frenchman serves to bring out ideas that tie up loose ends of the plot. The French archaeologist's views, a major element in this character's portrayal, were inspired by the Russian author Mérejkovsky's book *Les Mystères de l'Orient*. This book obviously influenced al-Hakim—there are repeated quotations from it and allusions to it in *Return of the Spirit*—but the ideas he borrowed from it were not given to Muhsin and may be taken with a grain of salt.[31]

Dr. Hilmi, Saniya's army doctor father, plays a part in the plot, but serves mainly to introduce a digression about the Sudan. The question of the political status and future of that land riled Egyptian-British relations for decades. With the anecdotes of life in the Sudan toward the end of the first volume, al-Hakim made a series of nationalist, Egyptian points about the possibilities of future Egyptian exploitation of that country's resources. These adventure stories told by the retired doctor outside the pharmacy also provide an example of Egyptian society's separation at the time into two gender worlds: one of men literally in the street and a second of women praying or playing the piano inside the house.

The unsuccessful attempt of Muhsin's blended family to hand over the household finances to Mabruk conveys a political message. Mabruk, although male, is uneducated and illiterate.

When he squanders "public" resources on personal prestige he violates the book's teachings, which strongly favor solidarity. He also provides a warning against handing power over to uneducated masses who may squander the nation's resources on prestige projects. There is thus an ambiguity to the political message, a fact that did not escape some Soviet critics.[32] The novel's waves flow back and forth between liberalism and authoritarianism.

The respect that *Return of the Spirit* shows for the Egyptian nationalist leader Sa'd Zaghlul, whose banishment led to the 1919 revolution, makes Zaghlul seem the Prince Charming whose kiss will awaken the Sleeping Beauty—Egypt. The novel implies that this Prince Charming could be another pharaoh and even an earthly manifestation of the divine. Al-Hakim later realized that this beautiful, romantic vision had less beautiful implications for human rights and freedoms. Even though the book's prediction that this new leader would bring forth from the Egyptian people another miracle like the pyramids appeared to set the stage for President Nasser's successful struggle to build the Aswan High Dam, it is not Sa'd Zaghlul who figures in the climax of the novel. Muhsin, the young man who aspires to be an artist expressing the feelings of his people, is the novel's hero. Moreover, Muhsin does not wish to become the nation's beloved, simply its tongue or mouthpiece. In al-Hakim's world, the artist inspires the politician. *Return of the Spirit* is a call not to arms, but to pens.

ASSESSMENTS

The strongest claim that *Return of the Spirit* makes for the attention of a non-Egyptian reader is its realistic depiction of life in Egypt at the beginning of the twentieth century. Roger Allen, in *The Arabic Novel*, termed it "the first novel which succeeded in giving a totally convincing portrait of a family."[33] Ali Jad wrote, "This is a novel about Egypt par excellence: here we find Egypt not only in the . . . daily life . . . of Muhsin and his uncles and aunt . . . but also in the crowded streets, coffee houses, tramcars and trains, in wedding parties and classrooms, at demonstrations and in prison."[34]

Ali Jad underscored the novel's comedy, reminding the reader of al-Hakim's early training in the Egyptian popular theater, in which vaudeville, slapstick, and farce were combined with music. Jad mentioned the book's "comedy engendered by the opposition of his characters' personalities and . . . conflicting interests" and "a series of outrageous . . . actions . . . followed by [a] hilarious comment." If "the characters in [*Return of the Spirit*] do not exactly go about throwing custard pies at each other. . . . Zannubah helped by a reluctant Mabruk bombards the two lovers (Saniyyah and Mustafa) with . . . garbage." Jad suggested that "the novel could readily be made into a musical farce."[35]

The Egyptian critic Hamdi Sakkut called *Return of the Spirit* "the first Egyptian novel which can sustain comparison with Western works."[36] He also commented that its popularity "helped to raise the prestige of the Egyptian novel."[37] Sasson Somekh said that the novel's dialogue, "given in vigorous vernacular—is probably among the best in Egyptian fiction."[38]

Richard Long said that *Return of the Spirit* "is by general consent the first real novel in Arabic." If that were not enough, he pointed out, "The first real play and the first real novel in Arabic, astonishingly, had issued from one pen, seven months apart in the same year."[39] He was, of course, talking about their publication dates, not the actual period of composition.

Ali Jad mentioned al-Hakim's "consistent characterization" as one of the novel's strengths: "Almost everything the characters do reflects and confirms the author's initial statements about them."[40] As is typical in al-Hakim's works, the language of the novel is clear and unpretentious. The noted Egyptian author Yahya Haqqi commented, "*Return of the Spirit* is written in the only style that can be considered suitable to the theme: an easy, uncomplicated, authentic style that conveys conversation through its spirit and describes and speaks in such a way that the readers, about and for whom it was written, can understand it." Haqqi continued by saying al-Hakim's "only aim is to be entirely natural, unforced, and unpretentious."[41] In this book al-Hakim used more dialect words than he would later, even some words said to be used only between women.

A nice touch of irony is provided by the fact that Muhsin and Zanuba inadvertently awaken and foster the romance between Saniya and Mustafa, even though this romance runs counter to the hopes and wishes of their entire family. An apparent structural problem—that the novel starts as a romance starring Muhsin and Saniya but ends up with a different male lead—may exist only in the reader's mind. One can argue that a single romantic event is seen in radically different ways by the various characters, whose differing perspectives merely give the story the appearance of being a series of unrelated romances.

Ghali Shukri found a creative tension in *Return of the Spirit* involving (a) its classical dramatic structure, in which the characters' development is determined by their symbolic roles and by a progression from beginning to crisis to resolution, (b) a middle-class romantic ideology, and finally (c) realism, which is received here more hospitably than previously in Egyptian literature. What is really at stake in the novel is not a classical theme like honor or revenge, or a romantic one like death, but the condition of the middle classes in Egypt at the start of the twentieth century.[42] Each of the novel's characters has a role to play by personifying this cause and milieu. Countless details that taken separately may seem of trivial importance are woven together to create a realistic fabric for the novel. According to Shukri, al-Hakim's blend of classical dramatic structure, bourgeois romanticism, and realism influenced Naguib Mahfouz (especially in *Palace Walk*) as well as other Egyptian writers.[43]

Some critics, admittedly, prefer *Maze of Justice*, which Roger Allen has called "a beautifully constructed picture of the Egyptian countryside."[44] Dina Amin, for example, in an extensive article about al-Hakim, praised *Maze of Justice* as "one of his finest prose works" and said of *Return of the Spirit* only that it was "reality-based" and "a fictional portrayal of the life of his paternal uncles and aunt in Cairo, with whom he lodged while completing his undergraduate education."[45]

For reasons that I have advanced in this introduction and elsewhere, however, I believe that *Return of the Spirit* is Tawfiq al-Hakim's single most influential and important novel, if only for the juicy slice of Egyptian life it offers. Roger Allen admitted that it "provides a lively colloquial dialogue as a means of introducing his readers to the tensions of a large Egyptian family . . . in Egypt in 1919."[46] Paul Starkey acknowledged that because it "captured the mood of the Egyptian people at a crucial point in their history," it "may well strike a more responsive note in the mind of the average Egyptian reader" than *Maze of Justice*, which combined "realism and immediacy" with an "avoidance of the structural faults [that] mar all his other extended prose works."[47]

M. M. Badawi wrote an excellent assessment of the novel: "*Return of the Spirit* represents a giant step forward in the writing of the Arabic novel: the art of narration, the skill in characterization, and chiefly the management of dialogue, in which al-Hakim boldly opted for the language of speech rather than that of writing. Furthermore, the work is characterized by al-Hakim's intelligence and urbanity of spirit, as well as the ability to see and create comic situations in which humour is often combined with pathos."[48]

CONCLUSION

Return of the Spirit is first and foremost a memorable and influential portrait of an Egyptian Muslim family living a century ago. The message of the novel is upbeat; it teaches that the solidarity of Egyptians of all walks of life will revive the age-old Egyptian spirit and chase away colonial oppressors, whose chief damage has been psychological and can be addressed, first and foremost, by waking the Egyptian people. The only true villains in the novel are inertia and ignorance.

Return of the Spirit did not merely celebrate the change that Tawfiq al-Hakim felt began in Egypt in 1919 but was itself a significant part of that change.

WILLIAM MAYNARD HUTCHINS

NOTES

1. Alaa Al Aswany, "Narrating the Revolution," interview in the *Cairo Review of Global Affairs* 1 (Spring 2011), 91–92.
2. Ghali Shukri, *Thawrat al-Mu'tazil* (Beirut: Dar al-Afaq al-Jadida, n.d.), 142.
3. James Joyce, *A Portrait of the Artist as a Young Man* (New York: Viking Press, 1978), 189.
4. Ibid., 252–53.
5. Johann Wolfgang von Goethe, *The Sorrows of Young Werther*, trans. Victor Lange (New York: Holt, Rinehart and Winston, 1949), "May 22," 8–9.
6. Ibid., "June 21," 24; "March 15, 1772," 68–69; "September 4, 1772," 79.
7. Ibid., "August 18," 48–49; "May 10, 1771," 3.
8. Ibid., "Introduction," by Victor Lange, ix, x.
9. Jean Lacouture, *Nasser: A Biography*, trans. Daniel Hofstadter (New York: Alfred A. Knopf, 1973), 28, 281; P. J. Vatikiotis, *Nasser and His Generation* (New York: St. Martin's Press, 1978), 28, 29, 43; Amos Elon, *Flight into Egypt* (New York: Pinnacle Books, 1981), 103, 159; Anouar Abdel-Malek, *Egypt: Military Society*, trans. Charles Markmann (New York: Vintage Books, 1968), 207–208; and Richard Long, *Tawfiq al Hakim: Playwright of Egypt* (London: Ithaca Press, 1979), 28.
10. M. M. Badawi, *Modern Arabic Drama in Egypt* (Cambridge, UK: Cambridge University Press, 1987), 66.
11. Ibid., 67.
12. Joseph Conrad, *The Nigger of the Narcissus* (Garden City, NY: Doubleday, Page, and Co., 1925), xii.
13. Tawfiq al-Hakim, "I Challenge," in *Shajara al-Hukm al-Siyasi fi Misr 1919–1979* (The Rulership Tree) (Cairo: Maktabat al-Adab, 1985), 272.

14. Ali B. Jad, *Form and Technique in the Egyptian Novel: 1912–1971* (London: Ithaca Press, published for the Middle East Centre, St. Antony's College, Oxford, UK, 1983), 51.

15. Hilary Kilpatrick, *The Modern Egyptian Novel* (London: Ithaca Press, 1974), 41.

16. Tawfiq al-Hakim, *The Return of Consciousness*, trans. Bayly Winder (New York: New York University Press, 1985), 79, note 47.

17. Shukri, *Thawrat al-Mu'tazil*, 138.

18. Naguib Mahfouz, "Return of the Spirit," *Al-Ahram Weekly*, June 29–July 5, 2000, 10.

19. Denis Hoppe, "The Novels of Tawfiq al-Hakim," senior thesis, Princeton University, 1969, chapter 2, available at http://www-personal.umich.edu/~dhoppe/THESEPIC.htm.

20. Nizami, *The Story of Layla and Majnun*, English trans. R. Gelpke with E. Mattin and G. Hill (Boulder, CO: Shambala, 1978).

21. Dwight F. Reynolds, ed., *Interpreting the Self: Autobiography in the Arabic Literary Tradition* (Berkeley: University of California Press, 2001).

22. Usama ibn Munqidh, *The Book of Contemplation*, trans. Paul M. Cobb (London: Penguin Books, 2008).

23. English translation in W. Montgomery Watt, *The Faith and Practice of al-Ghazali* (London: George Allen and Unwin, 1967).

24. Ibn Tufayl, *Hayy ibn Yaqzan*, trans. Lenn Evan Goodman (Chicago: University of Chicago Press, 2003).

25. Tawfiq al-Hakim, *The Sacred Bond*, trans. Mohamed S. Ghattas in "Balance Through Resistance: The Novels of Tawfiq al-Hakim," PhD diss., Oklahoma State University, May 2000, 109.

26. Jad, *Form and Technique in the Egyptian Novel*, 74.

27. Tawfiq al-Hakim, *Bird of the East*, trans. R. Bayly Winder (Beirut: Khayats, 1966).

28. Shukri, *Thawrat al-Mu'tazil*, for example, complained: "We are unable to see the characters of *Return of the Spirit* as personalities of flesh and blood," 131.

29. E. M. Forster, *Howards End* (New York: Alfred A. Knopf, 1951 [1921]), 295–300.

30. Tawfiq al-Hakim, *The Prison of Life*, trans. Pierre Cachia (Cairo: American University in Cairo Press, 1964).

31. See, for example, Dimitri Mérejkovsky, *Les Mystères de l'Orient: Égypte-Babylone*, trans. Dumesnil de Gramont (Paris: L'Artisan du Livre, 1927), 109–111, 112–113, 117, 165–166, 169.

32. See K. O. Yunusov, "Introduction," in A. A. Dolinina and N. M. Zand, *Tawfik al-Hakim Biobibliograficheski Ukazatel* (Moscow: Kniga Press, 1963).

33. Roger Allen, *The Arabic Novel* (Syracuse, NY: Syracuse University Press, 1982), 38.

34. Jad, *Form and Technique in the Egyptian Novel*, 38.

35. Ibid., 92.

36. Hamdi Sakkut, *The Egyptian Novel and Its Main Trends 1913–1952* (Cairo: American University in Cairo Press, 1971), 89.

37. Ibid.

38. Sasson Somekh, *The Changing Rhythm* (Leiden, NL: E. J. Brill, 1973), 19.

39. Long, *Tawfiq al Hakim: Playwright of Egypt*, 27–28.

40. Jad, *Form and Technique in the Egyptian Novel*, 40.

41. Yahya Haqqi, in Roger Allen, ed., *Modern Arabic Literature* (New York: Ungar, 1987), 111–112.

42. Shukri, *Thawrat al-Muʻtazil*, 133.

43. Ibid., 135, 139.

44. Roger Allen, *The Arabic Literary Heritage* (Cambridge, UK: Cambridge University Press, 1998), 306.

45. Dina Amin, "Tawfiq al-Hakim (1898–1986)," in Roger Allen, ed., *Essays in Arabic Literary Biography, 1850–1950* (Wiesbaden, DE: Harrassowitz, 2010), 104.

46. Roger Allen, *An Introduction to Arabic Literature* (Cambridge, UK: Cambridge University Press, 2000), 185.

47. Paul Starkey, *From the Ivory Tower* (London: Ithaca Press, 1987), 228.

48. M. M. Badawi, *A Short History of Modern Arabic Literature* (Oxford, UK: Oxford University Press, 1993), 120.

Summary and List of Characters

A NOVEL IN TWO VOLUMES OF EIGHTEEN AND TWENTY-FIVE CHAPTERS, RESPECTIVELY

PLOT SUMMARY

A sensitive Egyptian lad matures through the early years of the twentieth century as romantic heartbreak and patriotic revolt against British colonial rule help him find his calling as an author who celebrates his solidarity with his extended family and with all levels of Egyptian society.

MAIN CHARACTERS

Muhsin, an upper-middle-class, provincial Egyptian boy who decides to become a writer

Muhsin's three uncles:

Salim, a vain and earthy police captain

Hanafi, the sleepy head of the blended family, a math teacher

Abduh, an irascible engineering student

Zanuba, Muhsin's homely and illiterate spinster aunt, who serves as housekeeper for her male relatives in Cairo but still hopes to marry

Saniya, the beautiful girl next door with whom all the young men fall in love

SUPPORTING CAST

Hamid Bey, Muhsin's henpecked father

Muhsin's mother, who is proud of her Ottoman/Turkish ancestry and dismissive of Egyptian farmers

Mabruk, the household servant and a family friend from their village

Mr. Black, a British irrigation inspector

M. Fouquet, a French archaeologist

Mustafa, the young man who steals Saniya's heart from Muhsin and his roommates

Abbas, Muhsin's school pal

Maestra Labiba Shakhla', a female entertainer who teaches Muhsin to sing and allows him to perform at least once with her troupe

SETTING

Cairo in 1918–1919, especially the area of Al-Sayyida Zaynab, which is named for a beloved granddaughter of the Prophet Muhammad, with some scenes in rural Egypt in and around Damanhur

Return of the Spirit

VOLUME 1

When time passes over into eternity
We shall see you again.
Because you are going there
Where all will be one.
  —Egyptian funeral lament, cited in Dimitri Mérejkovsky,
    Les Mystères de l'Orient

PROLOGUE

They all caught flu at the same time. The moment the doctor laid eyes on them, he was stunned, because they were all crowded into one room, where five beds with flimsy mattresses were lined up next to each other. The single armoire, reminiscent of cabinets used by public scribes, had lost one of its two doors and held clothes of every color and size, including some police uniforms with brass buttons. An old musical instrument with bellows—an accordion—was hanging from the wall.

"Is this a barracks for a military base?"

The doctor was certain he had entered a house. He still remembered the street and the address. When he finally reached the fifth bed, he couldn't keep from smiling. This wasn't a bed; it was a wooden dining table that had been converted into a bunk for one of them.

The doctor stood for a moment gazing at his patients lying in a row. At last he took a step forward and said, "No, this isn't a house; it's a hospital!"

He examined them, one after the other. When he had finished and was ready to depart, he looked back in amazement at them—crammed together into that room. Why did they put up with this crowding when there was room elsewhere in the apartment—the sitting room at least? When he asked, a voice replied from the depths of a bed, "We're happy like this!"

This declaration was uttered simply and sincerely, like a profound truth. A person pondering it would sense an inner joy at their communal life. It might even have been possible to read on their sallow faces the glow of a secret happiness at falling sick together—succumbing to one regimen, taking the same medicine, eating the same food, and suffering the same fortune and destiny.

The doctor's visit concluded, and he prepared to depart. He reached the threshold but stood there thoughtfully. He turned to the invalids in their beds and said, "You must be from the country!"

The doctor left without awaiting a reply. His imagination had sketched a picture of subsistence farmers, and he told himself: *Only a peasant could live like this, not anyone else. No matter how spacious his house, the fellah will sleep with his wife, children, calf, and donkey colt in a single room!*

CHAPTER 1

The lunch hour having ended, the family members went off on their separate ways, even Mabruk, the servant. He finished helping Miss Zanuba clear the table and wash the dishes and then he too departed to sit with the fruit seller next to the Bab al-Mayda quarter. Miss Zanuba remained at home, alone, far from anything that might disturb the serenity of her solitude. She went to her small room and sat down gravely on her cabbage-colored pallet. She looked for a long time at the cards she had lined up in front of her on the faded red kilim carpet.

Time passed. The call to the afternoon prayer rang out. Zanuba was still sunk in her dreams. All she saw was the blond boy beside the dark maiden; both were overcome by happiness. One of them would travel and . . . and . . . and everything else from the world of mystery and symbols.

The door to the room opened suddenly, and Muhsin appeared with his books, ruler, and compass under his arm. He shouted at her in his merry, boyish voice, "Haven't the folks come home yet?"

She did not move, nor did she answer right away. She continued sunk in her reverie. At last, without looking at him, she said, "You're back from school?"

"We got out a long time ago, but I was at the tailor's!" He adjusted his clothes with great care and sat down beside Zanuba on the edge of the mattress. He was silent for a bit; then he fidgeted and looked at her. He hesitated as if he wanted to say something but felt embarrassed.

Zanuba seemed to remember something suddenly. Without raising her head from the cards she said, "I imagine you're hungry, Muhsin. Go get a cucumber to munch on. That should hold you over. It'll be a long time till supper."

She looked up to show him a basket she was hiding from

Mabruk behind the door. The moment she peered at Muhsin, though, she shouted in astonishment, "My God! God's will be done! You're wearing a new suit?"

The boy bowed his head and did not reply. Zanuba continued in her amazement: "Fantastic, sister! A person seeing you would say you're a different person. So your family sent you money? Isn't that fantastic!"

Muhsin asked her with some embarrassment and hesitation, "Fantastic? Why?"

Zanuba did not stop gazing at his new clothing with an astonished and admiring eye. "Because it's not like you. You've never been willing to wear a new suit except for the Feast of the Sacrifice, like your uncles. It's amazing! Today, like this, you've turned into a handsome swell! By the Prophet, anyone seeing you would say you're the sultan's son. May the Prophet's name protect you! You're a sight for sore eyes! It might as well be Thursday! Thursday!"

Muhsin blushed a little at this lavish tribute. The praise, though, instead of filling his heart with satisfaction and joy, created a strange pang in his heart. He immediately changed the topic: "What's for supper tonight?"

Zanuba replied lackadaisically after returning to her cards, "Same as lunch."

Muhsin raised his voice a little: "Goose leg, again?"

She brought her head up abruptly and, giving him a reproachful look, asked, "What's wrong with goose leg? Even you, Muhsin, who I say is smart? Okay, by the Pure Lady, tomorrow they'll see what this ingratitude brings. Is our Lord going to bless someone who sticks up his nose at a bite to eat? Don't be like those uncles of yours—they're unbearable. God preserve us. Don't be like them."

The boy replied gently, "But Auntie, this goose leg we've seen in front of us for three days—at every meal. Uncle Abduh swore on the Holy Qur'an today at noon . . ."

He did not finish, because Zanuba waved her arm furiously and shouted, "Abduh! Who is His Lordship Mr. Abduh? Is he the respected head of the household or is that the eldest? Shame on Mr. Abduh! Shame! Since when, fellow, has this house had a head other than the eldest, who is rightfully and justly the senior: your uncle Hanafi, may God protect him. He works, pays the bills, and cares for us. He never complains or breathes a word. May God never deprive us of him! Then there's that boy Abduh. All he does on the face of the earth is to shoot his mouth, yell, and attack."

"He'll be making good money tomorrow, aunt. At the end of this year he's going to get his diploma and become an engineer."

Zanuba did not reply. Her expression was still sullen. She had gone back to the cards—arranging, sorting, and lining them up.

After a moment, though, she raised her head suddenly and asked, "Does he think I'm going to be frightened by his pointy fez? That pipsqueak kid . . . God's name; just because he's nervous and impatient . . . No, by the Mighty Lady, I'm not afraid of anyone."

Muhsin smiled sarcastically and asked, "Could you say that to his face?"

She turned toward him fiercely and asked, "What are you saying?"

Muhsin did not want to quarrel with her, especially not today, and seemed to regret what he had said. So he laughed, or pretended to laugh, to make her think he was kidding and did not expect to be taken seriously. Then he said earnestly, "Do you want the truth, auntie? Uncle Abduh has a good heart and is a fine person like all the others."

Zanuba did not reply. She was silent for a moment and then leaned over the cards again, busy and preoccupied with them. Before long she was immersed in her previous musings and thoughts. Muhsin began to watch her, following the movement of her hands as she picked up and set down the cards. He observed the expression of her face as if eager to discover her secret. His eyes shone with an innocent, childish skepticism.

Finally he approached her familiarly and sat beside her. He asked with a mischievous smile, "For whom are you reading the cards? For a bridegroom?"

As soon as she heard these words her eyelids, which were heavily daubed with kohl, began to tremble. She raised her hand nervously to rearrange her scarf—which did not need it—over her henna-tinted hair. Then, her eyes downcast, she replied with embarrassment, "No, by the Prophet. That's not what I was thinking about."

Muhsin kept up his veiled sarcasm. "Then about what? Am I a stranger you should hide things from? You know, auntie, by God Almighty, no one has chased away bridegrooms except Uncle Hanafi. The mistake is entirely Hanafi's—he's the one who's run off the suitors."

"No, by the Prophet, that's not what I'm thinking about."

She kept her eyes modestly downcast as though she were a girl of twenty. Muhsin was silent for a moment while he stealthily began to study the lined and misshapen face of this old maid. He seemed to be wondering whether this modesty of hers was an affectation or genuine. Then, as his boyish sarcasm was quickly overtaken by a kind of melancholy, he bowed his head.

Zanuba grew up in the country, where she was neglected and left uneducated. She served her father's wife and raised chickens for her. When her brothers Hanafi and Abduh came to Cairo to study, she came with them, together with Mabruk ibn al-Khawli—her classmate from the village Qur'an school, who had not prospered there. She was to look after them and to manage the household. Her long stay in the capital had had no real effect on her; she remained just as she had been. The life of the commercial center and metropolis had intruded on her only superficially, its influence limited to her clothing and speech. In these she mimicked the standards of her Cairo girl-friends and modern neighbors without understanding what she was imitating. Muhsin said he once heard her greet some female visitors before noon with "*Bonsoir*, ladies." Zanuba, like many other homely women, was aware of everything except her homeliness. She was quite amazed when she saw one of her acquaintances and neighbors become engaged and marry. Although she was lovely, thrifty, the lady of her house, perfect in every way, she still had no offers. She consoled herself by ascribing that to: "Luck, bad luck! May you never experience it! Nothing but that!" This she repeated to herself and others.

Even so, matchmakers had come to her more than once. One of them stopped her pitch as soon as she saw Zanuba, stood up, and, tucking her wrap around her, hastened to leave. Zanuba was sure the matchmaker was delighted and was going immediately to inform the groom. She scurried along beside her to the door of their apartment, whispering, "So, say nice things about me to him."

The matchmaker's smirk was hidden by her veil. She replied maliciously and sarcastically, "Well, sister, no one deserves praise but you!" and departed, never to return.

One day, however, there occurred a historic event in the life of Zanuba. On a day that hardly seems to have been part of her life, a rare, never to be repeated opportunity was offered her, but, alas, Mr. Hanafi, through his stupidity, idiocy, and naiveté, forfeited that unique opportunity. One afternoon, as luck would have it, good fortune—apparently grumpy at being slandered and unfairly censured—sent Zanuba a suitor who was an educated gentleman, a perfectly acceptable person, to ask for her hand directly, without recourse to a matchmaker or mother. He was apparently a good-hearted gentleman with upright intentions, or else a pious person who placed blind and unlimited trust in God.

This man came and met with Hanafi Effendi, a math teacher at the Khalil Agha school, since he was head of the household and its ranking member by age and position. He discussed the matter with him, saying that there was no need to delegate someone from his side to see the bride and that he would be satisfied with asking whether she was ugly. So long as she wasn't ugly or misshapen, he wouldn't demand anything more.

He asked the alleged "president" of the household his opinion of her with a polite, reserved look. The honorary head of the household, as they termed him, raised his head to the other man and gazed at him with nearsighted, inflamed, and diseased eyes. He turned toward him his misshapen, dust-colored face, which sun and sores had scorched and turned the color of the mud bricks used to build village houses, and put his hand to his fez, which he pushed back, revealing an ugly, scarred forehead. Then he said to the suitor warmly and vehemently, "No way! Never! Have no fear! Not bad at all! Rest assured! A piece of cake! This woman is as sound as a gold guinea—twenty-four carat! Look, sir. Have you observed me closely? The bride is my spitting image, a chip from the same block, because she's my full sister, born immediately after me."

The gentleman suitor was surprised and temporarily flustered. When he calmed down a little he began to look stealthily at Hanafi's ugly face, trying to hide his distress, disgust, and distaste. Finally, he muttered in a kind of whisper to himself, "Impossible . . . no way!"

Hanafi heard him and quickly tried to reassure him, "Impossible how? It's a sure thing, a fact!"

"Impossible!"

"Just don't trouble yourself at all, sir, about that aspect. You, sir, have nothing to worry about! She resembles me perfectly, my guarantee. Nothing for you to worry about."

The gentleman had scarcely succeeded in getting out of Hanafi's house; nothing was ever heard of him again.

Muhsin repeated his words in a flattering and cajoling way. "It's true. It was all Uncle Hanafi's fault."

Zanuba lowered her head and did not reply. She had to restrain herself from sighing. Muhsin was silent for a moment. Then he suddenly sat up as though remembering something. A smile, which he attempted to conceal, came to his lips. He tried to look earnest and said at once, "Auntie! Have you heard? Mustafa Bey downstairs is sick."

Zanuba raised her head. This woman who was almost forty blushed slightly, although she pretended to be calm. Trying to make her voice sound normal, she asked, "Sick? Who told you?"

Muhsin, noticing the effect of this news while pretending not to, said, "This morning I ran into his servant on the stairs. He was carrying a bottle of Epsom salts."

She fixed her eyes on him as though wanting to interrogate him and pump him for more information but gained control of herself right away. Then she lowered her eyes in embarrassment. She was silent for a long time. Muhsin began to survey her stealthily, with a merry, childish smile on his lips.

At last he pointed to the cards and asked mischievously, "Didn't the cards tell you?" She was temporarily flustered and did not answer. Muhsin looked at her for a moment. Then he asked abruptly, "What are you thinking about?"

The woman shuddered and stammered anxiously, "I'm thinking about something else."

Muhsin would not let her off the hook. "Something else? Like what, for example?"

His knowing tone embarrassed her, but she remained calm. At that moment her mind rescued her and her memory came to her aid. She found the presence of mind to reply in a reasonably relaxed voice, "I've been busy since this morning thinking about the neighbor's handkerchief that disappeared the day before yesterday from the roof." As soon as Zanuba said this, Muhsin's face changed color, turning first red and then yellow. He bowed his head straightaway. Zanuba didn't notice what had suddenly happened to Muhsin but seemed to feel she had discovered a topic that would rescue her from her plight. So she rattled on: "Saniya's silk handkerchief! Do you think it's true, Muhsin, that the wind blew it away?"

Muhsin did not reply; he wasn't even able to raise his head.

Zanuba continued, "By the Pure Lady, that talk just doesn't make sense to me. The wind blew it away? Does the wind make handkerchiefs fly off?"

Muhsin stammered, "Then what?"

She answered immediately, "No way! Do you take me for a fool? By your life, it was stolen!"

The boy looked at her fearfully and did not utter a word.

She continued, "By the dear Prophet, it has been stolen. Do you know who stole it?" When Muhsin didn't respond, she went on, "The person who stole it . . . is Abduh!"

Muhsin suddenly raised his head with obvious astonishment and joy. "Uncle Abduh?"

She answered critically, "He's the only bad character we've got."

Muhsin bent his head and did not utter a word.

She declared forcefully, "By the Prophet, I'll consult the astrologer tomorrow and find out."

Muhsin raised his head. "Astrologer?" he muttered anxiously and fearfully.

She continued, "If it's not that boy Abduh, I deserve to be beaten with a slipper." She was quiet for a moment, but then a thought crossed her mind. She said suddenly, "Oh! What a pity! I forgot someone!"

Muhsin trembled a little while silently waiting for her verdict. She turned quickly toward him and asked in a satisfied tone, "Who do you think stole the handkerchief?"

The boy stirred anxiously, but she didn't notice. She exclaimed, "Salim!"

Muhsin gasped and looked up at her. He mumbled, "Mr. Salim?"

She said, "That ne'er-do-well—God's truth, have you forgotten his stories and adventures with women? Enough boasting and swaggering to turn our brains inside out! Fie on that one! Why does he tilt his fez, twist his mustache, and start playing that musical crock of his with the bellows? What? He thinks he looks swell? Outrageous! By the Prophet, Muhsin, then you favor him with one of your sweet songs. He thinks we have forgotten about him and his famous story that got him suspended by the government? The escapade with the Syrian lady from Port Said! My cousin Salim—how different from you! Is anyone as sneaky as him?"

Muhsin relaxed. The tense expression left his face, and he smiled innocently. Then he gently moved closer to Zanuba and asked in a voice marked by a slight quaver, "Auntie, did you see her on the roof today?"

Zanuba said, "Who? Saniya?"

The boy nodded his head affirmatively. He asked, attempting to speak naturally, "What did she say?"

Zanuba replied, without noticing his concern, "About the handkerchief? She laughed and said, 'If it truly was stolen, the thief deserves the gallows.'"

Muhsin's face turned as red as the carpet. He lowered his eyes and looked at the floor.

CHAPTER 2

It was time for supper, and the folks gathered in the apartment's entry hall around a cheap white wooden table covered with an oilcloth. Time had drunk and eaten away on this table just as they had. Time perhaps had slept on it too, like the servant Mabruk, whose bed it became at night when he spread his pad, covers, and fleas on it. In the morning it changed back into a table, with a big dish of fuul midammis and loaves of bread for breakfast. For lunch or supper there was a trencher of farik or fuul nabit.

At this hour the familiar trencher was in place, and steam was rising from it, but everyone was abnormally silent and still. They hadn't begun to eat yet and seemed to be waiting for someone. In fact, Hanafi's place was empty, but was that why they were so quiet and despondent? Here was Zanuba placing her hand on her cheek as though sunk in distant dreams. Mabruk, for his part, sat as usual at the table's end, where he was inhaling the aroma of the steam rising from the trencher. He was looking most impatiently at the empty place near him where Hanafi Effendi always sat. Yet, he did not dare, even so, break this pervasive silence. From time to time he would stare across the table at Muhsin's new clothing with a dejected, servile look. Mabruk wasn't an ordinary servant; he was a childhood friend of the family. In his youth he had played with Hanafi, Abduh, and Salim in their village of al-Dilinjat. For this reason he was the family's honorary servant, just as Hanafi was the honorary president of the household. Muhsin, in his place at the table, was busy too, stealing glances at Abduh and Salim as though he wanted to discover the secret of their strange silence. Abduh and Salim were without doubt the ones responsible for the gloom this evening. It was obvious that something unusual was troubling them and depriving the supper of the enjoyment, uproar, and good humor customary among the folks whenever they gathered around the table. Salim Effendi, the merry reveler, was unusually solemn. His head bowed, he was twisting his long mustache silently and thoughtfully. Abduh was rigid and sullen. His large nose was swollen and redder than usual, a sign of his intense anger and alarming nervous agitation this evening.

They continued to be silent, their eyes downcast, for some time. At last Abduh abruptly raised his head. He struck the table nervously and forcefully with his fist; all their heads shot up at that. He shouted, "Damn the father of anyone who waits!"

Startled by this cry, the servant Mabruk jumped to his feet at once and headed toward the bedroom. After casting a glance at Hanafi Effendi's bed he returned to say, "Hanafi Effendi is stretched out in his bed. He is eating, excuse the expression, rice pudding with the angels."

At that point those present heard a voice from the bedroom saying, "Rice pudding with the angels? I hope our Lord hears you, Mabruk Effendi! It's been a long time since I've eaten rice pudding. Not since I started working and entrusted the household finances to Zanuba."

Zanuba raised her head and said angrily, "Since when? Lie! You, Your Lordship, by the holy name, by the Prophet, won't you rise and shake yourself? Don't be sluggish! The food's been cold since morning."

From the bedroom Hanafi called, "You all think I'm sleeping? You're retarded. I've got piles of work—piles!"

Then Abduh shouted restlessly, "No waiting! No more waiting!"

The honorary president replied from the bedroom, as if chanting a ballad, "Folks, be patient! Patience is good, though bitter. It won't harm you. I just have a notebook and a copybook to grade. Sir, a notebook and a copybook! Sir, a notebook and a copybook! Sir, a copybook! Even if there are two—so what? It doesn't matter."

Abduh restrained his rage while Hanafi remained in the bedroom with its four beds, busily correcting his pupils' copybooks. He was reciting and singing, "Sir, a notebook and a copybook! Sir, a notebook! Sir, a copybook! Oh, sir, a copybook. . . ."

Of those present, only Mabruk responded to the singing. He stood in the middle of the hall, looking toward the bedroom and the president's bed. He began to clap his hands like a member of a claque, exclaiming, "God! God! 'Sir, a copybook,' one more time."

Finally Abduh's patience gave way. He screamed, "I swear by God Almighty, I won't keep still. That's it!"

He reached for his spoon nervously and raised it forcefully and violently. He thrust it into the trencher of bread crumbs in sprouted bean broth and then began to eat, paying no attention to anyone else.

At that, the others exchanged looks, as though Abduh's action had stunned or displeased them. Nonetheless they didn't dare say a word.

Zanuba, however, shortly remarked, in a voice that sounded as though she wanted to justify Abduh's action, "Yes! So! The fault is with His Lordship, the great head of the house, who is always stretched out as lazy as a sultan's three sleeping jesters. By the life of our dear Lord, the house is spoiled because of him."

She turned to Abduh to flatter and cajole him in order to calm him down. She seemed to want to change the course of the conversation and the flow of their thoughts to another subject and commented, "Mr. Abduh, don't get yourself all riled up. Don't worry about the food and drink and his conduct!"

Then she suddenly changed her tone and asked, "I wonder if one of you found Saniya's missing handkerchief."

Abduh had begun to quiet down, secretly regretting his extreme vexation and anger, or at least letting these show. But as soon as he heard Zanuba and the words "Saniya's handkerchief" in particular, his expression changed and became worse than before. Zanuba's attempt to calm him with these words had been like calming a fire with oil.

Abduh bowed his head for a moment while his neck veins swelled and his nose turned red. When he could no longer contain himself, he burst out shouting, "You mean you don't know who has the handkerchief? We all know who has it!"

Muhsin trembled and looked at the floor, but Abduh turned to his cousin Salim and gave a significant, hostile nod of accusation toward him. He continued, "If we were fools, he could put it over on us. But—praise God—we aren't. He can tell you where the handkerchief is!"

He pointed straight at Salim, who was twisting his mustache deliberately and now asked frigidly, "What are you saying, sir?"

Abduh replied in a dry, caustic tone, "There's no need for talk. We all know."

With equal coldness, Salim asked, "Know what?"

Abduh didn't respond and instead turned his face away. Salim shook his head in amazement and said, "Bravo to you! You steal it and accuse someone else? But that's how clever young people are today."

Abduh turned forcefully and violently and shouted at him, "If I had a record of previous offenses in such matters, it might be true."

Salim was a little taken aback and muttered, "Previous offenses?"

Abduh continued insidiously, "If I were a captain, and they had suspended me from my job because of a certain Syrian woman . . ."

Salim steeled himself, raised his head forcefully and proudly, and asked, "Meaning what?"

Even so, he recognized that he had lost the support of his audience. That incident, which they kept bringing up, indicted him in advance, without any need for evidence. They all knew he was a police officer who had been suspended from work for the past six months, charged with abusing his authority. He had been accused in Port Said of flirting with a Syrian woman who resided in a house opposite his police station. Had the matter been limited to flirting, posturing, sending signals, greetings, and smiles, and to twisting his mustache and wriggling his eyebrows at that fetching woman whenever she appeared at her window, that would not have justified his suspension. But Salim

Effendi went further, wishing to approach the beautiful crea-
ture. For a long time he sought for a way, and finally Satan
guided him. One summer afternoon, when it was very hot and
emotions and bodies were aflame, Salim Effendi, the police deputy, in his official uniform—its brass buttons and the three stars
on the shoulder shining in the glaring sunlight—rose quickly
and proceeded to the pretty woman's building. He went up to
her apartment and knocked on the door, saying, "Open up,
ma'am. Don't be afraid. I'm the police chief."

"Why? What's the matter?"

"Just let me in for a bit."

"For what reason?"

"For what reason? Glory to God, what a nature you've got.
In order for me to search. I've got to search your flat. Won't
you let me search?"

Thus he had affirmed falsely and deceptively that he wished
to search her apartment. The trick was discovered, the news
spread, and it was a scandal. He was suspended for a year.

All this flashed through Salim's head like lightning. So he
was silent and didn't offer any rebuttal. Abduh observed this
and said in the tone of an enraged assailant seeking revenge,
"Right! It's better for you to say nothing. The matter is as
clear as the sun."

Salim raised his head and asked coldly, "What do you mean?"

Attempting to appear calm, Abduh said, "There's no need.
We know everything!"

Salim straightened up and said sharply and earnestly, "Listen then. Enough! We're not gulled by your con job. You think
you're being clever. No, shame on you! If you actually were
clever, you'd confess and not deny it. Nevertheless, this much
is clear—I'd just rather not have to speak. If you don't believe
me, I'm ready to prove my words with the others present as my
witnesses."

Abduh interrupted him: "Prove your words?"

Salim replied immediately, "Certainly. Want me to prove it
to you? Just let me keep my eyes on you while I search your
clothes and belongings!"

At that Abduh released a loud, sarcastic laugh and asked,

"What did you say? Search! God's will be done! Sir, aren't you still forbidden to conduct searches?"

The others followed this debate in total silence, young Muhsin the most intently of all. As he listened attentively, fear and anxiety took turns racking his heart. Yet he had reason to be quiet and calm—who would accuse or suspect a boy of fifteen?

While they were thus engaged, Hanafi suddenly appeared at the doorway leading from the bedroom to the hall and began to stare nearsightedly at them. After a moment he asked, "What's up? Why are you so rowdy tonight? Were you drenched in afreet water? Fine! Here I am. I've arrived. I'm here."

No one answered him. Only Zanuba reacted, by raising her eyes and glancing at him indifferently. Then she looked away and went back to her previous thoughts. The honorary president of the family advanced toward the table as he said, "I mean, I don't see anything to eat or drink! Where's the supper you were talking about? We heard there was a supper. Seems that was a rumor!"

Zanuba raised her head and pointed to the trencher listlessly. "Don't you see this?"

Hanafi adjusted his spectacles and directed his gaze at the trencher and its contents. Then he exclaimed, "Fuul nabit? May Umm Hashim come to our aid!"

Zanuba didn't look at him but rose at once and set off to the kitchen, saying, "There's this other dish too." No sooner had Zanuba departed than a motionless silence returned. Hanafi sat down at his empty place near the servant Mabruk.

He waited a moment for them to say something. Finally he cleared his throat, adjusted his spectacles, and began to stare at his companions' faces in turn. Their mood appeared to astonish him. He wanted to unravel the secret of their strange conduct this evening.

"What's it all about? What's wrong with the folks?"

But no one present stirred or tried to answer him. The servant Mabruk finally looked at him and said in a serious but barely audible voice, "The folks—I'm not kidding—have been quarreling."

Hanafi asked in amazement, "Quarreling? Who's been quarreling?"

Mabruk answered tersely, "Everyone."

Hanafi sought some clarification: "Everyone! Why? What's happened? May God protect us."

Mabruk said, "To put it bluntly, everyone—they all felt like quarreling."

Hanafi's curiosity was whetted, and he asked, "But what was the quarrel about then?"

Mabruk remained still and did not respond. He cast a quick glance at the others and found them silent. So he kept his peace too, as though relieved and pleased to be a member of the silent group. Despite Hanafi's insistence, winks, and prodding with his elbow, Mabruk remained quiet, not caring to speak. He moved only his large eyes, which traveled back and forth between his plate and the trencher. Hanafi gave up on him and turned away, muttering, "How strange, people!"

The family's president tried in vain to make them talk. Then bored and enervated, he threw himself totally into eating and began to swallow silently like the others.

A short time later Zanuba returned with a dish in her hand. With one quick look from his sharp eyes, Mabruk discerned its contents and announced, "We have the honor of a goose leg."

Hanafi, the family's president, shook himself in a mock, theatrical way and protested, "No!" He rose to his feet at once, adjusted his spectacles, and stared. He affirmed, "No doubt about it. It's true, lads."

Then he suddenly straightened and changed his tone. He shouted, "Your excellency, the goose leg!"

They looked up. Once they had identified the dish, they started to exchange glances. Their eyes finally came to rest on Abduh. They seemed to be asking his opinion and plan of action, especially this evening when he was so angry and agitated.

Abduh, however, did not move or utter a word. Instead he let Zanuba place the dish confidently in the center of the table. Then he raised his eyes and gazed for a long time at the goose leg, which was resting quietly in its dish. But, suddenly, like a predatory kite, he swooped down on that leg. Grasping it, he ran to the window and threw it down to the street. Then he returned to his place without uttering a word.

Faced with this silent drama, the folks were dumbfounded for a moment. Then, with the exception of Zanuba, they all started cheering happily and laughing. Hanafi and Mabruk, naturally, were laughing, yelling, and roaring the hardest. The family's honorary president and servant were laughing straight from their pure, innocent hearts. They wanted the laughter and hubbub to continue now that they had finally found an excuse for it. Hanafi started to prolong his laughs and link them together while he looked at Mabruk, who was the only one still laughing with him. He said, "Oh! Oh, what a goose leg!"

As though he had suddenly remembered something, he turned abruptly toward Abduh and said, "But Mr. Abduh, you forget that Master Shahhata's coffee shop is below us, across the street. I bet the goose leg fell on a patron's head."

The servant, Mabruk, replied immediately, "We are God's and to him we return."*

Hanafi agreed just as solemnly: "Life is full of lessons and sermons."

Mabruk sighed and said, "My goodness gracious! A guy is sitting there, and, no kidding, everything's hunky-dory. He's ordered himself a cup of coffee—not a skewer to strike him unexpectedly."

Hanafi interrupted him in the same vein: "Descending upon him! May God preserve us and deliver us from evil!"

Zanuba was beside herself with rage. She was no doubt the only one Abduh's action had angered, but she suppressed her fury and said nothing.

Shaking his head, Mabruk continued, "There's no way around it: This world is made up of lessons and sermons."

Then Zanuba exploded and shouted at him, "Shut up then, servant, glutton, plate licker!"

Mabruk was silent for a time and asked, "Did I say some-

---

* Holy Qur'an, "The Cow," al-Baqara, 2:156.

thing? This is, to put it bluntly, a very big sermon. A customer orders at most a cup of coffee costing a piastre or a pipe for two milliemes. Then, without so much as a 'by your leave' there falls on him out of the sky, without warning, a country-style goose leg worth a pound."

Zanuba said sharply, "I told you to shut up." Then she turned on Abduh. Emboldened by his silence she exclaimed, "You, by the life of our dear Lord, will see what happens to-morrow. Spit in my face if you think you'll gain from it."

Abduh's face became flushed from anger; he shouted, "What are you saying?"

But Zanuba steeled herself and continued, "Tomorrow you'll see if our Lord forgives you or acquits you. You'll be up against me, if you get transported to paradise or a prophet intercedes for you."

Abduh gestured nervously with his hand, frightening her, and she fell silent at once. Apparently thinking it best to placate him, she asked, "Was I bringing that for you? By the precious Prophet, this wasn't for you. I was bringing this bird for Mabruk. Isn't that right, Mabruk?"

Mabruk glanced at her and then looked anxiously and hesitantly at the others, feeling trapped, not knowing what to say. Finally he agreed with her in a mildly sarcastic tone: "Oh . . . the bird!"

Zanuba continued, ignoring Mabruk's response: "Because this fellow Mabruk likes cold fowl."

Mabruk, who had no choice but to agree, nodded and said, "Right, like, no kidding, the English."

Hanafi, the president, looked at him and asked, "How do you know what the English eat?"

Mabruk replied, "What do you mean? Wasn't my cousin taken by the authorities during the war along with the other camels, donkeys, and conscripts?"

"True!" Hanafi said. "So did he eat cold fowl? By God, fantastic! It appears Miss Zanuba wants to turn us into Englishmen."

Zanuba realized that Hanafi was making fun of her. So she

turned on him and shouted sharply, "By the Prophet, knock it off you, too. Put a cap on your failure. What are these calamities, sister? I know what's come over you; by the Prophet, you've become absolutely unbearable!"

No sooner had Zanuba completed her words than Abduh looked up and screamed in his terrifying voice, "Hush! Shut up! Not a word!" Then he continued, menacingly, "I swear by God the high and mighty, I won't keep silent about you. You think we're dogs and feed us this kind of food. We're not!"

Zanuba looked at him fearfully. Then she said meekly and gently, "Didn't I tell you I was bringing it to Mabruk?"

Abduh immediately replied, "Isn't Mabruk a human being? Isn't Mabruk one of us? Since when has Mabruk been treated any differently from us? Since when has there been discrimination in the house?"

Abduh's statement was at once affirmed and applauded by the folks, who were filled with unusual resolve and zeal. Mabruk, the servant, looked down in embarrassment, and his fingers began to fiddle with the buttons of his torn and stained caftan. In the depths of his heart he sensed things he did not understand. He felt a secret desire to steal a glance at Muhsin's expensive new clothing, although something restrained him. Then he felt the urge again to sneak a peek at those costly new clothes.

Those naive glances were innocent of any ulterior meaning, but even so they conveyed his submission, defeat, and dejection, without his being conscious of that, perhaps. At that moment he may have sensed a certain dividing line that would continue to separate him from the people with whom he lived. He wasn't conscious of any of this. He didn't focus on anything in particular. It was just a quick sensation that flashed past like lightning.

Abduh went on speaking harshly and gruffly to Zanuba, "We give you our money to spend on us—not on magic and astrology."

Hanafi, the honorary president, hastened to lend his support. "Bravo, Abu Abduh! The whole budget, on your honor, is wasted on incense, charms, and shabshaba spells."

Zanuba shouted in protest, but Abduh screamed her down: "Hush, not one word! You should realize that we're not fools or little kids sucking our fingers. We all know. You economize and manipulate the expenditures so you can waste what you save on astrologers and charlatans. Ignorant woman, do you think this kind of activity is going to get you a husband?"

The honorary head of the household spoke next. "Instead of depriving us and spending the budget on—in the name of God the Compassionate, the Merciful—afreets, spend it on us. We come first. Do you mean we're less important than the afreets?"

Zanuba didn't dare speak and pretended to be busy eating. She began to consume her food silently, her face gloomy and dark, her forehead clouded and furrowed. Silence and stillness quickly dominated the room again. Everyone else started eating too, without a soul raising a topic for conversation. Soon the only sounds to be heard were those of the spoons and of chewing and sipping. The folks seemed to have finally submitted to the will of their bellies and forsaken everything else.

Nonetheless, anyone looking at Muhsin would have seen that some secret concern was troubling his mind at that moment. He was eating gravely, as though something was upsetting him. Moments before he had glimpsed that submissive, embarrassed, innocent glance that Mabruk had stolen at his new clothes. Perhaps such an innocent and naive glance meant nothing. No one should pay attention to it. But a soul like Muhsin's was capable of discerning its significance and being affected by it. It woke in him an old memory from his childhood, back when he was eight and a pupil at Damanhur Elementary School. His young companions were poor. He was the richest of them and from the most prominent family. He was Muhsin al-Atifi, son of Hamid Bey al-Atifi, one of the wealthiest and most respected local residents. Hamid Bey's wealth came from his mother, not his father. She wasn't Hanafi's or Zanuba's mother; they were his half brother and half sister. For this reason, they were poor, while Hamid Bey was rich. He had resolved to raise his son, Muhsin, elegantly, surrounded by every kind of luxury and comfort.

Muhsin, however, was one of those souls who find elegance and luxury distasteful, who perhaps are distressed by wealth. Muhsin was secretly embarrassed and pained by being rich. Time and again he had struggled, wept, and screamed to keep his family from dressing him up in fancy clothing. Time and again he had begged, pleaded, and shed tears to prevent them from sending the carriage to wait for him when he got out of school. Young Muhsin wanted only one thing: to be like his impoverished young comrades. Nothing embarrassed him more than being set apart from his peers by a garment, money, or a semblance of wealth. He felt so strongly about this that he used to keep his family name secret from his school friends.

Thus he remained one of them for a long time; they thought he was an ordinary, simple pupil like them, a boy whose parents were poor or middle class, until an ill-omened day spoiled it for Muhsin. Once, when he was in poor health, his mother was so concerned about him that she ignored his entreaties. Unbeknownst to him, she sent the carriage to wait on him. The young pupil Muhsin emerged as usual in a band of youthful comrades, who were laughing together happily, innocently, ingenuously. Then he found himself face-to-face with his parents' stately carriage. It was an unforgettable moment of embarrassment. He quickly steeled himself and ignored the carriage and its driver. He wanted to walk on by, as though he had no relationship to it. But Mr. Ahmad, the driver, noticed his young master and called him. Muhsin shuddered, pretended not to hear, and squeezed in among his companions. He wanted to hide in the group and flee, as though he wasn't the boy being called. The driver saw what he was up to and called him again by name: "Master Muhsin Bey! Master Muhsin Bey! Come here!" Then he ran after him to bring him back to the carriage.

It was at this moment that Muhsin's companions realized who their friend was. They looked back and forth, from him to the elegant carriage with its pair of fine horses. Theirs were innocent, artless glances expressing a certain humility and subservience.

What an indelible impact these glances made on Muhsin!

Actually, his friends hadn't meant anything by them, not those simple children.

At that pure and innocent age, their looks couldn't have implied anything, but Muhsin bowed his head in despair and walked toward the carriage as if to the gallows, as though he heard deep within him the echoes of an irreversible verdict proclaiming, "Muhsin has left our pack forever!"

CHAPTER 3

"Master Shahhata!" shouted Salim Effendi grandly. Then with a slow gesture of affected gravity he cast out over the table, "Bring me a shisha!" and began to twist his waxed, military-style mustache. He was deliberately attempting to give his gestures and pauses the stamp of an important person, someone with status and influence, as, from time to time, he shot stealthy glances at the balcony of Dr. Hilmi's residence. This was a wooden balcony of the old type enclosed with windows like the mashrabiya latticework you see on the waqf, or religious trust, buildings on Al-Khalij Street.

Salim Effendi noticed that although he had called al-Hajj Shahhata, the summons had not been obeyed. He immediately turned his bare head, which he had perfumed with a bouquet of colognes, and looked into the coffee shop.

It was shortly before noon, and the sun felt burning hot. Even so, Salim was sitting on the pavement outside the coffee shop in his customary place. He was not one to pay attention to the heat of the sun. His fez, which he had taken off and placed on a chair beside him, bore witness to that. He did, however, keep taking his cheap silk handkerchief out of the sleeve of his jacket to dry his forehead with affected delicacy, care, and circumspection to prevent the handkerchief from mussing his hair or even touching the pointed tips of his mustache.

Captain Salim Effendi called out once again, "Master Shahhata!"

But Master Shahhata appeared not to hear anything. The clamor and tumult inside the coffeehouse were deafening. No request could be heard over the guffaws, coughing, spitting, and hawking of the customers. Master Shahhata's patrons weren't Salim Effendi's type; they were inferior to him in rank and status, in temperament and sensitivity, and in their present circumstances. While Salim Effendi sat alone and aloof outside the coffee shop, preoccupied by his emotions and beautiful dreams, the rest of the clients were inside, busily shouting and making a racket, virtually tearing the place down around them. Al-Hajj Shahhata's patrons carried on like that every day. They all knew each other. They all frequented that small coffeehouse at the same times to fulfill a duty they could not neglect, the duty to laugh. These people seemed to have no profession other than laughter and to have been created for that alone. They spent all their life, so far as could be told, guffawing between sips from their shisha or their straight Turkish coffee. They were always in their customary place, grouped around one man who was their leader. He was an outstanding and distinguished wit and comedian. Their eyes were fixed on him even when this mighty buffoon wasn't uttering a word. They would all burst into laughter to the point of choking from their bellowing and mirth, whether what he said made any sense or not. They seemed to find in the very act of laughing and shouting a sensual pleasure. Master Shahhata and his waiters went here and there among them, bringing their orders and laughing too, not knowing why at times. They seemed to catch the contagion of it, or else they wanted to increase the uproar and merrymaking and to stoke its furnace. Not a minute would pass without Master Shahhata clapping his hands and shouting in a totally unnecessary way, as though he wanted the tumult and exuberance to reach their ultimate: "Proclaim the oneness of God! Whoever prays for the Prophet gains."

Nothing could be heard over his voice except the call of a patron: "Waiter, a glass of arrack," or the echo of a backgammon piece striking the board powerfully and forcefully in a corner of the room as the player said, "My move . . . six-four!"

But the loudest voice was always that of the grand buffoon along with his claque, who surrounded him as though he was an idol encircled by devout worshippers. He would talk to them, ordering and forbidding: "Listen, fellow, you and him!"

Then voices rose: "Listen. . . . Hush!"

When he spoke, he blended jests with song and mixed ordinary conversation with ballads. While addressing those closest to him in a whisper about some observation he had made or about some private matter, he would suddenly raise his voice without warning: "Seven waterwheels pouring couldn't put out my fire. . . ."

They would all respond, "God!"

"Seven waterwheels pouring couldn't . . ."

At this point Master Shahhata passed by carrying an order. The singer stopped singing and, turning to his associates, said loud enough to be heard, "Seven waterwheels pouring couldn't wash Master Shahhata's face."

They all laughed in sync with the song's beat: "Ha . . . ha . . . ha!"

They kept laughing till their throats went dry and the master of ceremonies silenced them. Master Shahhata wasn't offended and laughed with them. Then he cast the grand buffoon a look of censure and entreaty and said, continuing on his way with an order, "Fine, Hajj Hasan."

Master Shahhata heard a voice calling him from outside the coffeehouse and shouted, "Coming, coming!"

In his haste, he collided with a chair and spilled a drink over the head of a customer. He bent down to pick the remnants of the glass from the ground, saying, "Bless the Prophet and gain. . . ." He ignored the patron whose face and cloak he had drenched.

The customer started drying his face with the end of his cloak and grumbled, "I'll gain what? . . . Can't you be a little more careful?"

Master Shahhata looked up at him and said, "Bless Fatima's father, fellow. By your Creator, that's arrack! How many people get a facial with arrack? That's better than holy water, fellow."

Everyone laughed, launching into one of those long, interminable, shared guffaws—like lunatics. They actually might have been mad or just a group enjoying communal laughter.

Salim's patience was exhausted, or, more correctly, he pretended it was. He gestured angrily while looking out of the corner of his eye at Dr. Hilmi's balcony. He clapped his large hands together like thunder and shouted, "Master Shahhata! What's up, Master Shahhata?"

A few seconds passed. Then the proprietor of the coffee-house emerged, saying, "At your service." Recognizing Salim Effendi, Master Shahhata rushed to him: "Your Honor! Anything you desire!"

He said that and stood respectfully before his regular, well-groomed customer. Salim seemed to like the deferential way he stood there, for he did not order at once. He let him wait while he enjoyed this respect and twisted his mustache, without forgetting to cast some discreet glances at the aforementioned balcony.

Finally he said in a deliberate, grave, dignified manner, while gesturing toward the pipe with the pretended ennui of a person of rank, "A light! Quick!"

He stole another glance at the balcony. Then he said imperiously to the proprietor: "You're still here! I told you: quick!"

Master Shahhata put his hand on his head, which was wrapped with a cloth, and said, "My goodness, sir. Your Excellency's orders! I'm yours to command."

He started to leave to fill the order, but Salim Effendi detained him to say, with his eye on the balcony, "Don't you know who I am, Master Shahhata?" Then in a haughty voice he added, "Don't let my civilian clothes deceive you!"

Master Shahhata quickly replied, "I know! I know—noble people from a fine and distinguished family. My God, wealth and blessings!" He went toward the door of the coffeehouse and cried out, "A light for the shisha outside!" Then he disappeared inside.

Salim turned his attention to the pipe, putting the mouthpiece in his mouth. He lifted his head to puff smoke into the air, gazing directly at the balcony of Dr. Hilmi's house this time. He fixed his eyes there but shortly looked down in despair. He did not observe any trace of a person within, neither a man nor a woman.

Salim finally got fed up and started to mutter in annoyance and displeasure. He felt weary and started to yawn. He had good reason, because it had been about three hours since he had deposited his massive body like a sack of cotton in this seat at the coffeehouse. How many times had he looked at the balcony in vain! How many times had he clapped his hands like thunder for Master Shahhata and his waiters, shouting at them in a tone he always attempted to keep—one of authority, like that of a police chief. In fact he did not limit his commands to the owner of the coffeehouse and his assistants; for three hours he hadn't allowed a single bootblack to pass by on the street without calling to him peremptorily: "Boy, come polish my shoes!"

He would thrust his foot at him, saying, "Dust it off properly. You don't know who I am."

He accosted any newspaper vendor he spotted with: "Listen, boy. Do you have *Basir*? If not give me *Ahram*, so I can read about promotions and transfers."

Any hawker he saw he stopped with: "Come here, fellow. Show me your German-made suspenders. No, no, no! That's fake. I buy exclusively from Sim'an's. Scram, chap."

His aim was to speak in a loud, resounding voice, while looking from time to time at the balcony. Unfortunately none of these maneuvers attracted anyone's attention, by God, except that of a customer sitting directly behind him. He had perhaps arrived without Salim Effendi noticing.

It was obvious that this patron hadn't missed a single one of Salim's maneuvers. Indeed, judging by his interest and furtive smile, he seemed pleased, diverted, and secretly amused by what he saw, as if he was watching a show. This customer and spectator was none other than Mustafa Bey, the neighbor who lived downstairs from Salim and his companions. Had Salim redirected his eyes even once and scrutinized the building next to Dr. Hilmi's residence—number 35, in other words the residence of the folks—he would have noticed the shadow of a woman at one of its windows. She too had been staring despondently, for twenty minutes, but at the coffeehouse. He would also have heard the racket and commotion the woman was producing at her window on the pretext of setting out the pottery water jugs, which had brass tops.

Salim wasn't aware of any of this, and perhaps Mustafa Bey did not notice either. His preoccupation with observing Salim's movements and moods, his interest in that spectacle, kept him from noticing the window in question or what was happening there.

The heat became intense, and the sun was blazing. Salim was forced to put on his fez. He cast one last look at the balcony and then took out his watch to consult it. It was not past eleven yet. The rest of the folks didn't usually return for lunch before one o'clock. What should he do with the time? Should he sit there any longer or go off? If he went off, where to? He hesitated, not knowing what to do.

Visions of the Soldier's Coffeehouse from the time it had been his favorite place flashed through his mind. He remembered those charming foreign women who frequented the top floor. He had—according to his boasts and perceptions—been adored by those shy gazelles who had thronged around him and gazed admiringly at his mustache, which was twisted to stand at attention. But, alas! God curse the stricken heart that had brought him to Shahhata's shabby coffeehouse to loiter there all day long, his eyes raised to the sky as though he were a pagan worshipper of an inanimate balcony.

He yawned again and then stretched out his hand languidly to grasp a newspaper from the table. He tried to read, but one of his eyes was always straying from the page, looking every which way and rotating anxiously in its socket like a marble in a cup until, at last, it came to rest on the designated balcony.

A period passed like that. Then suddenly something happened that caused Salim to let his newspaper fall to the table. He began to look attentively in front of him. He had seen the servant Mabruk come out of the house carrying a small bundle under his arm. What attracted Salim's attention and interest, however, was that Mabruk was wearing his good cloak, the one clean garment he reserved for feast days, holidays, and other religious celebrations: his best caftan. And even more remarkable was that Mabruk was heading toward Dr. Hilmi's house.

In fact, Mabruk, after he appeared at the door and surveyed the street, turned his head and walked a few steps in the direction of the beloved neighboring residence, singing, "What's it to me? What did she tell me?"

At that moment Salim rose halfway and shouted, "Mabruk!"

The servant turned toward him and smiled but didn't stop or say a word. Instead he continued singing, "Go get drunk! Come along, without a veil."

Salim rose and began to shout and beckon dramatically: "Shut up! Listen: I'm talking to you, Mabruk. Listen: I'm speaking to you! One word—then you can go."

Mabruk didn't reply. Instead he stopped and looked at Salim but kept on singing. Then he turned his back on him and started to walk off with dancing steps. When he reached the door of the doctor's house, he stopped at the threshold and glanced back at Salim. He gave him a wink out of the corner of his eye, wriggled his eyebrows, and popped inside.

Salim stormed and snarled between his teeth, "What an animal!"

Mustafa Bey, who was sitting behind Salim, didn't miss any of this. He smiled. Ten minutes passed. Then a woman enveloped in a black wrap appeared on the stoop of building number 35, in other words Salim's residence. This woman stopped for a moment and froze, giving long, direct glances at the coffeehouse from eyes that flashed on either side of her face veil's brass nosepiece. Then, with an abrupt motion suggesting vexation and annoyance, she turned her back on the coffeehouse and walked down Salama Street heading toward Al-Sayyida Zaynab Square.

As soon as Salim saw her, he rose, forgetting his newspapers and stick on the table and chairs, to hasten after her. With his long stride he caught up to her in three paces. She was swaying and swinging her body in front of him, slowly and deliberately as though she were the ceremonial camel litter bound for Mecca.

Salim gave a quick twist to his mustache and moved alongside her. He cleared his throat and whispered, "Good gracious, what about this! Peaches and cream! Your servant, lady: A carriage or an automobile?"

She recognized his voice at once. So she stopped and looked at him. With discernible sorrow and disappointment she said, "So it's Your Lordship?"

Salim was flabbergasted. Slightly embarrassed, he muttered in astonishment, "Zanuba?"

She smiled dejectedly beneath her veil. Without bothering to wait for his answer, she started to look stealthily and anxiously at Shahhata's coffeehouse behind her, as though searching for something or someone.

Salim sensed the awkwardness of this situation. Disconcerted, he said, trying to cover with a laugh, "Ha ha! God reward you! I was thinking . . . In short, then—where are you going?"

Distracted and absentminded, Zanuba asked, "Me?"

At that, Salim seemed to remember an important matter and quickly observed, "By the way, that boy Mabruk just went into the doctor's house."

He waited for some response or explanation, but she remained silent. Then she finally asked grimly, her eyes searching the chairs of the coffeehouse at the end of the street, "Who?"

He looked at her for some time. "What do you mean, 'Who?' I told you: Mabruk!"

She came to herself, turned toward him, and said, "Mabruk? What about him? He just went on an errand."

"Errand?"

"Oh, he went to take a dress to Saniya Hilmi. I was using it as a pattern."

Salim was satisfied and paused for a bit. Then he started speaking again in a strange voice: "And for an errand like this of two steps the beast wears his best caftan?"

Zanuba replied indifferently, "That's what he does whenever he goes there."

Salim stared at her. "Strange! He's always that way when he goes there?"

Zanuba answered absentmindedly, "He has a right. He doesn't like to visit people in dirty clothes."

Salim stammered, not fully convinced, "True, that's right. In short, where are you going?"

She hesitated and looked at him uneasily. Then she said, "Me? I want to go to . . . Zahra the seamstress!"

Salim asked, "Here in Al-Baghala?"

She replied quickly, "Ah . . ."

Salim moved to depart and as he left said, "Okay then, I'm going back. So give my greetings to Zahra—if she's pretty and her cut is too."

Then he turned around and walked back to his place at the coffeehouse.

Zanuba stood frozen for a moment, hesitating, as though prey to some unseen force. She began to think as best she could—as well as anyone with her mental training could. She didn't know what to do. She threw one last glance at the coffeehouse and then looked away in disappointment. She proceeded slowly on toward Al-Sayyida Zaynab Square. As soon as she reached the mosque, she stood and peered through the bars of the tomb's grille. She stared at the resting place of the granddaughter of the Prophet of God, with its rich decoration. Then she began to recite sadly to herself the opening sura of the Qur'an in honor of the Pure Lady. Al-Sayyida Zaynab Square was the chief station for the vehicles of the Suarès omnibus line. A person passing there would soon have his ear assaulted by the voice of a conductor or driver shouting at intervals, "Let's go—Al-Muski! Al-Sayyida Nafisa! Al-Muski! Muski! Muski!"

Zanuba was the first to respond to this voice. The name al-Muski reminded her of something. She hesitated a moment. Then, suddenly, she made up her mind, walked purposefully to the omnibus stop, and quickly boarded the front of a vehicle that was preparing to depart.

For half an hour the Suarès wove through the streets and ancient alleys, cutting through the old quarters of Cairo until it finally reached the Muski. Passengers heading there descended while the others craned their necks to look out both sides at the countless shops and stores. Eye-dazzling wares were displayed—silk and velvet textiles, brocades with gleaming gold and silver thread and glittering sequins; jewelry of real gold or in fish-scale patterns; shoes and slippers, with heels or flat, in the latest fashion; haberdashery, laces, household linens; brass and china vessels;

metal and wooden spoons and ladles; in short, all the goods available in this renowned market.

As usual, the congestion was severe, and the Suarès had difficulty cutting its way through the waves of people gathered like ants on narrow Al-Muski Street. Their shouts became loud, and their movements and clamor intensified: the whole lot of them, merchants and vendors, buyers and lookers. The merchants and vendors were calling out their wares, competing for customers with alluring words and cheap prices as well as oaths and asseverations on their honor and integrity that the product was excellent, that this was a real opportunity, a bargain—gentleman's honor.

The buyers—women and men—were looking, bickering, fingering, and taking the textiles in their hands to rub them and test their strength vigorously. They were also haggling and wrangling. Voices rose. Oaths multiplied. Pushing and shoving grew worse. Sweat poured over brows and faces. Added to this hubbub was the sound of the finger cymbals of the licorice drinks vendor, who was crowding against people, his red jug in front of his belly and his brass pitcher in his hand. He had set a block of ice on the jug, where it cooled nothing and had no contact with the drink. It was employed, rather, merely for advertising. "Hold on to your teeth! I sell drinks. Your teeth are none of my business." Then he would snap his finger cymbals or fill a glass for a customer, shouting in another tone, "Patience is beautiful! Real wealth is to be poor but debt-free. Watch out for your teeth!"

The passengers of the Suarès watched all of this from the windows of the vehicle; Zanuba alone remained frozen and still, oblivious to the Muski and its contents. She didn't move or awaken from her reflections and broodings until she reached her stop at Sayyiduna al-Husayn, where the omnibus came to a halt and Zanuba descended. She seemed to know exactly where she was heading, because no sooner had she stepped to the ground than she proceeded through that district from street to street and alley to alley, not turning aside for anything, not wasting a single second.

In the heart of this district was a small, dark, dead-end alley. It wasn't a place a stranger to the district would happen upon by chance. This alley was Zanuba's destination, and she took fifteen minutes to reach it. She stopped at the door of the last house and hesitated before knocking gently. After a bit it opened, revealing an old woman who looked at her with a frown of inquiry. Zanuba said to her with some embarrassment, "I've come for Shaykh Simhan."

The old woman stepped aside to let her in and replied gruffly, "Come this way."

Zanuba entered, and the old woman closed the door behind her. Then she led her to a spacious, sparsely furnished room and pointed her to an empty pallet on the floor beside a woman nursing a baby, saying to Zanuba, "Sit and rest till it's your turn."

She exited through a door at the far side. Zanuba sat down on the pallet and began to look around her. Women, seated like her on the ground, were also waiting their turn. They were all pressed together, and their faces were focused on the door at the end. They remained silent, staring at that door as though it were God's portal. A single notion was sketched on the features of these women, and thus a spectator might well have imagined that a single thought was passing through their minds, uniting all of them. They might well have been participating in the communal Friday prayer, when souls part for a moment from their separate bodies and each spirit forgets its individual existence. All gather and dissolve together, focusing on one thing: the prayer niche. Zanuba forgot her personal concerns briefly under the influence of that feeling to which the other women had succumbed. For a time she sat motionless and silent, looking, like them, at the door at the end.

Finally she turned quietly and gently to her neighbor, the woman with the baby, and whispered a question to her: "Have you come for the shaykh, you there?"

The woman looked at her and replied, "Yes, sister."

Then she gave her baby a breast like a cow's udder and added, nodding at him, "Because of the child; may it never happen to you."

Zanuba moved her mat closer to the woman and leaned

toward the baby tenderly. She said, "The protection of God's name for him. What's the matter with him?"

The woman raised a blue blanket from the face of her small son. Then she answered, "His eyes! May our Lord protect you! Look!"

Zanuba glanced at the baby's eye, which was severely inflamed. "Haven't you taken him to a physician?" she asked.

The woman raised her head and turned toward Zanuba argumentatively. In a knowing and confident voice, she asked, "Physician? Do those doctors know anything, sister? I've tried everything. Oh, what they prescribed for us, sister. God only knows. So is there anything stronger and more effective than molasses, kohl, cassia powder, and leeches—even, may God protect you, a poultice of warm donkey droppings? None of that was any use or help. What do you say?"

Zanuba was silent for a moment. Then she asked the woman simply, "Does Shaykh Simhan know about eyes?"

The woman puckered her mouth in regret at Zanuba's ignorance. Shaking her head in its black scarf, she said, "Know? You ask if he knows? What doesn't he know? It's clear, sister, you haven't heard about him. What a shame! So the person who directed you to Shaykh Simhan al-Asyuti didn't tell you about his miracles?"

Zanuba replied politely, "They told me a lot, but I haven't tried it yet."

The woman interrupted her: "No, sister. This is tried and true. I'm not the only one. Before I had this baby, I was—may it never happen to you—unable to bear a child. And what I did to try to get pregnant! What's happened to me has been a catastrophe. My husband had his heart set on children. Morning and night he would tell me, 'Woman, either you get pregnant or I'm going to take another wife. I'll bring you a co-wife.' So tell me, sister, what was I to do? The Lord knows, I tried every medicine and remedy, magic and practice. And none of it, on your life, did a bit of good. One day, my neighbor Umm Hasanayn, God bless her, told me, 'Get up, sister. Go see someone named Shaykh Simhan beyond Sayyiduna al-Husayn. People have spoken to me about him and said . . .' By God and

your life, it turned out to be true. Do you know how long I had
to wear the amulet? A month passed and as the crescent moon
rose at the beginning of the next one, I felt my belly and let out
a trill of jubilation."

Zanuba asked with innocent wonder, wanting to be sure,
"He made you pregnant?"

The woman replied immediately, "What else, sister! May
you become pregnant that quickly! Just a month after the
charm! What more could you ask for than that?"

Then the door at the end of the room opened. The old
woman appeared at the threshold and gestured to the woman
with the infant. She said dryly, "Let's go. Get up. It's time for
you and your son."

The woman leaned down over her child to look at him.
Then she turned to Zanuba and said, "Sister, the baby is sleeping. All last night, sweetheart, he didn't sleep a wink. If you're
in a hurry, sister, you go on ahead of me."

Zanuba rose swiftly. She thanked the woman and asked
God's help for her along with that of the Prophet and of Sayyiduna al-Husayn, that they should grant her wish and bless her
son with a cure. Then she hastened to the door and followed
the old woman.

Immediately after crossing the threshold of the rear door,
Zanuba found herself in the shaykh's room. It was square in
shape and dimly lit, with no windows except for an opening
with an iron grate near the ceiling. Its furniture was limited to
a few pallets on the floor around a small table that sat on an
antique Persian carpet.

In the center of this room stood the shrine of Shaykh Simhan. It wasn't a shrine or tomb in the normal sense. It was,
rather, a kind of cage hidden from sight by a heavy black cloth.
On top of it was a row of ancient brass candlesticks, and its
small door was like a little window with gold-colored bars.

At that golden door to the tomb or cage, a middle-aged
woman sat. She was plump and her face was not unattractive.
This, they said, was the shaykh's wife. She, alone, could contact him through this small golden door. Then she transmitted

his cryptic words to visitors who came with requests. No one had ever seen the shaykh himself. How and why was he imprisoned in this cage or tomb? No one knew. Perhaps no one had ever asked. People simply knew that Shaykh Simhan al-Asyuti had mysterious powers and knew genuine secrets. He was in constant contact with—"In the name of God the Merciful the Compassionate"—the beings from below.

Zanuba stood there frozen, staring at the mausoleum. The shaykh's wife gestured silently for her to approach and sit on one of the mats near her. So Zanuba sat down in the place indicated. The woman scrutinized her and in a low, even voice asked, "Have you thought it over?"

Zanuba was quiet for a moment; then she answered hesitantly, "Yes . . . but, just . . ."

The woman knit her brow, which was almost hidden, swaddled in a navy blue kerchief, and asked, "But, just what?"

Zanuba answered in embarrassment, "A pound! That's a lot!"

A contemptuous smile traced itself on the woman's lips. She demanded, "A lot? One pound a lot . . . for what you plan to receive? What if I had told you five pounds like the woman just before you?"

Zanuba said softly, "By the Prophet, if I were rich, I wouldn't hesitate."

The shaykh's wife replied gently, "Bless the Prophet, sister, do you think I'm asking for this money for myself? Do you think this is something that goes into our pockets? Never, by your head's life! We are not in need, may evil stay far away! Good gracious! With your pound, sister, we're going to purchase on your behalf, may God's name protect you, a white sheep without any marking to sacrifice here at this door in your name. Then we will rub the threshold with its blood so God—by the blessing of his saints, who hear us—will open the door of happiness and bliss for you."

Zanuba's heart pounded suddenly at this thought. She lowered her gaze for a moment in embarrassment. Then she regained her poise and composure, removed her handkerchief from her bosom, and untied its knotted ends. She extracted a pound note from the money in the handkerchief and placed it with a trembling hand on the small table. She asked, "Just a sheep? No amulet or anything?"

Staring at the pound on the table out of the corner of her eye, the shaykh's wife replied, "Well, sister, well, an amulet, incense, the material for the spell . . . I know the right incense for you, never fear: gum ammoniac, jet, verdigris, Persian gum, euphorbia, and jinni's eyelid! You must have an amulet you wear at all times and never remove—may God's sovereign name protect me—because you are vulnerable. Be patient a little more, until I ask the shaykh for you."

She put her mouth to the aperture or golden door and called, "Shaykh Simhan!"

They heard a faint voice, which seemed to come from a corpse in a tomb on the day of resurrection, issue weakly from the gloomy depths of the shrine. The woman turned to Zanuba quickly and demanded, "Tell me at once your name and those of your father and grandfather."

Zanuba replied hurriedly, "My name is Zanuba. I'm the daughter of Rajab, who was the son of Hamuda."

The woman returned to the door of the mausoleum and shouted: "Shaykh Simhan! Her name is Zanuba, daughter of Rajab, who was the son of Hamuda."

A deep and terrifying silence reigned for a moment. Then, suddenly, that weak, indistinct, distant voice came again. The woman put her ear to the golden door and began to listen attentively. Zanuba in her concern watched the woman closely with impatient eyes. She craned her neck and positioned her ears to try to catch a few words.

The woman finished quickly, left the door of the shrine, and approached Zanuba to reveal the results to her. "Listen! The shaykh says he wants a clipping from his hair, but it must come from the part at the top of his head."

Zanuba stammered in a low voice, embarrassed and agitated, "Whose hair?"

The woman looked at her wickedly and exclaimed, "Whose hair! The hair of the man you have in mind."

Zanuba repeated to herself, "A clipping from his hair?"

The shaykh's wife added by way of confirmation, "From the part at the top of his head. Don't forget. If you're clever, you'll have a word with the barber who cuts his hair and get him to supply what you need. Listen too, sister. The shaykh says you must have, as well, the heart of an orphan hoopoe."

Zanuba inquired innocently, "The heart of a hoopoe?"

The woman affirmed: "An orphan—the heart of an orphan hoopoe. Be careful not to forget."

Zanuba asked, "Just that?"

The shaykh's wife answered, "Bring those first. An amulet made from these will never fail—the shaykh said so from below, and he is the supreme authority on the mysterious and miraculous. Whoever wears this amulet, man or woman, will be able to cast anyone he has in mind at his feet."

Zanuba was convinced and blushed.

CHAPTER 4

That afternoon was just like a spring day. The sky was pure blue without a dollop of cloud in it. Egypt's sun seemed rejuvenated in its eternal, flaming vigor and sent down on Cairo a scorching heat, which was partially alleviated by a heady Nile breeze.

At that hour Zanuba and Muhsin were on the roof, sitting on a small mat they had spread by their neighbors' wall for shade. This wall separated their roof from that of Dr. Hilmi's residence. Zanuba was busy stitching on a dress, and her face had a thoughtful expression. Muhsin, who was wearing his new suit, had a book in his hand. He was turning its pages without showing much interest in reading. They had been silent for a long time and seemed disengaged from each other, lost in thought, forgetting the other person's existence. Finally Zanuba noticed and decided to break the silence. She asked Muhsin casually and without stopping her work, "What's your book?"

Without looking at her Muhsin answered tersely, indifferently, and listlessly, "A poetry collection."

Zanuba pushed the needle against the thimble on her finger and asked, "A collection of what?" Muhsin didn't answer.

Zanuba was silent for a moment. Then she sighed and said, while cutting out a piece of fabric: "How unlucky I am! If only I knew how to read and write! What a pity! All I lack is reading and writing."

Muhsin raised his head with a smile and glanced at her wryly. He repeated her word mischievously in a whisper. "All?"

Zanuba didn't notice his sarcasm. She fixed her eyes on a section she had finished. She lifted it in her hand and drew her head back to examine and scrutinize it. Then she said to Muhsin with pride and satisfaction, "Look, Muhsin! Tomorrow you'll see it when it's finished."

At first Muhsin looked with little interest, but suddenly he remembered something that made him blush slightly. He said with almost fanatical admiration, "God! It couldn't be more beautiful."

Soon he added hesitantly with embarrassment, "It looks just like a dress of . . ."

Zanuba quickly added proudly, "Saniya! Exactly! It's patterned after Saniya Hilmi's new outfit. Have you seen it?"

Muhsin stammered in his agitation, "Seen?"

Zanuba said, "Her outfit, Saniya's new suit. Haven't you seen it? It's enough to make a person delirious. The latest fashion! You'll see it now with your own eyes too, Muhsin; in just a moment Saniya will come to their roof to hand it over the wall."

Muhsin's heart throbbed, and he looked incredulously at his aunt, as if seeking confirmation. But Zanuba lifted her head, looked at the top of the wall, and explained, "I arranged that with her this morning. I wonder why she's late."

Muhsin trembled and asked, "She's coming here, now? I mean her suit? That is to say, the suit. . . ."

He got tangled up in his words and immediately fell silent. Then, as though his heart had been filling with repressed delight, he burst out suddenly with unusual enthusiasm, "Yes, aunt, yes! I certainly want to see the model for your new dress. I just have to see it and examine it. If only you knew, auntie! By God Almighty, I always love for you to be well dressed. A pretty person must dress well."

Looking at her new dress, Zanuba replied, "Of course!"

Muhsin continued enthusiastically, "That's true! You know, auntie, tomorrow people will be going wild over you. By God Almighty, tomorrow you'll be in good shape. People will be saying, 'Wow!'"

Zanuba lowered her eyes bashfully as though she were a girl and said in a voice that was slow and soft with a ring of forced modesty to it, "Don't fib!"

Suddenly she thought of something that agitated her a little. She once again busied herself with her work as though nothing were troubling her, but her mind began to reflect and brood.

Muhsin continued chattering enthusiastically. She was eager

to listen to his praise to satisfy her vanity, but something still preoccupied her mind.

Finally her face revealed that she had found what she sought. She turned to Muhsin and said with unusual affection and sympathy, "You're handsome too, Muhsin, by the Prophet, in your new coat and trousers."

He replied in a tone of innocent, childish pleasure, "Really?"

Zanuba responded while looking at his hair, "By the Pure Lady, it's just that, well, what a pity."

Muhsin anxiously asked her, "What?"

Zanuba inquired hesitantly, "Where do you get your hair cut?"

Muhsin quickly raised a hand to his head and began to comb his hair with his fingers.

Out of the corner of his eye he cast a quick, stealthy glance at the top of the wall. Then he asked, "Why? What's wrong with my hair?"

Zanuba said tenderly, "Nothing. . . . All I mean is that your barber isn't as good as he might be."

Muhsin asked, "Master Dasuqi?"

Zanuba said, "Do I know him? Isn't there anyone else in the area?"

Muhsin replied, "What's the matter with him? He's the barber for all of us, for me and my uncles and . . . and all of us."

Zanuba added snippily, "And for the servant Mabruk?"

Muhsin replied instantly, "So what? What's the matter with his haircuts?"

Zanuba was perplexed and fell silent. After a bit she retorted, "No, all I mean is that someone wearing a suit like yours deserves to have his hair cut by a barber for quality people."

Muhsin lifted his eyes and looked straight at her as though trying to grasp her meaning. He was afflicted by a light anxiety concerning the intent of her remark. Was she directing covert criticism at him and his new clothes and his fresh interest in his appearance? Did she mean to insinuate that his clothing and elegance now set him apart from his uncles and companions? Her tone and facial expression, however, weren't critical. Zanuba continued, "Oh, if I were you, I'd get my hair cut by a barber for well-to-do, respectable people. I know why you let this happen. Your father is rich, but you may not know where to find a good barber. Oh! See, what good luck! There's our rich neighbor, the investor, who lives below us. He must have a superb barber."

With a sigh of relief and a smile of understanding, Muhsin asked quickly, "Mustafa Bey?"

Zanuba said hesitantly, but with her concern showing in her eyes and a slight blush on her face, "Smarty-pants, do you know where he gets his hair cut?"

Muhsin looked at her out of the corner of his eye and answered with a smile on his lips, "Yes, well . . . I know. I saw him once sitting at the large barbershop across from the mosque—the one with 'Perfection Salon' written above it."

Zanuba wanted additional clarification and asked, "Opposite Al-Sayyida Zaynab Mosque? Do you mean in the square beside the store . . ."

She didn't finish, because a sweet, musical voice called from the adjoining roof, "Abla Zanuba, where are you?"

Then a beautiful face with glistening black hair appeared above the wall. Zanuba looked up. Muhsin's face suddenly turned white and then red. He froze, lowered his eyes, and fixed them on the book in his hand.

Zanuba called out, "Come here, Saniya."

But Saniya noticed Muhsin and said delicately and graciously, "Oh . . . no. It's not important. Another time."

Her beautiful face disappeared immediately behind the wall. Zanuba shouted at her and rose to chase after her, "Come. Come, Susu! There are no strangers here. This is Muhsin. Are you going to hide and conceal yourself from a small child? Are you—name of God protect you—who are well schooled, embarrassed to see him? Come on!"

Saniya returned to the wall with a polite but enchanting smile on her lips. She said, "I didn't notice." Then she turned toward Muhsin cautiously and circumspectly and said engagingly, "*Bonsoir*, Muhsin Bey."

Feeling flustered and confused, Muhsin quickly rose to his feet and stammered out an answer while looking at the ground: "*Bonsoir!*"

Zanuba put her hand over the wall, which wasn't much more than a meter high, and accepted a small parcel from Saniya, after asking, "You brought the dress? Give it here, sister. Come, cross over the top of the wall and jump down here with us like always."

Saniya apologized sweetly. "I can't stay, sister. Mother is waiting downstairs for me to play the piano for her."

Zanuba asked, "Now? Right now?"

Saniya answered with a smile, "Yes, now, right now!"

Zanuba urged her, "Just stay for five minutes. What difference does five minutes make? Just sit down, and then I'll go with you."

Saniya asked happily, "Is that true, abla?"

"Yes, by the Pure Lady. Just sit down here first so you can see how I have cut out my dress. Then we'll go down together."

Saniya replied, "I accept, for your sake. Give me your hand, abla, please." She rested her soft hand on Zanuba's broad shoulder and hopped down to the mat. Then she announced with a smile, "So here I am on your roof." The two women sat beside each other while Muhsin gradually scooted away from them till he reached the very edge of the mat, leaving himself no room to retreat.

Zanuba quickly took the parcel and opened it. She chattered on, although her voice had a serious tone to it, mixed with some astonishment. "Since when, sister, has your mother liked listening to the piano?"

Saniya replied, "Always, abla. Mama loves the piano, especially when she's feeling tired. Today she's home alone and doesn't have any visits or errands scheduled, or anything. Papa left early as usual to hold forth at Al-Jawali Pharmacy. Oh. Look, abla! By the Prophet, Mama wanted to call on you today, and I'm the one who prevented her."

Zanuba protested, "Why, Saniya? What a shame!"

Saniya replied in a merry, playful voice, pointing to Zanuba's dress, "Because I knew you were busy with your dress. I was afraid the visit would delay you. Didn't I do the right thing, abla?"

Zanuba patted beautiful Saniya's shoulder and said, "Many

thanks for your taste and graciousness, but, by the Prophet, you were wrong. How would your mother delay me? In short let's quickly look at the way the garment is cut out and go down. It certainly wouldn't be right to leave your mother alone."

She picked up her dress at once and showed it to Saniya, saying, "Here, sister, in all its splendor, is my new dress. Look at the fabric—first quality crepe de chine. But it's not like your fabric. What could I do? I asked at Palacci, al-Mawardi, and al-Jamal. Sister, I kept looking until my knees gave out. But I came back saying: It will do as well. Don't imagine it was cheap. The same price, sister, by your life. My dear, ask . . ."

Then she turned to Muhsin, "Is my dress going to turn out like this?"

The boy's face became as red and hot as fire. He replied enthusiastically in a quavery voice, "It is really outstanding!"

Zanuba turned to Saniya and lightly rapped her soft arm, saying, "See how your dress pleases him, Susu?"

The beautiful girl raised her head and looked at Muhsin demurely. He lowered his eyes and mumbled his confirmation: "Really." Then his hand groped for his book while he avoided looking at Saniya.

The girl noticed his confusion and concealed a little smile. Then she turned her black eyes, which resembled a gazelle's with long black lashes, to the book in Muhsin's hand. She asked with modesty that was not innocent of coquetry and enchantment, "Is that a novel?"

Without looking at her, Muhsin answered as he pointed with a trembling finger at the title of the book, "No, it's the diwan of Mihyar al-Daylami."

Saniya asked in her delicate voice, "Do you love poetry?"

Muhsin hesitated a moment. Then he raised his head suddenly like someone determined to be a little more courageous and replied, blushing but smiling, "Yes . . . how about you?"

She answered, "I actually prefer stories. All the same I love some of the verses and lyrics I sing at the piano."

As soon as Zanuba heard the word *sing*, she put her dress in her lap and turned excitedly to Saniya. She said enthusiastically, "Muhsin, too, sister . . . don't you know he sings? This fellow has quite a voice, Miss Saniya. Haven't I told you that when he was young—may the name of God protect him—he used to sing with the vocalist Maestra Shakhla', in her troupe?"

Saniya was astonished and asked, "Are you kidding or is that for real?" She looked inquisitively at Muhsin.

Muhsin, however, avoided her glance and started to leaf through his book. Then he mumbled, "That was a long time ago."

Smiling, Saniya asked him pleasantly, "Is it true you were in the troupe?"

He attempted to look at her this time when he answered, "I was an amateur," but soon lowered his gaze from her engaging black eyes.

Zanuba quickly asked entreatingly, "Muhsin, sing us, 'Your Figure Is Prince of the Boughs.'"

Beautiful Saniya shouted in amazement, "The famous song of Abduh al-Hamuli? But who can sing that? It's ancient and terribly difficult."

Pointing at Muhsin proudly and confidently, Zanuba immediately replied, "He knows it, may the Prophet's name protect him. Sing, Muhsin!"

The boy blushed. Flustered, he eventually stammered, "I don't know it now. I've forgotten."

Saniya smiled slyly and artfully. She said, "Perhaps Mr. Muhsin can't sing it without instruments."

Muhsin sighed deeply. He said, nodding his agreement vigorously, "Right . . . true exactly!"

But Zanuba looked at him out of the corner of her eye and said, "Liar! You were singing it to me just yesterday downstairs in the hall. Your problem is that you're embarrassed now."

Muhsin raised his head, trying to be courageous, and said, "No, not at all. Yesterday I sang because you accompanied me on the soup dish, like a tambourine."

Saniya burst out laughing so hard her mouth opened wide, revealing regular teeth like inlaid precious stones. At first Muhsin didn't understand why she was laughing; his last words had been straightforward and unadorned. He turned

toward her cautiously, modestly, and politely. As soon as he realized that he had succeeded in making her laugh, he blushed.
After that he felt proud—as though his heart was being ca-
ressed by the delicate, invisible fingers of a novel happiness. He
had never experienced anything like this before. Saniya rose,
smiling, and proposed seriously. "Fine, what if there's a piano
instead of the tambourine?"

Zanuba cried out: "The Prophet's light upon you! But do
you think your mother would object?"

Phrasing her words coquettishly Saniya replied, "To the contrary, Mama loves the songs of Abduh al-Hamuli, because when
she was young she heard him a lot, when he was still living."

Zanuba turned toward Muhsin as she too rose, saying,
"Come with us then, Muhsin."

Although the boy's reaction to this invitation was indescrib-
able, heartfelt happiness, he hesitated in embarrassment.
"But . . . just . . ."

While heading for the wall, Saniya said sweetly, "Come,
Muhsin Bey! You've no right to hold back. I've promised to accompany you on the piano . . . *parole d'honneur!*"

Muhsin's heart pounded as though he was afraid, but at last
he rose and headed for the wall with the two women.

It took only a moment for the three to cross the dividing
wall to the neighbors' roof; that is, the roof of Dr. Hilmi's residence. From there they went to the door of the steps leading
down into the house.

Then they found themselves in a spacious and beautifully
furnished hall filled with carpets and sofas covered with bro-
cade. Hung on the walls were stuffed heads of Sudanese gazelles and elephant tusks. A terrifying stuffed crocodile from
the Sudan was similarly hanging above the entry.

Muhsin wondered why these Sudanese trophies were in the
house but remembered all at once that Saniya's father, Dr.
Ahmad Hilmi, had been a doctor in the Egyptian army and
must have spent time in the Sudan like most of the troops.
Saniya left her guests in the parlor and hurried to look for her
mother, whom she found in her bedroom, where she had

spread a small prayer rug and was concluding the afternoon prayer. Saniya waited for her to finish and then approached her to say, "Mama! I've brought some guests—Abla Zanuba and . . ." She stopped and hesitated.

Her mother began to arrange the white silk prayer veil around her head after folding the small prayer carpet. She rose, saying cheerfully, "A blessing by God! Welcome to her!"

Saniya quickly added with apparent indifference, "And her nephew, Muhsin."

Her mother looked at her and asked, "Her nephew?"

Saniya replied resolutely, "Yes, her nephew Muhsin."

Her mother frowned slightly and said, "That's really not quite right for her to bring a man here."

Saniya laughed scornfully. "A man? Is he what you'd call a man? A small boy like this!" Then in a serious tone of voice she added, "Haven't you heard, Mama? They say his voice is very beautiful. He's going to sing for you now the songs of Abduh al-Hamuli."

The mother found the situation too much to deal with. She asked in disbelief, "What are you saying? God's will be done! He's to sing for me? A man?"

Saniya replied a bit sternly, "Again you say 'man'! I told you, ma'am, he's not a man. He's like your son or grandson."

But the mother didn't want to listen. Turning her back on her daughter, she asked, "Have we come this far? Is this the latest fad too? You'll drive me out of my mind eventually."

Saniya didn't respond. For a moment she remained quiet and looked at her mother with rage. Her mother began talking again. "Fine, daughter. You're one of today's generation, marching through the soot of fashion. You won't even let anyone tell you what a third of three is. And your mother as well—what do you want from her? No! Do me a favor. Leave me as I am. Excuse me as a favor to the Prophet. May our Lord guide you!"

Saniya was upset. She took her mother's hand, wishing to lead her. She said a bit sharply, "Don't be silly. I told you he's a child, a boy. Come see for yourself. Come!"

Her mother hesitated, feeling afraid and weak. She protested, "But, daughter . . ."

Saniya at once said forcefully, "No 'but.' You make a big deal of it and exaggerate far too much. Come see him first and then talk."

"Well, daughter, just don't drag me this way. Do me a favor. You're always dragging me behind you. You'll make people laugh at me. This time, by your life, I won't listen to your words at all." She attempted to free herself from her daughter's hand.

But Saniya would not release her. Although she retained her earnest and commanding mien, she said graciously and gently, "No, Mama, you must listen to me, because I know more than you. Come!"

The mother said in despair, "You go. You go by yourself. Why me too? Oh, what a fate is mine! Where has this been lying in wait for me?"

Saniya said in an angry voice while dragging her mother, "You must come with me, Mother! It's not right at all. I promised. I can't go back on my word. What will they say? Let's go then. At once! They've been cooling their heels in the parlor forever."

Looking at her fearfully, her mother said, "All right. Wait. Since you insist, let me put on a veil then."

The girl lost patience and shouted, "Veil! What a calamity! A veil because of a small boy? You are definitely going to make people laugh at us. Listen, Mama, I beg you. It's not necessary. Believe me, if it were improper Abla Zanuba would be the first to notice. Won't you trust Zanuba either? Someone like you, of your generation? She's the one who brought her nephew to see you. If she thought that scandalous, she wouldn't do it."

This final argument seemed to have convinced the mother. All the same she looked quickly at her daughter's eyes one last time, searching for some sign to convince and reassure her. Then she carefully covered her hair, which was streaked with gray, with the white scarf, attempting to conceal most of her face, and asked, "Where are they?"

Saniya sighed like someone God has finally aided, and led her mother silently to the large parlor. Saniya left her mother and went quickly to Muhsin and Zanuba, who were sitting on a sofa. She said by way of apology to them for the delay and slowness, "Please excuse us. Mama was praying."

Saniya's mother came forward at that moment, leaned over to kiss Zanuba's cheeks, and said, "Welcome, Miss Zanuba! Welcome a hundred thousand times!"

Then she turned to Muhsin and extended her right hand to him in greeting, while with the left hand she tugged at her scarf to hide her face. "An honor, Muhsin Effendi."

Then in a tone that an inattentive observer would have thought welcoming or complimentary, she added, "This, by God, is a man!"

Muhsin uttered two or three words that could hardly be understood. He kept his head bowed and his eyes on the ground.

Saniya's mother seemed to show that she welcomed Muhsin by addressing him in an earnest and sedate tone. "Muhsin Effendi, your mother is a fine, princely lady."

Muhsin raised his head in shame and embarrassment to ask, "Tiza, do you know my mother?"

Zanuba quickly intervened. "Oh, what a shame! So! Didn't you know, Muhsin? But this goes back quite a time!"

Saniya's mother agreed. "A very long time ago, God save us. By now she will have forgotten me. It goes back to the days when we were little girls. We were neighbors and grew up in the same area. All of us girls used to play together in front of their house. Your mother was Turkish, from a Turkish family. She was the youngest but was our leader. We feared and minded her. She was the daughter of a Turkish soldier with a blond mustache! Whatever game we played, she was the boss. We called her the queen and the sultan's daughter. She loved to set herself apart from us. If we wore red for the holiday, she wore green. And if we wore green, she wore red! Woe to us when she got angry! She used to say, 'Tomorrow, I am going to be extremely rich, and I'll buy you for my maids and slaves.' Oh, those days have passed. How sweet they were."

She stopped talking and looked heavenward, as though yearning for her happy childhood. There was a moment of stillness and quiet that Saniya finally broke. In a merry, cheerful voice she said, "Let's all go to the piano . . . to the salon . . . away from here."

She proceeded to lead them to the salon, which had a wooden balcony overlooking Salama Street and Shahhata's coffeehouse. It was a medium-size room furnished in European style with stuffed armchairs, cushions, electric lamps, and a black piano in a corner opposite the balcony door, which was wide open.

Saniya sprang to the piano with the lightness of a gazelle and, without waiting for them to take a seat, passed her expert fingers over the ivory piano keys, producing a swift sound like the warbling of sparrows. She stopped suddenly and turned toward her guests. Addressing the youth who had taken a seat at the edge of the room, she said, "Why are you sitting so far away, Muhsin Bey?" Pointing to a chair next to her she said, "Please come here."

Muhsin rose quickly as though pricked by a pin and sped to the chair indicated, like a hypnotized person responding to a command from his hypnotist.

Then Saniya commented with a smile, "Yes, that's the way. Now you can sing along with me. So show me how this old-time song begins."

She played a melody with one hand and began to hum it softly. But then she turned vigorously toward her mother and Zanuba, who had not stopped chatting from the moment they entered. She cried at them, "So will you please listen? We're about to begin."

Zanuba replied, "Right, begin, may our Lord give you strength. Here we are, ready to listen." Then she turned to Saniya's mother, who was beside her, and told her with pride and admiration, "Now you're going to hear Abduh al-Hamuli!"

The mother was astonished and asked in amazement, "By the Prophet, is that true? Does he, by the name of God, know how to sing Abduh's songs—young as he is—by heart?"

Saniya motioned to her for silence and then looked at Muhsin. She said, "Let's go, Muhsin Bey!"

The lad trembled but saw no alternative to obeying. So he

rose and moved closer to the piano without knowing what he was doing. Saniya looked at him, her fingers on the keys. She said with an intoxicating smile and look, "I've got to tell you the truth, Muhsin Bey. Don't count on me to get it right."

Her voice was like music. The boy felt the blood rise to his head and sensed a warm intoxication. He found in himself a drunken courage and said in a tone of mild censure, "Is that what you promised, Miss Saniya? Do you mean, at the last minute, to make fun of me?"

Saniya laughed, revealing a mouth like a magic goblet capable of dizzying heads at a distance even before they take a sip. She answered, "I assure you, I'm not making fun of you. It's just that the song is hard, and I haven't studied it yet. You begin first, Muhsin Bey; I beg you." She straightened herself as a sign to begin. Muhsin hesitated a moment, feeling flustered. Then he opened his mouth and closed it without uttering a word or emitting a sound. Saniya looked at him, inviting him to sing with a look that could not be defied. Then in order to encourage him, she began to play on the piano what she thought was the song's opening melody.

At that, those present heard a voice emerge and slowly increase, quivering a little at first but becoming more assured and balanced. It spread a warm sweetness through the air of the room with a variegated and tender tune.

Zanuba didn't pay attention or listen so much as watch the face of Saniya's mother to gauge from it how the song affected her. When she was assured of her astonishment, amazement, and admiration, she began to nod her head with self-satisfied pride. She gestured toward Muhsin, showing her confidence in his ability and genius.

Saniya's mother was genuinely amazed by Muhsin's expertise and mastery and began to listen with unusual attention.

Saniya too was listening to Muhsin with contentment and pleasure. She gazed at the ceiling, smiling tenderly and repeating some of the tune to herself along with him. But she did not at all grasp that the singer was referring to her and thinking of her when he sang Abduh's song:

Your figure is prince of the boughs
Without any rival,
The rose of your cheek is sultan
Over the flowers;
Love is all sorrows;
O Heart, beware,
Rejection and separation are
The reward of the daring.

CHAPTER 5

It was evening when Muhsin and Zanuba returned home. No one in the whole world was, or could have been, happier than Muhsin that night.

Like the impact of a shock that is felt only after it occurs, Saniya's existence dazzled and overwhelmed young Muhsin. He didn't realize how much happiness had conquered him until he left her. What a beautiful dream! Was what happened this afternoon possible? Although he had been expecting no more than a peek at her, he had seen her and been able to converse with her, after never having spoken with her at all. The only time he had ever seen her before was with his uncles when he had peeked through cracks in the door when she came once to visit Zanuba.

That had been about two months earlier, on a Friday when the folks were a happy, congenial community. Mabruk had come running to them with a twinkle in his eyes and pointed toward Zanuba's room, saying, "She has guests and one is a lady."

Then he kissed the tips of his fingers. The folks rose, led by Captain Salim, and hastened to the closed door of Zanuba's room. There they all bent down by the cracks in the door, pushing each other aside with their shoulders. They were laughing together under their breath, innocently, like happy youngsters. When they looked into the room, they were astonished by a beauty such as they had never seen before. After that, they raced each other to the holes of the door whenever they learned she was visiting Zanuba. That had been Muhsin's first vision of her when he scampered to that door with the others. He gazed with them in adoration at that image. But now, how did they compare with him? He had just been with her a moment ago. He had spoken with her. He had sat beside her and had possibly gained her admiration. He would be seeing her frequently, very frequently, because she had asked him to teach her to sing according to the principles of the art. Her mother had agreed and consented to that. Was it possible for all this to happen between the afternoon and evening prayers? What happiness and what a miracle!

Muhsin felt a need to confide his total bliss to someone. But to whom? He remembered her silk handkerchief, which he carried at all times, the way pious people carry the Holy Qur'an. Let him confide his feelings to her handkerchief, then.

His soul yearned to be alone and secluded in some remote place, so he could be by himself, kiss this cherished handkerchief, and reveal to it many things, chatting with it at length. But the group had returned from outside and supper was ready.

Muhsin sank into his beautiful dreams and did not hear the tumult and uproar rising around him. They were searching for Mabruk. Salim and Abduh were looking with annoyance at the door leading outside.

Twisting his mustache, Salim said, "This isn't like him at all to be late for supper. His whole life he's been the first." Abduh responded with nervous gestures of his hands.

Perturbed, Zanuba observed their distress silently and anxiously. From time to time she attempted to calm them, telling them, "It's still early for supper. Why are you in such a hurry? Mr. Hanafi is sleeping. When I went to wake him just now he yelled, with his eyes closed, that he's not getting up or moving so long as the sky hangs over the earth."

Both Abduh and Salim cast a swift look toward the bed of the honorary president. Abduh grumbled and huffed, "God deliver us from such laziness!"

A period of silence ensued. Then Salim suddenly turned toward Zanuba and asked her mischievously, "You mean you don't know where Mabruk went?" Zanuba, however, looked away evasively and walked quickly toward Muhsin.

Abduh, finally noticing Muhsin's solitary seclusion in a corner, rose and approached him. He asked, "And you, Muhsin, are you hungry or not? God! Why are you so quiet today, sitting by yourself?"

At this moment Salim approached Zanuba as though he had remembered something. He asked her in a meaningful tone, "Mabruk hasn't gone on an errand . . . to . . . for example . . . ?"

Zanuba pretended not to hear. Trying to change the topic, she tapped Muhsin on the shoulder gently and turned to Abduh to say proudly, "May he have the protection of God's name—Muhsin enchanted Dr. Hilmi's family today with his sweet voice. The old lady, Saniya's mother, swears it's a performance exactly like Abduh al-Hamuli, and Miss Saniya, who plays the piano to perfection, asked him, who knows the songs by heart, to teach her to sing."

When Muhsin heard her say this, he was displeased and fearful. He didn't want any of his uncles to know about this, at least not so soon.

He was right, for Zanuba's release of this information produced an immediate effect. On hearing it, Abduh appeared dazed and incredulous. He looked at Muhsin with doubt and suspicion. Then he seemed to have grasped at last the secret of his silence and seclusion. Similarly, Salim didn't fail to notice on the young boy's face the profound impact this visit to the neighbors' home had made on his psyche. Salim twisted his mustache and cleared his throat and in a cold, stinging tone remarked, "God's will be done! A fine craft that provides honey to eat: a paid singer in private homes! I wonder how much you charge for that, Mr. Muhsin." Muhsin raised his eyes and glared harshly at Salim but did not condescend to answer him.

This increased their doubts. Abduh turned on Zanuba and said to her sharply, "Madam, so you take him around to sing to people? That's the last straw!"

Muhsin suppressed his rage and gained control of himself. He replied quietly, "What's it to you?"

Abduh flared up in anger and raged, "What did you say? What's it to me? Do you think you're an adult? You're a little boy! You came here to concentrate on your studies, not to work as a song stylist. You sit your competency exam this year. By God, if only your parents knew!"

Muhsin couldn't stand this and screamed, "It's not your job!"

Then he rose violently to move away, fighting to control his outburst of temper. Zanuba stopped him and asked mildly and gently, "Where are you going, Muhsin?"

He didn't reply. He freed himself from her and went off toward his bed. Zanuba followed after him a step, asking, "Aren't you going to have supper?"

Without pausing, Muhsin answered tersely and gruffly, "No!"

Zanuba went back to Abduh and gave him a look of blame and censure. She said, "You have no right to get angry. By the Prophet, that was not at all necessary. What's wrong with him teaching Saniya to sing when she, name of God, is going to teach him to play the piano?"

Abduh shook with rage. "What are you saying!"

Salim emitted a forced laugh and said to Abduh, "Do you hear? He teaches her singing and she teaches him piano. How extraordinarily beautiful!"

Zanuba turned toward him and stared at him for a long time. He grasped the meaning of her look and wanted to retreat a bit. Trying to seem an impartial counselor, he said, "Of course, our only goal is his welfare, because of his studies and . . . and his parents . . . and . . ."

Abduh nodded his head in agreement while his eyes wandered through space. At that moment, the two felt the mutual accord between them being reestablished—that old, harmonious entente between them.

Muhsin undressed and climbed into bed, retreating inside the mosquito net draped over it. He sought the solitude and independence that only a person with a private room can enjoy.

For the first time Muhsin resented this style of living: five individuals in a single room. For the first time he felt exasperated by their communal living that had always been a source of happiness, contentment, and joy for everyone—for him, his uncles, and Mabruk, the servant; in other words, the folks, as they chose to call themselves.

Muhsin hid his head beneath the covers, wishing to block out the cold, merciless voices of his comrades so he would hear nothing but the beautiful, enchanting, musical voice of Saniya. He began to recollect, trying to remember the events of that happy day.

Muhsin didn't omit anything, not even the most trivial details. He didn't overlook even ephemeral gestures and passing words that memory usually doesn't retain. He began to set out in his imagination everything related to the day's events. Finally he lingered over his memory of how appreciative and enthusiastic Saniya had been when he finished singing . . . and that smile she cast him when she offered him the rosewater punch and explained that it was his reward. Those hands and fingertips that presented the glass, those sweet smiles, her teeth, her looks, her eyelashes!

Muhsin closed his eyes to see her. Then he tried to fall asleep, hoping she might appear to him in a dream. But how could he sleep that evening when his heart was so awake it seemed divine?

Sleep fled from Muhsin's eyes, and he realized he would not sleep that night unless she gave him permission. He remembered the words of Mihyar al-Daylami:

> Send me your dream visions in my sleep,
> If you permit my eyes to slumber.

CHAPTER 6

Abduh's and Salim's patience had limits. Zanuba's attempts to pacify and calm them were futile. They finally resolved not to wait for Mabruk and went to the dining table, grumbling and fuming. Abduh ordered Zanuba in a nervous voice to wake Hanafi and Muhsin at once and to serve the meal without further delay.

No sooner had Zanuba obeyed and stepped toward the bedroom to rouse the sleepers than the outside door opened and Mabruk appeared, panting like a tired dog. Between gasps of breath he exclaimed, "Oh, oh! I've totally destroyed myself walking around, you Muslims!"

Abduh and Salim turned toward him in amazement. Abduh asked, "What's the matter? Where've you been?"

Mabruk answered in the voice of a person on the point of death, "The orphan hoopoe . . ."

Salim put a hand to his ear, trying to understand. "What?"

Mabruk moaned, "The orphan hoopoe! May God requite and bless us for this hoopoe, this orphan! Oh world! Oh people!"

Zanuba stopped in her tracks, struck by fear. She began to look stealthily at Abduh. He was frowning and asked Mabruk dryly, "What orphan hoopoe? I don't understand you at all!" He turned to ask Salim, "Have you understood him, Mr. Salim?"

Salim twisted his mustache and put a finger to his brow. He replied, "I'm still investigating this puzzle in my bean."

Zanuba regained control of herself and began to gesture secretly to Mabruk not to say anything. But Mabruk appeared not to understand her signs, for he began to rub his knees, saying, "Oh, my knees! Starting this afternoon, by the life of the Prophet's beard, I have been running around—from Al-Husayniya to the Citadel, to Zaynhum, and to Al-Darrasa."

Then he raised his head, turned toward Zanuba, and said,

"All of this because of you and because of—I'm not kidding—
the orphan hoopoe. I have asked throughout the town and
found only one hoopoe. I don't know whether he's an orphan
or not. I didn't ask him. Am I someone, Miss Zanuba, who
understands, no joke intended, bird talk?"

He still did not get the message from Zanuba's winks, which
were secretly signaling him to be quiet in front of those present. He continued, "The upshot was that when I was on my
way back I met a fellow named Balaha, who's the butcher's assistant. He said, 'No problem! Give me a riyal, and I'll get you
a fine piece of hoopoe, just like you want, an orphan on both
his mother's and father's side. If you find any of his family, return him and you won't need to say anything to me.'"

Salim burst out laughing and told Mabruk, while nudging
Abduh with his elbow to try to get him to laugh too, "The best
thing would be to look for him in an orphanage."

But Abduh didn't laugh. He did not wish to jest or joke
around. Instead he continued to frown and asked gruffly, "Tell
me, what's the point of this story?" Then he turned on Zanuba
and asked her, "What's this orphan hoopoe you're after?"

When Zanuba didn't reply, Abduh cast her a frightening
glance and shouted, "Magic again? Haven't you given up on
magic and wasting money on nonsense?"

Zanuba recovered some of her composure and protested,
"What magic? Don't say that. This is medicine."

Abduh replied angrily with chilly sarcasm, "Medicine!"

Zanuba responded forcefully, "Yes, by the Prophet! Real
medicine—a doctor's prescription!"

Salim guffawed. He said, "Hold on! Let's get serious! What
physician, then, clever girl, prescribes hoopoe? I want to know
the name of this physician. I suppose he wrote 'hoopoe' on the
prescription for you. I beg God's forgiveness: 'orphan hoopoe.'
Yes, he's got to be an orphan, because if his mother or father
were still alive that will ruin the effect of the medicine?"

At that point, Abduh shouted at Zanuba, "No way is the
money going to stay in your hands after today! No way!
Enough's enough! We can't stand for things like this. Food like

tar and the money wasted on magic—our money being wasted. Our whole budget is spent on spells for bridegrooms."

Enraged by his words, Zanuba burst out screaming, "Cut out a tongue that says such things of me . . . that I do magic for bridegrooms! Lies! Fine, by the Pure Lady, if you don't stop that talk, I'm not going to have anything to do with you again. Take your money, for what it's worth. You be the ones to plan, spend, cook, and see to the housework. By the Prophet, I'm not going to lend a hand to anything. I don't see what you'll do without me. If it weren't for me, your worn-out clothes would be lying at your feet."

Abduh's anger and nervous agitation intensified. He shouted in a terrifying voice, "What are you saying? You think you can threaten us? Fine. I swear by God Almighty that you won't cook or serve meals. Bring the money you've got at once. Give us back what you still have of the month's account immediately. We don't want your guidance. Enough! We know how to care for our affairs. Bring the money!"

Clenching her teeth, Zanuba managed to say, "Fine. Gladly. By the Prophet, a blessing from God, rest for the brain. Does anyone dislike rest? Okay. I'm going to hand back what I have left of yours."

She headed straight for her room and entered it.

At that, Abduh turned forcefully toward Salim and said, "Let her boil! It's the best thing for us a thousand times over. Don't you agree?"

Salim answered in a jesting tone while twisting his mustache, "I agree totally. Our food was really awful, and our dear, distinguished governor was spending our funds on her personal affairs and nonsense."

Abduh quickly added, with no change in his serious expression, "It's enough to drive a person insane. It's infuriating. She leaves us hungry, yearning for a crumb, without a piece of meat to be found."

Salim concluded, "And if she errs and buys a goose one day, we have to keep eating on it for two months."

Meanwhile Mabruk was propping himself up with his arm

on the edge of the table, silently watching the action, like an ordinary bloke at a fancy play.

Abduh happened to glance at him and asked him at once, "What about you, Mabruk? Why are you silent? Don't you agree?"

Mabruk roused himself from his stupor, rubbed his eyes, and replied, "By God, I don't know. May a calamity strike the father of the orphan hoopoe. It's all the fault of his crest. But just the same, there's no need to make Miss Zanuba angry."

Abduh shouted at him, "Don't you be a fool too! We just want you to answer this: Do you like to eat well or not? That's the question."

Mabruk replied immediately, "No, by the life of Saint Zaynhum, I like to eat well."

Salim smiled and said quickly, "Of course!" His face suddenly became serious. He motioned to Abduh as he said, "We ought to tell the others too."

Abduh concurred with the suggestion, nodding his head. He rose straightaway and headed to the bedroom to inform Hanafi of the new revolution. The tried-and-true method of waking Hanafi quickly was simple and known to everyone. It was to yank the covers off him in one jerk and then to scream in his ear for a long time. Abduh resorted to that method directly without wasting time on useless preliminaries. Hanafi Effendi moved at last, bellowing angrily, "People! Hey! I'm in the glory of the Prophet. Can't I have a little nap? I taught five classes today, people."

Abduh said resolutely, "Wake up! Get up and hear the important news, Mr. Hanafi. It has now been confirmed that the government is wasting the budget on its own pointless, personal affairs."

Hanafi yawned. Closing one eye, he said, "How does that concern me? I'm not involved in politics."

Abduh frowned and retorted sternly, "How so? You're the senior member of the household." Hanafi shut his other eye and asked listlessly and indifferently, "Which paper reports this news?"

Abduh replied with some amazement, "What do you mean,

which paper? No, no. This isn't in the papers. I mean our own government here in our house. I'm talking about Zanuba."

Hanafi rolled over in bed, turning his back to Abduh. Trying to resume his nap, he said, "Fine then; spare me, for the sake of the generous God."

A thick snore issued from his nostrils, marking his actual return to sleep. Abduh tried with all his might to prevent him. He stripped off the bedcovers once again and shook his shoulder violently. He threatened seriously to pour a glass of cold water on his head if he did not wake up at once. In short, he employed all the strongest procedures used in such circumstances. Finally the honorary president found he couldn't avoid rising. He sat up halfway in bed, grumbling, scolding, raging, and cursing. When Abduh was convinced that he was wide awake, he left him and went toward Muhsin's bed.

But as he neared it he heard all of a sudden the sound of a quarrel erupting in the hall and recognized Zanuba's voice. He left the bedroom at once and went straight to her, asking gruffly, "Where's the money?"

Zanuba did not answer or budge. Salim pointed to the sum of one pound on the table. "Help yourself," he said. "This is all that's left."

Abduh looked at the pound and then at Zanuba. He shouted in a grating voice, "Impossible! It's only the nineteenth! Twelve days remain. One pound is going to suffice for twelve days? Nonsense!"

Zanuba didn't respond. She was cloaking her rage with a calm exterior. At last she said coldly, "You don't believe it? Suit yourself. That's all of your money I've got. If you don't believe me, go ahead and search."

Salim gestured secretly to Abduh to come and whispered to him provocatively, "Right. Let's search!"

Mabruk caught that, because he was close to Salim and could crane his neck and eavesdrop. He grasped what Salim said and, clearing his throat, whispered, as though to himself, "By God, Mr. Salim, all he knows how to do is search." Then out loud, he continued, "The best thing is to pray for the Prophet. There's no need to . . . May God protect us from evil. What is predestined will be seen, even if only after a time. Beg pardon, but is a pound nothing? Praise God. . . . Our destiny. What will we do? Nothing: Here's the sky and here's the earth."

Abduh gave him a long, strange look. An idea seemed suddenly to fall on him from the heavens. He quickly placed his hand on Mabruk's shoulder and said in a firm, thoughtful, calm voice, "Listen, Mabruk, God will make it possible to do without her. You keep the funds. You will be our government from now on. Understand? You! Because with you at least there won't be any fear of squandering and wasting money on foolish nonsense."

The servant cast a quick look of inquiry or petition at Zanuba. Then he said anxiously and nervously, "But . . . only . . ."

Abduh contracted his eyebrows. "What?" he asked. "'But only' what? You think the amount is small? Is your point, namely, that it's impossible for us to live on a pound to the end of the month? But that's the problem which your good management is going to solve for us. This is your genius. Aren't you our government? Cope. There are twelve days left to the end of the month. Get us successfully through these days. Do a good deed. Feed us as you will. The goal is for this pound to last till the end of the month without our needing to rely on Zanuba."

Zanuba emitted a sarcastic, angry laugh and turned her back on them. Through her teeth she said, "May God make it easy for you. Oh my luck: peace of mind. A lazy man blames the mosque when he misses the prayer."

She headed swiftly for her room, slamming the door violently behind her. Abduh saw the door slam and heard the deafening sound. He said angrily, "Sixty disasters!"

Then he turned to Salim and Mabruk and continued, "So we've agreed, haven't we?"

Salim concurred enthusiastically: "We have!" Then he punched Mabruk's shoulder and said, "Long live Mabruk! Long live Mabruk! Our bellies rely on God and you, Mabruk Effendi."

But Abduh interrupted at once with a shout. "Not during this period, my dear. Till the end of the month it's going to be fasting and moderation. One pound, of course, is not going to suffice. Listen, Mabruk. Do the impossible. Feed us for this period with lentils every day like the boatmen . . . or cottage cheese and corn bread like the fellahin . . . or fuul midammis, salad, and ta'miya bean fritters like . . ."

Salim added quickly, "Like students at a mosque."

Abduh continued seriously, "Right, Mabruk, do as you think best. Act. The whole idea is to have the pound last to the end of the month without us dying of hunger on a sum like that. Take it, Mabruk. Proceed by reasoning, brains, and sound management. You don't need any guidance." Then he handed him the pound.

Mabruk took from the pocket of his tunic a large pouch made of cloth the same color as the waistcoat he wore, as though the leftover cloth from it had been used for a bag.

After he thrust the pound in it and returned it to his pocket, he said, "By the blessing of the lady Umm Hashim, have no fear! The believer does not die of hunger. Bless our Prophet who said, 'God repays those who rely on Him.'"*

---

* One of the many hadith, or authenticated sayings, of the Prophet Muhammad.

CHAPTER 7

When Muhsin went to school the next day his face was beaming with happiness, and joy almost leapt from his breast. While he was in the streetcar on his way to school he imagined that God had never created a more beautiful morning. The streetcar passed by Lazoghli Square, where lush trees surrounded the statue, birds sang as they flitted from branch to branch, and kite and hawk called as they flapped their wings in the sky. Amazing! He saw and heard all this today; it drew his attention. He had passed there hundreds of times before without seeing anything. Had the world changed that morning, or was he the one who had changed and developed new eyes?

Muhsin entered the courtyard of his school wanting to speak to everyone he met, even the janitor, but he was astonished to find the place empty. Had he come extra early today? Yes, the wall clock in the guard's room struck seven, right then.

Muhsin started pacing back and forth, dreaming of beautiful things. At times happiness would press his heart so hard he would race with strange hilarity to the great staircase. Then he would descend it in leaps and bounds and head for the water tap as though he wanted to drink. He didn't drink but went to another room and from there to a third and a fourth.

Any of his acquaintances seeing him then would have been astonished and would have denied that it was Muhsin. At last he calmed down a little but began fretting that his colleagues—especially his close friend Abbas—were so slow to arrive.

Compared to other boys his age, Muhsin was serious and sensible. Unlike most of his peers, he had little taste for youthful games. He was rarely seen running and jumping. His amusements and diversions were mental rather than physical. His sweetest times were spent in poetry competitions and slams with Abbas and others who shared their artistic temperament. For this reason, he seemed older than he was—compared with his classmates, who were tireless, prattling, and boisterous. His teachers thought of him that way too. They treated him well and predicted brilliant results for him on his competency examination that year.

Muhsin didn't like to mix much, preferring solitude at school. Although he seemed to scorn youthful frivolity, most of the pupils respected him and liked to listen to him when he spoke. The pupils would frequently gather around him and Abbas, if they noticed them by the walls, debating with each other under the great staircase in their usual meeting place during the noon break. But Muhsin himself wouldn't seek out anyone except Abbas, for in him he found a temperament to match his own. There was something more important too: Abbas believed in Muhsin and was devoted to him. He acknowledged to himself that Muhsin influenced his ideas and thinking.

Muhsin awaited Abbas's arrival with a bounding desire he couldn't explain. Did he want to confide something to him? Was Abbas worthy of that? Was it right? Yes, Abbas was his dear friend, but did he have the capacity to understand such things? Over and beyond this concern, did Muhsin have the right to reveal something that did not concern only him?

But he wanted to talk this morning. He wanted to lighten the burden he felt. He calmed down again. When he saw a number of pupils entering the courtyard, he rushed to them, greeting them and chatting with them merrily. He talked freely with them and joined in their laughter. Words filled his mouth. They were amazed by all this coming from him and began to exchange glances among themselves, because Muhsin was known for his aloofness; they were the ones who had to chase after him to try to get him to converse.

At last Abbas appeared. As soon as Muhsin saw him, he left the boys he was with and rushed toward him. He grasped his arm and took him off in another direction, rather than to the wall of the great staircase, where the others would think they were having a debate or poetry slam, which they would hurry to observe.

Muhsin began by asking him why he was so late—in such a concerned tone that Abbas was astonished. He replied straightforwardly that he had come at his normal time and wasn't tardy at all. But Muhsin insisted determinedly, making clear the importance he attached to it.

Abbas replied with equal certainty, "Not at all, brother. You seem to have come early today."

Muhsin, however, retorted in his unaccustomedly eager voice, "No way . . . you're late!"

Abbas's astonishment heightened, but he limited his response to: "Fine. What's happened?"

Then Muhsin stopped talking and lapsed into anxious confusion. His zeal abandoned him, and he found nothing to say.

His silence lasted till he sensed that Abbas, who was looking at him with astonishment, was waiting for an answer. So he suddenly pretended to laugh. Moving closer to his friend, he made him think it had all been a joke. He began to chatter and laugh, attempting to turn things around. He talked about all sorts of subjects quickly, moving from one to another without any tie, as though he simply wanted to talk and wished for nothing more than to be immersed in chatter, merely to relieve himself and lessen the pressure on his heart. Sensing Muhsin's nervous state from his excited, breakneck manner of talking, Abbas turned on him suddenly and asked, "Muhsin, what's wrong with you today?"

The boy looked at him inquisitively and fearfully and blushed. Then he said hesitantly, "Nothing. . . ."

At once he changed the topic to something commonplace, but this time he tried to speak in a calm, coherent, ordinary way. So the two started discussing their lessons, their homework, and the day's classes. Then Abbas suddenly remembered something and shouted, "My God! Today there's oral composition in Arabic! Remember?"

Muhsin asked him mechanically, "Which period?" Meanwhile he had allowed his thoughts to drift to the far horizon.

Abbas answered without noticing that Muhsin wasn't paying attention to him. "Sixth period, at the end of the day."

Muhsin didn't reply. Once again happiness flowed through him. He wanted to burst forth, fly, leap, or speak.

Thinking his comrade was listening to him, Abbas continued, "Whose turn do you suppose it will be? The shaykh chooses the name from the roster. Oh Lord, I hope he doesn't call my name today. I haven't prepared a topic."

Muhsin did not respond to that but said suddenly, "Abbas, life is beautiful!"

Abbas looked at him with surprise, but Muhsin went on, not paying attention to him. "Do you know what that happiness we hear about is? Be a good fellow and tell me what happiness is."

Abbas repeated in astonishment, "Happiness? Do I know?"

Muhsin asked him forcefully, "Don't you know when you're happy?"

Abbas thought for a moment before saying, "That will be when I pass the competency examination."

Muhsin's face displayed a mix of disappointment, annoyance, and scorn. Through his teeth he told his friend Abbas, "You're a dunce!"

At this point the school bell rang, and they sped off to join the queue. Muhsin felt a desire within him to speak about this topic all day long. Abbas, on the other hand, was surprised by Muhsin's last remark and wanted to know why he was a dunce.

The pupils took their seats in the classroom. Abbas sat on the bench behind Muhsin's. He couldn't bear to wait and whispered to Muhsin, "Why am I a dunce?" But Muhsin gestured to him to be quiet and straightened himself to attend to the lesson with more than usual delight and energy. He was very quick to answer questions and to understand their obscurities. His enthusiasm and vigor pleased and gladdened the teacher.

At the noon break, Muhsin and Abbas met beside the wall under the great stairway. Muhsin wanted to recite love poetry and with that in mind had brought along Mihyar's diwan, which he adored. The students from the class, however, had since the fourth period been absorbed by the question of choosing the school to enroll in after the competency examination. The math teacher had raised the question today in the algebra lesson, although it was premature. When the pupils saw Muhsin and Abbas in the spot set aside for debate and discussion, they asked Muhsin the following question: "Which are you going to select: arts or sciences?"

Muhsin replied without hesitation, "Arts, of course!"

Abbas, however, hesitated a little. "I like the arts section, but my father wants me to be a physician."

Muhsin yanked Abbas toward him and said, "Listen to what your soul says, to what you want." It was not just today that he was choosing his path but since infancy a person senses where his natural inclination lies. Taking Abbas's arm and squeezing it, he said, "Abbas, you've got to enter arts like me. . . . I must convince you to enter arts like me."

One of the pupils present objected at this point. "What future does arts provide?"

Muhsin turned toward him and said, "You mean in terms of money and wealth; I don't care about money and wealth."

Another asked curiously, "So what do you care about?"

Muhsin pointed to himself and Abbas. With youthful braggadocio he replied, "Tomorrow we'll be the eloquent tongue of the nation."

He looked at Abbas as if to give him extra courage and resolve. He wanted to continue, but he thought of a phrase that made his face beam. It was a phrase that could only seem to kids of his age and education to be a revelation. He burst out, "Abbas! Our occupation tomorrow will be to express what is in the heart of the entire people. Do you understand? My goodness! If only all of you knew the value of being able to express what is in the soul, to express what is in our hearts!"

He thought a little. Then, his eyes gleaming with another idea, he said, "Think of the maxim in our book of memory pieces: 'A man is known by two of his smallest parts: his heart and his tongue!' The nation also has a heart to guide it and a tongue to direct the physical forces within it. Wealth by itself is nothing." He began to spout words in enthusiastic bursts to develop this idea.

The bell rang and the pupils went in for their afternoon lessons. By the time the sixth period arrived, Muhsin wanted nothing more than to leave. His emotions were close to the flash point. Shaykh Ali, whose beard was thick and demeanor solemn, appeared. The students rose respectfully, not sitting back down until he did. He started by looking around the room. Then he opened his roster. At that, the young students began to exchange glances, wondering who would be called to speak on a topic of his own choosing in an extemporaneous fashion. Some who hated the class trembled and held their breath while the teacher ran his eyes up and down the column of names before him—each fearing he would hear his name. Finally the teacher spoke. The name was: "Muhsin."

The teacher looked at Muhsin and commanded him: "Muhsin! Come up to the blackboard." The pupils calmed down. They were pleased by this selection. Muhsin didn't hesitate; he rose at once and went to the blackboard.

At that, the teacher ordered him, "Muhsin, choose a topic; then speak on it." The boy stood, hesitating anxiously. He hadn't prepared a topic, and nothing came to his mind then. He stood there indecisively for a long time. Then the teacher said in his deliberate way, "Write the topic heading on the blackboard. Then divide it into subheadings as usual."

Muhsin asked himself: *Do I know what the topic is?* Suddenly he thought of an idea that made him blush. He dismissed it from his thoughts at once, but it soon returned. He didn't know how he found the courage or what force was pushing him to it. Perhaps his powerful feelings at that time convinced him he could not speak then at length or with pleasure on any other topic. He took the chalk at once and wrote impetuously, "The topic heading is: Love."

As soon as this word appeared on the blackboard, the class grew boisterous and rowdy. The teacher, who was astonished at the insurrection of the class in front of him, did not know the cause yet. He rapped his pencil on the table for silence and shouted, "What's up?"

He saw that they were looking at the blackboard and, turning toward it himself, he saw the word "love." He could not restrain himself from screaming out in disbelief, "God, God! God's will be done. Step down! Go back to your seat. We can't allow shameless wisecracks."

Muhsin was taken aback; he wasn't used to treatment like this from his teachers. He stood there in anxious confusion but had not lost the confidence and strength that had impelled him to write that daring word in front of the poor students, who were accustomed to hearing words like "knowledge," "study," "learning," and "perseverance," but not words like "love," "emotions," or "heart." If they did hear them, their meanings were reduced to the least common denominator, as though life provides only two options: learning and corruption. For them, learning was synonymous with studying and success on the examination. Corruption was synonymous with love and the heart and everything else that wasn't an exam subject. Virtue and vice were presented in this manner to these young people.

Shaykh Ali saw Muhsin standing there, confused and courteous in spite of everything. He remembered that his record was good and that he had been well behaved since he started at that school the previous year. The teacher relented a little. All the same, he said in a voice not lacking a sting of censure, "What's come over you today? Are you bewitched?"

Muhsin didn't reply. The idea of rebelling against this shaykh, who understood no more than any of those pupils, passed through his head. Muhsin imagined he was seeing and sensing stupendous things—extremely stupendous—that a person like Shaykh Ali would never see.

Shaykh Ali looked at his roster to pick another student, but the class as a whole summoned the courage to say with unaccustomed enthusiasm, "We want this topic! We want this topic! Speak, Muhsin, speak."

Muhsin looked at the class and realized that this word had aroused a great curiosity among these young and ignorant fellows. These pupils clearly showed a thirst for a topic like this. Muhsin saw that his friend Abbas was a leader of those requesting it. He was waving his hands at his friend, and his smile spoke for itself. The clouds were dispersing before his eyes.

Muhsin gained courage then and resolved to speak no matter what the price, but saw from the Hanbali shaykh's body language that there was no way to get around him.

Then Muhsin had an idea that showed a certain brilliance. He took the chalk at once and wrote under the word *love* these lines: "There are three forms of love: (1) love of God, the High and Exalted, which is humble submission and acknowledgment of grace, (2) love of parents, which is based on kinship, and (3) love of beauty, which is love of the heart."

The class was jubilant and, with Abbas as chief advocate, sought the shaykh's acceptance of the topic since it was totally literary. The shaykh turned toward the blackboard again after putting on his spectacles. As he read the first division, then the second, his voice had a ring of acceptance and agreement in it. When he reached the third division, however, he became distressed and hesitated again. He looked at Muhsin and said, "Erase number three!"

Muhsin was reluctant, but Shaykh Ali would not relent or budge this time, despite the objections and pleas of the class. Finally Muhsin saw no alternative to erasing the third section, although he resolved secretly to address it during his discussion of the first two, as though comparing causes and reasons.

Thus Shaykh Ali consented to allow the word "love" to remain on the blackboard. Muhsin began to speak while the boys listened more quietly and attentively than in any class all year. Whenever Muhsin inched toward the topic of the heart, Shaykh Ali grumbled, scolded, and murmured like a cat that sees a mouse. But the class focused their attention on Muhsin and soaked in through their eyes and ears what he said with unusual delight and joy, as though they were really benefiting somehow. Indeed it was more than that, much more. They seemed to be hearing something they had all sensed for a long time but hadn't dared express or hadn't realized they felt, because they lacked knowledge of the existence of beauty in the world. They were ignorant of the heart's role in their lives and didn't know the sublime meaning of life.

Muhsin felt that about them. He also felt that the secret of their amazing attentiveness and overwhelming contentment with him and his speech—clearly visible in their eyes—was attributable to one thing: that he was expressing what was in their hearts.

CHAPTER 8

Looking out at Salama Street, Saniya and Zanuba stood at one of the windows of the wooden balcony in the piano room watching for Muhsin's return. It was afternoon, but Muhsin hadn't come back from school yet. He was, however, due to head directly to Dr. Hilmi's residence to give Saniya her first singing lesson. They had agreed to this the day before. So Zanuba had come to wait for him at Saniya's.

The two women began to look about discreetly and to pass the time by observing things. Quite naturally, Shahhata's coffee shop, which was opposite the house, drew their attention. As usual at this time of day, it was swarming with its regular customers, inside and out.

No sooner had Saniya cast a glance at the chairs and tables lined up on the pavement than she nudged Zanuba with her arm and whispered to her, "Look, abla, at the effendi with the shisha. What's with him? He can't keep his eyes off our balcony. Look! Every so often he twists his mustache in a way that could make you die with laughter."

Zanuba stared at that effendi. Then she turned quickly to Saniya and said immediately, "Yes! Absolutely. Don't you know him? That gentleman is my cousin."

Surprised and a little embarrassed at what she had blurted out, Saniya apologized. "Shame on you, abla. Why didn't you tell me right away?" She was quiet for a bit and then said, "So is he the engineer?"

"No, sister," Zanuba replied. "The engineer is my brother, Abduh. This one, he's the officer, the one Muhsin was telling you yesterday has a musical instrument with bellows."

"An accordion?"

"Right, sister, that's it. You see the light."

Saniya looked at Zanuba's cousin again and lavished praise

on him to make up for her previous slur. "The truth is, abla, each of his gestures shows his dignity, prestige, and rank."

Zanuba looked at Salim in the coffeehouse. Then she laughed with gentle scorn. "Sister, why does he act like that? May God's name protect us from such conceit!"

At that moment Saniya suddenly emitted a small cry of amazement. She grasped Zanuba by the arm and with a ripple of enthusiasm directed her attention toward the coffee shop. "Look, abla! See—with the blond hair and the trim little mustache—that effendi who only just arrived. What a coincidence! He sat down directly behind your cousin." Zanuba looked and her heart suddenly began to pound. The color of her face changed, but she hid her feelings.

Gazing at the newcomer to the coffeehouse, Saniya continued, "See how he laughs as he watches your cousin. Does he know him? But he didn't greet him."

Zanuba replied in a slightly altered voice, "They don't know each other yet."

A little surprised at this choice of words, Saniya repeated, "'They don't know each other yet?'"

Suppressing a sigh, Zanuba said, "Right, I mean they may possibly meet one day. . . ." She was silent for a moment. Then, as though she feared her words might betray something, she amended them: "You see, he's our neighbor."

While looking at the man, Saniya asked in a rush, "This fellow? Is he really your neighbor, abla, or are you joking? Does he live alone? What's his profession?"

Zanuba replied absentmindedly, her eyes fixed on the coffeehouse, "Yes, his profession? He's rich! An investor!"

Zanuba became self-conscious and noticed that Saniya was staring too. So with a quick, brusque gesture she immediately drew Saniya away from the balcony, saying roughly, "Come back. You shouldn't peer out like that so much, Saniya."

Saniya withdrew into the salon and remarked cheerfully, "I don't make a habit of looking down from this balcony, but it's truly a sweet spectacle. Do you suppose there are men like this in the coffee shop every day?"

Zanuba did not reply. Saniya returned to the balcony for yet another look but right away called out enchantingly, "Here's Muhsin! He's come." She was silent for a bit while she followed him with her eyes. Then she picked up again. "He's gone first to the coffeehouse to greet your cousin and has left his books with him too. That's a good idea. He can come here directly, by the street door."

Zanuba had not heard a single word Saniya said. She was, rather, silently observing the coffeehouse, her thoughts adrift in dreams. Then she straightened quickly and moved toward the salon. She had seen something that made her decide to depart at once. She had seen Salim rise from his place in the coffeehouse and head for their residence, carrying Muhsin's books, while the young lad was knocking on Dr. Hilmi's door.

What interested Zanuba about all this was that she saw Mustafa Bey sitting there alone now. She cast him a final glance before leaving the balcony window and going to fetch her wrap from the bench in the hall. Saniya perceived her intention and asked, "Where are you going, sister?"

Zanuba answered quickly and anxiously, with feigned indifference, "I'm going to the dressmaker and will be right back— just long enough for the errand."

Saniya commented with mild censure, "You're going to leave me alone? You know Mama isn't here."

Cloaking herself in her wrap, Zanuba replied, "By your life, I'll be back in ten minutes."

Saniya complained, "Is the dressmaker really necessary right now?"

"Yes, sister," Zanuba replied, preoccupied with her appearance. "I've remembered something very important. There's nothing to fear. If I'm so much as five minutes late, then you can complain."

In front of the mirror she began to arrange her garments carefully. She adjusted the way the fish-scale patterned bridge of her face veil fell on her nose and made sure that locks of her tinted hair were visible on both sides of her head. She focused on her toilette with the eagerness of a girl of twenty, making Saniya smile in spite of herself.

At that moment the black maid came to announce Muhsin's

arrival to Saniya. A minute later the youth appeared at the door of the salon. He stood there hesitating in embarrassment for a time. Then he went to Saniya and greeted her politely and with profound respect.

Zanuba took advantage of Saniya's preoccupation with greeting Muhsin to slip to the balcony. She looked out the window and stood leaning there so her torso could be clearly seen by the men at the coffeehouse. That accomplished, she swiftly stepped back to Saniya and Muhsin and assured them of her early return and short absence. She bade them farewell and departed quickly. Muhsin and Saniya were left alone, face-to-face.

At that, the young boy felt his reserve and embarrassment increase to the point of fear and dread. He sensed that the courage that he had worked up during the day and that he had meant to hoard for this moment had abandoned him in the twinkling of an eye. He stood there silently, looking at the floor like a guilty child facing punishment.

Saniya wasn't afflicted by embarrassment, reserve, or fear. Although she was a girl of seventeen, or only about two years older than Muhsin, she was self-assured and even womanly in her physical and psychological development. If at times she lowered her long, lovely eyelashes while speaking to Muhsin, laughed in a quintessentially feminine way, and limited her eyes to polite, bashful, reserved glances, none of that came naturally to her. It was, rather, a stratagem. This is perhaps the most refined magic of the Egyptian woman, for the truth is that she is gifted at perceiving instinctively the impact and effect a single glance can have. For this reason she does not gaze much at the person with whom she is speaking. She does not glance idly or randomly as daring, frivolous, European women do. Instead, she keeps track of her glances and holds them between her languid lashes—like a sword in a scabbard—until the desired moment arrives. Then she raises her head and releases a single, devastating look.

Saniya finally broke the silence by saying in a friendly and congenial way, "Come right in, Muhsin Bey." She directed him to a large chair next to the piano. Then she smiled and added, "What are you going to teach me today, professor?"

Muhsin answered with such superfluous good manners, reserve, and decorum as to be tedious, "Just as you wish."

Saniya replied with a smile, "I don't know why I love today's pop songs, but what you sang yesterday, though it's in a very old style, still, I can't tell you how much I liked it. That's the first time in my life I've liked the old style, but the merit is yours, Muhsin. You truly sang it in an exemplary way. It was really very beautiful!"

Muhsin blushed, and his heart throbbed with joy at this enchanting praise. Apparently deriving some daring and courage from it, while attempting to raise his head, which he had kept bowed all this time, he said, "Thank you, Miss Saniya. You're too kind."

Saniya replied, "I assure you, Muhsin Bey—you have an amazing talent in singing. It's this art that I want you to teach me. Isn't that so?" She smiled graciously, went to the piano, opened it, and took her seat there.

Totally charmed, Muhsin rose and approached the piano, as though wishing to put his embarrassment behind him and relax by conversing with her a little. He said, attempting to imitate her recent phrasing deliberately and gracefully, "Here's the piano I want you to teach me. Isn't that so?" But his face flushed as soon as he got these words out.

So Saniya sent him a look that could have softened the heart of a rebellious Amalekite and said, "No doubt about that. I guarantee that you'll progress rapidly, since you told me you know how to play the accordion."

She turned back to the piano, running her fingers over its keys. Muhsin stood behind her. His anxiety had calmed a bit, and he relaxed. She could not see him where he was standing, so he started to glance at her stealthily. For the first time he noticed that her hair was cut in the latest fashion. His eyes began to gaze at her ivory neck, which was superlatively white. Above it rose a beautiful head with a circle of intensely black hair, which gleamed in a captivating way like an ebony moon. Muhsin remembered a picture he had looked at frequently in the year's assigned text for ancient Egyptian history, a picture he loved a great deal. He spent lengthy portions of the history class gazing at it while swimming through a world of dreams from which nothing would bring him down to earth except the teacher's voice when he began to explain the lesson. That picture portrayed a woman whose hair was also cut short, gleaming black as well, and rounded like an ebony moon: Isis!

Saniya raised her head unexpectedly and turned toward Muhsin, smiling. She said, as though remembering something suddenly, "Look—I've been forgetting something terribly important."

The boy was taken by surprise and looked at her like a person roused from a dream. He trembled slightly, for he was afraid she had caught him sneaking a glance at the back of her beautiful head. He pulled himself together nevertheless and stuttered, "What?"

Saniya continued, "I wanted to ask you about Maestra Shakhla'—the singer who taught you her craft."

Muhsin was silent for a bit, until he could calm down. Then he said, "Oh! But that's a very old story."

Saniya pleaded delicately and somewhat coquettishly, "I want to hear it. I'm very eager to learn it."

Muhsin asked with delighted amazement, "Are you really?"

"Yes, I want you to tell me how you met Shakhla'."

Muhsin paused as if trying to remember things long gone. Earnestly and pensively he began, "Shakhla'! I had forgotten. At the time I was very young. All the same I remember. Those were wonderful days. I was happy, even if I don't know why. Yes, I recall that now. I remember!"

Then Muhsin's face took on an unusual expression. His was no longer the face of an innocent, embarrassed child. It had become in a moment a man's face that expressed deep feelings. "Yes! It's impossible for me to forget." He said that in a whisper, as though to himself.

Saniya was surprised and began to look at him in confusion. She gazed at the face of that young lad, the feelings it revealed, and his imaginative eyes, which were like ethereal veils over the past.

CHAPTER 9

Muhsin was six years old when Maestra Labiba Shakhla' was a frequent guest in his family's home. There was more than mere coincidence to the story of that artiste and her close friendship with the family. Muhsin's grandmother at that time was suffering from a nervous complaint for which no treatment or medicine could be found. Many physicians had treated her to no avail. At last, one, after trying everything else, said, "The best thing for a condition like hers is tranquility, calm, and a cheerful outlook. Entertain her as much as possible. A hearty dose of pleasure and joy may improve her health."

"Entertain and delight her how, doctor?"

"I mean sing to her. Cheer her up. Song and instrumental music will be the best remedy for her."

The coincidence came later. Muhsin's mother heard Maestra Labiba Shakhla' at the wedding reception of one of her relatives and was immediately taken by that famous artiste's manners and decorum, modesty, and taste. She found her exquisite. Shakhla' likewise picked out Muhsin's mother from the crowd of ladies. A certain aloofness in her personality caught her eye. So they made each other's acquaintance. On that occasion Muhsin's mother mentioned the sick lady whose cure was music and seized the opportunity to invite Shakhla' to visit.

From that time on, the Maestra Labiba Shakhla' visited Muhsin's family every summer in Damanhur, accompanied by her troupe and their instruments. She would stay all summer, or part of it, as their honored guest. She revived her soul with the sights and air of the countryside while entertaining the ailing old lady and filling the house with animation, joy, and pleasure.

Those days that Shakhla' and her troupe spent in the house of Hamid Bey al-Atifi were her best, she said. Nothing interrupted them unless al-Hajj Ahmad al-Mutayyib sought her

and the troupe from time to time for an unscheduled performance or a good contract.

Especially for little Muhsin, those days were without doubt
the happiest of his life. He waited for them all year long, counting the months on his fingers in anticipation. It was a matter of
great joy to him whenever a month passed.

What sweet and innocent dreams they were! How agreeable
the magnificent childhood mirage was that passed before the
boy's amorphous soul, which was hard to pin down, even at
that age.

What pleased and flattered Muhsin was being considered a
member of the troupe. He wasn't satisfied unless he sang, ate,
sat, and squeezed in among the artistes. Woe to anyone who
did not specify he was a member of the ensemble! Many a time
he had wept and raged because someone forgot to realize that
he was a member of the chorus exactly like Hafiza, Najiya, and
Salm, who was blind. Time and again he had raged and stormed
to make them teach him the argot that they, the fellowship of
artistes, employed.

His identification with the troupe and his imitation of its
members were such that he became known for his sincere respect for the leader, Maestra Labiba Shakhla'.

Yes, he would never forget his happiness when he sat on the
floor with the ensemble around the maestra, who loomed above
them in a large chair in the center, holding the lute in her arms.
He would look up at her as though observing a goddess on a
marble plinth. He would turn his small head right and left to
his colleagues in the chorus with psychological satisfaction that
could not be described or characterized.

At times he felt a strange sensation looking at that charming
woman of about thirty, particularly at evening receptions or
parties, when she appeared decked out in glittering jewelry before the female guests and visitors who came especially to hear
her at Muhsin's home.

He sensed at times that he understood nebulously the spell
that Shakhla' cast over him. Actually, in addition to her magical singing, Labiba had a merry nature and a light and grace-
ful spirit. She provided her listeners bliss and delight.

Muhsin loved to sit with her, flattering and praising her after he had spent the morning plucking and gathering bishop's weed, which she would boil and drink to clear her throat. He would beg her, in return for that, to tell him some of her anecdotes, which she would recount at length to him and the others, without the repetition detracting in any way from their charm.

"Tell me the cook story," little Muhsin would ask her plaintively.

She would laugh and then pretend to frown, telling him and those around, "Cook? What a disaster, kids! Whatever I forget, will you remind me?"

The starting point of the story was that the real cook fell ill one day, and Maestra Labiba suggested seriously and earnestly that she should take her place. She affirmed that no one had ever tasted anything more delicious than the food her hands would produce. She advised everyone to take care not to eat their fingers along with the food, since it would be so tasty. She claimed she was a gourmet cook and that a person eating her Alexandria-style fish might well say that he had never eaten fish before in his life.

They were happy to let her try. So they led her to the kitchen and brought her the vegetables, fish, and all the other necessary ingredients. She set to work . . . but what work?

She hadn't spent five minutes in the kitchen until it started to look like a market late in the afternoon. She got down all the copper vessels, trays, bowls, and containers and placed them on the floor, scattering them every which way. There was no corner or spot without a tray, dish, or pot. Why all this?

Perhaps she didn't ask herself. No one dared approach the kitchen, because she had categorically refused help from anyone so she could claim all the credit.

She left some empty cooking pots on the hot stove for a time, while she began to run here and there in the kitchen with a fish in her hand. She was crooning, "O Reviver, O you with the almonds . . ." while tripping over the trays and containers strewn in disarray across the floor.

Fish was also scattered throughout the room. No one could imagine how that happened with such speed. There was fish on the floor, on the shelf, in the bowls, and in the basin under the spigot—as though the kitchen had turned into a fish market.

But Maestra Labiba Shakhla' doubtless paid no attention to the condition of the kitchen, for she was truly caught up in her work; enthusiasm for it had grasped hold of her. She called out from time to time, laughing, "God, God, darlings! Where's the audience now to watch Maestra Shakhla' at the height of her powers?"

At last she threw together a number of dishes and emerged from the kitchen with sweat dripping from her and food dribbling from her white apron. In the parlor she shouted, "It's done, darlings! I've stewed the eggplant and trimmed the ends of the okra. And the fish . . . O my spirit! I've fried it in a way to bewitch and enchant the mind."

She suddenly fell silent and her face went pale, because just then Dr. Farid, who had been summoned to examine the sick cook, appeared at the parlor door. This Dr. Farid was one of Maestra Shakhla''s most enthusiastic patrons and most avid fans. He saw her frequently and heard her at wedding parties and soirees. No sooner had he seen her there in a kitchen apron with scraps dribbling off it than he shouted in astonishment, "God! Are you working as a cook here or what?"

But Shakhla', the moment she recovered from her surprise, turned tail and fled, hiding her face with a hand one moment and slapping her side curls the next. In a weak, choking voice she begged, "Hide me! Hide me!"

This was not all that her volunteering to cook brought down upon her that day, nor all the Alexandria-style fish cost her. Another crisis threatened to prove more serious, because unbeknownst to her, the fish was spoiled. She ate a lot of it, as did all the members of the ensemble, because she had fixed it. Unfortunately she and the troupe were booked that very evening to perform at a soiree in the home of one of the local notables.

She went and sang till the festivities were at a climax of commotion and joy. The guests were assembled and the excitement and agitation were intense. It was then that Maestra Labiba suddenly felt acute pains throughout her digestive tract. At first she tried to conceal it for fear of a scandal, but she had hardly staggered to her feet when she saw that all her musicians were suffering from the same indigestion. Each of the accompanists was leaning on another, writhing, a hand on her belly. She grasped the truth of the situation. It was quite a scene, as recounted afterward by Shakhlaʿ with her lighthearted spirit, weeping and laughing at the same time. Immediately thereafter the guests witnessed all the members of the troupe reeling and writhing. They rose quickly at the same moment, each with a hand on her belly. All the artistes rushed off, clearing a way for themselves through the crowd, in search of a bathroom or toilet.

But the most pitiful sight of all, in truth, was Salm, the blind woman, whose colleagues had abandoned her in that predicament. She stood in the center of the room, anxiously groping about, one hand on her stomach and the other beating the air as she sought her way. She was calling out, "O what a disaster! Bring me a basin or a chamber pot. Those who love the Prophet! May God protect you one day!" At first the invited ladies laughed, but then they rushed to her assistance.

Young Muhsin wasn't with the troupe that evening. Despite his tears and pleas, his mother had not permitted him to accompany the artistes. He had therefore to satisfy himself with hearing the story, like the others, from the mouth of Maestra Shakhlaʿ. She narrated and recounted it frequently in a diverting manner. Muhsin would laugh with childish good humor and feel consoled at hearing that account. He would forget his wish to accompany them.

Shakhlaʿ would scarcely have finished her story before Muhsin quickly begged, without allowing her time for a cigarette, "Tell me the story of the Jewish wedding."

Maestra Labiba and her troupe had been invited to perform at a wedding party at the home of a well-to-do Jewish family.

That was in the Coptic month of Tubah, when winter is at its coldest. The maestra sat in the center of her troupe, awaiting the arrival of the bride from her bath and toilette. Shakhlaʻ explained that one of the Jewish marriage customs was for the bride to bathe in cold water mixed with holy water sprinkled by the rabbi. After this bath, the bride is dressed and adorned. Then, it is forbidden for anyone who isn't Jewish, whether Muslim or Christian, to touch her. If that occurs, she must bathe again in the cold water.

Labiba Shakhlaʻ waited until the bride appeared, strutted forward in her gown and finery, and took her seat. Then festivities commenced and heated up. As the climax approached, the wind was howling, and the rain that night was coming down cold and freezing in Cairo in an unprecedented way. Labiba rose without warning and approached the bride to admire her magnificent clothing. Wanting to scrutinize and check the fabric in the bride's gown, she stretched out her hand and touched the bride. No sooner had she done that than an appalling cry rang out in the room, stunning her. Voices were raised in anger from every direction. Caught by surprise, she recoiled and stood frozen where she was, not moving. When she looked up, she saw that everyone—the bride, her family, and her attendants—had left, frothing and foaming, in spite of the roar of thunder outside. They were leading the bride to the bath a second time, the bitter cold notwithstanding.

The poor bride eventually returned from the cold bath, moaning, her teeth chattering. Her male relations heard the commotion and came to see what was happening. The women from the bride's family and the women guests hurried to them, yelling, "May Labiba be diced up! May Labiba be burned! Labiba touched her!"

Labiba heard that while cowering among the members of her troupe. Her body was trembling in fright and terror, and under her breath she had begun to recite the Throne Verse from the Qur'an. From time to time she peeked out to see whether the family's fury had abated. Then she would cling to the musicians near her and whisper, "Move a little closer, Najiya! Hide me. Do me a favor. Hold me, Salm. Have mercy on me.

Ransom me, children! O Master Abu al-Su'ud, by your miracles—half a dozen candles. Just permit us to escape from here unharmed."

Even though she was more fearful than Shakhla', Salm tried to calm her and scolded her maestra in a whisper, "Drat! I mean, what can they do to us?"

Najiya answered in a whisper, "The least they can do is plunge us in that soot bath too."

Salm's teeth chattered and she said, "Shield us, Lord. Are we responsible for all this?"

Then the shouting calmed down, and it seemed the hosts thought the stream should now return to its banks so the evening would not end badly. They became quiet and at once signaled to Maestra Labiba to resume the singing and music. Shakhla' decided to obey the order immediately to avoid causing any new problem and to distract them from what she had done. She straightened herself in her seat and ordered the troupe to pick up their instruments. She said to Najiya quickly, "Tune the lute for Hijaz-kar."

Then she raised her voice and sang "The Jealous Critic's Ruse."

She had barely finished the preamble when she heard whispering and a commotion among the members of the troupe. She noticed Salm's voice calling out and drowning hers: "God! God! Maestra Shakhla', you Egyptian . . . Pride of the kings!" Salm then bent over her and whispered, "God! . . . God! That's Discord-kar!"

Shakhla' turned on her sharply. "What's come over you, girl?"

But Shakhla' immediately realized she was singing off-key because of her fear and terror. So she composed herself and smiled. "What shall I do? They brought this calamity on me. Sing, children; sing no matter how. Just let's get through this evening with our skins . . . They can do what they please with 'The Jealous Critic's Ruse' when we're on the way home."

But among all those memories there was one night Muhsin would never forget. It was a night when he, although young, saw things that engraved indelible pictures and sensations into his memory and the depths of his soul.

One afternoon al-Hajj Ahmad al-Mutayyib asked Maestra Shakhla' to perform for a great wedding, emphasizing its magnificence and importance. He counseled her to be in top form. The news spread through the troupe and had a marked effect. They all started to get ready. One rehearsed. Another tuned the instruments. A third got the glittering costumes and jewelry in order, along with their cosmetics: the powders, perfumes, kohl, and eyebrow pencils. In no time flat the members of the troupe were all bustling about, full of happiness and energy.

Only one person stood looking forlorn and feeling heartbroken amid that movement and clamor. This was young Muhsin.

He stood sadly by the wall, realizing that he had been chasing a mirage. He wasn't a member of the troupe, nor had he ever been. Here the entire ensemble was preparing to leave him behind. The troupe could do without him and his services. They went to weddings and parties without him. Here were his colleagues Hafiza, Najiya, and Salm, each concerned with herself and not thinking about him. Indeed, not even one of them was aware of his existence.

He began to watch Maestra Shakhla' while she primped in front of the mirror. His eyes were pleading in entreaty, but she too at that time was unaware of him and totally preoccupied with her own affairs. Even she seemed to have forgotten that he was an important member of the ensemble.

That thought hurt him a lot, and he burst into tears. He started stomping his little feet and screaming, "Take me with you! I'm going too!" But his mother refused.

Muhsin rebelled. His howling and storming intensified. The maestra and the artistes tried to calm him, but that was impossible. His anger escalated now that he had determined he would accompany the troupe, no matter what it cost him. "What's wrong with me? Alas! I must go! I must go! I want to see the wedding. I've never seen a wedding!"

Shakhla' laughed at him a little but then took pity on him. She went and whispered tenderly to him, promising to persuade his mother to give permission for him to go.

The child hushed at once and gave the maestra a look that

ran the gamut from gratitude to hope. He knew his mother trusted Maestra Shakhla' implicitly. She had lived with the family so long that they had complete confidence in her.

Shakhla' actually managed to persuade his mother, although she hesitated a little at first. She ended up giving her consent and permission based on the maestra's vow: "There's no need to worry about him while he is with me. I won't let him out of my sight. Let him see a soiree for himself."

Muhsin was listening from the other side of the door, his heart quivering with fear and hope. As soon as he heard the permission, he let out a whoop of joy and raced at once through the house to look for his new clothes, while telling everyone he encountered—all the servants and artistes—that he was going with the troupe too.

In the depths of his young heart, he treasured a feeling for Shakhla' stronger than mere thanks and gratitude. It was a deep feeling he had never experienced before.

That evening the carriage transporting the artistes stopped before the wedding house, in front of which a large and magnificent pavilion had been erected. It was decorated with various types of hanging lamps and chandeliers, and with small rectangular and triangular banners of different colors: red, yellow, and green. Posts with gas lamps had been set up on both sides of the road leading to the house, as though they were the rams lining the road to the Temple of Karnak.

The pavilion was filled with hundreds of chairs, seats, and wooden benches. These were occupied by a number—known only to God—of guests. Not even the hosts shared that knowledge with him. Of course, there were the guests who had actually been invited, but along with them had arrived a vast number who had invited themselves and who had no idea whether the bride was named Zaynab or Shalabiya.

Dressed in their formal black jackets, waiters and servants circulated with large trays of red-colored drinks. Hands reached out; that multitudinous crowd swarmed around, each person seeking his share.

In one corner of the pavilion, the official (or semiofficial) army band was installed with its drums, winds, and brass instruments. It added to the clamor and deafening sound that are requisite for weddings of this importance and significance.

As soon as the artistes arrived, there was an additional commotion among the throngs. Two butlers hurried to meet the carriage and to assist the golden-voiced maestra to alight.

Shakhla' got out first, with great dignity. She dazzled the eyes with her ornaments, dangling gold jewelry, clinking anklets, and silk gown, which was embroidered with gold and silver thread and bangles, and was visible beneath her black wrapper. All this shimmered in the dull light of the lamps. She seemed to be a luminous piece of jewelry, constantly in motion.

Maestra Shakhla' took the ends of her shawl and wrapped it tightly around her. Then she looked behind her to the chorus, the members of the troupe. She directed them to carry their instruments carefully and attentively, each bringing her own. The maestra sashayed ahead, trailed by little Muhsin, who was wearing his suit purchased for the Great Feast.

Muhsin saw at once that Najiya was carrying the lute, Hafiza the darabukka drum, and Salm the tambourine. So he blustered, grumbled, and threatened to cry. He wanted to carry one of the instruments. Wasn't he a member of the troupe? Shakhla' vainly attempted by plea and guile to silence him. Finally she ordered that Muhsin should be given the finger cymbals. She told him, smiling tenderly, "You carry the castanets. They're the right size for you." She took his hand, wanting him to walk beside her, but he wished to follow her exactly like a member of the troupe. At last Shakhla' led the way, followed by her accompanists. They were escorted by butlers and servants to the door of the women's section. The looks and smiles of the male guests followed them. Words of flattery, courtship, and banter rose from the throngs: "Oh, my Lord! My Lord! Like that! Like that! Make way, fellows! You and the other one! One look, Granny! Watch out for her wrap, you! Ha ha!" and so on and so forth.

This continued until the artistes disappeared from sight behind the door of the women's quarters. As Maestra Shakhla' entered, she found herself in a spacious chamber filled with ladies who sparkled like stars in their gowns and magnificent jewels.

As soon as she appeared at the threshold, the party's hostesses came toward her, the mother of the bride among them. They gave her a welcome fitting a famous artiste and conducted her to the place set aside for the troupe. It was a spacious corner furnished with silk cushions and soft mats arranged in a circle. In the center was an armchair reserved for the clarion-voiced maestra.

Then the members of the ensemble entered along with Muhsin. He caught the attention of the hostesses, and the mother of the bride asked Shakhla', "God's name protect him, is he your son?"

Muhsin, however, did not allow Shakhla' time to reply. He said at once in his piping voice, pointing to the finger cymbals he carried, "No. I'm in the troupe!"

The bride's family laughed, amused by his serious tone, which was filled with determination and decision, despite his age. The bride's mother wanted to kiss him, but he fled, clinging to his colleagues and squeezing among them. They had taken their seats and were busy setting out their instruments and preparing them. Shakhla' excused herself then and immediately followed Muhsin.

Each of the artistes sat on a cushion or pallet around the maestra, who was elevated on a chair in the center. They began to chatter among themselves using their special argot.

They began as usual to criticize everything their eyes saw. Blind Salm asked if the house, the wedding party, and the people were really as advertised: a household where both the people and the food were rich and the family and the bread refined. Her colleagues turned their keen and critical eyes round the room. They looked for a moment at the bridal dais, which was in the center. Entirely covered in white silk, it held chairs for the groom and the bride and was extremely elegant. Then they gazed at its baldachin, which was also lined with white silk and resembled a waxen sky. Hanging from it on every side were garlands of jasmine, white roses, and other flowers. But the bride and groom had not arrived yet. For that reason the artistes trained their critical judgment on the guests. In any case, all signs indicated that it truly was a magnificent wedding.

Finally Najiya the lute player said, "Aye, in truth, the people are well-to-do, but they should have the courtesy to offer us cigarettes so we can relax with a smoke."

The maestra scolded her in a whisper, "Hush, triller, the bride's mother is coming toward us."

In fact, the bride's mother came up to Maestra Shakhla' and asked graciously if she would favor them with even one song before the buffet was opened, since the guests were longing for that.

Shakhla' answered politely, "Most gladly. At your service, madam, but the troupe would like cigarettes and I would like a cup of coffee, without sugar, and the protection of God's name on him—"

She pointed at Muhsin and tried to complete her sentence, but the young fellow interrupted. "I get whatever the troupe does!"

Shakhla' chided him disapprovingly. "Cigarettes? Anything but that! No, Muhsin, shame!" She turned quickly to the bride's mother and whispered in her ear, "For him, God's name, a glass of fruit punch."

The bride's mother answered, "Only that? Such a cheap request, when we hold you so dear? You will have it, sister! Most gladly! Listen, Maestra Shakhla', by the Prophet, feel no reserve. This house is yours. Whatever you want, ask for it. We want this night to be the night of a lifetime, one we will remember you for, Madam Shakhla'. Glow, shine, and let your voice resound. Make it incomparable!" She went off quickly to fulfill the troupe's requests.

Shakhla' raised her eyes and cast a comprehensive glance over the guests. She saw that they were looking at her with admiration and anticipation. She smiled at them.

At once a daring voice called out, "Maestra Shakhla'! Please, the song 'My Darling's Gone, My Heart Dissolves.'"

Shakhla' politely nodded her consent while the ladies laughed—some uninhibited and encouraging, others disapproving and surprised. Their eyes searched for the lady who dared say out loud, "My darling's gone; my heart dissolves; I've endured a long time without a letter from him."

An hour passed while the artistes did nothing more than tune their instruments, smoke cigarettes, drink coffee, sip fruit punch, chatter, and criticize. Perhaps their most important accomplishment was to vex the audience and exhaust their patience. Actually, this is an element of the art of the people of that profession. Indeed, perhaps the sole art that Egyptian artistes have perfected is the art of vexation and keeping the audience waiting.

But no one was quite so impatient as little Muhsin. This novice did not understand yet why the troupe was deliberately drawing out that tedious delay and procrastinating. Stirred by a fever of enthusiasm, he wanted the troupe to sing at once. He asked the maestra innocently and forcefully, "Why are you all silent? When will we sing? The people have been waiting for us to sing for a long time!"

Shakhla' gave him a look of pity and compassion, like someone eyeing an infant or an ignorant, inexperienced simpleton. Then she leaned over and whispered confidentially, "This is our craft, dummy. This is the whole secret of the craft. The more you bore the audience, the more they fall into your fingers. Do you understand, son?"

Hafiza, the drummer, added, rubbing the head of the drum with her palm to tighten it, "Whoever said that it's an art to bore people was right."

Shakhla' agreed. "That's so true!" Then she held the cigarette in her mouth toward Hafiza to light for her.

When Shakhla' determined that according to the dictates of the art the moment had arrived to sing and gave the order to pick up the instruments, it was too late. The hostesses came to announce the opening of the buffet.

So the maestra ordered the instruments set down again. Smiling, she said to the troupe, "A blessing, group, thanks to you as much as me."

The mother of the bride came to invite just Shakhla' to the

buffet, apologizing that it was too crowded for her to invite the other members of the troupe. She suggested they eat at their places and said a large tray with a wide variety of dishes on it—just like those at the buffet and better—would be served them while they sat peacefully in their corner, far from the turmoil and from anything that might disturb them while they ate. The maestra agreed but asked if it would be possible to bring young Muhsin with her to the buffet. The bride's mother answered immediately as she attempted to kiss Muhsin, "So! Sister, good gracious! He's goodness and blessing!"

But Muhsin refused to leave his colleagues again this time. Faced with Shakhla''s urging, he shouted, "No, I don't want to. Why should I? Alas!"

Remembering what she had told Muhsin's mother and her promise to look after him and keep him near her, Shakhla' insisted he accompany her. She told him rather frankly and angrily, "Come with me, I tell you!" Then she whispered gently in his ear, "The buffet's better. You'll eat delicious things there."

Clinging to the arm of the chair, Muhsin answered stubbornly, "I don't want to eat better things. I want to eat here with the troupe."

Two maids appeared at that moment, carrying a large tray, which they set on the floor between the artistes. There was a large platter on it filled with couscous and roast turkey, along with various types of vegetables and meat, kebab and kofta, and different varieties of sweets, pastries, and fruit.

Muhsin didn't hesitate and crowded in at once among his colleagues, not paying attention to anyone. Shakhla' hesitated a little over what she ought to do but quickly reached a decision too. She turned to the bride's mother and declined the buffet. Then she sat on the floor beside Muhsin to eat with the troupe, like him.

Blind Salm smelled roast turkey. She asked her colleagues to confirm it really was turkey.

The artistes commenced with the couscous. At that point it became clear that the servants had forgotten the spoons. Blind Salm stretched her hand out in the air, saying, "Where's the spoon, sisters?"

Eating with appetite and delight, young Muhsin answered, "There's nothing but forks. Will you take a fork?"

The blind woman said in doubt, "A fork? What do you eat couscous with, you there?"

Muhsin replied immediately with a smile, "With a fork. We're all eating that way. Eat like us."

Salm said sharply, "Couscous with a fork? What an idea! Don't kid around, by the Prophet, Muhsin. Bring me a spoon at once, may God reward you. Shame on you! This isn't a time to joke. Get me a spoon quickly. Do me a favor."

Shakhla' intervened and said with affected gruffness, "There aren't any spoons. He's telling you to take a fork. Won't you listen and quiet down?"

Salm stretched out her hand and took a fork, scolding, "Still a fork? Does this work with couscous?"

She plunged the fork straight into the couscous as though spearing a piece of meat. Naturally, not a single grain struck to it. She raised it to her mouth, but found not a speck of couscous.

Her colleagues roared with laughter. Little Muhsin in particular was laughing, innocently and boyishly. He said, "Look! She doesn't know how to eat couscous with a fork."

He wanted to teach her how to position the fork—horizontally, not vertically. She should shovel and scoop with it, not plunge and stab. Her other colleagues, however, signaled to him secretly to refrain. Najiya said out loud, while giving him a wink from the corner of her eye, "Leave her alone. She's eating just fine. Is she lacking in any way?"

Then she whispered in his ear, "If she keeps that up, by God, she won't get more than ten grains all evening. Leave her be, by the Prophet, Muhsin. Let's see what she does. It's amusing. Let us laugh at her a little."

Muhsin consented at first and put a hand over his mouth to hold back his childish giggles. But he thought it over. Then, simply and innocently he said, "You mean she's not going to eat? Salm's not going to eat with us? That's wrong! She must eat with us. Look, Salm." Then he proceeded to teach her how to eat couscous with a fork, till she was able to eat like the others.

Shakhla' observed all this silently with interest. Touched, she said, as though to herself, "What a good heart you have, Muhsin."

Toward midnight the wedding festivities reached a climax of joy and commotion. The troupe had sung several long numbers and some short popular songs, each separated from the next by long intervals.

The audience of enthusiastic female guests surrounded the troupe like the crescent moon around the star on the Egyptian flag. They listened as though they were all a single individual. They weren't quiet and still with their heads bowed; to the contrary—their cries of admiration, approval, and enthusiasm were louder than the singing. Yet their faces all had the same expression: one of boisterous happiness. They had a single expression because the music had that effect on them. There wasn't even one of the guests who set herself apart from her sisters to wrest some other meaning from the music or some different emotion from that sweeping the others. They all became a single person as they responded to the music. The music itself seemed a beloved capable of turning all creatures back into one person.

Just a little after midnight, someone came to whisper softly in Maestra Shakhla''s ear, and she at once passed the word on to the members of the troupe under her breath. The news prompted them to straighten up, and their faces took on an air of earnestness and consequence. They lifted their instruments energetically and enthusiastically, like soldiers raising their weapons after receiving the order to attack. Suddenly a shrill and prolonged ululation, like the whistle of a houseboat on the Nile, was heard throughout the house, and the bride appeared— fresh from the hand of the bridal stylist—in her white silk gown, with the bridal tiara on her head. Her family and relatives and the women of the household followed her, with the stylist on her left, scattering salt in every direction and crying out, "If you love the Prophet, pray for him."

The bride strutted to her chair on the dais and sat down. The stylist sat near her and held out her kerchief to receive wedding money from the guests. Meanwhile the troupe was singing so boisterously that their music filled the room.

As soon as the bride was settled, a person came to announce the arrival of the groom. He appeared at the door and entered with embarrassment, after smiling at the men assembled to see him off at the door of the women's quarters. They were also trying to catch a glimpse of the bride, but that didn't prevent them from looking at the beautiful women among the guests and smiling at them. The groom made his way between the ladies, who were almost devouring him with their eyes while they whispered their opinion of him to each other. When he reached the dais, he paused hesitantly. Then he collected his courage and with his right hand raised the tiara's white silk veil to reveal the bride's face.

At this, necks craned and the people present stood up. They were staring in a dreadful silence, hardly breathing, as though awaiting a verdict not subject to reversal or challenge. Even the troupe, although they were singing and playing enthusiastically and vigorously, kept their eyes fixed with intense concern on the groom's face.

When he lifted the veil, the groom seemed slightly surprised and astonished but quickly recovered himself and smiled. He bent over the bride's hand and raised it to his lips to kiss. Then he mounted the dais and sat down beside her.

At that, sounds of joy and jubilation rose from every side, and deafening ululation resounded. The singing of the artistes grew louder as the commotion and uproar increased.

Suddenly the sound of finger cymbals rang through the hall as Shakhla', half-naked in a glittering gold dance costume, made her appearance. She advanced to the middle of the chamber, dancing with every sinew of her supple, slender body. Her torso was in play as though it were a thong of taffy. The castanets rang from fingers decorated with henna.

The room fell silent as the commotion of the guests died away. Everyone was staring with enchanted, admiring eyes that followed the movement of this extraordinary body and the pulsations of that slim belly and of her breasts, which resembled ripe fruit. All this was aquiver in a beautiful vision to the accompaniment of the drum and the tambourine.

Among all those dazzled eyes, Muhsin's were the most dazzled and amazed, in an extraordinarily innocent way. It was not the first time he had seen her dance. Indeed he had seen her dance time and again. Tonight, however, when she was the object of all those admiring, hungry looks, Muhsin—because he knew her and lived with her—felt for the first time a kind of glory and pride. He was a member of the troupe, her troupe. Then he felt, in addition to that, other vague sensations. Before Shakhla' finished her dance, the wedding family, followed by relatives and then the guests, took turns going up to her and pressing on her forehead a gold coin: a pound or a napoleon, as though sticking stamps on an envelope.

Whenever her forehead became heavy with gold, she wiped it off with her kerchief, so to speak, to let it be covered a second and third time.

She received banknotes as well as gold, and a large sum was showered on her by the groom's family. The artistes crowded around her, gathering money from the floor, along with the servants, hangers-on, and dependents.

By two a.m., after much singing and dancing, the bridal pair made known their desire to leave the room for the nuptial chamber.

They stood and descended the steps of the dais slowly, arm in arm. Then the family, relatives, and hangers-on fell in behind them. Maestra Shakhla' rose with all her ensemble, their instruments in their arms, and they were followed by the guests. Thus the wedding procession, amid cries of praise to God and ululation, advanced till the couple reached the door of their chamber. They entered and the door closed. Then, after a final trill of joy resounded through the house, the party started to break up and the commotion, hubbub, and turmoil began to dissipate. Everyone went pell-mell to the wedding family, invoking blessings on them and saying, "We look forward to the birth of the children."

Thus ended the wedding. The hosts and guests fell upon

Maestra Shakhla', heaping her with words of praise and expressions of wonder and admiration for the success and regard
she had earned during that glamorous evening.

Shakhla' was intoxicated by this victory and began to separate herself graciously from the guests and to make her way
through the crush, while she hummed with pleasure, back to
the troupe. She was preparing to depart but suddenly remembered Muhsin. She struck her breast in anxiety and fear. "Woe
is me! What a fix! Where's Muhsin, kids?"

The fact was they had all forgotten poor little Muhsin. They
were distracted from him by the wedding procession for the
bride and groom. None of them had remembered that it was
after two a.m. and that the child could not fight off sleep forever.

Shakhla' searched with anxious, worried eyes until she finally found him on the floor, fast asleep, half-hidden under a
chair. She took him in her arms quickly and firmly and then
covered his face with kisses.

He opened his eyes.

When he could see her clearly, sleep left him all of a sudden.
His lashes trembled and his cheeks flushed. He felt a little uneasy. He didn't know why. Then he quickly released himself
from her embrace and ran off.

The passing years will never erase from his memory that sweet
and happy moment when he opened his eyes to find himself in
her arms, treated to her kisses.

When eventually Shakhla' married al-Hajj Ahmad al-
Mutayyib, Muhsin felt distressed and disappointed. A mirage
seemed to have vanished. Despair settled deep inside his soul
without his knowing why.

CHAPTER 10

The time passed without their noticing. They had not been singing, nor had she been playing the piano. Instead the two were silent, with their heads bowed, as though they had something on their minds. The expression on Saniya's face was serious and concerned. Muhsin was beset by hesitation and fear for a variety of reasons.

This wasn't because of the story that Muhsin had related concerning his childhood. Although Saniya had certainly enjoyed it, that story would not have been able to generate such preoccupation and concern in her.

Muhsin, however, when he finished his account of his early days, had found the courage to tell her—without any preamble and all in a rush—about her silk handkerchief. He informed her that it had not been lost and that the wind hadn't blown it away. It was still around and in the possession of a man who carried it always, protecting and treasuring it. He did not, however, tell her the name of that man. Despite her urgent entreaties, he remained silent without answering, feeling alternately hesitant and fearful. She gave up on him and began to wonder who might be keeping her handkerchief. From time to time she gave Muhsin a pleading look. She was perplexed. He was the one who had started it and sparked her curiosity. Finally she raised her head resolutely—the matter was beyond her—and shouted at him, "Won't you tell me who has my handkerchief?"

She softened her shrillness a little and continued in an enchanting tone of censure, "Why don't you want to tell me? Shame on you!"

When Muhsin did not reply, she continued, "You know him, of course."

The youth trembled and immediately stammered, "Who?"

She did not notice his agitation and observed thoughtfully,

"You said just now that the handkerchief did not necessarily land on your roof. . . ."

Muhsin calmed down and smiled, because he had thrown her off the scent. He said mischievously, "Right! Not necessarily!"

She said, as though to herself, "Okay, whose roof might it have fallen on then?"

At once an idea flashed through her mind, and she rose quickly to head to the balcony. She looked and whispered to herself, after scrutinizing al-Hajj Shahhata's coffeehouse before her, "It's possible. . . . Impossible. . . . Why . . . why not?"

Then, turning her eyes to the building next door, but to the lower apartment, she whispered to herself, "The floor below them has a balcony!"

Muhsin followed her with his eyes without understanding this movement of hers or why she went to the balcony, although he felt somewhat depressed.

At that moment Zanuba appeared at the door of the room. She must actually have gone to the dressmaker, or someplace far away, to take up all this time. She must equally have failed in the project she had resolved upon, for Mustafa Bey was still sitting in al-Hajj Shahhata's coffeehouse. He hadn't budged an inch.

From the threshold Zanuba noticed that Saniya was looking out the balcony window. She couldn't keep herself from shouting at the girl and scolding her in a way that was extraordinary and coarse. "What are you doing there at the window?"

Startled, Saniya turned in surprise and saw Zanuba at the doorway. She said, as though stunned, "You've returned, abla?"

Zanuba gained control of herself and realized that she had spoken harshly. So walking in, she said in a calm voice, as she removed her wrap and put it on a chair, "Is the piano lesson over?"

Saniya answered as she returned from the balcony and took a seat, "We were too lazy to study today. The time was all consumed by talk. How about you, abla? Where did you go?"

Zanuba was somewhat rattled but replied at once, tersely, as though trying to avoid the topic, "The dressmaker."

"All this time?"

"Aye." Zanuba remembered immediately, however, the half

hour that she had omitted from this reckoning—the cursed half hour she had spent on Salama Street walking back and forth in front of the coffeehouse while that blind fool gave no sign at all of noticing her.

They were all silent for a moment but finally Saniya turned to Muhsin and asked softly, "Why are you standing so far away, Muhsin Bey?"

Muhsin was leaning against the piano. He hadn't moved since his conversation with Saniya and was brooding about what she might have understood from this whole story of the handkerchief. What had he secured or gained from telling her? What was the effect or result of all that on her? Why had she gotten up and gone to the balcony? What did that mean? There were things that escaped his ken, and he had begun to feel fearful about this mystery.

At that point the black maid came to inform them that Mabruk had arrived. She had scarcely announced him when he appeared in the salon in his best caftan. Zanuba stared scornfully at him and asked, "And you, sir. What brings you here?"

Mabruk was a little deflated after his grand entrance and cleared his throat. Then he replied gravely, "I have come to tell you . . ."

Zanuba asked with biting sarcasm, "To tell us what, fellow?"

Mabruk was silent for a bit, feeling embarrassed. He looked at Saniya humbly and then glanced at the floor. Finally he started peering around anxiously, like a simpleton.

Zanuba watched his antics for a while and then suddenly asked, "What is it? Sister, what's wrong with him that he's acting like the village fool at the wedding? Won't you speak?"

Mabruk straightened up at once and turned toward her. He cleared his throat and said, "I've come to tell you . . ."

Zanuba could not control herself; she shouted, "Sister! We've heard that a thousand times."

Mabruk steeled himself and protested, "Won't you wait for me to speak?"

Zanuba said scornfully, "Fine, tell us, fellow, the important news. Speak."

Mabruk was silent for a moment. He looked at Saniya, then at Zanuba. He cleared his throat and said weightily, "Dinner."

At that point, Zanuba's sarcastic laughter rang out, producing a cold sweat on the servant's body. She asked frigidly, "Is this the news? You make a calamity for me because of this? So, you, sir, came, wearing your dress caftan, decked out twenty-four carat, in order to tell us something that is neither here nor there?"

Saniya felt like laughing but saw that Mabruk was upset and in an awkward situation. She didn't want to make him any more uncomfortable or embarrassed. Indeed she wished at that point to relieve him and get him out of his fix. She said flatteringly, "By God, Mabruk in his caftan looks exactly like a village headman."

Mabruk, the servant, advanced a step toward Saniya and cleared his throat, holding his wide sleeve over his mouth. Then he said earnestly, "You're right, by God, Miss Saniya. I used to be an *umda*."

Muhsin couldn't keep himself from laughing, in spite of his agitated condition. Zanuba raised her head and threw Mabruk a sarcastic glance. She asked, "Just when was that, Light of my Eye?"

Mabruk winked at her from the corner of his eye, imploring her to be still. But she would not. Perhaps out of revenge she declared, "You were a peasant in the village hostel, sleeping and living with the donkey colts, the calves, and the water buffalo. We brought you to the capital, fixed you up, and provided for you. We taught you how to live in a house, and you became a human being."

Mabruk looked so defeated that everyone laughed. Saniya, however, after she laughed, at once felt sorry for him. She said with enchanting sweetness, "No, abla. Don't say that. By God, Mabruk is the spitting image of the headman in Papa's community, except that ours wears glasses."

Mabruk felt his self-respect return with these words. He turned to Saniya and said, "Okay, by our lord Husayn, I have—no kidding—a pair of glasses."

They all laughed.

Zanuba said at once in a stinging tone, "Glasses! Name of God! What do you do with them? If you knew how to read and write, we could say you read the papers with them. You have eyes strong enough to repel a bullet."

Mabruk did not answer her but looked instead at Saniya. He said, "Miss Saniya, believe me, by the life of the Prophet's beard, I was a headman with glasses."

This time not even Saniya could suppress her laughter, which trilled out. Muhsin approached Mabruk and told him, "Ninny, it's better to be a headman without glasses, if your eyesight is good."

But it was pointless to try to get that idea into Mabruk's head. He did not want to hear talk like this at all. He turned to Saniya and gestured to her, as if to say, "Don't believe anyone but me."

CHAPTER 11

The next day was Friday, a day of rest and relaxation. Hanafi Effendi and his comrades—the folks—spent the whole day at home, waiting for a substantial meal, as was their custom on that free day. So, once President Hanafi heard the voice of the muezzin calling the Friday prayer from the minaret of al-Sayyida Zaynab Mosque—"Come to prosperity"—he put his hand on his stomach and shouted to announce his hunger. It wasn't long before Captain Salim and then Muhsin followed his example.

Abduh alone, out of stubbornness, did not want to acknowledge he was hungry. Instead, he began to take issue with his comrades, advising them to be forbearing and encouraging them to be a little patient. He addressed them as though delivering the Friday sermon, telling them they should learn moderation if they wanted to stay alive and have anything to eat till the end of the month.

The folks were quiet then for a time as Hanafi Effendi rambled around the apartment, going in and out of the rooms in order to keep his mind off his hunger. At last he said all of a sudden, "Where's Mabruk, gang?"

Abduh answered confidently and reassuringly, "In the kitchen!" Then he added, "Perhaps we're going to eat lentils in a cloak today."

Hanafi, who was rubbing his belly and moaning, asked, "In a cloak and caftan?"

Abduh replied immediately and somewhat sharply, "Right! In a caftan, cloak, and turban. So what do you want, sir? I suppose you're hoping for roast turkey at a time like this?"

Captain Salim, who was also putting his hand on his stomach, hastened to say, "Hush! It's forbidden to utter the word 'turkey' now! Danger! Withdraw it. Spit 'turkey' from your mouth."

They were silent till Hanafi started again. He laughed sarcastically and said, "By God, it doesn't look like we're going to eat today."

Salim added, "True! I don't hear the sound of a dish, cook pot, or mortar, and there's no aroma of cooking."

Abduh said angrily, "I told you: lentils."

President Hanafi replied, "By God, the kitchen doesn't have lentils or turkey or Mabruk in it."

Abduh inquired anxiously, "How's that? Mabruk's not in the kitchen?" At once, they all rose in disorder and disarray to storm the kitchen. They were astonished to find absolutely no one there. They searched then in every room—in the large sleeping chamber, under the five beds lined up there, under the table and chairs—without finding any trace of Mabruk. They saw no one in the house, except for them and Zanuba, who was in her room. She had not intervened since the housekeeping and kitchen were removed from her control.

Salim wondered aloud, "So where has he gone? Now, at lunchtime, when it's time for the Friday prayer?"

Abduh scratched his head and said thoughtfully, "Perhaps he's gone to perform the Friday prayer."

Salim countered wrathfully, "God's will be done! He performs the Friday prayer while we eat each other here. This fool prays before he cooks? Are we going to dine on his prayers?"

Hanafi commented sarcastically, "He may have gone to implore the Master, may He be glorified and exalted, to throw us down a two-course meal."

But Abduh shouted suddenly as though he had discovered something. "Hush! Listen. I've understood at last! I know where Mabruk has gone. Perhaps he's found that cooking food is expensive. Of course it costs something to cook, that's obvious. For example, he buys a match for . . . and . . ."

Hanafi asked sarcastically, "So you mean a box of matches worth a millieme has shut down the world?"

Abduh silenced him with a violent gesture and continued, "I mean cooked food is expensive, and that's that. That's obvious. For this reason, Mabruk, who is a clever, perceptive person, noticed that and intends today, for example, to feed us salt-cured fish. What do you think of salty, little fish? Isn't it an astonishing idea?"

Hanafi, who was trying to understand, asked, "Is that your deduction in your capacity of chief engineer . . . or . . ."

Salim started to complete his sentence. "Or are you sure he's gone to buy—" but did not conclude his phrase, because at that moment the door opened and Mabruk appeared.

Everyone turned quickly in his direction and leapt to welcome him as though he were a messenger from heaven.

But it was only a moment before they all emitted a single cry, because Mabruk was empty-handed. He clearly had brought nothing—no lentils, no salt-cured fish. He had just one thing: a brand-new pair of glasses that he was wearing.

Mabruk stood there a moment, looking at the stunned folks through his new glasses. Then he suddenly went to Abduh, spread out his hand, which held forty-five piastres, and said, "I've changed the pound you gave me yesterday. Here's what's left. So take your money. I resign from this job. It seems the money's not going to last to the end of the month. You have a Lord who is called 'the Generous.'"

Abduh was aghast. He opened his mouth but did not utter so much as a syllable. He glared at Mabruk for a long time before turning to his comrades. Then he looked back at Mabruk. Finally, gazing at what was left of the pound, he asked, "What's this talk?"

Only Mushin understood, and he savored the situation. He looked at Mabruk's new glasses and smiled. Then he whispered to him, "Now you're a headman with glasses."

Abduh couldn't get over his astonishment. He fixed his eyes at times on the depleted funds and then on Mabruk, until Salim got his attention with a nudge of his arm. Tapping Abduh on the shoulder, he remarked sarcastically, "The only thing worse than the lady is the gent! So here's what is left of your government and our budget."

Mabruk shrugged his shoulders at them and declared dismissively, "Neither my father nor my mother was a government. I never told you to make me a government. There's your money. Free me and release me from this charge, as a generous deed in honor of Umm Hashim."

CHAPTER 12

Abduh glared at Mabruk with a mixture of exasperation and anger for a moment more. His hopes had been dashed. Finally he shouted, "Is it my mistake? I was duped. I thought he was a human being. But the truth is that once a servant, always a servant."

The servant, Mabruk, didn't hear a single word Abduh said. He had removed himself to a corner, where he was busy cleaning his new glasses with a gauzy cigarette paper the way Hanafi Effendi did.

Abduh kept on talking, without looking at Mabruk. "The proverb says: 'A man's fingers are not all the same.' I ought to have understood that from the outset. If all natures and minds were of one type, the world would be a different place."

He wanted to continue with this line of talk, but Salim tapped his shoulder, directing his attention to Mabruk, who was oblivious, preoccupied with his glasses. He told Abduh, "Spare your brain this philosophy. Your friend is in another world, and what's happened has happened."

Abduh turned toward Mabruk. Seeing him, he raged and rose fuming. He shouted, "Still polishing the glasses? Scram, get away from me! May your day be like tar!"

Mabruk stirred himself and headed for the door. He said calmly, "You're right—no kidding—it's true. Today is Friday, which contains an unlucky hour."

Abduh shouted at him. "I'm telling you to leave. Scram! I don't want to see your mug."

Mabruk put on his glasses and, looking through them at Abduh, responded, "Fine. If you'll pardon my asking, why are you angry? Why are you so out of sorts? Anger is outlawed and quarreling is forbidden." He then departed, escorted by the fiery gaze of Abduh.

The subsequent silence was finally broken by Salim, who asked, "What do we do now?"

Abduh did not reply; he seemed not to have heard. Perhaps he didn't know what to say or was preoccupied thinking about how to escape from that abyss.

Abduh realized that the experiment hadn't succeeded and that Zanuba would certainly mock them, take revenge on them, and glory in her triumph over them, but all the same, here he, Abduh, saw that there was no choice but to go back to her, to her fire instead of cursed Mabruk's paradise. What tormented Abduh's mind was how to return contritely to Zanuba. How could he overcome his pride and inform her of his defeated hopes and of the need to rely on her to straighten matters out as she saw fit to survive to the end of the month?

Apparently God did not want to humiliate Abduh; at times, God prepares for each person the circumstances that are most congenial to him. Zanuba suddenly appeared at the door. She advanced hesitantly, with a serious look on her face, as though she had important information she wished to convey.

Abduh raised his head to look at her without uttering a word but didn't frown at her. Zanuba said at once, impetuously, "The neighbors' electric line's cut!"

Abduh looked at her with curious astonishment, as though asking how that concerned him. Zanuba informed him immediately that the neighbors—that is, the household of Dr. Hilmi—had wanted to ask one of the electricity workers to come repair the wiring now, fearing that night would overtake them, but since it was Friday, they were afraid none of the company employees could be found. So Zanuba had suggested to them that Abduh, who was practically an engineer, should repair the damage with the utmost speed, sparing them any need to find an employee of the company or to cause a fuss over so trivial a matter.

As soon as Abduh heard that, he was up on his feet as if he had touched a live wire, for he had learned he would go to the neighbors' house. He looked at Zanuba with interest and realized that he had forgiven her every offense and shortcoming in a moment. "Should I go now, at once?"

"Now or later in the afternoon. It's all the same."

Abduh walked around looking in every direction, as though searching for something. He said, "Where's the hammer? Where are the pincers? Where are the nails? . . . Where . . ."

Salim, who was not very happy about this news, started carefully observing Abduh and the transformation that had swept over him. Salim twisted his mustache, pretending to be calm, while his eyes showed his scorn and envy. When he saw Abduh hasten to look for the tools, he said in a stingingly sarcastic tone, "Not so fast! Slow down! Haste is from the devil!"

Abduh looked at him askance and said, "Do us a favor and be quiet, please."

Twisting his mustache, Salim replied with annoyance, "You visit people at the lunch hour?"

Abduh did not answer him. At that point, Hanafi Effendi, rubbing his eyes with one hand and preparing with the other to put his glasses on his nose, asked, "With regard to lunch . . . what have you done about the issue of our lunch?"

Abduh turned not toward him but toward Zanuba instead and asked, "That electric wire, how was it cut?"

She replied, "The maid, Fatima, was cleaning the hall today. The broom struck the wire on the wall and it fell down along with the nails."

Abduh continued to think for a moment. It occurred to him that it would be best to go later so he could prepare, not just by gathering what he needed to fix the wiring but by changing his clothes and look.

It was naturally not difficult for Abduh then to show Zanuba the forty-five piastres on the table and to ask her, without any servility or entreaty, to manage things till the end of the month. He conveyed the information quite tersely in an abrupt and decisive tone, to prevent her from fathoming what had happened. Zanuba should not feel they were humbly coming back to her. When she saw the sum she felt like shrieking in astonishment and disbelief. "What a calamity!" she said. "Is this all that's left of the pound?"

Abduh at once answered tartly, "There's no need for a lot of talk. You make it work. Spare us the headache."

She took the money from the table silently and went off with it to her room. She had realized that there was no call for going into particulars and trying to unravel things. She was satisfied, feeling that they had failed and been forced to return to her.

At about two p.m., the group observed that Abduh was acting strangely. He was going from room to room with a towel around his neck, soap on his chin, and a razor in his hand. He was looking for Mabruk, or anyone who would clean his jacket for him and get the spots out of it with benzene.

Mabruk shouted, "If we can't find food, how should we be able to find benzene?" Abduh, however, scolded him. Scowling and screaming, he ordered Mabruk to help him get dressed, because the time had come.

They were all watching him and most of them were neither amused nor pleased by his concern and fastidiousness. Salim sat silently, as though he had a pain in the chest. He began to twist his mustache and stealthily watched Abduh, who, after shaving, was in front of the mirror sprinkling his face with Zanuba's powder, which she had brought him from her room at his request.

Salim's patience gave way, and he looked at Hanafi, who despite his nonchalant appearance was also following Abduh's actions through his thick glasses. Salim winked at President Hanafi and pointed toward Abduh. With weak sarcasm he said, "Wouldn't you say he's going to a rendezvous?"

Hanafi pretended not to hear and continued watching Abduh as he finished dressing and placed the fez on his head with careful deliberation. He settled its tassel over his right ear. Then he shouted at Mabruk to wrap the hammer and pincers in an old newspaper with the utmost speed. He walked a few steps toward the door.

At that point the honorary president asked Abduh in a halfway serious jest, although gently, "Don't you need a boy?"

Abduh answered with decisive brevity, "No!"

Hanafi insisted, "To carry your equipment, boss."

"No." Abduh uttered this second "no" in a dry, definitive

tone that revealed his displeasure. Hanafi turned to Salim and said, "No, no—God will provide."

Abduh went to Dr. Hilmi's residence, where he found Zanuba waiting for him at the door of the living room, ready to accompany him to the spot where the wire was cut. He had barely set foot inside when he started looking discreetly right and left, not turning toward Zanuba, who was pointing out the place that needed repair. All the doors leading into the hall were closed except for one that was half-open. This was the door leading to the piano salon. But Abduh could not see so much as a shadow or ghost inside it. Finally he said in a voice that filled the whole hallway, "Where's the ladder? Isn't there a wooden ladder here?"

His voice resounded with command and self-confidence. Zanuba hastened toward the half-open door and called, "Fatima! O Fatima!"

She did not wait for the maid to come and went quickly through the door into the salon, leaving Abduh alone in the hall gazing at the gazelle heads hung on the wall and the stuffed crocodile over the main door. Then Abduh's heart suddenly fluttered because he heard the sound of a piano giving forth beautiful melodies. He listened, smiling joyfully, almost tipsy, until Fatima, the maid, appeared all at once carrying the wooden ladder. He turned toward her, took it, and propped it against the wall. Then he began to climb its rungs while alternately listening and wondering, *Why is she playing the piano now?* Did she perhaps do that when she learned he was in the house? Or was it a coincidence? Did she practice at this time every day? He, however, proceeded to discount the two last hypotheses with various arguments. He favored the first possibility: that she had started playing when she learned he was present, that he had come. Yes, all signs pointed to that!

Zanuba returned to ask Abduh whether he needed anything else and to see if the work was proceeding without a hitch. At this moment the sound of the piano ceased. Fully alert, Abduh soon heard the rustling of a dress behind the half-closed door and a soft voice whispering, "Abla! Abla!"

Zanuba turned in the direction of the voice and headed

toward it. Just before she reached the door, however, the voice asked, in a clearly audible way this time, "Shall we offer Abduh Bey coffee or fruit punch?"

Zanuba stopped, turned to Abduh, and said, "Miss Saniya asks if you would like coffee or fruit punch."

Abduh had heard the first time. There was no need to repeat the question, but she did that to flatter Abduh. As soon as Saniya heard Zanuba mention her name to Abduh, though, she laughed or pretended to laugh on the other side of the door. She murmured with affected modesty, "Is that the way, abla? Shame on you."

Before Abduh could reply, Saniya leapt away to conceal herself. In the distance, the fleeting pistachio green color of her dress was visible and filled Abduh's eyes. He no longer saw anything except the color green passing before his distracted mind.

Abduh did not awake from his surprise and his dream until he heard Muhsin's voice. The boy had popped out of the salon door and was asking Zanuba languidly whether this story of the wire had ended yet or not.

Abduh looked at him in astonishment and scowled. He asked coldly and sternly, "God! You're here? What are you doing?"

Muhsin answered tersely and noncommittally, "The lesson."

"What lesson?"

"The piano lesson!"

A cloud passed through Abduh's heart with the speed of lightning and spoiled the delicious moment that had just preceded: the music and the voice whispering his name, begging him to drink coffee or fruit juice. He wanted to respond to Muhsin. He had started to frown, but the rustling of the gown returned and the eye-dazzling green color was visible beyond the door. A voice was calling gently, sweetly, and coquettishly, "Muhsin! Where have you gone, leaving the lesson?"

Muhsin started toward her, saying, "Here I am, Abla Saniya. Coming at once!" He did, however, turn to look at Abduh and told him with a voice laced with chilly, vengeful sarcasm, "Fix the wire well. Be careful not to electrocute yourself."

Abduh cast him a fiery glance from the top of the ladder, but Muhsin quickly disappeared from sight. Abduh, who was filled with rage, soon heard a pretty tune being played on the piano by an excellent and accomplished performer. He listened but some of his anger lingered on. He heard that beautiful melody cease suddenly. Its place was taken by the sound of someone who was clearly a bumbling beginner. Only a moment later he sensed the rustling of the dress and spotted its fleeting green color passing the half-closed door. Abduh's eyes froze in the direction of that door. Suddenly, he did not know if his hand had touched a live wire, for he felt his heart throb with the speed of lightning in one powerful pulsation. His eyes had encountered two other eyes—black eyes more beautiful than any he had ever seen. They had a magical impact. Then the rustling dress flashed past again. The green color crossed before his earnest eyes and vanished.

When Abduh had calmed himself, he started asking himself again happily and with the intoxication of conquest, why had she shown herself to him so frequently? Was she doing that deliberately?

His eyes and face came alive, and his heart filled to bursting with vitality in an unprecedented fashion. He grasped the wooden ladder in his hands and moved it to another place on the wall. He sprang up it vigorously and enthusiastically, as though his heart was climbing the rungs of love.

CHAPTER 13

Abduh returned home shortly before sunset after prolonging the work next door as long as possible. He was filled with a gentleness, lightness of spirit, and happiness the folks had never seen in him before. He began to move from room to room, jesting gently with Hanafi Effendi, trying to get him to put aside for a moment the copybooks, which he was busy correcting, and to talk. He did not, however, get a particularly favorable reception from him.

Then he sought out the servant Mabruk, wanting to kid around with him and remind him of the new glasses he had purchased with their food money. Even Salim with his forced smile, who pretended to be engrossed in reading a newspaper, wasn't overlooked by Abduh, who grabbed the paper away from him suddenly, as though wanting to start a conversation. Salim, though, gave him a cold look, picked the paper up off the floor, and began reading it again. He said, as though to himself, "What's happened? What's the reason for this nonsense?"

Abduh heard him and asked jokingly but grumpily, "Yes, Mr. Salim?"

"Nothing, it just seems to me you're being uncommonly jolly, for no reason."

"Because you're here, because you haven't gone down to the coffee shop the way you usually do."

Salim did not respond. He started reading, moving his lips like a person caught up in his reading to the exclusion of everything else. So Abduh left him, vexed, and turned to Hanafi. He found he had gone back to correcting the notebooks. The fever of work seemed to have rendered him oblivious to his surroundings. Abduh felt a distressing chill encompass him. He was left with no one but Mabruk. He spoke a couple of words to him and then got fed up. He hesitated, not knowing what to do.

His entire body felt so unusually alive that he wanted to speak, to move, and to be energetic, but today when he searched for life all he found was stillness. If Abduh naturally hated being still one carat, today he hated it twenty-four. He couldn't imagine listening quietly to his soul, giving it free rein over his imagination, or retreating into solitude like Muhsin in similar circumstances. For this reason Abduh walked around the house not knowing what to do. He wished he could find someone who would listen to him and shoot the breeze.

Finally he headed for the communal sleeping room. Finding it empty, he quickly turned around to leave. It felt oppressive to him and wrapped his hot, eager, raging heart with a cloak of stillness and solitude. In his imagination he pictured these beds, lined up one beside the other, in the bedroom. Visualizing that for the first time, he felt odd about it.

He sensed exactly what Muhsin had when he too returned from the neighbors' house the first time. He felt a revulsion against five people living in one room. Muhsin had sensed that and had sought seclusion and solitude in order to give free rein to his imagination. Abduh, however, felt an aversion to it because he grasped suddenly that this strong bond between five people sharing a room was bogus. Here he was experiencing solitude and boredom, unable to find anyone to speak to, anyone who would understand his language.

Abduh's distress increased. A nervous person like him could not bear to be patient very long. Thus the peaceful, gentle, happy look with which he had returned quickly deserted him and his typical frowning scowl returned to his face. The slightest provocation would cause nervous Abduh to explode in a screaming rage, as was his wont.

Abduh spent several anxious days not knowing what to do to stay in touch with the neighbors. He was afraid that what he had achieved so far was the most he could hope for. Despite his virility and vitality Abduh lacked the daring and brashness to undertake some bold, proactive deed without regard for what people would say.

Therefore the most he could do was ask Zanuba—repeating the question every day—whether the electric wires were functioning properly at the neighbors' house or whether there was any problem that needed repair. When Zanuba replied that everything was fine, Abduh would insist with nervous harshness, "How do you know? Have you asked them?"

His mates noted how insistent he was, and Muhsin remarked in a cold, dry tone, "The electricity is working great!"

But Salim, who was infuriated, would not let the opportunity pass without a scornful word or two. "Mister, the electricity is working fantastically well. Maybe you should sabotage it? Mister, find yourself some other employment besides this."

Abduh finally could not take any more and screamed in his face, "And you, what's it to you, stupid?"

Calmly but incredulously, Salim asked, "Am I stupid?"

"Sixty times over."

"Group, are you witnesses?"

"What right do you have to pry into my affairs?"

"God forgive you! I'm to blame!" So he fell silent.

Muhsin began scrutinizing both of them. Zanuba wasn't there, for she had gone up on the roof to attend to the laundry with Mabruk's help. The only other person present was Hanafi, but the honorary president was in bed and did not care to interject a word to heal the rift, by God, although as he laughed under the covers he asked, "What's this charming conversation? Why are you angry, Mr. Abduh? If the electricity won't do the trick, look for some other task. Don't you know, for example, how to repair a Primus stove, lamps, or a window blind?"

Abduh turned toward him and said scornfully, "Yes? You too, blanket-face? Sleep—sleeping's what suits you best. Won't you let me speak?"

Pulling the covers over himself, Hanafi Effendi answered immediately, "I sleep? Do I sleep a lot? At school, when I enter the classroom, the class is rowdy. At home, when I get in bed a ruckus breaks out. I'm beaten and so is my ass."

Then he straightened the covers, closed his eyes, and turned his back on all of them, his face to the wall. He began to snore audibly as he gradually fell asleep. It wasn't long before his braying became even noisier. Muhsin turned to Salim as though affectionately taking him into his confidence and, pointing to the sleeping Hanafi, said almost in a whisper, after he had given Abduh, who was moving away, a look of aversion and loathing, "This Uncle Hanafi! What a shame! All he's got is sleep."

Salim answered with scorn and pity, "Do I know what he teaches? Someone like this—his pupils must run circles around him!"

Muhsin felt uneasy about his relations with the neighboring household despite his frequent visits there, because he still did not understand Saniya's soul. She seemed to have some mysterious secret, and he had sensed something different about her and Abduh the day Abduh went to fix the electricity.

Muhsin had noticed something about Saniya's behavior that hadn't pleased him, although Saniya's treatment of him had not changed to corroborate his strange feeling. So this cloud soon left his heart, although he remained concerned and uncomfortable about Abduh. Base feelings toward Abduh had been awakened in him, making him shudder. Saniya's simple acts that day had granted him a distressing revelation that women value men above all else for having a powerful body. Men should be brawny, tall, and broad, and have a deep voice. Women are motivated by unconscious desires, possibly motivated by some sexual instinct. Perhaps compared to Abduh he seemed a child or boy who would not inspire that emotion in a woman. Muhsin began to remember Abduh's voice as it rang out in the neighbors' hall and his powerful forearms propping the wooden ladder forcefully against the wall.

This memory tormented him, and he didn't know nor could he express the reason for this vague feeling that made him smart and prompted him to hate Abduh.

Abduh's attitude toward him, after he returned from the neighbors' house, contributed to this feeling. Instead of quarreling with Muhsin or getting angry and enraged at him as he had on previous occasions, now Abduh paid no attention to Muhsin or his existence. Indeed, the arrogance of all his gestures suggested that he was a person who felt he had scored a total victory. Muhsin played no part in his reckonings. Even if there had been someone in his thoughts he considered a potential rival, it wasn't little Muhsin. It was rather someone worthy to compete with him in this field—a man like Salim.

Little Muhsin sensed all this with his perceptive, discerning heart. He was pervaded by self-doubt; the idea that he was too young to be considered an adversary or rival pained and troubled him.

CHAPTER 14

No one knows whether it was a jest of fate or of some human being, but one day Zanuba brought back the news that the neighbors' piano was on the blink and that she had promised Saniya she would ask Salim about a shop that repaired pianos because Salim owned a musical instrument resembling it, namely his accordion.

Salim listened to her with intense interest, and she had barely finished speaking when he rose. Zanuba assured him straightaway that there was no need to wear himself out. All he had to do was write the name of a repair shop he trusted—along with its address—on a slip of paper; Saniya would take care of the rest.

But Salim was not satisfied with this; he was not about to let this opportunity escape him. If Abduh, that rash and thoughtless youngster—born yesterday, Salim thought—had gone to fix the wiring in the neighbors' house, shouldn't he, a versatile and experienced specialist, visit the loved ones' house on some pretext?

Salim, therefore, wasn't slow to display his knowledge of the piano and of musical instruments in general. He mentioned the names of various shops. He concluded his case by saying these shops charged exorbitant rates. One shouldn't have recourse to them except in cases of urgent and dire necessity. Who could say—perhaps what was wrong with the neighbors' piano was something quite simple that an expert like Salim could diagnose. He could advise what it needed without their having to resort to one of those swindling shops. "Right, then! The piano must be examined. I need to examine it first thing in any case. So I can investigate what it . . ."

The servant Mabruk was listening. Smiling, he said, "Yes.

So Mr. Salim can investigate." He winked at Muhsin, but Muhsin didn't smile back. He was pale-faced, and finally he asked, "Who said the piano's on the blink?"

Zanuba replied, "Saniya told me when you weren't there."

His face darkened a little, and he said, "I just played it yesterday! She must have said it needs cleaning . . . not that it's on the blink."

Salim intervened somewhat angrily. "No, sir. She said 'on the blink.' Have some respect."

"Impossible! Just yesterday I . . ." Muhsin was speaking with despair; his face was flushed.

The argument might have gone on longer if Hanafi Effendi had not come in from the street carrying a bundle of copybooks, which he placed on the table. "What's up?" he asked.

When Mabruk gave him the news, he cleared his throat and looked at Salim. "Congratulations!" he said.

Salim responded coldly, "Yes, Mr. Hanafi?"

"Nothing! Just, won't you need a boy? This is a piano, not a piece of wire."

Salim smiled a bit but grew serious and cool again. "By God, we're a pretty strange lot. The neighbors seek our assistance, and we make a big story out of it? The question couldn't be simpler. I'm going there to check the piano to discover what it needs and to see—"

Looking at Salim through thick spectacles and smiling slyly, Hanafi interrupted him: "You mean, in brief, you're going to investigate!"

"So, what's it to you?"

"Did I say something? I take refuge in God!" Hanafi moved off, heading for his bed. He was going to change from his street clothes to his jilbab and skullcap, so he could stretch out as usual.

Fortunately for Salim, Abduh wasn't home when Zanuba returned with the news about the piano. When he came, he found Salim in a state of preparedness. He had brought out his police uniform from the large armoire, planning to wear it despite his official suspension and everyone's opposition. Abduh asked what was happening. When he learned about it, his face grew dark and gloomy. Then he brought himself under control. A cold smile of rage appeared on his trembling lips. He began to look at Salim, whose mustache was expertly twisted with wax. He was combing his hair with extraordinary care. Pointing to the uniform's brass shoulder stars, which had grown tarnished from long neglect since he left the service, he ordered Mabruk, "Shine the stars quickly, boy."

"Right away, Your Excellency the Commandant."

He went to fetch a rag and began cleaning the stars. He looked at Abduh and Muhsin, who seemed frozen by an unseen force. He winked and smiled at them.

Salim finished pulling on the trousers with the red stripe and came for the jacket, saying in a bogus tone of command, "Enough on the stars!"

Mabruk replied quietly, "The stars and tars, all finished."

Then he held the jacket for him and helped him into it, while telling him, as though giving him earnest advice, "I mean, Mr. Salim, if they catch you in this uniform, will it be all right?"

"Who's going to catch me?"

"The government—no kidding."

Then Abduh's patience evaporated and he interjected, "Leave him! He doesn't know he's been discharged from the service."

Salim turned on him and said coldly, "Will you be so kind as to take back your words? I'm not discharged—just suspended."

"What's the difference?"

"I think anyone with an education knows the difference between a person who's discharged and one who's suspended, Mr. Engineer!" Salim continued primping.

At this moment Hanafi rose from his bed sluggishly. As soon as he saw Salim, he shouted in astonishment, "What! You've put on your dress uniform?"

Salim answered nonchalantly without looking at him, staring instead full face at the mirror. "So . . ."

Hanafi Effendi cheered, "Super! Go, uncle! Congratulations

to you! May the same thing happen to us too! Let them ask us to correct . . . what?"

Salim speedily supplied the missing word: "Correct copybooks!" He grasped his officer's leather whip and slashed it through the air to announce his departure.

By afternoon Salim was at the neighbors' house. Zanuba and the maid led him to the piano room, which he scouted thoroughly but found empty. So he went to the piano, raised the lid, and ran his fingers over the keys. Then with one hand he picked out a lively melody from a popular song. He turned to Zanuba and asked, "What's wrong with the piano? It works great."

"Sister, so why would Saniya say it's busted?"

"Possibly there's something in it that needs repair. I think the best thing would be for you to ask Miss Saniya to show us herself what it needs."

Zanuba went off with that request, followed by the maid. Shortly thereafter he heard footsteps approaching. Salim got ready and gave a quick twist to his mustache. He straightened his jacket and checked his appearance. He turned to the door and saw Muhsin. Salim frowned and said with cold displeasure, "God! What brings you?"

The boy answered anxiously and angrily, "I come here all the time."

Salim didn't respond, turned his back, and began to pace back and forth in the room.

It was an awkward, chilly situation, Muhsin felt. He wanted to depart, but the door opened. Zanuba came in to ask Salim to leave the room so Saniya could demonstrate what was wrong with the piano. She opened a door to a small foyer and motioned for Salim to follow her. She stationed him behind the door. Then Saniya arrived. She paused at the salon door, asking in a voice modulated by captivating coquetry, "Shall I enter, abla? No one's in the salon?"

Salim heard this voice and forgot his situation. He stretched out his head to have a look with roving, wandering eyes, to investigate that beautiful gazelle. In a mellifluous voice, which he tried to make gentle, he said, "There's nobody here, miss. Come in!"

Zanuba immediately went to escort her to the piano and asked her to tell Salim Effendi herself what she thought. Salim added quickly, "If you would be so kind, Miss Saniya, as to play a song so I can hear the sound of the piano."

Saniya pretended, modestly, to laugh. She was clinging to Zanuba and said, pointing to one of the piano keys, "It's the 'do' only, sister, which is out of whack. See!"

She played the "do" several times, but Salim, who was peeking at her from behind the door, objected, "That's not enough, Miss Saniya. You ought to play a tune. Play 'Star of Happiness,' for example. It's a very pretty tune. Before my transfer from Port Said, I had a police band that included mounted and foot police. Every morning after the lineup, I would give them the command to play that tune. All the same, I used to play the tune better on my accordion than the police band could. Now it's been some time since I gave up the accordion. That's why I would love to hear the tune played on the piano by the hand of Miss Saniya."

Saniya smiled, pretending to be embarrassed, and looked at Zanuba and Muhsin, who was beside her, quickly and unconsciously. She was blushing. She whispered to Zanuba, "What will Mama say?"

But she didn't wait for an answer. She sat on the piano stool at once. From behind the door Salim was following her motions and almost went berserk when he saw her svelte body bend and her breasts tremble as she sat down.

She began to perform the tune "Star of Happiness," playing forcefully at times and delicately at others. All that Salim noticed of this from behind the door was that her rounded breasts quivered with each crescendo. They seemed to be dancing to the melody of the song.

Salim, deep inside himself, was shouting, "O my life! O my life! What boobs! An Egyptian orange still on the tree! O my soul!"

Saniya finally finished and rose from the piano, saying with such embarrassment that her voice sounded even more coquettish, "Did you hear, Salim Bey, how the sound of the piano is off? I don't know if this was because of the 'do' or whether the whole mechanism needs cleaning."

Salim answered at once, "By God, Miss Saniya, I . . . I didn't notice because your rendition of 'Star of Happiness'—there was no way it could have been better. Allow me to tell you that I've never in my life heard better than that."

Saniya looked at Zanuba. She was blushing in a way that made Muhsin flinch. Then she said in a faint voice that Salim could hear, "Merci!"

The conversation progressed next to the question of cleaning the piano. Salim advised it and promised to return in a day or two with an expert repairman. Salim would be responsible personally for this repair and for this piano from now on. Whatever Miss Saniya commanded would be obeyed and attended to immediately with pleasure and delight.

Saniya thanked him decorously and modestly for that offer with delicate and polite expressions. Then the maid brought coffee, which Salim drank before he departed, affirming in a proud and masterly tone, "God willing, today I'll send a patrolman or an officer to the finest repair shop."

He made his way to the hall grandly and pretentiously, moving his shoulders with the gleaming stars. He created a clamor, commotion, and racket in the house with his government-issue boots and their spurs.

Salim went straight home to remove his uniform at once before anyone caught him. He entered like a triumphal conqueror among the folks. The ends of his mustache stood erect as he swelled with pride, like someone who has just achieved something major. His happiness and joviality were clearly evident in his expression. President Hanafi got the first word in: "What did you do, hero?"

Salim looked down his nose at him and barked, "Shut up! Be quiet!"

Hanafi persisted, "What? What happened, honestly?"

Salim replied quickly while entering the communal bedroom and unbuttoning his jacket, "The girl's smitten with me."

Hanafi tried to obtain some clarification, but His Honor the officer wouldn't volunteer any further information. He was, rather, looking at the bedroom and the four beds lined up there, one next to the other. His disdain was visible on his lips. For the first time he felt the strangeness of this way of living. He was astonished that he had been able, till now, to live four or five to a room. This sensation sprang from his feeling of superiority and exaltation over his comrades. For that reason he tossed his jacket far away, on one of the beds. He emerged to say, "Are we dogs, or what? I need to move my bed to another room so I can have some privacy. Half a dozen in a room like a burrow? Are we not dogs?"

Abduh had tried in vain to control his feelings, but his flushed face revealed his suppressed anger. He replied, "All our lives we've lived like this. Is it only today, sir, you've learned you're a dog?"

Thinking it a joke, Hanafi laughed. Mabruk likewise laughed from a pure heart, but Captain Salim's face grew dark. He said, "Are you trying to disparage me?"

Abduh responded nervously, "What I mean to say is that we don't have another room. Anyone who likes it the way it is— fine. Anyone who doesn't . . ."

Salim asked him coldly, "What's it to you? I'm going to move upstairs . . . to the room on the roof, the laundry room, without a roommate!"

The quarrel ceased when Zanuba and Muhsin returned. Quiet prevailed. Salim went to finish changing, humming the melody of "Star of Happiness."

Then Hanafi called to him, asking him with hope and delight, "Tell us, then, Salim, how the girl fell for you."

Muhsin heard this expression and trembled. He choked. The blood drained from his face all at once, but he kept quiet. When Salim emerged again, he said with admiration and pride, "Boys, does she have boobs! Bless the Prophet! Small, sweet oranges hanging on the tree!"

The boy Muhsin reacted like a devout and ascetic worshipper who catches someone profaning his beloved with obscene language. Zanuba, however, began to boast about her friend. She asked, "Did you see, Mr. Salim, the dress she was wearing?"

The captain tried to remember and answered, "Dress? By God, I wasn't paying attention."

At that moment a shade of green passed before the mind of the silent Abduh, who was suppressing his feelings. This color expanded until green filled his eyes and thoughts; green silk rustled by him like the breeze on spring leaves. He felt his heart almost burst into flame in revolt. He wanted to rise and slap Salim or box him and turn the house into a free-fire zone but steeled himself.

Hanafi, the honorary president, at once replied to Zanuba's question with some of his typical, innocent sarcasm—the sarcasm of a person whose heart is empty and at rest and whose mind is free of troubles. "You ask him about the color of her dress? Did Salim see anything except her breasts, belly, and calves?"

Young Muhsin heard these words and visualized Saniya's angelic form. His soul revolted as he tried to banish those obscene, brutish words from his thoughts. He harbored for Salim something he could not limn. He felt that obscure sensation once again in a clearer way: a feeling of deficiency and humiliating weakness when compared to Salim. He imagined Salim to be so virile he would easily conquer a woman; she would be unable to resist him. Salim was a man who knew things he did not . . . or . . . or . . . Young Muhsin could not say. These were just vague feelings he could not analyze. All he understood from them was that he was learning to hate Salim and to fear him. Salim made him feel inadequate. Muhsin began to incline instead toward Abduh, to see him as a comrade or at least a human being who resembled him a little, a person who did not see a woman as breasts and belly but as something more, someone who was dismayed and hurt to hear such revolting and demeaning language.

The young man's feelings about Abduh were justified. Abduh had risen in disbelief and rebellion when he heard that talk. He went to Zanuba and demanded, "What's this foolishness and bad manners? Are you happy when you take men into people's homes so they can come back and say this kind of thing?"

Abduh left, abandoning the arena to them. He left because he couldn't bear to hear any more than he had.

This protest fell like cool water on Muhsin's flaming heart. He felt a little better and found solace from this for the humiliating anxiety in his soul.

CHAPTER 15

Some days passed during which the piano at the neighbors' house was tuned. Muhsin hadn't visited there all that time. Days passed while, with burning impatience, he awaited the hour they would summon him to return for lessons with Saniya once the piano was fit to play. He tried to keep his mind off the wait by reading the novel *Magdeleine* in al-Manfaluti's translation.

One day he came home from school early and found no one there except Abduh, who was at work drafting an engineering project that he would present at the midyear examination. Muhsin changed out of his street clothes. Needing something to occupy his free time that afternoon, he looked for the novel, intending to finish the last pages. When he didn't find it in the usual place, he asked Abduh, who didn't know anything about it. The young boy was a little surprised but was soon distracted by thinking about Saniya, himself, Abduh, and Salim.

Did she like one of them better than the others? Which did she prefer?

His heart pounded when he remembered Salim's statement: "The girl is outstanding." His soul recoiled, and he asked himself: *Is it actually possible for someone like Salim to win her heart?* He consoled himself a little when he remembered Abduh and his fate. Someone like Abduh at least deserved her admiration more than Salim. But here they were, he and Abduh, ignorant of their destiny, while Salim, since that day, had been merrily going and coming. He went and came, full of energy, good cheer, joy, pride, and vanity, as though he had won and been assured something.

While he was thinking these things, Abduh was nearby, bent over the drafting board set on the hall table, but then the servant Mabruk entered with a letter. He waved it in his hand as he smiled mischievously. "A letter for Mr. Salim! A letter addressed to Mr. Salim!"

Muhsin was agitated, and Abduh raised his head. He looked at the letter in Mabruk's hand, but did not break his long silence. Instead he leaned over his work again as though focusing on it to calm his heart and mind. He could not, however, prevent his thoughts from dwelling on this letter. He wondered: *Who can it be from?* Salim hadn't received a letter from anyone since he started living with them. What relation might this letter have to the recent events? Doubt crept into his heart. The strange thing was that all the ideas going through his head went through young Muhsin's at the same time.

Muhsin rallied and asked Mabruk, "Who's it from?" The servant shrugged to show he did not know. Since the letter was sealed, of course, how could he know who had sent it?

Abduh raised his head again and looked at the letter. He stretched his hand out to Mabruk and said, "Hand it here. Let me see the postmark." The servant gave it to him. Abduh read the postmark, which showed it had been mailed at Al-Sayyida Zaynab station. He began to turn the letter over in his hands and to scrutinize the handwriting on the address. His doubts increased, his face became pale, and he put the letter down on the table near him. He told Mabruk in a calm but somewhat altered voice, "Fine. Leave it here for him till he returns."

He went back to work. Muhsin also retreated into himself, brooding about that letter. Was it possible it was from . . . ? Mabruk turned from one of them to the other. When he found they were ignoring him, he went off, after saying he was going to sit by the door to wait for the others to return. As soon as the servant was out of the way, Abduh raised his head and picked up the letter a second time. He stared at it and turned it over in his fingers. He looked at Muhsin, who was peeking at him. Then Abduh observed, "The envelope isn't tightly sealed."

Muhsin grasped the special meaning of this phrase. With impetuous and intense desire he agreed: "I wonder what's in this letter."

Gazing at the letter with greedy curiosity, Abduh said hesitantly, "It would be possible to open it and glue it back."

Muhsin replied enthusiastically, "Yes, by God! There must be some amusing things in it."

Abduh turned the envelope over and said hesitantly in a faint voice, "Come, shall we see what's inside?"

Approaching him, Muhsin replied immediately with childish glee, "Right! Go ahead. By the Prophet, let's see what's in it."

Abduh raised his head and gave Muhsin a piercing look. "You won't tell?" he asked.

"Don't worry. Am I crazy?"

Abduh immediately started opening the envelope with care and circumspection—so he could seal it again and return it to its original condition. He took the letter out, unfolded it, and began to read with eager anticipation. Muhsin crowded up to him to read along with him avidly. At first they didn't understand anything. When they saw the signature at the bottom of the letter, however, everything became clear. They started laughing, their mouths agape, feeling malicious revenge.

The letter had originally been sent by Salim to his sweetheart, but she, instead of answering him, had returned it forthwith, not adding the least comment.

As soon as Abduh and Muhsin grasped this, they amused themselves by reading this love letter. They sarcastically declaimed aloud some of its phrases, calling into question the veracity of the emotions expressed in it. The letter's text was as follows:

Darling of my heart, Miss Saniya,

I have loved you with a love such as no one before has ever loved. I have been true to you with sincerity that not even a brother nurses for his brothers, nor a parent for his child. I have revered you the way a worshipper reveres his Beloved.

I have filled the entire emptiness of my life with you. I look only to you. I feel only for you. I dream only of your image. I respond to the sight of the sun at its rising only because I see your form in it. I am moved by listening to the warbling of birds in their variety only because I hear in them the melody of your conversation. I am touched by the sight of flowers laughing within their calyxes only because they represent the

diverse perfections of your beauty. I have not wished for
happiness for myself except for the sake of yours. I have not
preferred life to death except so I may live beside you and
rejoice in seeing you.

   If you think I do not deserve to be with you, then tell me to
expend my life for you in tears, pains, sorrows and grieving.

                                        Peace in conclusion,

                                        The Passionate Lover,

                                        Captain Salim al-Atifi

   They finished reading it, and Abduh turned to Muhsin to
ask sarcastically, "On your honor, is it conceivable that Salim
would know to write a single one of those words?"

   Muhsin was silent for a time, as though trying to remember.
Then he shouted suddenly, "Good grief! Do you know the
novel *Magdeleine*? He copied page 173 word for word."*

   Abduh said with vengeful delight, "Bravo to him!"

   Muhsin added in happy confirmation, "I think I know what
happened. I was just reading that page the day before yesterday. Oh! I understand. Didn't I tell you that the novel wasn't in
its right place?"

   At that Abduh took the letter quickly and put it back inside
the envelope the way it had been, with deliberate care and cau-
tion. He sealed it again, so it was just as though it had never
been opened.

   Salim returned home not long after that, humming cheerfully. Mabruk, the servant, informed him at the door that he
had a letter. He quivered as soon as he heard that word and
asked, "Where? Where is it?"

---

* *Magdeleine: Sous les tilleuls* by Alphonse Karr (1808–1890), translated
into Arabic by Mustafa Lutfi al-Manfaluti (1876?–1924) as *Majdulin, aw
Taht Zilal az-Zayzafun* (Magdeleine, or Under the Lindens). The letter
quoted is in *Majdulin*, 5th ed. (Cairo: Al-Maktaba at-Tijariya al-Kubra,
1928), 172.

Mabruk, who was smiling at his agitation, told him that the letter was upstairs in Abduh's custody. Salim didn't allow him to finish; he had already left and charged up the stairs three at a time. He accosted Abduh and before Abduh could say anything asked, "Where's the letter?"

Abduh raised his head somewhat scornfully as if to say: *No way—say hello first.* But Salim paid no attention to him. Instead, he repeated his question forcefully, losing his patience: "Where's the letter?"

Abduh couldn't see any way around directing him to the letter on the table near him. Salim pounced on it, grasped it, and made off with it to be alone when he read it. He left behind him Abduh, who was sharing sarcastic, vengeful looks with Muhsin, who was crouched in his corner.

In no time at all Salim came back with the letter in his hand. His face looked terrifying. He approached Abduh and showed him the letter. Then he screamed, "The letter's been opened!"

Abduh pretended to be astonished and to know nothing of the affair: "Opened how?"

"Opened and stuck back down again! The envelope is still damp. Am I a fool? You can't use my head for a skillet." He said this in a menacing tone no one had ever heard him use before.

Abduh trembled a little but steeled himself, and said rather curtly, "What need is there for talk like this?"

Salim shouted back with frightening anger, "It's this letter that makes it necessary. I wasn't the one who received it. By God, I didn't receive this letter! By God, I did not receive this letter!"

Abduh got riled up and answered nervously, "Whether you received it or not, why say such things to me, sir?"

Salim, frothing and foaming, said, "Whoever opened this letter is base, low, and vile. For sure, he's despicable, base, low, and badly brought up."

Abduh answered coldly, lowering his head and pretending to look at the drafting board, "Whoever opened it . . ."

Salim stared at him and asked aggressively, "You, sir, don't know who opened it? The wretch who opened it?"

Abduh flushed and shouted, "I've told you a thousand times: no! Are you going to drive us crazy with your letter?"

Salim said, "By God Almighty, I won't be quiet till this has been investigated. I won't let it rest this evening. Everything but opening personal letters!"

Abduh said coldly, "Go do whatever you want. Just let me work. I don't have time. I've got an exam!"

After putting the letter in his pocket, Salim left him and made for the door, saying, "You have an elder to whom you're accountable. The house is not a free-for-all. It's not anarchy!" He said this and slammed the door behind him. He was gone.

At that, Abduh looked at Muhsin, who was frowning slightly, and said to reassure him, "Forget about him. Let him go. The reason he's so hot and bothered is the rebuff he's received. His letter was sent back to him."

Muhsin expressed his agreement with a pallid smile but remained silent. He was wrestling with his conscience.

When Salim left the house, he headed straight for Khalil Agha Elementary School in order to confront Hanafi Effendi, who by virtue of being the eldest was head of the household. He was going to lay out before him what had happened to see whether he was pleased about this and whether he would let something like this slide by without intervening. This time would he display some of the authority, dignity, and gallantry that were rightfully his?

All the way Salim was thinking and saying to himself that Hanafi Effendi, regardless of his character, was the master of the house, the last recourse, and someone who would no doubt act resolutely about this incident. That was why he could depend on him. He considered this the wisest and most reasonable plan.

Hanafi was still at school that day, since it was his turn to supervise the athletic games along with a gymnastics coach. He had to stay at school until six thirty that evening and had alerted his comrades before leaving home in the morning. Salim therefore thought he would meet him at the school to tell him about the matter before he returned home. Otherwise

Abduh would muddle his thinking with disruptive interruptions and spoil the matter for Salim.

When Salim reached the school at last, he looked for the doorman or janitor in his cubbyhole but did not find him. He walked into the school courtyard, looking right and left. Perhaps he would run into someone. Finally he encountered a young pupil who was going to get some water, kicking stones and pebbles. He motioned to him to come, which he did, and asked, "Hey, smarty, where's Hanafi Effendi?"

The pupil looked at him and immediately shot back, "Spindle-shanks Hanafi Effendi?"

Salim was somewhat startled. As though to himself, he repeated, "Spindle-shanks?"

The pupil straightaway pointed to a portion of the courtyard concealed behind the school building and asked, "Sir, do you want him? He's there with the first year, third section."

At that moment the sound of small boys laughing wafted through the air. When the pupil heard it, he left Salim suddenly. He ran toward his pals, laughing and calling out in a low, cautionary tone, "Spindle-shanks Hanafi Effendi! Spindle-shanks Hanafi Effendi!"

Salim shouted for him to stop. He followed him and asked him to summon Hanafi Effendi at once.

The pupil obeyed and left Salim to wait. Doubt over the success of his initiative with Hanafi filled his heart, and he wondered: *What benefit do you suppose can be hoped for from someone like this Hanafi when even little kids call him "spindle-shanks"?*

Salim did not have long to wait; Hanafi Effendi soon appeared, wondering why Salim had come and suspecting that something serious had happened at home. His suspicions did not seem to be unfounded, because Salim launched into an exaggerated and hyperbolic account of what had occurred. He portrayed the deed to him in the most extraordinary way and in the harshest possible light.

The master of the house remained silent throughout all of this, his head bowed. He listened with deliberation that an onlooker could have mistaken for serious resolve. Finally Salim stared at him, shaking his shoulder violently, and asked, "Why are you silent? Won't you give your opinion, brother?"

The honorary president raised his head and answered immediately, "In my opinion, the right's on your side."

"Isn't that so? It's Abduh. No one but the lad Abduh did it. I'm sure. I'll shave my mustache if I'm wrong!"

"As for me, I'm so sure, I'll shave my beard. It's no one but that kid Abduh."

"What happens now?"

"You've been wronged."

"Me being right isn't enough. You, Mr. Hanafi, as head of the household, senior member of the family, and president of us all, will you keep silent about this too? You need to exert your authority."

Hanafi puffed himself up and turned toward him forcefully and proudly. "I've got to exert my authority!" He put out his hand and pulled Salim along with him. "Come with me. Have no fear! We'll destroy their house!" He said this so enthusiastically and vigorously that Salim believed him and, thinking all would be well, felt reassured.

When Hanafi and Salim reached home and entered the apartment, Salim stood back and pushed Hanafi in front of him, prompting him in a whisper, "Be firm!"

"Have no fear!"

On entering, Hanafi saw Abduh bent over the drafting board. He affected a frown and a scowl. Feigning anger, he asked, "What's the story of this letter? How does it happen that a letter is opened in a house like this?"

Abduh raised his head without speaking. He cast Hanafi a frightening look and suddenly shouted nervously that he wasn't responsible for anyone's letters and that he would not allow anyone to accuse him of anything. He left the drafting board and approached Hanafi Effendi. Then he shouted, "And you! There's no need for you to get mixed up with an inane matter like this!"

The honorary president fell silent at once and bowed his head.

Abduh asked, "Why are you silent? Won't you talk?"

Hanafi Effendi raised his head, cleared his throat, and then hesitated. Finally he stammered, "You're right!"

When Salim heard this, he became frantic. He grabbed Hanafi Effendi's arm and pinched him. He shook him, reminding him of his promise to devastate them. Then he reminded him of the accusation directed against Abduh and asked him once again, in front of everyone, to express his opinion frankly.

The honorary head of the family looked at him and said, "You're right."

At that point Abduh shouted at him, trying to force him to understand that whatever Salim said did not pertain to him, did not relate to him, and did not pin anything on him. And that . . . and that . . . But Hanafi, who had heard enough, turned to him and said, "You're right."

Observing this, the servant Mabruk laughed, as did Muhsin, who, however, felt anxious and had a guilty conscience. Everyone knew that Hanafi was a joker from whom nothing could be hoped. He had twisted the incident and turned it into a joke.

Salim had wanted him to join the dispute and get angry. He went to the large armoire to gather his possessions and clothes, intending to leave the house. He declared, "This house is a bad joke! A house with no leader! A house of anarchy! But it's my fault for relying on Mr. Spindle-shanks."

Hanafi Effendi, however, did not allow him to leave and tried to calm him, flattering him and joking and laughing with him. In an attempt, so it seemed, to flatter and make him feel good, he said, "Why are you angry, Mr. Salim? You ought, rather, to be delighted, because the question is one of two sorts. Either the letter was an ordinary one that was opened, in which case there is no harm done. Or, it was a letter full of love, desire, passion, and romance. In this case, it's really great!"

Through his teeth Salim asked, "Really great, how?"

Hanafi answered with equally good intentions, thinking he was cheering Salim up, "Well! By God, it's your good luck it was opened. The critic will be nonplussed and silenced. This is in your best interest, dummy! Has anyone during these days had even a quarter of a love letter? My goodness! How lucky you are, Salim! You really should have opened it and read it aloud to us so we could rejoice with you and celebrate the happy event."

Muhsin, on hearing this, could imagine the impact that words like these would have on Salim in view of his disappointment with the letter. Almost overcome by laughter, he ran to the toilet so he could laugh freely. Passing through the hall he saw Abduh, who was covering his face with a hand to hide his laughter.

CHAPTER 16

Not many days later Muhsin received a letter! The word "letter" at this time was enough to turn inside out the youth's heart or that of any other member of the household. But he soon learned that his letter was from his parents in Damanhur. They were sending him his allowance and the monthly sum for Hanafi Effendi for Muhsin to live with him. They expressed their surprise in the letter that although the midyear vacation was at hand Muhsin hadn't expressed any desire or set any time for traveling to them as he did each year. The fact was that this year Muhsin had not happened to think at all about traveling or about the vacation. His thoughts had been wrapped up in his affairs and those of his comrades. He had also isolated himself from his friends at school. School did not interest him, aside from studying the lessons. He would complete his work there and impatiently watch for the end of the day so he could go home. Frequently he spent his free time at lunch and during other breaks on homework so that he could rush home afterward, free of any commitments.

Now, however, he was caught off guard by this letter asking him to travel. It seemed he had opened his eyes after a delightful trance and seen the real world. There was no way to avoid the trip.

Even though the vacation was short, only ten days, that appeared long to him. Yet he saw in his mind the image of his parents and yearned for them, so he was happy about the trip if only to see them.

Muhsin wasn't the only one who had forgotten about the trip this strange year; Zanuba had too. She usually kept track of its date precisely in order to prepare the present she would send with Muhsin.

Muhsin was a little surprised that Zanuba had forgotten.

When he went to remind her about his imminent departure, he found her in her room shaping dough to make a pastry called ka'b al-ghazal. He told himself: *She didn't forget. She was just pretending.* When he asked her what she was doing, without telling her about his trip, she hesitated a little. Then she blushed and said, "It's just that the servant of our neighbor downstairs brought a tray with flour and clarified butter so we would make him some ka'b al-ghazal."

Muhsin was a little surprised and asked, "Mustafa Bey?"

Zanuba added while she worked without looking at him, "The thing is that he doesn't have anyone here who knows how to make it. We should care for him. The proverb says: The Prophet entrusted to our care even the seventh neighbor."

Muhsin hid a smile, remembering then that when he was coming home from school the day before he had noticed Zanuba speaking with Mustafa Bey's servant at the entry to the stairway. He had thought she was telling him to sweep the portion of the stairway that was his responsibility, because he had heard her say that when she saw him come up. Now Muhsin grasped what that conversation with the neighbor's servant had been about. Who could say? Perhaps she had proposed helping whenever his master needed something, since he was unmarried and had no one who could prepare for him pastries like ka'b al-ghazal or other such delicacies.

Muhsin's thoughts turned to Saniya after that. He wanted to go tell her about his trip and to learn her reaction. He imagined she would be as annoyed as he was by this news. His heart pounded at this idea, and he began to rehearse what he would say. He thought he would be more courageous this time and use news about the trip as a pretext for disclosing to her some of what he had been keeping hidden for months.

That afternoon when Muhsin returned from his last day of school before the vacation, he went directly to the neighbors' residence and entered the piano room as usual. He saw no one there at first. Then, turning toward the balcony, he noticed Saniya looking out its window. She had her eyes fixed on the little coffeehouse. She was wearing a bright yellow dress of the latest cut, and her hair was very beautifully coifed. His heart pounded. For a moment he stood there without her sensing his presence.

Finally he found the heart to walk toward her quietly till he was beside her and could see where she was looking. There was Mustafa Bey sitting at his place in the coffeehouse. His eyes were raised, smiling. Muhsin shuddered, and Saniya sensed he was there. She was a little startled but straightened up and put her hand out to greet and welcome him with pleasure and enthusiasm, calling him "my professor," as was her habit. She greeted him in such a way that he forgot about himself and everything else. He blushed and was silent, not knowing how to reply. So she led him to the piano, saying in a sweet voice, "It's been a long time since we've had a lesson."

She started passing her hand over the piano keys while Muhsin watched her in silence. Finally he mumbled, "This is the last lesson."

She raised her head without understanding. Then Muhsin calmed himself and began to tell her why he had come today; his aunt Zanuba was busy preparing what he needed for his trip. She had said she was going to visit Saniya Hanim the next day, but he could not bear to wait till tomorrow. So as soon as he got out of school, he had come straight to her. Then he was silent for a time and looked at Saniya. She was silent too, looking at him. He was out of breath from talking.

He spoke again, saying he was sad. He fell silent, unable to continue with the speech he had rehearsed.

Saniya asked with warm tenderness, "Sad? Why are you sad?"

The youth answered hesitantly, "Because."

Saniya suggested, "Because you're traveling?"

Muhsin responded in a faint, stammering, unconvincing way, "Yeah." She seemed to perceive or suspect what he felt from the way he looked. She softened a little, and her voice became more tender and feminine without her realizing it, as though something deep inside had prompted her to encourage him or at least to grant a hearing of what he had to say on this subject.

She pretended to be surprised that he would grieve over a brief trip like this and told him with an enticing smile that she couldn't believe he was sad just for something like this. But Muhsin did not answer. Whenever he attempted to speak, all that happened was an intense pounding of his heart. Saniya continued gently, "So why, really, are you sad? Shame on you! Don't you want to tell me?"

Muhsin mumbled some barely audible words and then said, looking at the floor, "Because . . . I'm traveling."

Saniya was a little vexed by this answer. She too was silent for a moment. Then in an ordinary voice with a ring of earnestness to it she asked, "Won't you greet Mama before you leave?"

Raising his head, the boy replied, "Sure!"

Saniya rose and clapped her hands to call the maid. When she appeared, Saniya asked whether her senior mistress had returned from outside. The maid replied in the negative.

Saniya glanced at Muhsin and said, "I don't know where she's gone! She went out early today without telling me—it's not at all like her."

She went with a bound to the balcony and stood there, looking out.

Muhsin raised his head and stealthily peeked at her. He felt dispirited, and an obscure doubt was troubling him. But she returned to him with a smile and suggested they play a farewell song at the piano. She did not give him time to reply. Instead, she went from talking about the piano to talking about Salim—how extremely kind he had been when he had taken responsibility for having the piano tuned in such an excellent way. Muhsin looked at her in surprise, remembering Salim's letter. He attempted to see through her or sniff out some scent of sarcasm but didn't find any. To the contrary!

When Saniya continued expressing her gratitude for Salim with beautiful phrases, Muhsin's heart trembled. It passed through his mind that Abduh had similarly repaired the electric wiring. Why didn't she remember him with a single word of thanks? Muhsin recollected that when he had arrived today Saniya had been at the balcony looking down at the coffeehouse. He asked himself: *Was that for Salim?* The boy felt deeply stung, although he quickly realized it could not have been, because Salim had stopped going to the coffeehouse some time ago. He was never seen sitting there anymore, not since the day he was asked to repair the piano. It seemed the coffeehouse route no longer had anything to offer him.

Then why and at whom was she looking and gazing in that fashion from the balcony now?

Muhsin felt almost resentful toward Saniya, as though he did not want to see her stoop to something like this. His heart was filled with a feeling he had nourished for her the day he noticed her conduct with Abduh when he was repairing the electricity and when Salim came to inspect the piano. In the depths of his soul, he had held this behavior against her, thinking it wanton and deliberately seductive.

This sensation overwhelmed Muhsin, and he was silent. Suddenly he saw Saniya rise from her place near him, as though she was uneasy or bored. She walked toward the balcony. As soon as she reached it, a rosy flush and a lively glow graced her face. Muhsin watched her out of the corner of his eye, observing all that in her. Was he imagining it or was she really sighing and smiling at a man outside? Muhsin felt miserable. A terrifying despair pervaded him. He realized in a moment that all his dreams were in vain. All his hopes concerning her were a mirage. He became certain that he had been a fool to romanticize what was actually happening and that he had hoped for more than someone like him deserved from a person like her. What was he? A young, competency-level student. What had his relationship to her been up to now? Wasn't it just a simple family friendship? If Saniya was sweet to him, wasn't that because he was a young boy? At least, she treated him like one. In her eyes, he would always be that young boy, one to whom she could be tender in her mother's presence without feeling any embarrassment. She could offer him drinks or fill his pockets with bonbons and sweets if she wanted.

Being tender and sweet did not amount to interest and affection. Had she ever been concerned about his coming or blushed the way she did when Salim or Abduh came or even acted the way she was now while gazing from the window at . . . at . . .

The room turned black before Muhsin's eyes while these

thoughts were going through his head with the speed of a
nightmare. He looked around him and saw he was sitting
alone; she had turned away and wasn't paying attention to
him. He felt the awkwardness and chill of his position. Why
stay here, forgotten and neglected?

He rose, his brow dripping with sweat. Saniya didn't notice.
He stood there, anxious and hesitant for a moment. Then he
put his hand in his pocket to search for his handkerchief and
came upon Saniya's silk one, which he always kept with him.
His heart pounded, but despair overcame him. He became
pale and stiff standing there and felt that he ought to weep or
shout or die. But he did not do any of these. He could not even
remind Saniya of his existence or that he had stood up. Finally
Saniya turned toward him, held out her hand, and asked, "Are
you going home now?"

Muhsin observed a certain languor in her appearance and
gesture and understood that she would not insist on detaining
him. He imagined that he had stayed longer than he should
have. So he put out his hand to her quickly and in a voice that
was barely audible said, "Yes, I'm going home."

He left her and went to the door. She looked at him, surprised by this person who had come to say good-bye and was
now leaving in this fashion. Muhsin, however, stood at the
doorstep and hesitated. Saniya noticed and went to see why he
was pausing there. Muhsin put a trembling hand into his
pocket and brought out her silk handkerchief, which he gave
to her without looking at her.

Saniya took the handkerchief. She turned it over in her hand
with astonishment when she recognized it. At first she did not
understand and shouted, "My handkerchief? Where did you
find it?"

Muhsin answered in a low voice, "I had it!"

This sentence sufficed for Saniya to understand. She looked
for a moment at the face of young Muhsin and gazed at his
gloomy features, his taut lips, and his drooping eyes, which
cast frozen, despondent glances at the floor. His appearance
then reminded her of the day she had seen him try to remember his past. His face then had suddenly taken on a manly

look, but today he seemed dangerous and frightening. He appeared to be struggling with something inside him. Saniya perceived some of what the lad was suffering and felt sympathetic toward him.

Muhsin wanted to depart, but she prevented him, asking him in a tender voice, "Have you had it for a long time, rascal?"

Muhsin did not reply but felt his blood boil. He thought Saniya was mocking him by using this stale term. He steeled himself. Saniya continued, "Why are you returning the handkerchief to me now?"

Muhsin answered in an impetuous, fierce tone, "It doesn't belong to me!"

Saniya was surprised but remained calm and, moving closer to Muhsin, held out her hand gently with the handkerchief. She asked sincerely, "What if I give it to you?"

Muhsin answered at once in a dry, decisive tone, "I don't want it."

Saniya's expression changed. This answer had taken her by surprise. She discerned from the youth's face that he was in a very angry and emotional state. She fell silent. They remained still for a moment. Finally she said to him in a changed, faint voice, "Muhsin! You're angry about something?"

He did not respond. When she raised her head to try to force him to answer, she saw two tears flowing from his eyes.

Her heart was moved a little. She put out her hand gently, took his, and led him to a seat. In a voice filled with emotion she said, "Muhsin! Are you weeping? Muhsin?"

She sat down and seated him beside her. Muhsin wasn't able to hold back his tears. They poured out without being willed or warranted. Saniya volunteered her silk handkerchief and dried his eyes. She asked him gently, "Are you angry at me? Are you angry at me, Muhsin?"

The youth did not reply except with nervous sobs that he tried in vain to suppress. Saniya, who was touched, continued, "Muhsin! Shame on you! Muhsin!"

Then she embraced him and kissed him at the bottom of his cheek. Despite the heat of this kiss, it felt cool like dew to the youth, who looked at her. She was crying too from emotion.

Silence reigned between them a moment. Saniya broke it when she asked why he was weeping. She insisted on knowing. At first he mumbled some words that were incomprehensible. Then he gained control a little and said he knew he wasn't anything special to her, that what hurt him was her hiding this from him. It would have been worthier for her to . . .

He couldn't go on with these words and started again, saying he wasn't criticizing her for anything at all. It was just he had hurt himself and was censuring himself for plunging into false and imaginary hopes and deceptive dreams.

He began to speak like this in a trembling, feverish voice. Saniya listened, moved and pleased, until he finished. Then she drew close to him, grasped his trembling hand, and, looking at him, said in a faint voice, "You're wrong, Muhsin! Is that the way it is? Shame on you! If you weren't important to me, I wouldn't have taught you piano and made Mama agree. You know it started the day I saw you on the roof?"

The youth's heart trembled. He smiled and turned toward her; it seemed his eyes were asking her: *Is that true?*

Saniya started speaking again in a faint, warm voice, upbraiding him for what he had said. He did not know what to say or do. He had no sense of where he was. He seemed to be in an ethereal realm where he felt nothing, not even the happiness perfuming that moment. He roused himself a tad and felt an urge to pour kisses on her hands, cheek, and face but did not dare do anything like that. He stayed frozen like a statue while time passed swiftly. Finally he collected the shreds of his resolve and moved to revive his leaping heart, but the occasion had been lost, for he heard the maid's footsteps. She came to announce the return of her elder mistress from outside. At that, Muhsin rose quickly to his feet, as did Saniya. He began to tidy himself and reached in his pocket for his handkerchief to wipe his face. Instead, Saniya quickly gave him her silk handkerchief without the maid seeing and whispered to him, "Keep it as a remembrance."

The lady of the house entered, clad in her black street wrap. Seeing Muhsin, she approached to greet him. Saniya told her he had come to say good-bye before his trip and that he had waited especially till she came home. The lady thanked him, wished him a happy journey, and asked him to give her greetings to his mother and to remind his mother of her if she had forgotten her. Then the youth asked permission to leave. The two women saw him to the stairs, which he descended quickly. He did not feel he was in this world. He seemed to be descending from another one.

CHAPTER 17

Muhsin returned home to find that Aunt Zanuba had prepared the present he was to carry the next morning. She was
there alone with the servant Mabruk, who was near her, busy
tying the package with twine. As soon as Zanuba saw Muhsin
come in, out of breath, she told him that everything had been
prepared. Nothing remained to pack but his clothes. She had
wanted to get out the ones he would take, and if Saniya's
mother had not come . . . When Zanuba mentioned that visit,
she quickly reconsidered and was upset as though she had
been wrong to refer to it.

But Muhsin noted this and asked her at once in disbelief,
"She was here?"

Zanuba wanted to make it seem a slip, but Muhsin went up
to her sweetly, filled with doubt. He continued to flatter her
and to curry her favor until she admitted, "Yes, she was here,
and do you know why? Just a word to you in secret, Muhsin!
Don't tell anyone!"

Her tone was confidential, and the youth at once answered
her earnestly, "Don't be afraid. Speak, auntie!"

She hesitated a little before bending over him to whisper
that Saniya's mother had come today to tell her that Dr. Hilmi,
her husband, had gotten hold of a letter from Salim Effendi to
Saniya. He was upset and annoyed but did not wish to publi-
cize the matter, in the interest of good neighborly relations. He
had returned Salim's letter at once and had not told his daughter about it or about what he had done. He only told his wife
so she could delicately alert Zanuba to this matter, which was
totally improper.

Muhsin bowed his head in thought on hearing this. His
happiness was marred a little by a troubling idea that occurred
to him: Saniya did not know about Salim's letter. So she wasn't

the one who had returned it in the manner he and Abduh saw. Who could say? Perhaps she would not have returned the letter if it had fallen into her hands. Indeed, she might have answered it in the most beautiful way.

The youth was depressed by this idea but recalled his recent encounter with her and dismissed the thought. Hadn't she told him just now while weeping that she, since she saw him on the roof . . . then, that kiss . . . No . . . this rotten idea should be rejected. Indeed, he had no reason to doubt his beloved Saniya from now on.

Zanuba started whispering again with dry sarcasm, "By the Prophet, I've had that number for some time. Is Salim someone to treat her right?"

When Salim's letter arrived, Dr. Hilmi was sitting in the place where he usually spent the afternoon, in front of Al-Jawwali's Pharmacy, drinking a cup of coffee brought to him from a nearby coffee shop. He was talking, in a voice like a storyteller's, to a few people, who were seated around him and who seemed by age and appearance to be retired civil servants like himself.

They were listening with pleasure, astonishment, and interest to his narration as he described his life in the Sudan back when he was an army doctor. This narrative was no doubt the continuation of a series of previous accounts he had delivered at yesterday's session and before. The doctor was silent for a bit while he sipped his coffee and recollected his memories, looking absentmindedly at Al-Sayyida Zaynab Square and at the movement and commotion in it. No one present uttered a word. Instead, they continued to gaze at him, waiting for him to resume speaking. The only one who stirred was a man who took advantage of that pause to pull a package of snuff from the pocket of his old-fashioned black jacket. After offering it silently to those around him, he took a little and inhaled it. Then he sneezed violently and said, "God! God! God!"

At that, the registered pharmacist sitting near him turned and asked, "Are you going to keep on sneezing at us, Sha'ban Effendi? We want to hear what the doctor has to say."

Sha'ban Effendi, a former head clerk of the Islamic legal archives office, took a large handkerchief from his pocket and wiped his nose with it. He said, "That's it, sir. Go ahead and speak, doctor."

The doctor put his cup on the small tray placed on a chair in front of him and glanced at his companions, as though asking them where he had gotten to in his account. One of them, a former health inspector from Markaz Ashmun, now a landlord, said quickly while fingering his string of amber beads, which he carried either for self-respect or respect for Judgment Day, "You were telling us about Bahr al-Ghazal province."

Dr. Hilmi said, as though to himself, "Right. Bahr al-Ghazal!" Then he was silent and gazed at the square blankly, trying to recall the past.

After suppressing a sneeze that took him by surprise, Sha'ban Effendi asked, "Is it true, doctor, that Bahr al-Ghazal province alone equals the size of all Egypt?"

The doctor did not answer his question. Instead he turned to his audience as if ready to resume his narration. They fell silent at once and looked at him attentively. He raised a fly whisk with an ivory handle, drove the flies away from the coffee tray, and said, "I'm telling you about Bahr al-Ghazal. . . . Oh, Bahr al-Ghazal! The Sudan!"

He uttered "The Sudan" with something like a deep sigh, an expression of regret issuing from his entire being, or a longing that shook his whole person. The hearer would have imagined that The Sudan was everything to this man. It was the entire life of this grizzled military doctor who had lived there for such a long time.

He began to recite for his audience in a firm, vibrant voice how he had accompanied an Egyptian expedition to explore unknown parts of Bahr al-Ghazal.

He said that when they were camped near Ghabt Shambe, they awoke early one morning and the soldiers lined up, each with a glass in his hand. He walked down the line with a bottle of quinine, pouring in each glass a sip or two, according to the drill in those areas, as a preventive measure against malarial fever. Then they carried their gear, tents, and waterskins and went deep into the dense and far-reaching forests and thickets. A black guide, one of the local inhabitants, preceded them. Whenever they had completed a stage and night overcame them, they stopped and lit fires to keep the beasts of the jungle away. Despite that, they would see by the light of the fire blazing in the dry twigs the eyes of leopards and lions that prowled around them in the distance. These eyes gleamed and glowed with strange and beautiful colors. Those nights were hot and at times magnificently moonlit and profoundly still. The only sound was the roaring of a lion prowling about in search of a portion of the meat from the wild teetal goats and water buffalo they roasted over the fire. Dr. Hilmi would squat on the ground with the soldiers, who watched intently, some holding their rifles ready in case of an emergency. Although those moments were full of terrifying anxiety, the doctor relished that adventure. He wanted to see a lion attack and be gunned down by their rifles. When he confided this desire to a Sudanese soldier detailed to serve him, the soldier told him, "You'll see something stranger than that when we get to Tungu. You'll see some of the natives hunt lions with short spears!"

In the morning the expedition traveled on. As they went, they hunted for their food. There were a lot of animals to hunt, from fatty wild teetal goats to greasy water buffalo. For long periods the doctor would split from the expedition in pursuit of fine game. It was the same with all new recruits who had been given a rifle: He shot, without thinking, at every animal he encountered, whether it was a predator or not.

The Sudanese soldier assigned to him noticed this and cautioned him one day, "Shoot any animal in these forests you want, whether life-threatening or not, but be careful not to harm the monkey or the entire expedition will be harmed. Don't get in a fight with the forest monkey."

The expedition traveled on for several days, until it was exhausted and the water gave out.

The guide said, "There's no hope for water until three stages further, where there is a single well. The bush country is sometimes like the desert in having everything except water fit to drink."

Finally the soldiers neared the well, where they would rest and quench their thirst after greasy food and an exhausting journey in intense heat. A few hundred meters before they reached the well, it occurred to the doctor to sneak off from the expedition and speed on alone via a shortcut through the jungle thickets to get to the well before them. He carried out the idea at once without telling even his Sudanese soldier. As soon as he arrived at the well, he stopped in astonished surprise, for he observed a ferocious-looking monkey standing motionless by the well.

He hesitated a little and then gestured at him with his hand, but the monkey did not move. He picked up a small stone and threw it, but the ape still did not move. So he aimed his rifle at him. The monkey gave him a piercing look but did not leave his post. The doctor grew nervous about his situation. He saw no alternative to opening fire on that strange monkey.

He did, and the monkey fell, stained with blood, into the well without uttering a cry. The doctor went forward at once toward the well and leaned over to look at the monkey in it and to see how much water it contained. What he saw there astonished him. He found more than a hundred monkeys had also fallen down it. He asked himself what had brought all these monkeys to the well. What were they doing in it?

He thought it over and came to an amazing realization: These monkeys had actually come to drink from the well and their method of reaching the distant water was for that large monkey to stand and grasp a second monkey who let himself down. This second monkey grabbed hold of a third who let himself down below him in the same way, and the third a fourth. Thus some of the monkeys made a ladder of their bodies inside the well so others could climb down and then back up.

The doctor could discern this from the position of the monkeys. Some were still clasping hands.

He was amazed and commented to himself on the solidarity of these monkeys and on the great sacrifice that large monkey had made on behalf of the group. This monkey had not wanted to move even after the doctor threw a stone at him and aimed at him. He was holding his comrades who were dangling down the well. He accepted death with steady eyes and a steadfast body and did not abandon his mission. It would have been possible for him to desert his comrades and save himself by racing and leaping into the bush as soon as he saw the doctor.

The doctor regretted killing that monkey a little, although his mind was troubled then by a much more important matter. The exhausted expedition would be arriving shortly and would throw itself upon the well in search of water. Now this well was fouled by blood and monkeys. To go on to another well would take further stages and require days and nights. Could the expedition continue marching on more days without water? And who had caused this? Who was responsible for what had happened and for exposing the soldiers to a danger like this? To contaminate or poison a well was a crime under military law . . . all the more so when the person who did it was the army medic, in other words the official who was charged with safeguarding the health of the soldiers and whose sole concern was the health of the soldiers. When all this flashed through the doctor's mind, he trembled and felt stunned for a time. But he roused himself suddenly and raced into the bush at once, because he thought the best way out of this predicament was to pretend ignorance of everything and return to the expedition, to trail along after it without anyone noticing him, as though he had not separated from it at all, had not preceded them to the well, and did not know what was in it!

It was not long before the expedition reached the well. The soldiers sped to it joyously and jubilantly after they put down their packs, removed the loads from their animals, and readied their empty waterskins.

When they saw what was in the well they shouted angrily and cursed. They became desperate. Their jubilation turned into moans of rage and grief. The doctor was at the very rear, observing silently and sadly, tormented by anxiety. But no one noticed how troubled he was.

The expedition began to brainstorm about what to do. The anxious doctor tried to hide and to steel himself. Then he suddenly felt someone behind him. He turned and saw the Sudanese soldier giving him a look that told him the soldier had grasped what had happened.

The soldier did not utter a word after that. Instead he took a sturdy rope from the supplies and went silently to the well. He fastened one end of it to a boulder and let the other end down the well. Then he shouted for everyone to get away and to hide in the nearby bushes. Once the members of the expedition were concealed in the jungle, staring dejectedly at the well, they all immediately saw, from their hiding places, a monkey emerge from the well after having climbed up the rope. The rest of the monkeys followed him. Then they watched in amazement as two large monkeys in the group carried away the dead monkey, which was soaked in blood. They raced off with him, and the other monkeys disappeared, leaping from tree to tree.

Thus the well and the area around it were evacuated. The expedition wanted to come out of hiding to run to the well to clean it and supply their needs, but the Sudanese soldier motioned to them to wait and keep still. He scolded the doctor in a whisper, "The monkeys won't allow the death to go unpunished."

In truth, he had scarcely finished his words when monkeys appeared out of the jungle again from every side. It seemed that this group had gone to inform all the monkeys in the vicinity and to mobilize them. One group approached the well and began to examine it with narrow, piercing eyes. They happened upon a soldier who, to his misfortune, had stayed behind his comrades. He was busy setting up tents and hadn't noticed that the others were hiding. The monkeys pounced on that man and threw him to the ground. They pulled him by his feet and dragged him across the dirt, taking him into the jungle. Before they disappeared with him, the other monkeys leapt into the trees nearby, tore off slender branches like whips, descended with the speed of lightning to that man, and rained blows on him.

The expedition could not rescue the poor soldier from their hands except at a high price—which was to resume their march at once, leaving that spot after taking a small amount of water, in spite of the fatigue of the exhausted soldiers and their extreme need for rest.

Thus the expedition left the area hastily and entered another forest, as vast as the ocean. All its trees were mahogany, the type of wood from which expensive furniture is made.

The expedition rested for some time in this location. The doctor had forgotten his deed and started thinking about other matters and considerations, spurred by his surroundings and the sight of these trees. He thought about the terrific fortunes that would be gained by anyone who could harvest the trees of a forest like this valuable one. The only barrier to that fortune was the difficulty of transport. But if a railroad connected that area with Egypt or the sea, the fortune would be assured. "In the future that will happen. This is why England wants the Sudan; not for today, but tomorrow."

He did not spend too much time on these thoughts, for the expedition quickly left the area and continued its journey elsewhere, and then to still another place, until they reached Tungu. They stayed there some time. The doctor was able to explore the place thoroughly and to see its wonders. The most astounding thing he remembered from it was watching a lion eat a gazelle held in its claws. One of the local inhabitants was spying on the lion from nearby, as though waiting for the opportunity to deprive the king of his food.

The doctor's Sudanese soldier was with him and said to him, "See what this man does next. There aren't many gazelle in this region and he wants to pry it out of the lion's claws." He had scarcely finished speaking when the doctor saw the man approach the lion and toss a pebble at him provocatively. The lion, however, did not pay any attention to it, as though the stone had been nothing more than a gnat that had touched him. The man repeated the attack with a rock that struck the lion on the head. The lion looked at him. Then it turned its head away as if in disdain and busied itself with its prey again. The man took a larger rock, aimed it at the lion's nose, and threw it hard. The lion's patience gave way, and it rose grumpily. Then it stretched and walked slowly toward the man. The doctor said to himself: *The man is lost and destroyed if he doesn't flee at once.* The man, however, did not budge until the lion approached so close that only three or four steps remained between them. Then the man took a short spear that was lying near him on the ground and confronted the lion. The attacking lion leapt at him. When the lion was about to jump on the man, the man bent down with the speed of lightning and caught the lower side of the lion's neck with the spear. Then the king of the jungle fell dead. The doctor in his amazement and bewilderment didn't know how that had happened in just a few seconds. This feat had fully demonstrated the expertise, deftness, and agility that this African had developed through long training since childhood. The man then went to the gazelle, picked it up, and carried it away, followed by the doctor's looks of admiration for this person who had snatched the prey by force from the lion's claws. The Sudanese soldier, however, was not much surprised and told the doctor that the important factor in fighting a lion is to avoid his blow, because all his power is in his blow. One day when he was on the shores of Bahr al-Zaraf, he had seen a lion come down to drink. A horrendous crocodile challenged it and clamped its jaws around one of his legs. There was a terrifying struggle between the two wild beasts in which one of the lion's legs was torn off, but the lion struck the crocodile's back with his claws and split it.

After a few more days, the expedition resumed its march, this time crossing savannah regions. High grass grew there, and people resembling Bedouins lived in the area. Their occupation was camel herding. They lived on the backs of camels in howdah-like dwellings that they carried with them when they followed the migrating herds of camels as they grazed. Thus these people were both sedentary and migratory in perpetuity. They resembled passengers on a ship lost in the middle of the ocean or the skippers of a houseboat on the Nile. Transactions among them were carried out in male or female camels, and it was the same when they traded with outsiders. Otherwise it was with camel milk, skins, and wool. The doctor observed this and mulled it over. He said to himself: *How fine it would be to make systematic use of these vast natural grazing areas and exploit the wool and milk.*

As soon as the doctor reached this point in his narration that afternoon, someone asked the pharmacist to fill a prescription. He rose and excused himself. So the doctor was forced to cut short his discussion. Sha'ban Effendi brought out his snuffbox and said, in amazement at what he heard, "That's something stupendous, doctor!"

The health inspector bowed his head in thought for a time. Then he inquired, "The land of Al-Jazirah, what's it like?"

Dr. Hilmi replied, "The land of Al-Jazirah—don't worry about it! This, sir, is an area suitable for everything: cotton, rubber. The easiest thing to plant is the rubber tree. It's one of the future treasures of the Sudan."

The health inspector nodded his head appreciatively and then silently bowed it. Suddenly he looked up to say, "I've heard, doctor, that you returned with a pretty penny from the Sudan."

Dr. Hilmi answered, "You mean the penny I got for the elephants?"

The head clerk asked, after sneezing vigorously, "Elephants?"

The health inspector said, "The doctor shot six elephants in the Sudan and sold their ivory for about four thousand pounds when prices were high."

Sha'ban Effendi said in awed astonishment, "My goodness! Four thousand pounds for elephants? What kind of elephants were those, brother?"

The doctor replied with a smile, "So what do you think? A single elephant has an average of sixty kantar of ivory, and the price of a single kantar today is ten pounds. In other words each elephant is worth approximately six hundred pounds. For that reason, anyone who wants to hunt elephants must get a license from the government, and the license fee is exorbitant."

Sha'ban Effendi said, "My goodness! Does the Sudan have all these enormous treasures?" Then he sighed and remarked, "How lucky you are, doctor! You fill us with desire. If I were young I would risk everything and go to God's country. Shaykh, while we're asleep here, farming, we won't succeed." Then he sneezed, wiped his nose with his handkerchief, and asked, "Was your family with you in the Sudan, doctor?"

The doctor and the health inspector replied in unison that he had not married yet.

Sha'ban Effendi said, "So you were a bachelor back then!"

Dr. Hilmi answered, "Naturally. I married and started a family on my return from the Sudan—how time flies—twenty years ago."

Sha'ban Effendi exclaimed, "Twenty years! So were you at the Battle of Omdurman?"

Dr. Hilmi's face was transfigured by pride and he boasted, "Omdurman and others. . . . That's well known! I've seen combat. I'm not just a doctor; I'm a soldier!"

At that moment the postman passed and looked at Dr. Hilmi, who cut short this discussion to ask, as usual, if he had any mail. The letter carrier was in the habit of stopping by the pharmacy to give the doctor his mail instead of going to the house. That day, however, he hesitated a little before replying. Then he mumbled in a low voice, while sticking his hand in the case of letters he carried, "No . . . just this letter . . . for . . ."

The mailman must finally have thought that it was none of his business to be too particular and that in any case the doctor was the father of the addressee. This was especially relevant because the letter was addressed to "Miss Saniya, Daughter of Dr. Ahmad Hilmi." So he felt obliged to give the letter to him. The doctor took the letter and opened it without looking at what was written on the front. At first he read without understanding anything. He reread it and still did not understand. Then he looked at the envelope and understood. He rose at once and excused himself. His expression had changed, because he thought his military honor had been besmirched. He headed straight home to settle accounts with his daughter.

When he entered the house, his wife welcomed him. He screamed at her and showed her the letter, summarizing its contents. She began to cajole him, trying to convince him that he should conceal the letter from his daughter to avoid causing a scandal and harming her neighbor Zanuba. She offered to go to complain to Zanuba about what had happened. She was going to work to rectify everything quietly and amicably. Then she helped him understand that their daughter Saniya might have been falsely accused and not know anything about the letter that the neighbor with bad manners and deplorable conduct had sent. Why should he get angry at their daughter and upset her over something for which she was not responsible and for which she bore no blame?

She continued in this way with him until he fell silent and the affair passed without incident.

CHAPTER 18

Mabruk, the servant, finished tying the package and set it aside. He came over to ask what he should do next to prepare for Muhsin's journey. Zanuba rose with enthusiasm and concern. It seemed she wanted to coddle Muhsin now that he was about to travel, so he would give a good report of her to his wealthy parents. She ordered Mabruk to go at once to the room on the roof to get Muhsin's suitcase. She motioned to the youth to come show her what he was taking and what he was leaving in her care till he returned. So they began to sort his clothes and personal effects. From the top of the stairs, Mabruk shouted down to Zanuba. She hurried toward him, and he informed her that Saniya was on the roof of her house and wanted to speak with her. Zanuba went up, leaving Muhsin by himself. His heart pounded as he wondered what she wanted to say now. About a quarter of an hour passed before Zanuba returned to resume her work. Muhsin looked at her with inquisitive eyes, but she had hers on a jilbab she was folding to put in his case. She was saying, "Don't forget the letters, Muhsin, and write to me too. Don't just think of your uncles and not me, the way you did last year."

Muhsin replied considerately, "Last year Uncle Hanafi wrote to me. I answered him and sent you my greetings. Shouldn't I reply to the one who writes me?"

Zanuba said immediately, "Have pity on me—if only I knew how to read and write. Last year I said repeatedly to your uncles they should write a letter for me. One time they were too lazy. The next they said, 'We've already sent our letter with more than enough news.' That's the way with letters. But this year, by the Prophet, you will receive a letter from me personally, because Saniya, may God's name protect her, is going to write it for me."

Muhsin became agitated and asked impetuously, "Saniya?"

She nodded her head yes and told him Saniya had called her just then to ask her to hurry and come over to their place as she had promised. She had apologized, saying she was busy getting Muhsin's things ready. At this mention of Muhsin, Saniya had asked Zanuba delicately not to forget to send her greetings and those of her mother whenever she wrote him. So Zanuba had told her that she was upset because her brothers wouldn't write a letter for her except under the most exhaustive pressure. Right away Saniya had proposed that she would write whatever Zanuba dictated. She was ready to write to Muhsin whatever Zanuba wanted: one letter, two, or three. So Zanuba had thanked her and was delighted. She praised God that He was going to spare her from depending on a person like Hanafi.

But Zanuba's delight could not be compared with young Muhsin's bliss. He was picturing himself receiving a letter written by Saniya's hand. His heart danced, and for the first time, he began to look forward to the trip, for the sole reason of waiting for this cherished letter.

Night fell, and the folks assembled around Muhsin before he went to bed. They bade him farewell and reminded him of the gifts they wanted him to bring them from the country on his return. One of them wanted pots of rice with pigeon. Another asked for curdled milk and sorghum bread . . . and so on.

Muhsin went to bed happy and instructed Hanafi to wake up quickly in the morning since he was to leave on the first train. It was Hanafi Effendi's duty to accompany Muhsin to the station and buy his ticket because he served as the responsible president of the family.

Muhsin did not sleep that night. Images from his happy day flowed in succession through his imagination. He kept impatiently anticipating the morning. He was delighted to be traveling to see his family after a long absence, to see the countryside, and especially to await the promised letter.

Dawn's harbingers appeared. Then the alarm clock, which they had set the previous night for five, went off. Muhsin leapt up and headed straight for Hanafi's bed to wake him. He knew he had an arduous task.

He removed the covers from Hanafi's head and called him, but Hanafi didn't respond. Muhsin repeated the call once, twice, and three times—to no avail.

Finally, Hanafi Effendi turned over in bed and said peevishly, "Good grief! You disturb my sleep in the middle of the night. It's not time to leave."

Muhsin shouted at him, "Middle of the night, huh? The sun's up!"

Hanafi grumbled, sleep weighing down his lids, "The alarm hasn't gone off yet!"

Muhsin said sarcastically, "Oh yeah? You were asleep. It rang and rang."

Hanafi wasn't convinced at first. So Muhsin began to try to persuade him with words. A discussion and debate arose between them over the hour, the alarm clock, and whether the bell had rung. This was all procrastination to gain time for Hanafi to lie in bed. Abduh finally heard the argument, rose angrily, and went to wake Hanafi in the tried-and-true fashion. He said it was the only thing that worked on Hanafi.

By six-thirty Hanafi and Muhsin were at Mahattat Bab al-Hadid, the railway station. Muhsin stood with his parcel and his suitcase under the station clock, waiting for Hanafi, who had gone to buy the ticket a quarter of an hour earlier and hadn't returned yet. Muhsin fidgeted and looked anxiously at the clock. He saw passengers rushing in droves to the train. Some more minutes passed. There were only five minutes left before the train was scheduled to depart, and Hanafi had not appeared.

The first bell rang, and Muhsin looked right and left in agitation, searching for him. But there was no trace of Hanafi. Time passed and late arrivals were racing toward the train. The porters were shouting that only a minute remained. In despair, the youth began watching the hand on the large clock over his head. Finally the conductor shouted, "Watch your feet!" Then the train whistled and moved slowly off . . . leaving the station and disappearing from sight. But Hanafi had not returned yet.

Muhsin suppressed his rage and decided to call a porter to mind his luggage while he went looking for Hanafi. Then, suddenly, the honorary president, who had the ticket in his mouth, came running up, dripping with sweat. When he drew near to Muhsin, he thrust the ticket at him and shouted, "Take it. Get on right away. There's no time."

Muhsin looked at him coldly. He stood frozen in place and asked him languidly but wrathfully, "Where's the train?"

Hanafi looked at the platform where the train normally stood. Not seeing it, he relaxed and calmed down. He took out his handkerchief and wiped his brow. Then he asked, "Hasn't it come yet? Didn't I tell you we woke too early?"

The youth flared up and said angrily, "Hasn't come? The train left an hour ago."

Hanafi didn't seem to believe him and asked, "What are you saying? Left? Are you sure?"

Muhsin asked him coldly, "Where were you? Where did you go, sir?"

The honorary president replied, "Brother, when I went to buy you a ticket, I found a terrible crowd of people at the window. So I told myself: I'll sit and wait a little on the bench."

"What bench?"

"Do I know? A green bench over there with a back."

Muhsin retorted quickly, trying to restrain in his rage, "You fell asleep!"

VOLUME 2

Arise! Arise, Osiris. I am your son Horus.
I have come to restore life to you.
You no longer have your true heart, your past heart.
    —*The Book of the Dead*

CHAPTER 1

Muhsin took the next train. Immediately after selecting a window seat in the corner of a compartment, he isolated himself from the other travelers to be alone with his imagination and memories and Saniya and what had happened the day before . . . and so on and so forth.

Gone were the clamor of the station, the anxiety of waiting, and the effort of traveling, of getting ready and prepared. Here he was now doing it. The train had carried him far away from his beloved Cairo. He had left Hanafi Effendi on the platform running behind the train waving good-bye to him and shouting with a moving artlessness, "Good-bye, Muhsin."

This President Hanafi with whom Muhsin had been furious shortly before—what a good person he was! Dripping with sweat, he had carried the parcel and suitcase for Muhsin into the second-class carriage.

Was this for real? Was he truly leaving Cairo with such speed? And his comrades, his uncles, the folks, with Hanafi their honorary president? Was he to spend the night in another community and another bed? Muhsin was moved and somewhat depressed. His one consolation was remembering that his trip was only for a short time and that he would gain a letter from Saniya, a letter that he was already anticipating even before it was sent. It would be his most precious possession.

One other thing helped console him about leaving Cairo: He would see his dear mother and his father.

When Muhsin eventually turned to his fellow travelers around him, he found there were a lot of them, some wearing traditional turbans and others modern fezzes. They filled the compartment, not leaving an empty seat in it. Till that time they had been quiet, although they had been glancing at each other as though they weren't comfortable with silence and isolation and wished someone would start talking.

It wasn't long before a man with a massive body looked in on them. He was wearing a broadcloth caftan and carrying a bundle. He began to scrutinize their faces as though to ask them for an empty seat. They had seen him before in the long corridor of the coach coming and going with his bundle, searching for a seat. They looked at each other for a moment. Then one of them cleared a space of two handsbreadth beside him by pushing sternly at the persons on his right and left. He told the man, "Sit down, sir. We're all Muslims. We make room for each other."

The man entered with his bundle and sat down. At that, an effendi among the compartment's passengers leaned toward his neighbor and addressed him in a voice that started out soft and deferential and soon became public and loud, as though he wanted everyone else to hear what he was saying. The others in fact began to turn their eyes toward him with pleasure and interest as though hearkening to an orator at a mosque or a preacher in a church.

The speaker was emboldened by the response of his fellow passengers and launched into an impromptu oration, gliding from topic to topic.

He began by commenting on how they had made room for the new passenger. He praised this gesture, offering a tribute to the sense of kinship and of heartfelt solidarity among the people of Egypt. He said, "If this had happened in Europe, not one of the passengers would have moved, even if he was acquainted with the newcomer and his friend. No one will decrease his comfort for the sake of another, no matter who he is."

He added, with reference to Europe, that he had once traveled by train in one of the countries there. Then one of the turbaned travelers interrupted him with naive admiration, "Sir, you've traveled overseas?"

The effendi smiled and answered him modestly, "I've been to Austria, England, and France on business."

The effendi returned to his topic and said that he was once a passenger in a train in Europe and spent a day and a night in it without a word escaping anyone's lips, neither his nor his fellow passengers' in that same compartment, as though each one of them was an extraterrestrial, not all earthlings with the same kind of heart and emotions.

A shaykh in a corner of the compartment cleared his throat and said, "It's a country without Islam."

The effendi did not respond. The color of his face changed a little. He put out his hand and pretended to be busy shaking the dust of the trip from his fez, as though slightly embarrassed and annoyed.

At that, one of the passengers noticed a cross tattooed on the man's wrist and realized that the shaykh had said something with the best of intentions but that his comment had not been well received. He intervened gently to set it right: "You mean, Mr. Shaykh, it's a land without hearts, not like our country where we are all brothers, whether Copts or Muslims."

Another passenger, an enlightened man, noticed the same thing. He entered into the discussion and began adroitly to amend the statement until he showed those present that the word "Islam," which was current in Egyptian use at all levels of society, really had no religious or sectarian stamp. Its meaning and import were, rather, the emotion of mercy, a goodness of heart, and a union of hearts. These were emotions to be found in Egypt and not in Europe. There, the poison of utility had spread through the souls of the Europeans. A dog-eat-dog strife prevailed with emphasis on the personal welfare of the individual.

Everyone, both the turbaned and the befezzed, pondered this statement and this gloss. He seemed to have disclosed to them a reality that had previously been concealed under the cloak of that word. They liked what he had said and appreciated it. The topic was closed.

One of those present still wanted to go back to the effendi who spoke first and to what he had said. He asked him, "So, Mr. Effendi, a person overseas can bear not speaking to his neighbor in a train?"

Another volunteered, "While one of us, no offense, rides our narrow-gauge railroad train for half an hour and gets off knowing all the passengers."

A third said, "Why look so far? Here we are—we're not to Banha yet—and we've been blessed by the company of all present."

Then he looked at each of them in turn with a smile as though greeting them. Finally his glance fell on young Muhsin, who was crouched in a corner, where no one had paid attention to him. His eyes rested on him a little, as though he was surprised at his silence when everyone else had spoken. Wishing to draw him out of his isolation, he leaned toward him politely and asked him gently, "Isn't that right, young effendi?"

The youth turned toward him in confusion and stammered shyly a few words. Then he turned his face to the window, going back to his quiet isolation. His interlocutor left him alone and did not persist. He attributed Muhsin's behavior to his youth, shyness, and diffidence about speaking when surrounded by adults.

They all recommenced their discussion of various topics, until they reached Banha station, where one of them leaned from the window and bought butter cookies, eggs, oranges, and tangerines. Another spread on his lap a napkin that was full of food and invited those present: "Help yourselves."

They responded, "A long life!"

The train started moving and left Banha. The passengers were busy eating for a while, except for the effendi who had spoken first. He started talking again and made this observation: "With regard to 'help yourselves,' one of those passengers in Europe would pull out a cigarette or eat and drink without so much as acknowledging the existence of his neighbor."

The people present incredulously asked God's deliverance. Each one had an opinion to express about that. The effendi went on to boast, "The people of Egypt are a deeply rooted nation. Why, we've been in the Nile Valley for seven thousand years. We knew how to plant and cultivate, had villages, farms, and farmers at a time when Europe hadn't even achieved barbarism."

The man with the bundle, after spitting voluminously out the window, said, "You're right: It all depends on one's lineage, Mr. Effendi."

Here, the enlightened effendi said, as though he had just thought of it, "You're right, sir. We are without doubt a social people by instinct, for we have been an agricultural people since ancient times. Back then, other peoples lived by hunting in a barbarous and isolated fashion with each tribe or family in a different place. We, however, from prehistory on, have had villages of a civilized type and have dwelt in the Nile Valley. Social organization was in our blood. Social life is a natural characteristic that has developed among us through many generations."

CHAPTER 2

When the train finally reached the Damanhur station, Muhsin looked down at the platform and found the Nubian butler and Mr. Ahmad, the coachman, waiting for him. No sooner had they recognized him than they attached themselves to the railway carriage and shouted, "Praise God for your safe arrival, bey."

"Fetch the luggage, Bilal, and be quick."

"What about the young bey?"

"I'll bring down the young bey. Come, bey."

Thus the youth got down and walked between the two servants as though at a loss. The word *bey* rang in his ears strangely, although for once he didn't mind. He felt an unaccustomed pride and wished Saniya could have been present to see and hear.

He climbed into the horse-drawn carriage, which transported him through this unpretentious city. People on both sides of the street, in coffeehouses and shops, gazed at him as though asking themselves who this youth was who was riding in the carriage of a local dignitary. When he reached home, he found his mother waiting for him at the top of the steps. As soon as she saw him, she opened her arms to him. The moment he saw her, he rushed to her instinctively. They embraced and tears of emotion and joy glistened in the mother's eyes. Whenever she finished hugging him, she started again.

At last she began to examine him from head to toe, inspecting him and touching him, as though conducting a limb-by-limb review. Finally she smiled, saying to him, "In God's name, God's will be done! You've put on some weight, Muhsin."

She brought him into the parlor and sat him down beside her. She began to ask him about Cairo and his aunt and uncles. Then his father came in. Muhsin rose and hastened to kiss his hand. He remained standing until his father sat down. His father then asked, "So, Muhsin, how was the midyear exam?"

The youth fidgeted a little and said, "There wasn't one this year. They canceled it."

His father replied with surprise and dismay, "Canceled it? How come? They don't have the right at all."

He then began to ask him about his courses and teachers and the competency examination that Muhsin would sit this year. Finally his mother intervened, chiding her husband, "Bey, you're wrong. Can't you let him catch his breath? Yes, ask him first about his health and that of his uncles. Why are you so thoughtless?"

Then, noticing her husband's shoes, she asked, "Are you still wearing them? Didn't I tell you to get rid of those shoes? It just doesn't fit your rank at all to wear shoes like these. You have a lot of shoes—why wear these? You're an important figure in this community."

Removing them, her husband replied, "I forgot. Here you go, madam. Don't be angry. Ali! Ali!"

Another Nubian answered his call, not the man Muhsin had seen at the station. He was wearing a white caftan with a red sash at the waist. The senior bey ordered him to bring another pair of shoes right away.

That was when Muhsin began to peer at the expensive carpets and sumptuous furniture surrounding him. He glanced politely at his mother and noticed the expensive clothes she was wearing.

His mother was looking at him at the same time. She immediately said, "I don't like what you have on, Muhsin." The boy mumbled some unintelligible words. His mother continued, "You just won't grow up like me."

Here his father cleared his throat and said, "Nor like me!"

The wife turned to her husband and said sarcastically, "Since when, Mr. Peasant Mayor? Do you deny I'm the one who civilized you and taught you to be proud?"

Her husband backed down and replied, "God, did I say something? Of course, madam, you are a Turkish lady and a descendant of Turks." He was silent for a bit.

She left him and started on Muhsin again, saying, "Truly it's strange—Muhsin hasn't turned out like me. Even when he was a child he cried and screamed the day we sent our private carriage to wait for him at the school gate. Remember?"

His father, pulling up his expensive silk socks, said, "Peasant! What can you say to him?"

Muhsin bowed his head on hearing this word. He felt an emotion like contempt but did not know whether it was for himself or someone else.

The supper table was spread, and Muhsin sat down with his mother and father. Bilal and Ali, the Nubians, each of them in a white uniform with a red sash like the Nubians at the Shepheard's Hotel, carried in plates and bowls filled with a wide variety of delicious foods. Muhsin, nonetheless, didn't have much appetite. He took a taste from each dish as though fulfilling a duty. His mother noticed how little he was eating and asked, "What's the matter, Muhsin? Don't you like the food? Is the food better at your uncles'?"

The boy almost laughed, remembering the trencher of fuul nabit and the goose leg that Abduh had tossed out the window. But all the same, those sprouted beans had been delicious when he devoured them with the servant Mabruk slurping his serving beside him, his gleaming eyes watching the steam rise, his nostrils sniffing around with great appetite. Hanafi Effendi, the honorary president, and the rest of the group had gathered around this trencher as though it were a shrine.

What a happy group! How fine that life was with the folks! Yes, that was why he ate. That was why he put on weight, even though the food was poor and monotonous.

Time for bed came, and they led Muhsin to his private room, a beautiful room with expensive furniture. Then they shut the door on him, each parent retiring to a separate bedroom. Muhsin looked around him. There was only one bed, and he was all alone. Quiet reigned supreme. It was as still as death. He was depressed by this solitude. The place distressed him. He longed for his bed beside those of his uncles in that communal room

with five beds, a room into which all the folks squeezed. He felt
even more homesick. It took him only a night to perceive how
comfortable he had been. That was where life was. What a
happy life! That communal life! Even during their troubles and
hard times!

CHAPTER 3

Muhsin awoke the next day feeling depressed and out of sorts. He began to prowl through the reaches of the spacious house, gazing without much interest at the elegant furnishings and magnificent curios he encountered. Suddenly he remembered Saniya and that changed his perspective. Pride swelled within him. He proceeded to look at his surroundings with new interest. His mother flowed toward him in a beautiful, trailing gown. Muhsin looked at her with admiration. He wished Saniya could see his mother looking like this. His father passed by in a different suit from yesterday. In his hand was an expensive, heavy walking stick with extraordinary gold designs on it. The youth remembered at once what his father had said the day before: "Peasant! What can you say to him?"

He felt a little ashamed of himself and found it odd that he was the son of parents like these, whom he did not resemble. He resolved to resemble them from now on. He was still young. It behooved him to grasp the significance of his status. This idea satisfied him. He approached his mother and patted her as though asking her to reveal the secrets of this life of splendor or to help him understand or savor this life.

But all this was wishful thinking. No sooner had the first day elapsed than boredom was killing Muhsin again. That enthusiasm and intoxication left him, along with his pride.

He sensed this truth in the depths of his soul: that he was a stranger in his family. Something he could not fathom separated him from his parents. Whatever he did, there was an inevitable reserve or awkwardness. So let them call him peasant as much as they wished. He would not be able to live the way they wanted. He needed the freedom and fresh air he could inhale when he was with his uncomplicated and unpretentious uncles.

Despite all the servants and comforts of this house, he felt himself weighed down by heavy chains that were intolerable.

Thinking about it this way brought him some peace of
mind. He detected a rebellious spirit he had not been conscious of before. The word "peasant" his father had used the
day before still rankled within him. Secretly he rebelled against
his father. He began a mental review of his father's personality
and upbringing. Wasn't he a peasant too, first and foremost?
Wasn't he a fellah, a man of the earth? Wasn't he still? How
had he changed? Did his clothes, his expensive walking stick,
his shoes and socks, and his diamond rings alter him?

Wasn't it just a set of conventions? Wasn't it his Turkish
mother who had influenced his father in the name of civilization? Yes, what right did he have now to look down on the peasant? Because the fellah was poor? Was poverty a fault?

Thus Muhsin continued turning over in his mind thoughts
of this type while he felt uncomfortable being there, conscious
of being estranged from this life. He couldn't imagine how he
would survive ten more days when he was grumpy after one
day. He longed for his home with his uncles like a fish longing
for water. It occurred to him he should think of a pretext to go
back. But he remembered Saniya's letter, which he was expecting. So he kept quiet and gave in. That reminded him he had to
write his uncles to inform them he had arrived. So he went at
once to the desk to write them a letter about his sincere longing to return. Then he wrote a separate, personal letter to his
aunt Zanuba, giving her his greetings and asking her to pass
on his respects to Saniya Hanim. He used expressions of the
utmost delicacy, since he expected Saniya to read the letter. He
wrote it as though writing to her.

His mother noticed his low spirits and suggested an expedition
for a few days to their country place, where the earth was now
covered with clover like a green carpet. When Muhsin agreed
happily, his mother ordered the carriage.

It was prepared and supplies were gathered for a stay at the
estate house.

By afternoon Muhsin and his father and mother, accompanied by some of the servants, were on their way to ___, which was at a distance of ___ from the city of Damanhur. As soon as the carriage reached the bridge and passed the massive syca more standing at the entrance to the threshing area, the farm dog began to bark. Behind him appeared the overseer, the headman of the farm community, and some of the farm workers. The dog fell silent once it recognized them. The overseer, the headman, and the others with them gathered around the carriage, welcoming them. They greeted Muhsin especially warmly as they helped him dismount, saying, "Three hundred thousand welcomes to the young bey! The farm shines brightly with the presence of the young bey."

The farm headman, whose stately white beard shook as he spoke, said, "Salutations, Mr. Bey! Salutations, Mr. Young Bey! Salutations, Mrs. Lady! Salutations! And more salutations!"

One of the men approached Muhsin and asked, "Don't you remember me, Mr. Bey? I'm Abd al-Maqsud. You used to favor me, back when you were in school in Damanhur, by letting me take you for a ride on Fridays so we could go fishing in the Abu Diyab canal. Don't you remember? You would grandly ride the young jenny halfway there. Then you would climb down and tell me, 'You ride, Abd al-Maqsud, you too.' I would tell you, 'Bey, I'm not tired. We farmers are used to walking.' You would get angry and say, 'You've got to ride, you too.' Don't you remember, bey?"

Muhsin smiled and did not say anything.

Meanwhile Muhsin's father and mother had been talking with the overseer and headman about agricultural matters, ordering and forbidding. The farm overseer answered politely, "Everything is just fine, Mr. Bey. We've cleaned out the drainage canals. The southern area we've devoted to corn. This year's clover, as Your Honor sees, will be as God wills . . . a fertile year in honor of the visit of the young bey."

The senior bey turned to the farm headman and asked, "And you, Shaykh Hasan—what about the story of Arjawi and the Bedouin watchman?"

"It all ended for the best, Mr. Bey."

"There are no problems, bey. We reconciled them in the presence of the mayor's deputy and the chief watchmen. The estate is calm, Bedouins and peasants, milk and honey."

The lady walked toward the villa. Her husband and Muhsin followed along with all the others. Shaykh Hasan began to say as they went, "You have honored the farm! By God, salutations! Salutations, respected bey! Salutations, respected lady! Salutations, young bey! So many salutations."

The lady, who had had enough, shouted at the poor headman, "That's enough racket for us. It's a whole lifetime of salutations. Why are you such chatterboxes, you fellahin?"

The headman was a little dismayed and embarrassed but said with a smile, "God grant us a long life for you. It's just that we're happy, respected lady, to have you here."

Muhsin was touched but continued walking silently behind his mother, his head bowed.

When the farm women learned that the owners of the estate had arrived, they emerged trilling. The boldest of them stepped forward, wanting to take the lady's hand to kiss it, but the lady scolded her and said dismissively, "Get back! Away! Take care not to soil my dress."

The beaming woman answered with docile good humor, a smile on her face, "Oh! Can't we kiss our lady's hand? Whose hand shall we kiss then?"

The lady gestured to her to move back. The overseer intervened to carry out the lady's wishes. He raised his arm in the air in a threatening way as though dealing with geese or chickens. He said, "Let's go, woman, you, and her . . . to your houses . . . back to your house!"

The women retreated, falling back toward their houses while they continued trilling. Muhsin approached his mother and asked passionately, "Mother, why do you drive them away? That's not right."

As she went through the door of the house, she replied sternly and with little interest, "Not right? Those are peasants!"

CHAPTER 4

Muhsin had not been in his room in the villa at the estate an hour when it was time to eat. The table was spread. The two Nubian butlers stood at the head of the table as usual. The lady came, followed by her husband and Muhsin. As soon as she saw the plate of whole wheat pita bread on the table she shouted, "My God! Where's the fino? Where's the good bread?"

One of the servants mumbled, "There isn't any."

The lady raged, "You forgot to bring fino bread from Damanhur? Isn't that great! What am I to eat now?"

"I'll go, lady, and get some from Damanhur. I'll be back right away."

The lady was quiet for a moment. Then after casting a glance at the blazing sunlight outdoors, she reconsidered. "It's too hot for you, Bilal. Send one of the peasants." Bilal started to leave, but she stopped him. "Listen, Bilal. Get me that dog of an overseer."

The servant went out and soon returned with the overseer. The lady asked him, "How do you expect us to eat peasant bread, man, you fool?"

The overseer replied with surprise and astonishment, "It's fresh, lady. Bread made this morning! My wife baked it herself, especially for you."

She shouted at him, "Don't disgust me. Do I eat bread like that? Go and send one of the peasants at once to bring me French bread from Damanhur."

"Now, lady, when it's so hot outside?"

"Yes! Now, while it's hot."

"Yes, lady. . . . It's just . . ."

"Just what?"

"It's just, Your Ladyship knows, those peasants suffer in the field from five in the morning and can scarcely wait for noon to come so they can stretch out under a tree to get a little rest."

"God's will be done! To get a little rest? Does a peasant rest? Since when has he had it so good?"

"Aren't they human beings, Your Ladyship?"

"Scram. No more coddling! Go get a fellah right away to bring bread from Damanhur. Otherwise, by the life of my father, the whip will fall on that turban of yours. Species of peasant!"

The overseer looked at the floor for a moment while the lady turned to her husband, the bey, as though to scold him for remaining silent and merely watching. The bey quickly agreed. In haste and confusion he said, "Right. So what? Send one of those peasants who are sleeping like water buffaloes in their houses."

The overseer raised his head and said, "Fine."

The lady added, "Or, you go yourself if you want to spoil them. You're just like them! I mean, do you have any Turkish blood?"

The overseer replied politely, "Fine." Then he went out to obey this grim command. Muhsin cast a sympathetic look after him. The youth lowered his eyes and began to toy with the buttons on his jacket, taking care not to look at his parents, as though ashamed of their conduct.

Muhsin was patient until the meal was finished. Then he left his parents and slipped outside to find freedom, open space, and the farmers, who were straightforward, uncomplicated, and generous. The first person he met was Shaykh Hasan, who was sitting on the stone bench outside the guesthouse. He had a string of beads in his hand. Pale of face and with a wavering voice, he was pleading with Abd al-Ati the Bedouin, a private watchman for the estate. The latter was shouting in his face in a menacing tone, "By God, by God, Arjawi won't take her. By the honor of a Bedouin, we'll blow his head off with this rifle."

"There's no need to raise a ruckus, Abd al-Ati. The bey is here. Do me a favor!"

"By God, this peasant will not have her."

"Wasn't peace established between you by the hand of the mayor's deputy?"

"We are Bedouin with honor. The word of a fellahin omdeh has no sway over us."

On saying this, he left Shaykh Hasan and swaggered off with a smirk of disdain on his lips. His path led him by Muhsin, who had stopped nearby to look and listen, not wishing to interrupt their discussion. When Abd al-Ati approached, Muhsin called to him and asked about what he had just been saying to Shaykh Hasan. Why did he hate the farmer Arjawi? The Bedouin guard replied arrogantly that the young laborer Arjawi wanted to marry his Bedouin sister, who was in love with this peasant. He hadn't succeeded in persuading her to give him up, although he had tried a heavy beating and sincere advice and had contrasted her Bedouin descent to that of the fellah.

Finally, she had reached an agreement with Arjawi to elope with him, against her brother Abd al-Ati's will. So he had sworn to kill this Arjawi on sight. They had tried to make peace between them. The Arab girl had attempted to appeal to her brother's feelings. She had pleaded with him to change his mind about her and her farmer husband, but none of that was of any use. Abd al-Ati insisted on carrying out his verdict. That was what Muhsin understood from the Bedouin. At this point he looked at him and asked gently, "So the Bedouin is better than the farmer, Abd al-Ati?"

The guard stared at him, surprised by his ignorance, and asked, "How, bey, could the Bedouin resemble the peasant?"

"What's the difference between the two?"

"How's that, bey? How's that? The Bedouin has a long and noble line of descent."

"And the peasant doesn't?"

"The peasant is a slave descended from slaves. We Bedouin don't tolerate abuse."

Muhsin left Abd al-Ati and walked on alone to think about what he had said. He remembered that his ancient Egyptian history teacher had said that the present-day Egyptian fellah was the very same Egyptian farmer who lived, plowed, and planted the same earth long before the Bedouin was a Bedouin. One age had followed another and one people had followed another, but because of the fellah's isolation from the cities and city culture and because he was tucked away in villages, far from the shifting political and social storms in the capitals, where the succession of new peoples normally lived and different ethnic groups mixed together—neither the length of time nor its vicissitudes had changed anything in him. Was this fellah someone who could be accused of having no lineage when he was directly descended from the original inhabitants? His shortcoming was not knowing this origin, whereas the Bedouin passed on his lineage from father and grandfather and from tribe to tribe. Moreover, wasn't one of the signs of a long lineage that goodness of character typical of settled life and stability? Meanwhile, this Bedouin continued to be wild and to love war, revenge, and bloodshed, which were carryovers from an earlier life that was aggressive, anxious, and unstable. It was based on raiding and pillage, with one tribe plundering another. But the farmer did not know how to defend himself. He should say that his goodness and love of peace were a consequence of his deeply rooted agricultural heritage. The farming life requires peace, tranquility, and a repudiation of raiding and plunder. When social, sedentary life is contrasted with nomadic life in desolate steppe or mountain regions, the calm and peace of the former reveal a noble origin, not slavery or debasement by slave descent.

Muhsin later went to Shaykh Hasan and sat down beside him on the stone mastaba. He looked at him and his white beard a little. Then he asked, "Uncle, Shaykh Hasan, is the Bedouin better or the fellah?"

The shaykh turned toward him. Running his beads through his fingers, he replied, "Those Bedouin, respected bey, are a bunch of rapacious jerboas. They have no religion and no creed. They are ignorant of divine compassion and of Islam."

"How so?"

"One of us fellahin will be very good to them. He will be generous to them, help them, and keep them company, while they hold him in contempt as though they are the only ones with real blood while we have water. They think the peasant's spirit isn't worth more than a piastre's load of shot. Consider this year: Abu Mutawalli al-Jarf was good enough to plow land for a man named Basis the Bedouin. He prepared it for cultivation and did the sowing, because a Bedouin doesn't know how to plant or weed. They are a people, if you'll excuse the expression, who are not good at anything except beating and snatching. The upshot of this aid and generosity was that people caught Basis the Bedouin beating Abu Mutawalli in the cornfields."

"Did he kill him?"

"Do those Bedouins know clemency? They're animals, respected bey. If you just watch them eating their flour gruel mixed with clarified butter when it's burning hot, you'll say they're not human beings."

He was silent for a time as Muhsin continued to look at him, waiting for him to speak. Shaykh Hasan started talking again after a moment. He told Muhsin, with regard to the eating habits of the Bedouin, that he had once been invited to an outdoor Bedouin wedding. After they had fired their rifles into the air and jousted around on horseback, they put out a big bowl filled with white rice. They then invited the guests to help themselves. That was during the khamsin windstorms when the winds were yellow with sand and dust and blew from every direction. Before the guests knew what had happened, the white rice in the bowl had turned as yellow as turmeric from the dust. He politely declined to eat. Naturally—was he going to eat dirt? Then the Bedouins came forward, bared their forearms, and attacked the bowl, without being about to tell rice from dust. They started devouring fistfuls of that rice and dirt as though dying of hunger.

Muhsin smiled and said enthusiastically, "The fellah's better than the Bedouin, more generous than the Bedouin, kinder than the Bedouin; isn't that so, Uncle Shaykh Hasan?"

CHAPTER 5

Two days passed without the expected letter from Saniya arriving. Anxiety began to pervade Muhsin's soul. He started spending the better part of his day on the mastaba bench waiting for the mail. He recalled Saniya and what had occurred between them the last time he saw her—that kiss she had granted him and his tears flowing out. As soon as he recalled this, his heart was oppressed. He imagined it had been a dream. He was amazed at how easily he had attained such happiness, without saying or doing anything. Had he been obtuse and heedless? Or had he been sleeping? Once again he was filled with the happiness he had not fathomed then but had become aware of only later. She had kissed him, and he could still feel the touch of that kiss on his cheek. His heart was agitated, and without being conscious of it, he raised his hand to his cheek and felt it, as though examining it and trying to assure himself that it had left a permanent imprint. He wasn't able to believe that a kiss made no more impression than air and vanished at once. No, this kiss meant something far more significant to him—that she loved him. At that time he had also not grasped the meaning of love. Yes, she loved him; otherwise what would have induced her, a bashful Egyptian girl, to take the initiative and kiss him when he hadn't kissed her? Moreover, wasn't it she who had suggested writing to him via his aunt Zanuba? So what did he have to fear? Why should he be anxious? Perhaps it was Zanuba's fault. She might have been slow to tell her about the letter concerning his arrival. So let him wait a little. There was no room for anxiety and for wanting things to happen too quickly. Instead of being anxious, he ought to rush out into the fields with his heart at rest, inhaling love from this pure, clean air and seeing love in all the pure, innocent creatures surrounding him.

Thus he got over it, and obeying his soul's counsel, set off running here and there, over vast stretches. He smiled at the lark in flight. He listened to the water flowing beneath the shade of the huge sycamore. It occurred to him to race to the threshing sledge that lay in a corner of the threshing area or to the waterwheel while it was turning. He would gaze at the two oxen operating it. Their eyes were covered so they would not see they were going nowhere.

But none of this had as much impact on him as the sight of the houses of the farm laborers. He went snooping cautiously down their narrow alleys, afraid of upsetting them. He saw an open door, poked his head inside, but found no one home. He realized that its occupants were out to pasture, so to speak.

He went inside hesitantly and started to look around. He saw a small courtyard, half of which was roofed with dry cotton and corn stalks, and then a small chamber. Its door was open as well. Muhsin looked in. He observed something he would never forget. He saw that this chamber was where the occupants slept. There was an oven with mats and covers spread on top of it. But he also saw a cow in one corner. Clover was piled before it, and between its back legs a beautiful suckling calf was reaching for a teat.

What astonished Muhsin the most, however, was to see beside that suckling calf a suckling child, presumably the son of the occupants. He was crowding against the calf and pushing him away from the cow's udder. The cow remained calm and still, not interfering with either of them, as though she did not favor one over the other. The calf and the child both seemed to be her children. What a beautiful picture! What a striking concept!

Muhsin looked at the nursing calf in its purity and innocence. It was lowing contentedly to show it was satisfied. Then he looked at the nursing child, who let out a cry of pleasure and contentment in its purity and innocence. It seemed to him that the two of them understood each other, as though they were linked and didn't see any difference between them.

Muhsin was delighted by this scene. It meant something to him at a deep, mysterious level. But his mind could not add anything to that deep feeling. Intuition is the knowledge of the angels, but rational logic is human knowledge. If one attempts to translate Muhsin's feelings into the language of logic and intellect, one can say he responded in his soul to that union between the two different creatures, who were joined by purity and innocence. But sadly, tomorrow that child will grow up and, as he does, his human qualities will increase while his angelic ones diminish. His feeling of union between himself and the rest of creation will be replaced by desires and wishes that prompt him to scorn everything that differs from him. These will blind him to all their resemblances. For this reason the angelic light that manifests itself as purity, innocence, and a feeling of unity and of group solidarity leaves him. Its place is taken by man's blindness, which shows itself in desires, passions, and selfish, egotistical feelings.

The feeling of the unity of existence is the feeling for God. For this reason, angels and children are closer to God than adults. Although Muhsin knew none of that with his developing intellect—the mind of a competency-level student—he perceived it through his heart and inner eye unconsciously.

Didn't Dostoyevsky say man knows many things without knowing it?

But there was one thing Muhsin was able to grasp with his intellect and this was thanks to his study of the history of ancient Egypt. This scene reminded him suddenly, without there being any particularly strong link, of what he had read about the ancient Egyptians worshipping animals or at least portraying the one God with images of different animals.

Why?

Muhsin wasn't able to discern the exact reason. Here as well he perceived vaguely through his emotions what might be translated discursively as follows. Didn't the ancient Egyptians know of the existential unity and the overall union between the different groups of creatures? If their symbol for God was half man and half animal, wasn't that a symbol of their perception that existence is a unity? They did not scorn animals any more than this child would scorn the calf. So if they made God in a man's form, they also represented him in the form of animals, birds, and insects. Aren't all these creatures God's handiwork? Doesn't everything created offer a portrait of its creator? So why shouldn't animals also be a portrait of the Creator or one of the images of the Creator just as man is?

The feeling of being merged with existence, of being merged in God, was the feeling of that child and calf suckling together. It was an angelic feeling. It was the feeling of that ancient, deeply rooted Egyptian people.

Even now, the farmers of Egypt had a heartfelt respect for animals. They did not scorn living with them in the same house or to sleep together in a single room.

Did not the angelic Egypt with a pure heart survive in Egypt? She had inherited, over the passing generations, a feeling of union, even without knowing it.

Muhsin left the farmer's house with this luminous intuition. He set off, his soul filled with a happiness he didn't understand. Perhaps God wanted prompt payment for this happiness with grief or to complete for Muhsin the picture he had sketched in his soul, for the youth heard shouts and wails from the threshing area. Women were slapping their faces. He rushed to ask what had happened. He saw a group of fellahin coming from the center of the clover field, carrying a dying water buffalo. The women following behind were weeping. Muhsin thought at first this bellowing and wailing was without doubt for a person who had died or suffered a calamity. When he saw them carrying the buffalo, he still did not understand what he saw. When the group neared him, he asked what had happened. They told him that a water buffalo from Arjawi's house seemed to have been poisoned. They would slaughter it and were consoling the owner for its death. Everyone appeared to be grieving and mournful, as though the deceased were a man.

Muhsin was amazed once he had calmed down a little. He repeated to himself, "A buffalo? A buffalo!"

He felt like cracking jokes while he walked by these peasants who were carrying on like this over a buffalo. What would they have done if its owner had died? A woman passed him weeping. He asked her, "All this for a buffalo?"

She stared at him in a hurt way and replied, "I wish it had been one of the babies instead." Then she went on, paying no heed to anything.

Muhsin was a little embarrassed, for it appeared to him that no matter who he was, he was still far from understanding the feelings of these people. Possibly life in the town and in the capital had corrupted his heart. His sarcasm vanished at once, along with his intellect and his logic. His emotions returned, and he mourned with the fellahin and admired them.

He heard someone pounding on a peg. He saw that nearby some individuals were putting up a wooden post in the middle of the threshing area. Then the buffalo was brought. They suspended it there and began to skin it. The people of the estate gathered after a bit, except for the buffalo's owner. He had no doubt gone straight home to weep over the loss of one he would never see under his roof again. It would never share the space or floor of his room again. When it had been skinned and butchered, one of the friends of the bereaved began to distribute the meat, selling it to the farm laborers. Everyone came forward to buy without any haggling or hesitation. They seemed to think they had a duty to provide more than spoken consolation. They had to lighten the burden on its owner by getting its price together and giving that to him in compensation for its loss. One of the farm workers told Muhsin that this was the normal practice, the custom followed whenever one of them suffered a loss from his livestock.

They were not, like the people of the district capital, a people who stopped at talk. They shared grief in a way that was more than phrases to be repeated. It was an actual sharing to lessen the burden. Each of them sacrificed part of his wealth for the sake of the other.

Muhsin was silent in astonishment. That luminous happiness, the essence of which was beyond his ken, returned to him; it returned to him this time from sorrow, like life returning from death.

What an amazing nation they were, these Egyptian farmers! Did there still exist in this world solidarity as beautiful as this and a feeling of unity like this?

The next day, when Muhsin opened his eyes he heard the chirping of little birds. He saw the first signs of morning and of the rising sun. Everything around him was quietly coming back to life. His soul was radiant and he felt at peace. He went to the window and opened it wide. There the green field, the blue sky, the birds, the light, everything was smiling in the stillness. Deep within him, for the first time, he felt the beauty of life. He perceived for the first time the spirit pervading nature's creatures and tranquil inhabitants. A vague, hidden feeling welled up inside him that eternity was just an extension of a moment like this.

This intuition of Muhsin's was sound. If he had known more about the history of the Nile Valley he would have realized that its long-gone inhabitants had believed in no paradise other than that paradise of theirs and in no other form of eternity. For them, the meaning of eternal life after death was a return to this earth itself and then death and a rebirth there again . . . and so on in perpetuity, because God had not created any paradise besides Egypt.

The youth dressed quickly and went out to the fields. He went far into them, breathing in the wonderful earthy air, air saturated with the fragrance of life and creation. In just the same way, the water and silt of the stream and the irrigation canals carried life and creation.

Muhsin felt power and energy in his body. He took delight in life. He accepted it joyfully. He felt the love in his heart swelling to life like this healthy, vigorous vegetation blessed by the warmth of the sun . . . and why not, when everything around him was strong, vigorous, and growing? How beautiful life was!

Lovely singing reached his ears then. He turned to look. The fellahin were grouped nearby with scythes in their hands, reaping the harvest, which was piled in rows. They were all singing. One of them would start and the others would join in. The breeze carried their voices to Muhsin's ears. The sun had just come over the horizon, and the dawn light was still bleeding red from its birth. What was this song or hymn? Were they chanting a hymn for the morning to celebrate the birth of the sun the way their ancestors did in the temples? Or were they chanting in delight at the harvest that nowadays was their Beloved to which they sacrificed their work, toil, hunger, and freezing in the cold all year long? Yes, they had sacrificed all they had for the sake of this Beloved so it might be gracious unto them, bring them prosperity, and fill their homes with comfort.

Muhsin went toward them and walked among them. They were caught up in their work and singing. He began to look at them and at their faces in wonder. Their features and expressions all conveyed the same sense. Despite their differences, they seemed a single person with regard to this sense of work and hope.

He watched them while each carried what he reaped to add to the pile. They were looking at the collected harvest with loving interest, as though saying, "Toil and suffering are of no concern when dedicated to the one we worship."

At the end of that day, Muhsin returned to the house. What he had seen had left a spiritual impression he could sense but not comprehend. Caught by the contagion, he started thinking of his own beloved. But he straightened suddenly when a thought passed through his mind that made him tremble. Would he too be able to sacrifice for Saniya's sake, plunging himself in pain and suffering for her? Or was he not of the same blood as these Egyptian farmers?

When night fell, the croaking of frogs reverberated through the air, while the birds and animals became still. The moon rose. The air was heavy, and Muhsin found himself unable to sleep. The beauty of the night disturbed his peace of mind. He would gaze at the moon for a moment and ask himself, "I wonder if she too is looking at you now?"

He went outside to the threshing floor with his heart in flames. Perhaps he would discover something to divert him. He found that the farm workers were gathered in a circle by the light of the beautiful sphere. In the center they had placed the tea things.

Tea had become another idol for the fellah. The wandering Bedouin had introduced it and taught the farmer about it. The latter held fast to it while the Bedouins, as was so typical, forgot it. They knew no permanence in work or love and would not limit themselves to one residence.

The fellahin, however, developed a taste for it and found they could not do without it. They drank it communally as if conducting a prayer service after they finished the heavy toil of the day. They had made a small wooden stand for the teapot and placed it there like a statue on a plinth. One of them assumed responsibility for passing around the cups. This drink, however, sometimes cost them more than they could afford. Many a prosperous farmer became impoverished by the excessive cost of preparing it, consuming it, and inviting his brethren to sit together to drink tea.

Muhsin approached them. When the headman of the estate saw him, he rose in Muhsin's honor. He invited him to drink and presented him a cup. Muhsin had no objections. He sat down politely and modestly among them, near Shaykh Hasan, who cleared a space for him and spread it with dry clover stems.

The boy was pleased by that. The fellahin were a little shy in front of him at first, but he graciously encouraged them to speak. They proceeded with their down-to-earth discussions. Whenever one of them finished a cup, he went to the teapot. Shaykh Hasan felt that Muhsin wasn't consuming enough tea and wanted to get him another cup. The youth smiled and showed him the contents of his cup. He had only drunk one sip. One of them asked in a straightforward way, "The bey doesn't like the fellahin's tea?"

Muhsin replied that this wasn't the reason, it was just he was unaccustomed to it being made this way. "Why do you make it like this? It's black as ink and bitter as colocynth."

One of the laborers spoke up. "What, bey? Tonight it's as delicate as pump water."

Muhsin burst into laughter. The laborers were happy that they had been able to make the young bey laugh and to delight him. The conversation turned to tea and the peasants' love of it. To make and prepare it in this fashion required a great amount of both sugar and tea. Even so, the fellahin wouldn't shrink from sacrifice for its sake and from extra fatigue and work to raise money for it. Some of them craved it so much they sacrificed all they possessed, or nearly.

When the conversation reached this point, one of the laborers turned to Muhsin and, pointing to the long spout of the pot, asked, "Would you believe, by God, that twenty camels and two calves have flowed out of this spout?"

CHAPTER 6

Muhsin's anxiety returned. Days had passed without the promised letter arriving. He became so upset that he was oblivious to everything. His eye no longer saw anything. It was incapacitated. He didn't want to stay and wanted to return to Cairo right away. Whenever he remembered Saniya, it seemed to him he had been separated from her for years, not a few days. He wondered how he could tarry here and put up with being far from her any longer. He went to his mother to tell her he wanted to leave but found the house all topsy-turvy. He heard the clatter of bowls and dishes and the sound of tables being set and food prepared. He asked what was happening and was told that his father was going to host a dinner party for the English irrigation inspector and a renowned French archaeologist in honor of their visit to the province.

He looked for his father and learned he had taken the carriage to Damanhur to meet the guests. His mother was engrossed in supervising the preparations. When she saw him, she smiled and pointed out the stuffed lamb the cook was decorating with roses, marjoram, and posies. "Look, Muhsin! Tomorrow they'll be saying that our banquet was better than the governor's."

At that moment the estate's overseer, dressed in his magnificent gown of striped homespun, entered with a basket containing several pairs of pigeons and chickens. The lady looked at him and then asked distrustfully, "Is that all you could find on the estate?"

The overseer replied apprehensively but courteously, "The peasants are dirt poor, madam."

The lady scoffed, "Dirt poor! If you had used the whip you

would have brought twice as many. But you're a dunce of an overseer."

The overseer was silent. When he raised his head he pointed at the stuffed lamb with a smile. In an attempt to humor the lady he said, "What a blessing that is, lady. One of us fellahin—all kidding aside—tastes meat only at festivals."

She did not respond. Muhsin edged up to her and said, "Mother, there's more than enough food for two guests."

She replied, "I want our banquet to be better than the governor's." Then she turned on the overseer and glared at his clothes. She rebuked him, "Get lost, man, you peasant. Put on your best clothes!"

The man bowed his head in embarrassment. He did not utter a word but blushed a little. Muhsin discerned this secretly and felt sorry for him.

The lady noticed the overseer's silent dejection and attacked again with renewed force. "My God! Amazing! Why are you standing there? What are you waiting for?"

The man replied in a weak stammer with an anxious, innocent smile of embarrassment while looking at the floor, "This is my best, lady." He remained silent for a bit with his head down. Then he raised his head and said with simple conviction, while taking a hem of the garment in his hand and showing it to the lady, "Is this ugly, lady? By the life of the Prophet's head, it's homespun."

The lady did not deign to look at his thawb. She turned her back on him and walked off to supervise another task. Muhsin trailed after her. He wanted to speak to her in private so he could entreat her not to be so hard on these people. He wanted her to understand that these poor peasants were not into pomp.

At exactly one p.m. the estate dog began barking to announce the arrival of a stranger. The dust from the carriage and its magnificent horses could be seen at the bridge. The carriage passed under the sycamore and entered the estate's threshing ground. Two Europeans, who were wearing hats, descended from it, followed by the master of the house, the bey.

The guests stood for a moment gazing at their surroundings. They looked at the fields, which spread out green like the sea. The overseer and Shaykh Hasan stood before them, politely awaiting a command or signal. One of the guests, the English irrigation inspector, expressed a wish to have a look around the fields for a moment to see the drainage ditches and make sure they were clear. He wanted to see the sluice gates to find out their size and how they linked the canal and the plots of land. Everyone set off for the fields, and the bey gestured for the overseer and the headman to lead. So they hurried off in front. The bey unfurled his white parasol with the golden handle and raised it over the heads of the guests while he described for them the method of irrigation and drainage in the eastern quadrant, through which they were passing. The French visitor smiled admiringly at the levelness of the land and at its olivine color. He was astonished that all Egypt was like this, as if the ancient gods had especially leveled it and prepared it for the fine inhabitants of Egypt.

The bey turned toward him and asked innocently, "Isn't the land in France like this?"

The visitor replied, "France is all valleys or hills. You rarely find a region that's this level." Then he looked at the bey and said with a laugh, "France wasn't fortunate enough to have once been a home for gods who smoothed it out—unlike your land."

The bey did not understand what he was saying very well. Nonetheless he replied, "You're right, honored inspector; our land has been cultivated since antiquity."

The Frenchman perceived a more profound meaning in this statement than the bey intended. He agreed, "Yes, yes. You are a people with a deep-rooted civilization, not like the arriviste peoples of Europe."

The bey did not respond. The Englishman bent over to pick up a handful of earth, which he rubbed between his fingers. He murmured under his breath in admiration of the fertility of the soil, "Gold . . . gold!"

Then he gave a sign to return. So everyone went back to the house, where the table was spread and the two Nubian servants stood with their clean white gowns and their red sashes. The meal was served.

Muhsin at this time was beside his mother in the hall between the kitchen and the dining room. She was supervising the arrangement of the different dishes and foods. She herself rearranged anything she thought substandard before allowing the servant to take it to the guests. Muhsin stood watching. His mouth was watering in hunger and anticipation of the stuffed lamb. He looked forward to the return of whatever remained of it after the guests finished. His mother asked him to be patient: "The right thing is to let the guests eat first." Then the two of them would eat. His mother, however, was at that time preoccupied and absentminded. She was running here and there, supervising. She was agitated and implored God that the meal would conclude successfully and that the guests would leave happy and pleased. She wished she knew what the guests were saying just then about the food and its presentation. At times she would leave Muhsin and follow the servant cautiously. Drawing close to the door surreptitiously, she would peek and eavesdrop. Perhaps she would glean a word of praise from one of the guests.

The visitors finished the meal except for dessert and fruit, and the two servants carried in the plates of sweets. At that moment the bey scurried out of the dining room and went straight to his spouse to ask in a quick, significant whisper, "Where's the cheese? Cheese at once!"

His wife frowned. She looked at him gravely without moving. "Cheese? What cheese?"

"Yes! Right away! They're asking for cheese. They eat cheese at the end of their meals."

"Cheese! After eating all of that!"

"Right! Save us! Do me a favor!"

The lady immediately summoned her servants in a whisper and asked about cheese. She was told there was none at all except for some fat-free white cheese soaked in whey in a pot. She slapped her face and asked herself how to escape from this crisis. Her husband was whispering as loudly as he could,

"Gibna arish in whey . . . that's totally out of the question! Are foreign gentlemen going to eat whey? Impossible! We're to serve them whey with maggots? That's just not possible."

With a voice choking with despair, the lady said, "What a disaster for me! What will we do now? What on earth can I do now, sisters?"

Her husband asked censoriously, "Didn't you know that banquets must have cheese?"

The lady regained her pride and self-respect. Placing her hands on her waist she shouted at her husband, "You, sir, what are you saying? Banquets? I'm the one who understands what the picture is. I was raised in the houses of pashas. I know how Ottomans eat. Who says that after lamb stuffed with raisins, hazelnuts, and pine nuts; chicken and pigeon prepared blanquette-style and also with hazelnut sauce; and stuffed grape leaves, people eat cheese?"

"Here they are, asking for cheese. What will we do now?"

The lady relapsed into anxiety and despair. She began asking the servants again, insisting, entreating. Finally a maid appeared shouting with joy that a piece of "Greek" cheese had been found in the pantry. As soon as she announced that, the lady rushed toward her, as did everyone else. It was as if they had made an important discovery. Despair turned to joy. The bey was reassured and left his wife. He hurriedly rejoined his guests after making it clear to his wife that this piece needed to be served immediately. Finally the servant brought the piece of "Rumi" cheese from the pantry, but it was brown with age. Everyone realized that this piece had been left in the pantry for such a long time to be used to bait mousetraps. The lady hesitated a little, and her distress returned. But finally she resolved to let it pass. She told the servants, "Mice or cats . . . it's better than nothing. I mean, will they know?"

She took it greedily and, carrying it to the tap, washed it to remove the look of age and filth. All the members of the household followed her, the hangers-on and the servants. They stared at that piece of cheese in the lady's hand as though looking at a precious gem. Since they were all so interested in that rare piece of cheese, they wanted to help the lady. They gathered around her. One of them turned on the tap. Another suggested it be washed with a sponge and soap so that it became pure white again. A third thought washing might harm it and said it should be only wiped with a damp cloth. A fourth did not like washing or wiping and recommended scraping— that is, scraping off the soiled surface with a sharp knife. While everyone was full of these suggestions and this concern, the lady, who was grasping the piece, suddenly shouted, because in her excitement it had slipped from her hand and fallen into the drain. They were struck dumb for a moment. When they came to their senses they all swooped over the sink at once. They got the piece of "Greek" cheese out with some effort after a desperate struggle. They saw no alternative to washing it again. Once it was put on the plate and presented to the guests, the lady raised her head and sighed deeply.

The two guests finished eating and were served coffee. Then the bey appeared hastily in the hall to ask for Muhsin. The lady went to him. The first words to cross her lips were a question about the banquet. What had the guests said about the food and the presentation? The bey, however, did not answer her. Instead he asked her quickly, "Where's Muhsin? Where is Muhsin? They want to see him."

He wanted to tell her he had said he had a son at the competency level who knew English and that the honorable English inspector therefore wanted to see him. But his wife interrupted him. "Fine . . . fine! The important thing is what did they say about the banquet? What did they say about the cheese? Tell me!"

He leaned toward her and whispered in her ear, "They're very pleased!"

The lady's lips opened in a smile. She said with pride, vanity, and arrogance, "So you see, I've civilized you and raised you, peasant, loafer. Won't you congratulate me then?"

The bey laughed and said, "Fine! I congratulate you!"

She asked proudly and boastfully, "Wasn't I the one who told you to invite them?"

"Yes, you did."

"Listen to me all the time and you'll do splendidly. Tomorrow invite the governor too, so he'll know."

The bey scratched his head. Then he exclaimed anxiously, "But the cost!"

The lady cast him a glance that silenced him at once. He stopped thinking about the enormous sums squandered on banquets and parties for years. He started looking around in confusion. "Where's Muhsin?" he asked. "Where is Muhsin?"

The two guests, meanwhile, were sipping coffee, sunk in large chairs, their faces directed toward a window that was wide open. There lay before them a limitless green expanse and the total stillness of the siesta hour. The farm laborers were resting in their houses or under the shady Nile acacias and lebbek trees by the waterwheels. The animals were quiet too. The farm dog was lying down with one eye closed. Even the birds—the larks and wagtails—seemed to have declared a truce. They had settled in the branches over the heads of the prostrate laborers. They had ceased their chirping and begun to pass the time grooming their feathers with their beaks.

A lovely breeze was wafting over the guests at that time. The Frenchman had his eyelids half-closed; his head was leaning back. He began to draw on the cigarette in his hand. He seemed to be in an enchanted dream, but his English companion had not lost any of his energy, nor had he relaxed. Instead, he stuck his hand in his pocket, brought out his pipe, and began to fill it with tobacco. He was sitting upright with an erect posture. His movements were steady and his glance strong. When he finished filling his pipe he put it in his mouth and lit it. Then he stood up. He wanted to pace back and forth in the room or go outdoors to the garden. But his French comrade thrust a hand out and motioned gently for him to sit back down. He asked in a sleepy voice, "Where to? Doesn't this delicate breeze have any effect on you, Mr. Black?" The Englishman looked from him to the window as if searching for this breeze to see it with his own eyes. The fellahin had started then to rise in groups or one by one. Each was carrying his hoe or scythe so they could resume their work in the field.

The Englishman said to his companion, "All I see are swarms of men in blue shirts."

The Frenchman looked at the fellahin and said admiringly,

"What wonderful taste they have! The color of their clothing is like the color of their sky!"

A sarcastic smile appeared on the Britisher's face. He said, "You go too far if you ascribe taste to these ignorant people."

The French archaeologist answered him forcefully and with conviction, "Ignorant! These ignorant people, Mr. Black, know more than we do."

The Englishman laughed and said just as sarcastically, "They sleep in the same room with their animals!"

The Frenchman replied seriously, "Yes, precisely because they sleep in one room with the animals."

Mr. Black scrutinized him carefully, with a smile. "What a clever joke, Monsieur Fouquet."

The Frenchman replied, "No, it's a truth that Europe doesn't know, unfortunately. Yes . . . this people you consider ignorant certainly knows many things, but it knows by the heart, not the intellect. Supreme wisdom is in their blood without their knowing it. There is a force within them they're not conscious of. This is an ancient people. If you take one of these peasants and remove his heart, you'll find in it the residue of ten thousand years of experiential knowledge, one layer on top of the other, although he's not conscious of it.

"Yes, he doesn't know that, but there are critical moments when this knowledge and these experiences come forth and assist him without his grasping the source of this assistance. This explains for us Europeans those moments of history during which we see Egypt take an astonishing leap in only a short time and work wonders in the wink of an eye.

"How could that be possible if it were not for the layers of experience from the past? These have become instinctive, giving them a push in the right direction and helping them through critical times without their realizing it.

"You don't imagine, Mr. Black, that these thousands of years that are Egypt's legacy have vanished like a dream and left no trace in these descendants. Even inanimate things are subject to at least that much of the law of inheritance, for what are the earth and mountains except a layer-by-layer inheritance? Why should that not be the same for ancient peoples who haven't budged from their land, when nothing in their environment or nature has changed?

"Yes, Europe is in front of Egypt today, but in what? Only in that acquired knowledge the ancients considered accident rather than substance, a surface indication of hidden treasure that is not of any particular significance by itself.

"All that we arriviste Europeans have done has been to steal from those ancient peoples this superficial symbol without the buried treasure. For that reason if you take a European and open his heart you'll find it empty and desolate.

"The European lives on what he gleans, what he learns when he is young, because he has no inheritance or past to assist him unbeknownst to him.

"Deprive a European of schooling and he'll be unspeakably ignorant. Europe's only power is in the intellect, that limited goddess we must flesh out with our will. The power of Egypt is in the heart, which is bottomless. For this reason, the ancient Egyptians did not possess a word in their language to distinguish the intellect from the heart. The intellect and the heart to them could be expressed by one word: heart."

The French archaeologist fell silent for a time and glanced at Mr. Black's face to gauge his reaction. He found his features rigid and his lips open in uncertainty and doubt.

The Frenchman resumed his comments: "Yes, Mr. Black. These fellahin have taste . . . good taste! If you asked them about the word 'taste,' they wouldn't know what it means. We know very well the meaning of the word 'taste,' but rest assured that there are a great number of us who have wretched taste. Yes, this is the one difference between us and them: They don't know the treasures they possess."

At that, the Englishman rose and said sarcastically, "You Frenchmen think nothing of sacrificing facts to eloquence."

Monsieur Fouquet motioned for him to sit down and responded sharply, "Facts? The facts are on my side, Mr. Black. You are hinting at the current weakness of this people, isn't that so?"

"I don't like their manners either."

"Their manners?"

"Yes!"

"Rest assured, Mr. Black, that any corruption of their manners is not native to Egypt but introduced here by other peoples, like the Bedouins or the Turks, for example. Even so, none of that has affected the eternally existing substance."

"Tell me what this substance is."

"You doubt what I'm saying. I'll limit myself to telling you to beware. You should all be on guard against this people, because it conceals tremendous spiritual power."

Mr. Black looked at him gravely for a moment. Then he resumed his sarcastic smile and said, "Where are they concealing it, Monsieur Fouquet?"

The French archaeologist answered with calm conviction, "In the deep well from which those three pyramids emerged."

The Britisher asked languidly, "The pyramids?"

The French scholar replied at once, "Yes, the pyramids! Champollion said of them, 'I cannot describe them. So it must be one of two things. Either my words can never express a thousandth part of what I must say or even if I wanted to paint the palest picture of the reality, people would surely consider me wildly partisan or crazy, but I will say one thing, those people built as though they were giants sixty meters tall.'

"Philo of Byzantium in his book *The Seven Wonders of the World* said of them, 'Those people ascended to the gods and the gods descended to them.'

"Even the experts say it's incredible a project like this could be carried out. As our archaeologist Moret observed, 'It is a dream that surpasses the human level that was realized on this earth once but will never return.' Such are the pyramids!"

The Englishman looked at him with a smile and asked, "All this emerged from a well. . . . Which well?"

Monsieur Fouquet answered calmly, "This one!" He pointed to the left side of his chest.

"The heart?"

The Frenchman did not respond, nor did the Englishman say anything after that. Both men were silent for a time, and the room was quite still.

That was when the bey appeared at the door with Muhsin in hand. During all that time he had been putting on his suit and combing his hair. As soon as the bey cast a glance at that still room he disappeared at once with Muhsin. They retreated, treading softly, and neither of the guests noticed them.

The French scholar eventually sat up in his chair and lit another cigarette. He puffed smoke into the air and then said, "I see my words have left you with little to say, Mr. Black?"

The English inspector turned toward him and said politely, "I acknowledge that."

The Frenchman was silent for a while. Then he said, "Yes! We may be excused if we don't understand this, because language for us Europeans is a language of sensibilia. We cannot conceptualize the emotions that transform this people into a single individual able to bear on his shoulders tremendous stone slabs for twenty years with a smiling face and a happy heart. He accepted the pain for the sake of his Beloved. I am convinced that those creative thousands who built the pyramids were not herded in against their will the way the Greek Herodotus stupidly and ignorantly asserted. They rather came to work in droves, singing a hymn to the Beloved—in the same way their descendants go to gather in the harvest. Yes, their bodies suffered, but even that gave them a secret pleasure, the pleasure in sharing pain for a common cause.

"They contemplated the blood their bodies shed with a pleasure comparable to their pleasure in seeing the blood-red wine presented in vessels to the Beloved. This pleasurable sense of communal pain, the emotion of gentle patience, and the smiling endurance of torments had a single reason that all shared: The emotion of belief in the Beloved and of sacrifice, sharing pain without complaint or a groan—this was their power."

The English inspector straightened up in his chair at that. His features had assumed a look of serious interest, as though he had been brought up short by some of what he heard. At that moment a breeze blew in, carrying into that total stillness the sound of the farm laborers singing beautifully in the distance. The Frenchman craned his head. Then he pointed to them and said, "Have you seen people more wretched than these poor fellows in any other country? You're an irrigation inspector and know full well, Mr. Black, whether you can find anyone poorer than this Egyptian peasant or with a more dreadful workload. I know that too. I've conducted excavations in the villages of Upper Egypt and have gotten to know some of the peasants. I've learned a great deal. They work day and night in burning heat or stinging cold. A chunk of corn bread and a piece of cheese with a few chicory leaves and whatever else is sprouting—that's all. It is constant sacrifice and endless forbearance. In spite of that, they are singing. Listen, for a moment, Mr. Black."

The French archaeologist was silent for a bit as though trying to deduce the spirit of this song, which was carried by the breeze. Then he spoke up again. "Do you hear these voices issuing in unison from numerous hearts? Wouldn't you think they all flow from a single heart? I'm certain that these people take pleasure in this communal toil. This again is a difference between us and them. If our workers suffer pain together, they catch the germs for revolution and rebellion and are malcontents. When Egyptian fellahin suffer pain together they feel a secret pleasure and happiness about being united in pain. What an amazing industrial people they will be tomorrow."

The English inspector put his hand to his forehead for a moment as though reflecting. Then he said, "I didn't think you were serious when you claimed there's a link between Egypt today and Egypt yesterday."

The French scholar answered, "And what a link! I said and say again that the essence is eternal. These fellahin who are singing from a single heart are many different individuals joined into a single person by emotion and belief. They still retain in their hearts, even though they do not know it, that phrase with which their ancestors mourned their dead at funerals: 'When time passes over into eternity, we shall see you again; because you are going there, where all will be one.'

"Here today these grandchildren, the fellahin, once again, sense in the depths of their hearts the all that is one."

The French scholar lapsed briefly into silence, which the English inspector broke, saying, as though still under the influence of what he had heard, "How amazing!"

The French archaeologist replied, "Yes, but even so, if you remember that it was these emotions that built the pyramids, it won't seem so strange. Otherwise, how do you suppose this people built an edifice like this if all the people did not at a certain time turn into a single human mass relishing pain for a single goal: Khufu, the representative of the Beloved and a symbol of the ultimate."

The Englishman's eyes gleamed with admiration or perhaps anxiety. Lost in thought, he whispered, "You're right."

The French archaeologist added, as if to conclude his previous reasoning, "This present-day Egyptian people still preserves that spirit."

The Englishman asked him immediately, "What spirit?"

He answered, confidently and deliberately, "The spirit of the temple."

The Englishman took the pipe from his mouth and fixed his eyes gravely on the window. The Frenchman looked at him as though perceiving the anxiety in the Englishman's soul. He smiled imperceptibly. Then he placed his hand on his companion's shoulder and said suddenly, "Yes, Mr. Black, don't disdain those people, who are poor today. The force lies buried within them. They lack only one thing."

"What?"

"The Beloved."

The Englishman gave him a look, but he could not tell whether it was skeptical or approving.

The Frenchman answered him after a bit. "Yes, what they lack is a man from among them who will manifest all their emotions and beliefs and be for them a symbol of the ultimate. When that occurs, don't be surprised if these people, who stand together as one and who relish sacrifice, bring forth another miracle besides the pyramids."

At that moment the voice of the bey was heard at the door, greeting them. He said he had thought they were having a nap and hadn't wanted to disturb them.

Then he called Muhsin and presented him to them. They rose to greet him graciously, affectionately, and cheerfully. Muhsin blushed with embarrassment and modesty. His father invited him to speak, saying proudly, "Say something to His Honor the Inspector in English, Muhsin."

CHAPTER 7

Only two days were left of the week, but Saniya's letter hadn't arrived yet. Muhsin was almost insane with despair. The only reason he had been willing to be separated from her for this period had been a desire for a letter written by her. Doubt pervaded him again. He fell prey to the most distressing images and phantoms. But hope came to his rescue in time. He began finding excuses for her. He put all the blame on his aunt Zanuba, who might have forgotten. She might have neglected to carry out her promise to ask Saniya to draft the expected letter. This explanation satisfied him, and his anxiety was somewhat allayed. This did not prevent him, however, from losing hope of receiving the letter. He was forced to stop thinking about it and went dejectedly to the field to divert himself with the sights. When the time for the mail delivery came he did not pay attention to it the way he had.

Then he heard a voice calling him. He turned that way and saw Abd al-Maqsud summoning him to the house at once because the lady wanted him. Muhsin hurried back to the house, his heart pounding. He went inside, and his mother met him with a letter in her hand. She told him it had his name on it. She did not finish her words, for Muhsin's hand stretched out and snatched the letter with a mechanical, nervous motion. As soon as he got his hands on it, he stammered while looking at the envelope, "Oh! . . . Right! . . . For me . . . for me!"

Then, carrying it off without opening it, he headed for the door and disappeared faster than lightning, leaving his mother behind him, staring in astonishment.

As soon as Muhsin was out of the house, he put the letter in his pocket and ran here and there as though crazed. The world seemed to be too small to hold his happiness. Then he started searching around for an isolated place, far away, where he could read the letter. It occurred to him to go to the end of the field by the watercourse: verdure, water, and Saniya's letter. At once he started to run. He pressed his hand to his pocket as though he was carrying a treasure he was afraid would fall. When he got to the place he had selected, he sat for a time on the bank of the stream. Then he rose, for the spot didn't satisfy him. He sat down in another location. Then he gazed at the sights surrounding him. He was deliberately taking his time, seeking calm, and proceeding slowly, but his heart was pounding. He felt something compelling him to put his hand in his pocket and withdraw the letter.

Finally he did, but he didn't open it. Instead he kept turning it over in his hand, looking for a time at the postmark and then at the address. He scrutinized the handwriting. All the time his hand was trembling from joy while he was torn between two impulses: the desire to open the envelope at once and the desire to delay and proceed slowly, as though wishing to prolong his delight at receiving it or as though he feared if he read it now his pleasure would dissipate as soon as he finished reading it. Thus he lingered while the two desires struggled within him for a time. In the end curiosity triumphed. He started to open the envelope slowly and cautiously for fear of tearing it any more than necessary. He seemed to begrudge even a scrap of this precious letter that might be carried off by the wind. At last he got the letter out, spread it open, and read:

The Very Respected Mr. Muhsin Bey,
  To begin:
  Many greetings and inquiries about you and your health and your well-being, which is the very thing we request from the Lord of creation. We received the precious gift of your letter and learned that in it you had asked after us and about our health and well-being. May God multiply your blessings and never deprive us of you. We, by God, are very eager to see you. If you love your aunt, Muhsin, do not delay your return to Cairo any longer. Make it soon, God willing, because Cairo without you is depressing. In conclusion, your uncles and everyone on our end convey to you, the senior

bey, and the lady, your mother, the best greetings. May you
all be well.

—Your Aunt Zanuba

Muhsin was stunned and felt glum. He felt a little disappointed. What most astonished and perplexed him was the absence of any mention of Saniya in the letter. But he reconsidered
and found an apology for her. He told himself: *She's the one
who wrote the letter.* She knew Muhsin knew that, so it wasn't
necessary to mention her name. Or perhaps shyness prevented
her. Or perhaps she wished to remain behind the cover provided by his aunt Zanuba.

Muhsin reread the letter, assuming now that Saniya had
written it and that she was really the one addressing him from
behind a veil. But what a veil! And why this trite language that
followed the pattern used by scribes in the market and that
would only come from the pen of a public secretary or a petition drafter?

Did she mean it as a joke? Saniya indeed liked a joke and was
playful but was also cultured and educated. She read stories
and books. He could not imagine that this would be her
style. . . . She must be teasing him. Yes, it was a charming jest
from her! Right away Muhsin smiled. He read the letter again
from the beginning. He paused over each word to laugh in
happy admiration at the wit of his beloved. An idea that flashed
into his head doubled his admiration. His eyes had fallen on
the signature. He told himself: Yes, out of good taste, since the
letter was from Zanuba, she had chosen a style that matched
the signature of an uneducated person like Zanuba. No doubt
Saniya was both jesting to amuse him and make him laugh and
being sarcastic in a sub-rosa parody of Zanuba. What a brilliant mind she had! Without doubt he had never encountered
such stunning brilliance as Saniya's.

Notwithstanding everything Muhsin had inferred from the
letter, his heart continued to be anxious. He wished she had
revealed some of her feelings toward him. She forgot he was
living here solely on her memory and the remembrance of that

kiss planted on his cheek. She forgot that no matter what she did for his sake, she couldn't dispel his anxiety. She could never grant him total rest and reassurance. He needed an expression that would convince him a little, bring him some comfort, and grant him peace of mind.

He started rereading it to try to discern something more than this jest, which he did not particularly require. When he got to the expression: "If you love your aunt, Muhsin . . ." and so on and so forth, his eye stopped and his face blushed. For it seemed to him that this expressed Saniya's feeling for him from behind the veil of Zanuba. Yes, that was it. Were it not for her bashfulness, she would have said: "If you love Saniya, Muhsin . . ." and so forth and so on.

Muhsin's heart pounded rapidly at this thought. He paused for a little while and sent dreamy looks at the canal water flowing beneath his feet. He felt pleased and happy. Then he went back to the letter after a moment. He started to scrutinize that enchanting sentence to draw new meanings from it, to get to the very bottom of it, to squeeze from it the veiled emotions. "If you . . . love . . . Muhsin, don't delay your return any longer, because Cairo without you is depressing!"

True? . . . Is Cairo without me depressing in Saniya's opinion? This was what Muhsin started whispering to himself. He was almost out of his mind with happiness and excitement.

He folded the letter with great care after bringing it to his lips to kiss it fervently. He put it into his pocket avidly, rose, and returned to the house. He felt he wasn't walking on the ground but in the air.

When Muhsin entered the house his mother met him. She asked about the letter he had just received and gone off with. He told her it was from his aunt. He put his hand hesitantly into his pocket. His mother noticed that and put her hand out for the letter. The way Muhsin was acting may have appeared a little suspicious to her. The youth did not hesitate long. He was obliged to bring out the letter for his mother. He smiled, blushed, and said with a bit of a stammer, "My aunt asks after your health and Papa's. That's all!"

Then he carefully opened the letter and handed it to his mother. She was watching his mercurial expression. When she took the letter and read it, she was surprised to find nothing in it. As she returned it to Muhsin, she smiled. She understood Muhsin's behavior to be the result of nothing more than childish interest in a letter addressed to him . . . no matter how empty and silly it was.

She also observed Muhsin's care in putting the letter back into the envelope and his concern, deliberation, and avidity as he put it back in his pocket, as though he was holding something of great value. She smiled again.

Muhsin stayed with her for a bit but remained silent, as if he could not think of anything to say. Finally he started to move away. He wanted to burst out into the open again, to be alone. She stopped him, however, and scolded him. "Muhsin, you're always in the field! Won't you stay with me a little?"

He came back and sat down. He masked his annoyance with a smile.

His mother came toward him. She felt that her link to her son risked being hardly more than a legality. She had observed how reserved their relationship was for a long time and didn't know whether the cause was his separation from her for the past years to go to school in Cairo under the tutelage of his uncle Hanafi, the schoolteacher, or a difference of their natures as the boy approached the age of reason. Their tastes did seem to differ. For a time she had noticed he preferred to be alone or to play with young friends rather than to sit with her. Or was it her fault and that of her temperament, which was less interested in motherhood and its cares than in other desires and hopes? She didn't know. What made her think of this now was a strange feeling—perhaps jealousy or selfishness—when she observed the interest of the boy in Zanuba's letter. After contemplating him for a long time, she observed, "I think, Muhsin, you love your aunt more than me."

The youth did not reply. What he had in mind was something else: to rush out to the field and sit, this time in the shade of the turning waterwheel, to read the letter again.

CHAPTER 8

Muhsin could not bear to be away from Cairo a second more after that. What would keep him now that he had received the letter and read it a hundred times till he memorized it?

He told his parents he intended to leave and when. He gently reminded them about the rural presents he ought to take to his uncles. He deftly let them know that they should be generous this time with the presents. His secret intention was to encourage his aunt Zanuba to share some of them with Saniya. By the next day everyone had started to make preparations for Muhsin's trip. The baskets and the parcels were ready. They were filled with pots of rice mixed with pigeon and chicken, pastries, minin biscuits, country-style sorghum bread, and thin phyllo sheets folded like handkerchiefs, along with two jugs of honey, two tins of clarified butter, two baskets of rice, and approximately five hundred eggs.

These abundant presents were lined up in a long row, which Muhsin inspected with pride and satisfaction.

It was time to leave, and Muhsin put on his suit. He was happy and joyous, because he would be in Cairo in three hours. Yes, in only three hours he would be arriving at the home of his uncles next door to Saniya's house. For the first time Muhsin realized that he was Saniya's neighbor. For the first time he sensed the meaning and value of this. How many truths pass by a man without his seeing or grasping them until too late, until these truths have turned into sepia prints? It almost seemed man was destined to see in life nothing but dreams and images. Yes, he had always lived in the building next to hers, but he had never focused on that or appreciated it until today, when he was far away.

He was in front of the mirror putting on his fez. His eyes wandered as he reflected on these thoughts. When he had that feeling of being separated from her only by the wall between the two buildings, he felt drenched with bliss. His eye fell on his image in the mirror. He was delighted by it and looked at his reflection for a long time. His father suddenly came in, holding a watch, to remind him of the time. Muhsin roused himself, somewhat anxiously, and began to look around as though trying to make certain he wasn't forgetting any of his things. Then he headed for the door, following his father.

His mother had finished supervising the transportation of the goods. It had been decided that the baggage should precede Muhsin to Damanhur in a cart drawn by a pair of mules, while Muhsin would follow after it in the stately carriage, accompanied by his father. Muhsin's mother came toward him. The bey turned to his son and exhorted him, "Say good-bye to your mother right away. Otherwise there won't be enough time."

The youth went to his mother, who embraced him, instructing him to write regularly. Then she turned to her husband and asked him if he had given Muhsin his allowance. He answered quickly, "At the station!"

She said to him, gesturing in a way he understood, "Give him just what I told you. Otherwise, he'll be giving the money to his uncles."

Muhsin was offended and gave her a critical look to protest about the money. He said that his uncles had no need to take his money and that they were too good-hearted to do that. The youth did not know why those words stung him or what he felt for his uncles, who were also his companions.

His father noticed and said quietly, to avoid angering his wife, that he sent Hanafi Effendi a regular amount every month for Muhsin to stay with him and that the amount wasn't excessive.

The lady said rather dryly that all she meant was that Muhsin didn't like money and hadn't shown any interest in it since he was a child. She still remembered festival days when she had given him a riyal for the feast, thinking he would spend it like other children to purchase a flute, a balloon, or chocolate, but no. He had played with the silver coin for a while and then returned it. Astonished, she had asked, "What happened, Muhsin?"

He had replied, "All done."

Amazed, she had pressed him to say more. "All done how?"

He had said, "All done. I've played with it and now I'm done."

The lady was silent for a little. The bey said to her, "But today Muhsin hasn't asked for any more than the normal monthly amount."

The lady grew angry and said sharply and coldly, "Fine . . . fine . . . I know! I'm the one who is wrong. My point is that you should keep track so afterward you don't say it's the banquets that have used up all the money."

The train came and the servants stormed it with the bags and bundles. Muhsin climbed aboard, and the train moved off. He waved good-bye to his father on the platform. Then he sat down and withdrew into himself, trying to reconstruct the impact of the countryside on his soul or at least to retain a last image of his parents, whom he had just left. He found, however, that his head contained only one picture: Cairo-Saniya. There was nothing in his heart except the letter from her in his pocket. This letter was his entire past. His entire future was Saniya. Meanwhile, his soul was empty even now, as though he had never been in the country, hadn't seen anything, and hadn't met anyone.

Similarly, Muhsin had no desire to look at his fellow travelers or keep track of what was happening around him. Instead he took the letter from his pocket and began to read and reread it, pondering every expression. When he reached Cairo, the letter was still in his hand. Muhsin's father had sent a telegram to Hanafi Effendi giving the arrival time of the train so Muhsin would be met at the station. As soon as the train stopped, Muhsin rose and dusted himself off. Looking out the window, he gazed at the platform with terrific happiness. He ought to let his uncle Hanafi know where he was. It amazed him to find not only Hanafi but all his other comrades. The folks, all of them—Abduh, Salim, Mabruk, and Hanafi—had been standing there, watching the train thunder down upon them. Mabruk with laughable naiveté had his arm in the air, waving to no avail at the coach where he thought Muhsin was sitting. Muhsin didn't have sufficient time or a calm enough mind then to wonder why they had all come to greet him. Were they that eager to see him? Yes, the comrades in fact felt they had lost something when their fifth member departed. As soon as the telegram arrived, they joyfully hastened to meet him. Was that the only reason? Muhsin didn't know but was happy to see them. When he looked out the train window and saw Mabruk, who was pointing and talking in his usual way, Muhsin's heart filled with laughter; he felt he had returned to his native habitat.

CHAPTER 9

The setting didn't allow Muhsin more than a first quick greeting. When he mentioned to them the quantity of luggage he had with him, everyone rushed onto the train, with Mabruk in the lead. Each one carried what he could till they reached the station plaza, where they asked Mabruk to negotiate for them with the owner of a cart. When they had finished piling the bags and parcels on it and putting Mabruk on top of the bags and parcels, they took the carter's number and told him, "Go, boss, to Salama Street, number thirty-five."

Captain Salim said, "Pay attention to the baggage, boss."

Abduh counted the parcels and said, "Watch out, boss. Don't let any of the parcels drop on the way."

Hanafi said, "If you can't find the house, boss, ask around Al-Sayyida. There are a thousand who can show you."

The carter pulled on the reins and answered, "Giddap, you dog's donkey! No fear! How could I get lost? Didn't you say Salama Street in Al-Sayyida district?"

President Hanafi added to be certain, "There's a coffeehouse facing the building. All you need, boss, is to ask Master Shahhata, the owner of the coffeehouse."

Here Mabruk shouted at them from the top of the cart to protest that they were ignoring his existence. "And me—all kidding aside—am I nothing but a package on the cart?"

Muhsin laughed and acknowledged he was right. Hanafi looked at him and said apologetically, "You're right, Mr. Mabruk. Our mistake. Drive on, boss, and if you get lost ask the effendi who's on top of the baggage."

The driver raised his hand with the whip, and the cart started off, heading tipsily through Maidan Bab El Hadid. The donkey wore brass anklets, and Mabruk on the summit swayed back and forth. He looked back to his comrades with a smile as they watched him disappear. He started waving for them to hurry to the house at once to meet him.

The comrades headed for the streetcar stop after that. They got on and rode to Al-Sayyida Zaynab district. All the way they were asking Muhsin about his parents, Damanhur, and what he had seen. He answered them while observing their faces and voices. He seemed to notice a change in them. There was an unfamiliar resonance to what they said. He couldn't tell yet whether his observation was correct or just the imaginings of a new arrival. He glimpsed a quiet sorrow on their faces. Their voices had a tendency to fade away, followed by a long silence. They seemed to feel no happiness or joy. Yet, amazingly, he sensed they were closer to him than before. He felt that the only happiness any of them experienced now was occasioned by his return.

Muhsin wasn't able to sort this out at the time; he was on the streetcar. But this was his first impression on seeing them. He kept wanting to ask about that on the way. He was afraid, however, that his feelings were erroneous and that all this was occasioned by the impact of their first meeting. Moreover he had to answer their questions and narrate the events of the journey. He didn't want to ask them too impetuously. There would be plenty of time. They too, for their part, withheld their news, as though they didn't want to be hasty or to seem preoccupied by their affairs.

They reached the house. When Muhsin's eyes fell on the neighboring residence that had a brass plate with the name of Dr. Ahmad Hilmi engraved on it, his expression changed and his heart beat faster. Abduh and Salim may have been watching him at this moment, for they exchanged glances. They were filled with something, but it was impossible to say whether it was peace or pity.

They all went up the stairs. On their way, Muhsin passed the first-floor apartment occupied by their neighbor Mustafa Bey. He smiled and remembered at once his aunt Zanuba. He turned to one of his companions and asked if this rich neighbor still lived here or whether he had moved. Glances were exchanged again. Then he heard Salim reply in an odd voice, "Still here, sir!"

They finally reached their floor and entered the familiar apartment. Zanuba met them, praising and glorifying God and welcoming Muhsin's return, asking him about his parents' health and looking at him. She said, "May you be safe and well fed here."

Then she commenced to recite charms over him and to pray for him to God and Umm Hashim. Muhsin looked around the house, acquainting himself with what he had left a week ago, as though he had been absent for a year. He looked at the table set in the middle of the hall. He remembered them gathering around it. Then he craned his neck to see the bedroom with the four beds lined up side by side. He turned his head to study the stairway to the roof, to the place he had met Saniya for the first time. He looked into Zanuba's room with the cabbage-colored mattress spread on the ground on top of the old red kilim where his aunt would sit with him while he naughtily devised stratagems to get news about Saniya from her without exciting her suspicion. He saw all of that; it shot through his mind in a flash. He found nothing changed from before in the apartment's arrangement or furnishings.

Yes, nothing had changed, but all the same he had some inkling that something had changed. What? Muhsin turned to his comrades' faces to investigate them. He found them silent and inscrutable.

He turned to Zanuba. At first he was unable to discern anything unusual in her expression or to observe in her voice and gestures anything to inspire some special feeling in him. Yet, it did not escape him, when he scrutinized her eyes, that there was something in them that did not fit with that happy smile and delight with which she received him. Yes, her eyes looked sad, but she lowered them at once when he gave her this searching look. She asked him if he was hungry. He replied he would only eat with his uncles after the luggage arrived, because he was bringing them pots of rice with pigeon and chicken. Their spirits were raised; they rejoiced and smiled when chicken and pigeons were mentioned. Zanuba told Muhsin to change his clothes while waiting for the luggage. Muhsin went to the communal bedroom, approached the large collective wardrobe, and opened it. He cast a glance at the clothing of different sizes and colors it contained. It reminded him of the displays at Suq al-Kanto. Then he went to his bed, which was next to President Hanafi's. While Muhsin was unbuttoning his clothes, Hanafi said cheerfully in welcome, "Greetings to my neighbor!"

Captain Salim gestured with his hand to the room and the bed and said to Muhsin in a playful way but with a murky, anxious ring to his voice, "You've returned to the barracks, hero."

Hanafi said with a smile, "The barracks are at full force now!"

He recalled that he had felt something was lacking whenever he had remembered that Muhsin's bed was empty. The feeling of deprivation had prevented him from sleeping at times.

Muhsin laughed. Looking at Hanafi he said, "Kept you from sleeping? Impossible! There's nothing that could keep you from sleeping, ever. Remember the day you fell asleep in the station and made me miss the train?"

He turned to the others, wanting to tell them what happened so they could join in the fun. But Hanafi signaled to him, entreating him not to share this information with the folks.

Silence crept over them for a moment. Abduh, who hadn't uttered a word since he entered, said, "We're short Mabruk." These words turned everyone's thoughts in another direction. They rose to look out the window for the arrival of the cart with Mabruk on top.

Hanafi got off his bed, where he had been sitting and said, "They must have gotten lost. With Mabruk in it, will it ever arrive? I bet he fell off the cart without the driver noticing or stopping."

A thought suddenly came to Muhsin. He stopped removing his clothes and rebuttoned his jacket. The presents would arrive shortly, and he could go meet Saniya. Yes, he knew it would be impossible to wait patiently until tomorrow to see her.

Muhsin had scarcely finished putting his clothes back on

when he heard his comrades shouting at the window, "Here it is!"

That was followed by the commotion President Hanafi stirred up when he crowded against his comrades at the window. He put his spectacles on his nose and focused his eyes where his colleagues were looking. He confirmed that the cart was in fact in sight, at the end of the street. It was shaking and jumping about like a sinking ship as it made its way over the washboard road and its potholes. On top was Mabruk. To those watching him from afar he seemed to rise and fall. Sometimes only his hand or arm could be seen directing the driver toward the house; at other times the entire top half of him appeared. He was clasping a small package!

The cart finally reached the house and stopped at the doorway. Abduh suggested they should all go down to help Mabruk get the parcels up. As soon as he said that, he headed for the door of the apartment and hurried down. The rest of the folks were right after him, including the honorary president. Muhsin remarked that Hanafi Effendi descended the stairs with amazing energy, ready for work. He laughed to himself, grasping the secret: *By God, what's set Uncle Hanafi in motion today is the pots of rice.*

Zanuba was at that time in her room waiting for Muhsin to finish changing his clothes. When she heard the noise they were all making on the stairs, she went out and looked down at them from above. She asked what was happening. President Hanafi answered her with innocent satisfaction, as he brushed against Salim's shoulder at the bottom step, "The cart's here! Get the trenchers, pots, and dishes."

In less than ten minutes the parcels were lined up in the dining hall. All the folks gathered after paying the driver for his services. Zanuba stepped forward. They had authorized her to open the items, distribute them, preserve them, and to deal with them according to the dictates of wisdom and justice. She took a knife and began to cut and undo the bands on the baskets and to take out the baked goods—minin, battaw, and ghurayba—to put in a large dishpan.

Mabruk watched the motion of her hand going from basket

to pan. He stared at the sorghum bread, and his mouth watered. Finally, no longer able to wait patiently, he hazarded a comment. "I'm telling you, Miss Zanuba, pray for the Prophet!"

Zanuba did not respond. She was preoccupied with her work and paid no attention to him. He grudgingly remained quiet for a bit. Then he resumed his attack by clearing his throat. He approached her at last and said, "I don't have any right to interfere—all kidding aside. Give me what's mine and then tell me to go to hell."

She looked at him askance without ceasing her work. She said, "By the Prophet, find something to do."

But Abduh, who thought Mabruk was right, suggested that the loaves be counted and then divided equally between them, so that none of the folks would take a single one more than his companions. Each of them would be allowed to go off with his share to do whatever he wished. He would be free to eat his entire portion in one day or spread it over several. The idea pleased everyone, and President Hanafi shouted enthusiastically, "That's fair!"

So Zanuba gave in and began to count the battaw and minin to divide them equally. Muhsin, however, remembered Saniya and her share of the present and became rattled and anxious. Finally he found the courage to say with some agitation, "I think, aunt, you ought to send a little to the neighbors' house. They must know of course that I've come from the country bringing—"

He choked on the rest of the sentence when he noticed a strange, sudden change of expression on the faces of his comrades and especially on his aunt's face. Zanuba stammered in disapproval, "The neighbors?"

Muhsin felt his heart sink. He turned to his comrades to clear up the matter with them. He found they looked annoyed and apprehensive. They seemed to wish to postpone something that would spoil their enjoyment of a moment like this. He noticed that Salim was twisting his familiar mustache for the first time since he had come. But this time he was twisting it gravely, compulsively, not with satisfaction and pride the way he once had. He noticed as well for the first time that

Salim's mustache had changed. It was no longer glisteningly erect. Instead it had become droopy, with the ends hanging down. He seemed to have given up using wax on it for a long time. He turned to his aunt Zanuba and noticed that her lips were trembling and quivering as though she was about to burst into speech. Her hands had stopped work. When she observed the silence, she got her nerve up and repeated in a fiery tone, "Neighbors! What neighbors?"

Muhsin felt a calamity brewing. It was taking shape, about to collapse on his head. His eyes wandered over his companions. At that point, Abduh raised his head and gestured nervously with his hands to Zanuba. In a dry, angry voice he said, "Be quiet now. There's no need!"

But it was enough for Zanuba to broach this subject for her mouth to open wide. She had not stopped talking about it for a week. Whenever she spoke about it, she felt she was quenching a thirst. For that reason, whenever she had met one of her acquaintances, whether close or distant, she had said the words she shouted now: "What neighbors, fellow? The house of Dr. Hilmi with the two horns! The house of Saniya, the whore!"

Abduh trembled with rage and shouted at her, "I told you, shut up. That's enough name-calling."

With affected disinterest Salim said, while twisting his mustache as vainly as a vanquished person, "There's no need for us to take an interest in a matter like this. Is your Saniya that important? I, by God, never cared for her."

Despite his nervous agitation, Abduh stared at him mockingly, as though to say: *The fox, unable to get them, pronounces the grapes sour.*

Zanuba gestured to Abduh and Salim to tell them to leave her and her concerns alone. She was screaming, "Right. Can't I tell Muhsin what happened?"

Yes, she would have told Muhsin what had happened while he was away, if Muhsin at that time had been among the living or in a condition permitting him to hear. Muhsin, as soon as her expression "Saniya, the whore" had lodged in the pit of his heart, had blanched, and his body had grown cold. He was oblivious to everything around him. He grasped the edge of the table to try to steady himself as he rose. He stared at the old, faded oilcloth spread over it, and his gaze froze. He no longer heard anything of that clamor, chatter, shouting, or fuss that Zanuba stirred up with her long, detailed story of what had happened that ill-fated week.

CHAPTER 10

The only sleep that Muhsin got that night came in spurts that did nothing for him. He dozed off occasionally from the fatigue of this day filled with travel and sorrow. Sleep would flow through his joints and quell the strife within him. But that lulling sleep lasted only a few minutes. Then a sound like a prolonged whistle or sharp scream would pierce his eardrums. When he made it out, it was a voice saying, "Saniya, the whore! Saniya, the whore!"

Sleep would fly away. He felt that his heart had been snatched or had fallen at his feet and sunk into the earth, opening two enormous red eyes in it. Then he would conjure up everything that had happened that day, remembering Zanuba and the features of her face contracted in rage. She had fumed and frothed as she narrated what had happened. Among other things, she told him, while he was only half-conscious, "From the day you left, Muhsin, she was flirting with him from the balcony."

Then, after that, she had said, "If only the matter had been limited to flirting from the balconies—but their relationship has now reached the point of exchanging letters and messengers. Not a day goes by without Saniya's maid, wrapped in her cloak, being seen heading in secret toward Mustafa Bey's. She stays in his residence in the downstairs apartment long enough to deliver the letter to him and for him to furnish her the answer."

She writes him . . . writes him messages and letters every day. Muhsin had been waiting for just one letter in Damanhur.

He remembered the truth that had spoiled everything for him. He remembered the letter that he had received at the farm and memorized. He remembered what Zanuba had said when he roused and braced himself enough to ask, "So, aunt, the letter I received from you—who wrote it for you? Not Saniya?"

Zanuba's reply had been, "Saniya? Does she have time for us or is her time devoted to the man, the giddy libertine, who lives downstairs?"

The youth mustered all his waning power to ask her despairingly, "So who wrote it?"

She replied, "The scribe opposite Al-Sayyida courthouse."

"A scribe?"

Yes, Zanuba's fury and anger had not been satisfied by exposing Saniya and making her faults known to people, with or without cause. Fury and anger had driven her to go to a petition writer for the court at Al-Sayyida Zaynab to get him to write an anonymous letter for her to send to Saniya's dignified father in order to expose the girl to him and stir up a storm in her house. She had done all that because Mustafa Bey had grown fond of Saniya and slighted Zanuba, although she had been the first to court him. For that reason Saniya was deemed a whore by her, and Mustafa Bey had become a giddy libertine.

That was her real reason for going to the public scribe of Al-Sayyida courthouse. She had merely seized this opportunity to ask him to write, as a little extra, a short letter for her to send to Muhsin.

Muhsin saw clearly now this was the truth about the cherished letter that he knew by heart. Saniya hadn't written him a single word. She knew nothing about him. It was of no interest to her whether he was in Cairo or away.

Muhsin couldn't bear the thought. He sat up in bed as though he had received a sudden blow and started hitting his head with his hands, wishing to end his life. What point was there to his life now? What was he to do with it when it was empty of . . . ?

He did not dare to mention her name. In fact, he almost moaned out loud but stopped his mouth with the covers. Then he looked around him anxiously and found they were all asleep. His neighbor Hanafi was snoring in his bed, his mind at rest. The rest of the folks were sleeping tranquilly. It was, however, the tranquility of people who have yielded and given in. Was it possible for him to yield too when he had lost everything in life? Why should he sleep? Why should he wake up tomorrow?

He pulled the covers over his face and body. His forehead was dripping with sweat. He began to pray to God fervently that he would fall asleep and never wake up. He closed his eyes with wild, nervous determination as though wishing to convince God of the force of his will. He remained for a while waiting for death and soliciting it, till sleep came to him. Then he slept deeply and experienced the most beautiful dream of his life. He saw first that everything he had heard about Saniya was a lie and an invention. Mustafa Bey had left the building and the area, even all of Cairo, to return to his farms in the provinces, where he had married the daughter of one of the local notables, a cousin of his. Muhsin, wearing his new suit, had gone to Saniya with the present he had brought her. She had greeted him at the top of the stairs clad in green silk garments that fluttered as though an unseen breeze was moving them. She put her arm out to him and kissed him on his right cheek. It was a fragrant kiss that filled his nostrils. He didn't know whether the fragrance was from her clothing or whether the whole room exuded a beautiful perfume. She gazed at him through her long black lashes until those lashes drooped like a tiny silk fan descending on her cheek. She began to fiddle with the buttons on her jacket without looking at him—as though chiding him. Finally he heard her whisper to him, "Didn't I tell you, if you love me, you won't stay away from Cairo any longer?"

Muhsin roused himself a little from the intoxication of the kiss. He told her he hadn't been slow to return. Just as soon as he had received that dear letter, which he always kept with him at his breast wherever he went—as soon as he had read and reread it—he had decided to depart. He had packed up his belongings and come to Cairo. She seemed to be half-convinced. At last she led him to the piano room and played the keys with her svelte fingers. The maid entered carrying glasses of red fruit punch. Muhsin trembled a little when he saw the maid. He didn't know why. He drank with pleasure. The maid exited. He watched her leave with a frightened look. Then he suddenly turned toward Saniya and caught her gazing at him stealthily in that languid way. When she saw him catch her by surprise, she lowered her eyes with their long black lashes and fell silent. Muhsin's heart pounded, and he felt tipsy.

Saniya rose suddenly and leapt back to the piano, wanting to play something else for him. After a delicate sigh, she smiled enchantingly at him. She said in a whisper as she gazed at him again, "Oh, Muhsin, if only you truly loved me as much as I love you!"

The youth did not know what to reply. Perhaps he was incapable of answering, for he was oblivious to everything, even to himself and to her. He perceived only one thing: that all the treasures of the earth and other worlds would not equal what he had won with this little sentence and that he was grasping his happiness—a happiness people describe without experiencing it—with his hand. Indeed here it was filling his palm. Here he was putting it in his pocket. No, in his heart. It was filling his heart to capacity, even weighing it down, as though this happiness were pure gold. Yes, it weighed his body down now too. It was currently pulsing through his entire body in spurts. He felt his body being stuffed with it, like a sack being filled with gold. He could scarcely breathe from joy. Happiness was strangling him. It had reached his throat. The joy would choke him if it didn't spill out. The happiness was about to pop out of his mouth. It was puffing up his chest and belly, searching for an exit. Yes, he needed to release some of it. He was in distress. How heavily this gold weighed on his chest!

Muhsin rolled over in bed with a smile on his lips, his mouth open, breathless from carrying the weight of his happiness. He wanted to do something. To run. To rise and tell . . . to tell people, to speak, to jabber, to leap, to wallow in the dirt, to roll about on the ground. The last Muhsin actually did. He rolled about on his bed till his head ended up at the edge. He opened his eyes and discovered that his head was hanging off the mattress, looking at the floor. His mouth was open as though he had been vomiting.

The harbingers of day showed at the window. The sun's rays took command of the large, communal wardrobe.

Suddenly poor Muhsin remembered everything. The grim truth in its entirety came back to him. He knew his happiness was a dream that had expired. He had vomited it and emptied his heart of it now at daybreak. Not a drop of it remained to nourish him or resuscitate him. The room went black to his eyes again as he looked at the sun's disk, which had risen fully. It seemed to him to be a black sphere . . . black ebony . . . black hair. It did not beam light and whiteness to the world. No, black . . . blackness.

He remembered that for fear of this day he had wanted to die during the night. In place of death, God had granted him a delightful dream in order to increase his torment when he woke and the truth became apparent to him. The image of Saniya in that beautiful dream—the kiss, the gaze, and her lashes—passed through his imagination. Saniya now would not know him, busy as she was with her love for Mustafa. She did not know or want to know whether he had returned. This terrifying split between dream and consciousness loomed before him, and he moaned to himself like an animal being slaughtered. He shoved his head under the pillow and panted out a plea to his Lord, mixing it with pain and censure: "Never! Shame! No way!"

CHAPTER 11

It passed through Muhsin's mind that the folks would wake shortly and see him in this state. So he rose quickly and slipped his clothes on in a few minutes. Then he left the house and headed for school without eating any breakfast. On his way he passed the doorway of Dr. Hilmi. He bowed his head in pain and didn't look at it. He walked beneath the infamous balcony without raising his head. It seemed he no longer had the right to look, not even at her wooden balcony, where he had frequently stood beside her and gazed out with her at the street and the small coffeehouse opposite. Then he suddenly remembered the last time he saw it—when he had gone to say goodbye to her shortly before his trip to Damanhur. She actually had been looking at the coffeehouse with such interest that he had felt apprehensive and doubtful. Mustafa Bey had been sitting on the street that day, looking furtively at her balcony too.

His heart had warned him then that all was not well, but she had known how to dispel his suspicions. She had acted toward him in a way that made him the happiest man. Yes, he could still feel her kiss on his face—had she been slyly seeking to deceive him? The tear she had shed for him, hadn't it been pure and genuine? Impossible! He could not conceive of her trying to deceive him. No matter how she was acting now, he couldn't doubt for a moment the nobility of her character. Then, what had happened? What had made her change so quickly toward him?

At that, an idea came to Muhsin and penetrated his heart with a flash of hope. Why should he judge her before seeing her? Why not go to her and ask for an explanation? Perhaps she would deny all or some of what he had heard. Or perhaps if she saw him, she would remember or repent or be moved to pity or . . .

Yes, he should go. He enjoyed some peace for the first time since learning of the disaster. This flash, however, was shortly blotted out by a black cloud that formed in no time. What a simple boy he was! Did he suppose that Saniya today was the same as yesterday? How could he—after this bond had developed between her and Mustafa, after the love letters—aspire to anything or imagine that he had any rights with her, starting with the right to visit her?

Then there was something else: How would he go? What pretext could he use when relations between the two households were now severed? His aunt Zanuba had cut them with her jealousy, and Saniya had moved farther away than the stars in the sky.

Thus he made his way through the streets, buffeted by these opposing ideas, moving from hope to despair, without fate leaving him the comfort of either. At last he reached the school and entered the courtyard with his head down. He kept his distance from the other pupils in order to be alone until the bell rang to go into class.

From time to time he raised his head and cast a glance at those droves of students gathered in numerous circles, each circle uniting a group of brethren who were laughing and joking together, relating what they had seen that was strange and unusual during the vacation or narrating what they had done during it and how they had spent it.

Most of the time, at the center of a circle was a pupil who was older, brighter, wittier, or funnier than the others. He was the one steering the conversation. He would narrate and relate stuff while everyone listened to him, laughing happily in enjoyment at every word he said.

Muhsin remembered that he had always been that beloved pivot for the listening pupils of his class to gather around. To his right had been his trusted friend Abbas, who buoyed him with his confidence and trust, his blind faith and total enthusiasm for everything Muhsin said.

Muhsin remembered the noon break, when he and Abbas, with the others crowded around them, had passed the time trading poems beside the school wall beneath the main stairway. When their quiver was emptied of poems, Muhsin would become a persuasive preacher, debating with eloquence, imagery, and allusions before this small crowd of admirers. When he happened to turn toward the place by the wall under the stairs, he was astonished to find a group of the students from his class there—Abbas among them—who kept looking at the gate of the school, as though waiting for someone to arrive. Who could they be waiting for now except Muhsin? But what could Muhsin say to them today? He who had left them just before the holiday the happiest of men returned to them as another person. He was afraid they would finally notice him, so he moved farther away and hid until the bell rang and the pupils lined up in the schoolyard. The queue began to move forward to the classes. At that moment Muhsin ran quickly and tagged along at the tail of his row without anyone noticing him till he entered the classroom last. They turned and recognized him, shouting at him. Abbas trotted toward him, and Muhsin pretended to be happy, affecting a smile. He tried to joke with them. To himself he was praying that God would speed the teacher's arrival so he could be spared having to pretend and the class would leave him alone.

The teacher came soon, and the students allowed Muhsin to go to his place. They all rose respectfully for the teacher, although Abbas, who sat behind Muhsin, kept nudging him with his arm, trying to get him to talk to him, not wanting to wait till the end of the period. Muhsin gently ignored him until the teacher calmly began to deliver his lesson.

This total calm proved to be the best environment for reviving Muhsin's thoughts and reflections. He was speedily submerged in seas within himself and forgot the class period, the lesson, and the teacher, who began to discuss his lecture with his pupils. Then it was Muhsin's turn. Till that day Muhsin's status had been high with his teachers and his peers. He was known for his seriousness, intelligence, and attentiveness. When the teacher asked him today about the lecture topic, it became clear at once that he had not been paying attention to anything said throughout the hour. His teacher, who was astonished and amazed at this behavior from Muhsin, asked in disbelief and surprise, "What's happened, Muhsin? What's on your mind?"

The youth, who had stood up, mumbled as though just waking up, "It's nothing, sir . . . nothing."

The teacher softened his tone and said, "A student returns from a vacation energetic, relaxed, refreshed, ready to study, and eager to learn—isn't that so, Muhsin?"

The boy hung his head in shame, confused and hurt. The whole class was looking at him. He heard Abbas whisper behind him. Abbas was sorry, grieved, and even angry. He didn't want this to happen to his friend, whom he cherished, believing him to be faultless and perfect. This hurt Muhsin all the more. He sat down, concerned and distressed. He was determined to pay attention to the lesson while he was in class. In a desperate, nervous motion he imposed the force of his will on the muscles of each of his eyes, which opened wide, gazing at the blackboard with long, steady looks. He emptied his mind of everything to focus on the teacher alone, no matter what it cost him. He kept struggling to achieve that and knit his brow as sweat poured from him.

Muhsin's willpower was fruitless. The poor fellow could not control his errant thoughts, which were stronger than he was. The day passed, and the pupils went home. He left with his head down, dragging his tail behind him, after making a bad impression on his teachers and most of his comrades. They were no doubt puzzled by him and what had come over him. The bewilderment of his friend Abbas was the most extreme, especially when he informed Muhsin that unfortunately his father wouldn't allow him to register for the arts section and that, for this reason, he was forced to break his promise to Muhsin. Abbas was anticipating that Muhsin would be angry, annoyed, or sorrowful at least. How astonished he was when he saw that Muhsin was unfazed by the news and that his face showed no interest.

Muhsin's head contained only one thing: the empty life stretching before him. How could he fill it? How could he patiently traverse the far-reaching future and the long days to come? He heard within himself a mocking voice answer sarcastically, "What were you doing before you fell in love? Go back to what you were before."

The youth smiled bitterly and gave the sky a rebellious look of anger, as though shouting from his depths: *Go back to what I was before? Yes, I lived without love and lived happily, but it was the happiness of a blind man who did not see beauty, light, or life. You opened the eyes of this blind man and made him see, dazzling him. Do you think if you put him back in his prior darkness he can recapture his prior happiness?*

Muhsin saw suddenly that he was in Al-Sayyida Square. He trembled when he remembered he would be forced to return home, where he would sit with his companions: his uncles and his aunt.

They would without doubt see from his face how he felt. He stood, hesitating, not knowing what to do. Then, suddenly, his glance fell on Al-Sayyida Zaynab's barbershop. All at once he became as pale and motionless as a corpse, because he had glimpsed Mustafa Bey coming out with white powder still on his chin. His small golden mustache had been trimmed in the latest fashion. He was strutting along in a beautiful suit. In his hand was a silk handkerchief the same color as the suit. He placed it elegantly in his left breast pocket as an emblem of his taste. His face was aglow with pleasure and contentment.

The square seemed a cheerless place to Muhsin. Without any premeditation, he made his way to the mosque. In his heart he felt dismay that this man might have seen him. Trembling, he quickly removed his shoes and crossed the carpet of the mosque to the shrine. He secreted himself in one of the corners of the dark mausoleum, which was lit only by a large chandelier hanging from the top of that magnificent, lofty dome. Muhsin grasped the brass bars of the grille and began to whisper desperately from his innermost heart in a staccato, nervous voice, "O Sayyida Zaynab! Sayyida Zaynab! Sayyida Zaynab!"

He began weeping, and his tears fell on the carpet of the shrine. He suppressed his sobs so the visitors around him wouldn't hear them.

CHAPTER 12

At the same hour, Abduh was in his school at a drafting table, determinedly working on the assigned engineering project. The fact was that since the day of the Saniya story his despair had been channeled into work. When he concentrated on his assignment at his college, nothing disturbed him except the image of Mustafa whenever it passed through his head. For this reason he could not bear to have that story mentioned in his presence, or the name Mustafa uttered. It humiliated and enraged him. He would shout at anyone who broached the topic in his presence, "That subject is closed, people. My brain is hurting me." Then he would leave the room at once, moving nervously.

Until the last moment his pride hadn't permitted him to imagine that Salim, the braggart show-off, deserved to beat him. Salim's claims and boasts about what had happened when the piano was repaired hadn't been enough to convince Abduh. As for the lad Muhsin, he was too young to be taken seriously. This was the way he saw things until the day the handsome, wealthy young man, Mustafa Bey, appeared in the field. Then his self-confidence took a beating. He was foaming and frothing to himself, making threats without being able to carry them out. He lacked a true feeling of malice. All this froth floating on top concealed beneath it nothing but pure water. The upshot of the matter for him was that after a few days he devoted himself to work, attempting by determined force of nervous willpower to forget.

His disdain for Salim turned into affection and solidarity. It had been like that between them before their competition and rivalry. Despite all that, however, he still had a feeling that some light within him had been extinguished. Neither work nor anything else could compensate him for that sweet hope and those few beautiful imaginings that had brought tenderness to his dry, stiff life.

The image of Saniya came to his mind then, and he couldn't keep from throwing down his pen. He left the drafting table and angrily went out into the gardens surrounding the school in Giza. He realized that his life lacked something. He perceived that intuitively. Neither his intellect nor his mouth dared put that into words. For this reason he attributed his depression, anger, and this exodus to the gardens to something else. He was either dissembling or lying to himself when he walked along, saying to himself in a peevish, rebellious rage, "Work, work, work! There's nothing to life but work. We were created only to work . . . like asses!"

He passed by a green field planted with lettuce, and his eyes were filled with this greenness. He trembled, remembering at once the day he went to the neighbors' house to repair the electric wiring. He had seen Saniya flutter from time to time before his eyes in her green silk dress. It had seemed she was intentionally letting him see her from a distance. Her delicate voice when she asked whether Abduh Bey would like a cold drink or coffee! Abduh sat down on a wooden bench he chanced upon. He freed his soul to dream of the past and to picture it however it wished, enlarging and exaggerating the image according to its desires.

He well remembered what he had said and knew the ring of her voice. Everything about her that day indicated she was interested in him and in his presence. The question of the electrical wiring might even have been a pretext.

He did not remember seeing her much. The first time had been the day he, along with his comrades, stole a look at her through the cracks in Zanuba's door. The last had been the day he repaired the electrical wiring. He had had an excellent opportunity that day to fill his eyes with her, even though she would appear from behind the doors like a fleet antelope. She had peeked out and tarried there once. But he had lowered his eyes in bedazzlement after they met hers. How beautiful she was, even though he had only seen her briefly. He remembered with a shudder his initial impression the day he saw her and his final feelings the day he parted from her: that she was the most beautiful woman he had ever seen. Abduh shuddered at this, for he remembered that the woman now belonged to one man, a man who was foreign to all of them. She preferred him to all of them. She loved him. She was writing to him and he to her. Envoys were going and coming between them.

Abduh suddenly stood up straight. He thought he should go straight to this Mustafa and pummel him. Or he might go to the landlord and ask him to evict the man. Or he would do something to harm Mustafa.

He made his way toward Al-Sayyida district. The length of the trip weakened his fury, and his pique cooled. He began to listen to reason a little, asking himself: Why harm Mustafa? Was it this man's fault if she loved him? Did he know of their love for her? Even if he did, what was he to do if she chose him?

Abduh turned his fury on her then and began to ask: How could this girl reject them? They were the ones who had been in contact with her and her family all this time. She had become entangled with a man without links to her or her family. She didn't know anything about him.

At that moment Abduh forgot his rage at Salim and Muhsin, the fury he had felt toward them whenever they flocked to Saniya's home on any pretext. He felt now that he would have liked it a thousand times better if Saniya had chosen one of them instead of this stranger. He felt affection, sympathy, and a tie uniting him to his comrades, who were out of luck too. He noticed that when he spoke and raged, he did it on behalf of all of them, not just for himself.

For the first time, he felt a need to be near them and to talk to them about this affair. They had shared the emotion—just as they shared everything—and then the disappointment and pain.

At that hour Salim was upstairs at the Soldier's Coffeehouse. He had returned to it the day after it became clear there was nothing to be hoped for from the neighbors' house. Salim had tried to convince the folks that the neighbors' household was of absolutely no interest to him and that Saniya was simply a girl like all the others. She did not concern him. A man like him would not pay attention to her. Even if he could convince others of this, he was the one most in need of convincing.

Thus Salim went to the Soldier's Coffeehouse, supposing that he had wiped everything away at this minimal cost. He afforded himself pleasure and consolation by saying, "What's Saniya? How does she compare with these high-spirited mesdemoiselles and good-time girls?"

He took his seat, looking right and left to reacquaint himself with the place, remembering his past there, a past filled with happiness and merriment. He began to scrutinize the faces of the young women sitting with the customers, those exiting, those waiting for a date, and those who were idle and scouting opportunities. It seemed he did not know any of them, even though he used to know every woman who entered this place, back when he was the most constant and regular customer. But he soon noticed one woman sitting alone at a table. She recognized him and smiled at him invitingly. He rose at once and approached her, twisting the ends of his mustache pompously. He gave her his hand in greeting. With the tone of an old friend he said, "How are you, Maria!"

He had scarcely taken a seat beside her when he was surrounded by waiters. He raised his head and asked with a frown, "What's up?"

But he got control of himself at once, for he knew them. He remembered he had pretended to them he was wealthy. He altered his tone and said to one of them, a stout Nubian, "So you're still alive, Pistachio!"

"So, Your Excellency, how may I serve you?"

Salim puffed himself up a little and motioned toward his woman companion. He told Pistachio, "See what the mademoiselle will order."

The waiter leaned over the woman to receive her order. She took her time. Salim waited for her words anxiously, as though awaiting a sentence to pay a fine. Salim had no capital other than pretense, boasts, and braggadocio. With these he had been able to frequent this drinking establishment in the past and to make an outstanding name for himself among its patrons and waiters. Finally the mademoiselle spoke. She told the waiter, "Bring me one Martell cognac with soda."

Pistachio left her and turned respectfully to Salim. "And the bey?"

Salim scratched his head. He pretended to think and have trouble deciding for a moment. Then he said, "Me? . . . Bring me a soda straight . . . with a bit of rose water. You know my digestion, Pistachio."

The waiter hesitated momentarily. Then he found no alternative to going for their orders. At that the woman turned to Salim and asked, "Salim Bey! Do you still have digestive complaints?"

"What am I to do, Maria! By the way, what's become of Katina and her sister Adèle?"

He began to converse with her on various trivial topics. He flirted, joked, and laughed with her, forcefully, boisterously, energetically, and contentiously, in a way she had not seen in him before. He seemed to be venting today and seeking revenge for a defeat he had encountered in another arena.

A new customer with the mark of true wealth entered and clapped his hands. Immediately the eyes of all the women were on him. Maria stopped conversing with Salim to stare at this new patron. Finally she rose, excusing herself for a moment to go to the restroom. She walked past the new customer with a swinging gait, leaving Salim behind with the orders. Salim settled back into himself. The dust of this false merriment that he had deliberately stirred up in his heart fell away from him. The depression and disappointment from which he had tried in vain to shield himself took root. The smile of pleasure on his lips turned into a smile of bitter derision. He looked at the girls and began to stare at their makeup, which sweat was causing to ooze down their sallow faces. He observed those gestures, affected voices, phony laughs, winks, and sniping. For the first time he asked himself how he had been able to frequent this place. How had these prostitutes been able to satisfy him?

Maria eventually returned to him, since the new customer had ignored her, choosing to sit with another woman. She found

Salim, his face grave and frowning, lost in thought. She asked him with surprise, "What! Salim! Aren't you very happy?"

He looked up at her and aimed a harsh, frigid stare at her. He answered coldly, "Very happy?"

Then he left her and turned his attention straight to the glass of soda with rose water. He concentrated on it, excluding her. She went on looking at him for a while. Then she turned her face away and shrugged her shoulders lightly. Salim began to move the spoon around in the glass. Looking at its color reminded him of a day he drank rose-flavored punch at Saniya's when he went to examine the piano. He was mistaken if he thought that girl had not made a lasting impression on him. Indeed, she had done more than make an impression. Here he was today disdaining these women for her sake. She had awakened in his soul a new emotion he hadn't known before, the emotion of honest admiration. That loathing and revulsion he felt now toward these mesdemoiselles had been inspired by his memory of Saniya's refined beauty, her charm, which wasn't hackneyed, and her sincerity of emotion. Salim perceived now that he could no longer settle for a prostitute. He sensed that his heart had been elevated. Indeed he sensed that he had developed a heart that wouldn't allow him to frequent prostitutes.

Captain Salim was feeling this now? What a change! He was amazed at this elevated feeling. He knew that Saniya had made him learn things about himself and discover within himself unknown regions. Had this captain known before today that he had within him pure sentiments? Indeed, would a person like that have known the meaning of the words *purity* and *nobility*? He himself had understood his love for Saniya as a trivial, fickle, trite love like his previous love for the Syrian woman in Port Said . . . or for these women. He hadn't realized he had the ability or sensitivity for a higher form of love. Salim took one sip from his glass. Then he spat and pushed it away with the tips of his fingers. He clapped. The Nubian Pistachio came. His eyes fell on Salim's full glass. He looked at him with questioning eyes: Why hadn't he drunk it? Salim's mouth revealed his revulsion. "It tastes bad!" he said.

The waiter wanted to object, but Salim motioned not to.

There was no need for words. He put his hand in his pocket, brought out the price of his order and of the mademoiselle's cognac and soda water, and added a tip. Then he rose and walked away after giving an abbreviated gesture of farewell to the woman. Surprised by his conduct, she incredulously watched him disappear down the stairs. She shrugged her shoulders as though annoyed and laughed scornfully.

Salim walked along the street, filled his lungs with the fresh air, and felt at ease. It seemed to him he had been breathing foul-smelling, polluted air in that place.

CHAPTER 13

In the hallway once Salim returned home, he ran into the servant Mabruk, who motioned for him to be quiet and pointed with a mischievous smile at the closed door of Zanuba's room. Salim trembled, hesitated a little, and then launched a gentle assault on the room, walking on tiptoe. He looked through the cracks of the door.

At that moment Abduh appeared, coming in from outside as well. Mabruk greeted him with the same gesture and smile. It was enough for Abduh to see Salim bent over at the door to have his heart affected in the same way as or even more intensely than Salim's. He instantly made for the door and jostled the captain with his shoulders. His heart was pounding. But Salim straightened up right away, leaving Abduh the hole with a bitter smile. He turned to Mabruk and asked in a whisper, "Who's the woman in there?"

Abduh straightened up too after that, his hope disappointed. He stood beside Salim as though adding his voice to the question while they waited for Mabruk's reply. Mabruk looked at them. He understood what they had hoped when they looked through the hole. He emitted a groan of confirmation, as though he too sincerely knew and felt what they did. He began to speak. "Those days will not return. The past will not return. Finished!"

But they pressed him to answer. With failing patience Abduh asked him again, "Who is that woman?"

Mabruk cleared his throat, approached them, and whispered quickly, "The undertaker's wife!"

The two of them repeated in astonishment, "Undertaker!"

Their lack of understanding was apparent. Mabruk pulled them away to the communal bedroom and explained in a tone of enjoyable revenge that this woman was the wife of the undertaker of Al-Sayyida Zaynab district. She was the one who was going to bring them a handful of dirt from the grave of a dead man who had not been buried three days.

Abduh asked forcefully, "Why? For what reason?"

Mabruk replied in the same vengeful tone, "For the 'job' we're going to sprinkle on the doorstep of that man Mustafa."

Abduh shook his head. He had grasped everything. He resumed his interrogation of Mabruk: "Of course this was Zanuba's idea?"

Mabruk confirmed this proudly and added, "Zanuba consulted the most famous expert for this prescription. It's tested. There's no fear it will fail. If Mustafa doesn't die within three days, the expert who provided it won't need to be paid. He's the one who laid that condition on himself, after he took only the amount for the consultation."

He, Mabruk, had spent several days searching for the undertaker's wife to invite her to come to Zanuba to reach an agreement with her. He had succeeded only today. Mabruk was silent for a moment. He looked at them as though expecting a word of agreement or encouragement. But they remained silent. Abduh was plunged into deep ruminations. It occurred to him that while they had yielded the matter to God and been impotent to do anything, Zanuba had not stopped her efforts. Neither religion nor conscience had prevented her from proceeding toward her goal. She wanted Mustafa to die in three days, and she was working to have him die . . . to have a man die whose only fault was not loving her. *How monstrous! Is this a woman? If she loves and is disappointed, does she become a predatory animal?*

Abduh's next intuition made the world look gloomy. By a strange coincidence, Salim thought of the same thing. Salim turned anxiously and suspiciously to ask Mabruk, "Are you sure it's only for Mustafa?"

Abduh added in a nervous tone verging on a scream, "It doesn't make sense that Zanuba would kill Mustafa and spare Saniya."

Mabruk grasped this suddenly, and his heart started pounding too. In a hoarse, anxious voice he said, as though to himself, "She only said against Mustafa. . . . I don't know. . . . Perhaps, additionally . . ."

Salim then began to outline for them what he suspected was Zanuba's intention. "She would not harm Mustafa. All the evil is directed against Saniya and no one else. This is only reasonable. This is what is in Zanuba's own interest. She wishes Saniya dead, because she's Zanuba's rival and foe. But in order to enlist naive Mabruk for the job she hid the true aim from him and led him to understand that the intended victim is Mustafa."

When Salim reached this point they heard the apartment door open and close. Thus they knew the visitor had left. They rushed to Zanuba. Abduh shouted at her, "Who was that woman?"

Zanuba was flustered to be accosted so fiercely but gained control of herself. She smiled and went toward him, relating what Mabruk had said shortly before. Abduh shouted at her with ferocious anger, "You're not, then, willing to give up this magic of yours?"

Salim added, "Fine, let's suppose you do a job on Mustafa. You'll be killing a man! You'll murder a human being? You have a clear conscience about that?"

She bowed her head for a moment, boiling with rage. Then she raised her head violently and shouted at them, "I'm not going to sit like a ninny in this house watching the messengers!" She turned on Abduh and demanded, "What should I do? I've worn myself out trying to get you to go to the landlord to tell him and explain it to him—to get him to evict this bachelor tenant, who has turned the house into a brothel."

The blood rose to Abduh's head. These foul words had stung him.

Whatever Saniya's tie was to Mustafa, she was still an honorable woman who should not be slurred in this way. Abduh didn't know why these filthy suggestions upset him when they were aimed at Saniya. Did he still admire her and consider her his ideal so that he wouldn't let anyone defile this magnificent marble statue, even if it did not belong to him?

Even stranger was the fact that Salim too turned his back on Zanuba in disgust.

They heard the door open and close. Muhsin appeared. They all looked at him. They were appalled by what they saw: a pale face and red eyelids, and legs that could barely support him. Zanuba couldn't keep from asking immediately, "Muhsin! What's wrong?"

He raised his head. He wanted to tell them it was nothing. Before he could get the words out, however, they were asking him, "Are you sick?"

He decided to tell them, "Yes!" Then he went to his bed, took off his clothes, and got under the covers. Meanwhile Abduh and Salim were watching him as though they grasped what was troubling him. Their hearts were smitten with pity for him. They approached quietly and sat on the edge of his bed. They would have liked to comfort him or bring him some relief but feared he would take their words of consolation the wrong way . . . that these might hurt his feelings. So they chose to remain silent, despite the affection and love they felt for him, and never so much as on that day. They lowered their heads when they saw he had closed his eyes from fatigue. They seemed to have gauged the extent of his pain and to have compared it to their own, finding his greater. They felt for the first time that they didn't measure up to him. He was set apart from them by the rare quality of his heart.

CHAPTER 14

None of Mustafa's neighbors in the vicinity knew anything about him except that he was a wealthy young man. Perhaps the first person to make inquiries about him was Zanuba. Since he had started living there at the beginning of the year she had been working up to asking his servant who he was and what he did. She had not yet been motivated by anything except curiosity about a new neighbor. The servant was busy carrying up a few household items delivered by a mule-drawn cart and answered her quickly, "His profession? He's one of the gentry."

The servant went on up, engrossed in his work, paying no attention to her. So she wasn't able to ask him what gentry he came from. Was he from Cairo, the countryside, or one of the provincial capitals? Zanuba caught sight of him after that from the window when he was at the coffeehouse opposite the house. She liked his looks but wasn't able to learn anything more about him. Perhaps modesty prevented her or fear of betraying her agitation, now that this person had begun to interest her. Or perhaps it was chance that kept her from that servant, who was seldom seen. The fact was that Mustafa Bey himself, when he first moved in, was often absent. If he appeared in al-Hajj Shahhata's coffeehouse one day, he would disappear from the district for days as though he had traveled. The same was true of his servant.

Yet there was nothing about the conduct of this young man to attract the attention of any of the neighbors. Calm prevailed at his residence. Tranquility slumbered at his doorstep. He entered and exited without anyone being aware of him. He seemed to strive for a good reputation among the neighbors or at least to avoid the suspicion attached to a bachelor living alone. Perhaps his personal acquaintance with the landlord and the confidence the latter showed in him by agreeing to rent to him without condition or stipulation made Mustafa extra careful to protect his reputation and to prefer solitude and quiet.

But something else prompted this wealthy young man to withdraw from the commotion and nightlife of Cairo and retreat to al-Hajj Shahhata's coffeehouse, where he spent long hours. Watching Salim Effendi try to flirt via the balcony was not his reason for spending long hours sitting there, because Salim was for Mustafa nothing but a diverting episode that came to him gratuitously to cheer him up. Mustafa at the time was peevish and out of sorts about something. He had returned to Cairo expecting it to be as he had left it five years before. He had been a pupil at the Muhammad Ali School, the large wooden door of which he could see when he sat at his place in the coffeehouse. Then he had been a student at the Nile Valley Secondary School, which he still passed whenever he went down al-Dawawin Street. At that time he had been dwelling in this very district, the air of which he was breathing now. Nothing was different, although the house he had lived in at that time was in Al-Baghala. Unfortunately, he had not been able to rent the apartment he had inhabited with his brother and sister as well as his sister's husband, who was an employee in the Ministry of Finance. He found that it had been occupied for a long time. But the landlord had purchased another house in the same area, on Salama Street. It was this one, number 35. He felt he had to live there. In any case, he would have the same landlord. In spite of that, Mustafa was cross and dejected. He felt disappointed with Cairo. So what had changed then, according to him?

Mustafa was sitting at al-Hajj Shahhata's coffeehouse thinking about his past in this district, his school days and friends, about playing ball with them near the Nilometer and their summer excursions in boats on the Nile as the moon rose. They brought along food and fruit such as watermelon and cantaloupe. They would eat, drink, and sing until the boat brought them close to the Abbas Bridge beyond Al-Qasr al-Ayni. They would put the oars up and let the boat float freely in those calm, tranquil waters under the bridge. The moon created beautiful patterns on the water with light and darkness. The Nile about them was silent except for the cry of a night bird or the sound of a fish leaping suddenly in the water beside them as it played among the stalks of grass and reeds springing up near the shore. They would sound off and make a racket, laughing together. At times they would be silent, as though the poetic sights around them stirred in them better feelings latent in them or some deep sense of sublime beauty. Young people have a special right to the heart. At that golden age, a person's first and last rebellion must take place so that he can discover by the flame's light the powers and treasures buried in his soul. But, unfortunately, this young man's time came to have his heart illumined before he had met a woman. None of the band of young men in the boat had been granted the opportunity to know a woman with a heart and soul who could inspire great deeds . . . unlike the prostitute they visited every Friday eve in exchange for twenty piastres.

For that reason, these moments of silence that this magnificent scene with its poetry elicited from them did not last. These could only exert a limited influence on the souls of boys who entrusted their reputations to prostitutes rife with base materialism.

The moon, water, and breeze moved the most poetic of them, and he started reciting verses from the poetry assigned them for the baccalaureate examination that year. His companions greeted this with coarse mirth and obscene jokes. So he fell silent in embarrassment.

Then he changed over shortly to join in their stupid banter and bestial clamor. He forgot that flash of exalted imagination and emotion that had shone in his heart a moment before. Thus those tiny sparks of greatness were extinguished in the souls of these young men filled with life.

They resumed their excursion amid vulgar songs and rowdy guffaws. At midnight they returned to their homes, stumbling through the neighborhood of Al-Baghala, which lacked lamps. They shouted a lot as though drunk.

But Mustafa did not recall the past in this fashion. He saw it instead as the first happy period of childhood, with its merriment and games and the total solidarity of his brethren. Where were these brothers now? Who could say . . . perhaps a doctor at a rural center, a superintendent in a district capital, a bureaucrat in a provincial capital, or an unemployed wanderer? Even his own brother, who had been a member of the group, had traveled years ago to complete his education in France. He had not returned yet and did not want to return, not even when they asked him to come for a pressing reason. Nevertheless Mustafa had been looking for his brethren from the past ever since he arrived in Cairo. He found some of them. At their first meeting they had been overjoyed. He had inquired what had become of them. They were employees in government agencies. They asked what he had been doing and why they had been separated all this time. He told them that after he received his baccalaureate, his father had wanted him to work for him in their famous textile firm in Al-Mahalla al-Kubra. He had remained in Al-Mahalla al-Kubra against his will all this time, until his father died at the first of the year. Then he wasted no time. He stayed only long enough to do his duty to the departed. After that he prepared himself quickly to travel. He brought along a servant and a few belongings. He left the large textile firm in the care of employees. He was determined to leave commerce to attempt to find employment in a government ministry so he could settle permanently in Cairo. But unfortunately he hadn't found the Cairo he had been longing for. To his regret he could scarcely recognize in it the town of his past. Everything seemed to have changed, even though nothing had.

Yes . . . those of the brethren he found had been able to dissipate that depression at first. They had led him through the city, exploring the new centers of amusement and entertainment. They took him by night to the drinking spots and then to the houses of prostitution. The glitter of the capital, which he was seeing again after his absence, captured Mustafa's fancy that day. It distracted him to some extent from hidden feelings of depression. His friends, however, repeated that excursion with him, and Mustafa noticed in them a frightening

change of character. He saw first of all that they were not seeking to revive an old friendship. They did not enjoy his company, nor were they befriending him for himself the way they
had before. They wished, rather, to exploit him, to curry favor
with him, so he would lavish his inherited wealth on them.
This was what he understood from them and their conduct.
He split at once from these companions, rejecting that side of
their character. He was amazed that childhood friends would
change that way.

For this reason he preferred the solitude he found at al-Hajj
Shahhata's coffeehouse and concluded provisionally that it
was impossible to revive the past. He got over his depression
bit by bit and began to think about what he should do. Should
he return to Al-Mahalla al-Kubra and take over management
of the firm as the successor of his industrious and diligent
father . . . or should he stick with his original idea of seeking
employment in Cairo after selling off the firm and dividing the
proceeds among the heirs: himself, his brother, and his sister?

His sister left the decision up to him. He received a letter from
Fayoum, where she resided with her spouse, who was now employed in the provincial administration. His brother likewise
wrote him from France saying, "Do whatever you want on condition you don't ask me to come back to Egypt and don't decrease my monthly allowance in any way."

He himself did not wish to settle in Al-Mahalla al-Kubra or
to be tied to the firm. It would be very easy for him to liquidate
it and sell it to a branch of a firm owned by a foreigner, C. S.
Cassoli, who had made an offer to buy the firm as soon as he
caught scent of a desire to liquidate it when he learned that
Mustafa, following the death of his father, would be traveling
to Cairo.

Yes . . . Mustafa was just a young man who had lost his am-
bition. He wasn't corrupt or dissolute. There was a lot of good
and virtue in his soul, but this goodness was buried under a
heavy layer of indolence and indecision.

He had had a long debate with himself over the question of
the textile firm, traveling repeatedly to Al-Mahalla. He and
his servant would go off . . . and then return. He would send

his servant there to provide him with news of the firm. He decided that was the easiest and best way to manage the business. But all of this only made him more certain that he wasn't strong enough for the burdens of commerce and the responsibilities of free enterprise. The firm had been in constant decline since he left. Its profits kept decreasing. He did not know whether that was because of his lax supervision of the employees since he had left them to sit in al-Hajj Shahhata's coffeehouse or because of a lack of direction, drive, and exertion. In any case, what was all this to him? Why not free himself from this entanglement? He should sell the firm to the foreigner Cassoli. Wasn't that best?

No one opposed him in this matter. His mother was dead. Her brother, who was an important cotton merchant, did go to him, incredulous and dismayed, on hearing rumors about the liquidation of the firm and its sale to Cassoli. He advised his nephew against selling. He pleaded with him out of concern for him, because it would be a big loss.

Mustafa Bey laughed sarcastically and nonchalantly said, "Loss! Are we dependent on this firm?"

His uncle answered, "My son, every blessing comes from this firm. It's this firm that has brought all the farms and properties." In fact, the inheritance of Mustafa and his siblings was not limited to the firm. Their deceased father had left them other properties and lands as well. For that reason, Mustafa was not too concerned about the firm. Yet his uncle said to him regretfully, "This isn't right for a merchant's son. Woe to businessmen if their heirs leave the profession to become low-ranking bureaucrats. Indeed, what a disgrace for an Egyptian to give up his commercial establishment and let a foreigner take charge! The famous textile firm of Raji will become a subsidiary of Mr. Cassoli the Greek."

But was this moribund heart in any condition to be moved by these words?

CHAPTER 15

Had it not been for Zanuba, Saniya's attention would not have been directed to al-Hajj Shahhata's small coffeehouse, nor would her eyes have fallen on this charming young man with the small blond mustache as he sat quietly in his solitary corner, oblivious to everything except the ridiculous antics of Captain Salim in front of him.

The same day she observed him, Muhsin came to her and revealed the story of the silk handkerchief. He was overly cautious, suggesting to her at first that the wind might have carried the handkerchief to one of the neighbors. She went immediately to the window and observed that the downstairs apartment, where Mustafa lived, had a small, open balcony that was almost next to the window of her room. She suspected the handkerchief might be with Mustafa and that he had kept the matter to himself.

This notion was quickly dispelled when Muhsin later confessed the truth to her. Even so, she watched Mustafa whenever he sat at the coffeehouse, just because she felt an urge to watch him—she didn't know why.

The day Muhsin said good-bye, she was sincere and truthful in all her indications of affection and emotion. Muhsin went off to the country. What happened? Nothing, except that she continued to amuse herself by looking at the coffeehouse through the window of the wooden balcony. She saw Mustafa in his customary place. He was even more withdrawn and solitary now that Salim had stopped coming to the coffeehouse. His face looked dejected and thoughtful. His gloomy look was no longer lightened by those suppressed laughs and smiles provoked by Salim, his twisted mustache, wide shoulders, commanding and forbidding, false pompous commotion, and looks directed toward the wooden balcony.

Saniya was uneasy though, because Mustafa never looked at the wooden balcony, not even in the days of Salim. Although he had grasped the reason for the gestures and glances, he had never looked up at the balcony, or only infrequently and then politely and modestly, like someone whose only goal was to keep up with Salim's news.

Salim deserted the coffeehouse, while Mustafa remained. He kept coming, driven by habit and because it was better than his empty house. He could at least drink a cup of tea there with a minimum of effort. Moreover, it was a good place for him to think over his worries about his future. Yet he had not looked at the wooden balcony, nor was he looking, for who would remind him of it now that Salim had vanished? For this reason, Saniya, after Muhsin left, began to spend most of her time watching Mustafa but didn't win a single look at her balcony from him. She asked herself in amazement what a person like him was doing in a coffeehouse like that. What was he thinking about? Why wasn't he looking at the balcony? This questioning and wonder reached the point of concern. She began to wear dresses of the most dazzling colors. She would play a well-known piece on the piano, one with a popular tune, after she had opened all the windows on the balcony, so the sound might reach the street. When she finished, she stood by the window. She made a show of busily opening or closing it, forcefully and noisily. Indeed it got so the only place she found suitable for calling her maid in a loud voice or for speaking and laughing vociferously was beside the window. It was because of all this that the battle erupted between her and Zanuba, who would visit her and see her do these things. When it became clear to Zanuba that Saniya was attempting to attract Mustafa's attention, she was unable to remain quiet. She scolded her and forbade her, but in a concerned tone that immediately aroused Saniya's suspicions. When she grasped what Zanuba felt, she burst into sarcastic laughter and asked, "Even you who are old enough to be my mother?"

This was a terrible thing to say. The moment she uttered it, Zanuba screamed and brayed like a camel in heat. She cursed and swore, using the vilest and most obscene words. Then she put on her black wrap, which she had been wearing, and departed in a way that ruled out a return. Saniya watched quietly and grimly, unable to respond or move. The maid came when she heard the shouting and caught some of Zanuba's words. Saniya turned to her and asked calmly, "Did you see, Nurse Bakhita?"

The maid answered her in disbelief, "Shame! What an absolutely dreadful woman!"

Saniya's mother, who was in her room performing the afternoon prayer, brought her devotions to a swift conclusion when she heard the row. She hastened to see what it was about and caught up with Zanuba as she descended the stairs. She worriedly sought to detain her, but Zanuba wouldn't stop, continuing down the steps. She shouted up in a piercing voice from the bottom step, "Go mind your daughter, the whore."

Saniya's mother was dumbfounded and somewhat alarmed but quickly roused herself. Her blood boiled, and she answered, peering down from the top of the stairs, "Anyone who says that about Saniya should have her tongue chopped off!"

Zanuba, however, departed. She vanished, muttering over and over, "Disgrace on your house! Disgrace on your house forever!"

The mother remained frozen there for a moment. Then she remembered her daughter and ran to her. She found her pale and with cold hands. When she calmed down and collected herself, she asked what had happened. Saniya told her everything: how Zanuba had come and looked at the coffeehouse as usual when she came, because she had a crush on a neighbor named Mustafa, who always sat in the coffeehouse. Zanuba had seen him alone there earlier that month, taken her wrap, and hastened down, without Saniya being at all suspicious of her then. But today, and even before today, Zanuba had remarked that she couldn't bear to see Saniya near the window. And today, all that had happened was that she had wanted to look out from the balcony. That had not pleased Zanuba, who had gotten angry. She had ended up cursing and swearing and had departed in this manner.

The mother bowed her head for a little. Then she said as

though to herself, "How sad . . . that she should be so petty over a matter like this!"

Saniya raised her head and added immediately, "I told her that, Mother, but she just flared up with anger and rage."

The maid, Bakhita, appeared. Saniya rushed to her mother and said, pointing to Bakhita, "Nurse Bakhita witnessed it. Ask her too, Mother."

The maid said at once, "For shame! She's a woman with no manners at all. An absolutely dreadful person!"

Thus the matter of the quarrel was ended. The mother took her daughter's head in her arms and cradled it against her breast. She tried to put her mind at ease and implored her not to upset herself on account of a woman like Zanuba, nor for anything in the world. Saniya put her handkerchief to her eyes as though holding back her tears in response to her mother's pleas. Then she gently escaped from her arms and headed for the balcony, holding her handkerchief like a fan to cool her flushed face. She emitted a little moan. She made it seem she was going to the window for no reason other than to get some invigorating fresh air. But the moment Saniya's eye fell on the coffeehouse, she saw Mustafa looking at the balcony as though waiting for someone to appear there. She withdrew at once and vanished from his sight. She was filled with amazement and throbbed with a kind of secret pleasure. In reality there was no reason for her to be astonished. She must have known that the sound of the quarrel between her and Zanuba had reached the coffeehouse, followed shortly thereafter by the exit of Zanuba, who was frothing, foaming, and gesticulating wildly all the way to her residence, which was number 35, the building in which Mustafa occupied the second floor. Mustafa, who was seated in his place at the coffeehouse, had seen all of that and wondered about this noise coming from the balcony and about this emotional woman exiting from the house to enter the building where he lived. Curiosity drove him to listen carefully and to try to observe what was happening beyond the balcony. Suddenly his inquiring eyes met, with no premeditation, two beautiful black ones. He immediately began to tremble. He saw a dazzlingly beautiful maiden, who no sooner revealed herself than she recoiled and vanished.

That was a simple vision that did not last more than five seconds, but all the same, Mustafa felt afterward as though a complete new world had suddenly been revealed to him. An unconscious feeling was born in him that the world now had a different flavor and that his life had taken a new direction in the twinkling of an eye. Yes, five seconds in the life of an individual is nothing. All the same, it can at times be everything. A person's whole life may pass without it budging an inch from its foundation until a mere five seconds arrives that may totally alter that foundation, turning it head over heels.

What had Mustafa seen? A girl who appeared and then vanished like a flash of lightning, like a flash of lightning that illuminated all the corners of his gloomy heart. . . . In five seconds Mustafa had glimpsed for the first time beauty that shook his heart. He had not known that this house contained all that. When he finally recovered from the intoxication of the surprise, he began to say to himself, "The tragedy is that I've been here since the beginning of the year without having any idea!"

He was overcome by a delirious happiness at his discovery. He attacked and scolded himself: *I'm a fool! An ass! Blind!*

His heart was pounding. He looked politely and contentedly at the balcony. He did not see anyone. He rose without regret and wandered happily through the streets, wishing he could traverse all of Cairo, up and down, with his long, happy strides. He remembered suddenly the hour he had arrived at the coffeehouse. He compared his state then to that on leaving it now. Not many minutes had passed between the two times. Yet he disavowed his old personality. He seemed to have become a new man.

At that moment Saniya was at the center of the room using her imagination to recall the same event. She too had trembled—and not just from surprise—when their eyes met. She had withdrawn immediately. She had not anticipated that their eyes would meet suddenly, nor that she would see that solitary, serious young man looking at the balcony.

At first she was happily going over it with herself. But all at once it seemed she was gripped by embarrassment. Affecting a frown and pretending to be cross and angry, she started asking: *Why should this man look at the balcony? By what right? The daring and nerve of this young fellow to permit himself to look at it!*

She imagined that if only she could, she would scold and chide him for that. She would speak roughly to him. All the same, only a moment after her peevish rage, she headed to the balcony, for no other reason than to know if this daring young man was still looking at her or the balcony. Saniya neared the window, after she had quickly and carefully arranged her magnificent hair in front of the mirror. How astonished she was when she saw that the person she accused of daring and insolence, who, she supposed, would be sitting staring at her balcony, hadn't left a trace at the coffeehouse. His place was empty. He had not only forsworn looking back at her, he had indeed left the coffeehouse with everyone and everything in it. This was how it seemed to her. What a disappointment!

The girl felt pain and then anger. She shut the window with a nervous, powerful motion, as though vowing never to look out it again. Her feminine pride had taken a beating. She felt as though tears would steal from the corners of her eyes. But she pulled herself together, remembering that there was nothing between her and this person to give her anything to be hopeful or despondent about. Who was he? What was he worth? What was he to her that she should accuse him this way? She went to the piano and began to play, attempting to forget everything.

At that moment the pale ghost of Muhsin passed through her consciousness. What a fine opportunity Muhsin would have had if he had returned to her at that moment. That would have been the ideal hour to win her favor. But, unfortunately, Muhsin was at the farm, out in the fields of green clover, waiting for a letter from her that she would never write.

CHAPTER 16

The following day Mustafa came to the coffeehouse as usual, but if the owner or one of those accustomed to seeing him every day had looked at him he would have been certain that Mustafa had paid special attention to what he wore. He had doubtless stood before the mirror for a long time prior to coming.

Mustafa took his place but felt he was coming to the coffeehouse for the first time. He cast his eyes about somewhat shyly. He felt that the men there, even al-Hajj Shahhata and the waiters, were looking at him and knew why he had come today. Or they realized at least why he was concerned about his appearance. But he found himself alone as usual, on the pavement in front of the coffeehouse. No one was looking at him. He regained his composure and waited for a moment as though struggling with himself. Finally he raised his eyes to Dr. Hilmi's balcony, cautiously and politely. He trembled. He lowered his eyes immediately on hearing one of the waiters ask for his order. He requested a glass of tea in a quick, mechanical way. Then he changed his mind and called the waiter to cancel what he had said. Instead he ordered a glass of the carbonated drink Spathis. He did not know why he was changing from tea today. Why did he change to a carbonated drink . . . unless the idea of change, which was floating in his unconscious reaches, inspired him.

The waiter was just as surprised as he was. Not merely because a regular customer suddenly changed his order but also because the name Spathis at this rather traditional coffee shop was not much in use by the establishment's patrons. This waiter wasn't accustomed to it the way he was to "a pipe" or "one coffee straight" or "one tea," or even "one Turkish delight" or "one pastry." For that reason he turned away and just called out, "One carbonated."

Mustafa returned to his internal debate. His glance at the balcony had informed him that there was no one there and that the windows were closed.

Could he hope to see her again or was yesterday a chance occurrence that would not be repeated? What guarantee did he have that she would show herself again? How was he to know? He could wait for months without seeing her on the balcony. Hadn't he already sat in this coffeehouse for months and yesterday was the first time he caught sight of her? Where had she been all that time? Where had he been? The past was over. There was no need to stir up regret for it, but could he hope for the future?

He was disturbed by use of the word *future*, since he suddenly perceived a tangible reality for this word. But doubt and anxiety plagued him. It occurred to him that she might be a visitor who had come to this house yesterday and left never to return. If she did return, who would tip him off? He didn't know yet who she was. This reflection brought a gloomy look to his face. Sitting in the coffeehouse now was pointless. He was waiting in vain.

He fidgeted in his seat. He took out his breast-pocket handkerchief, which was the same color as his suit, and wiped his forehead with it. Then he bared his left wrist to look at his gold watch. It seemed to him that he had been sitting there a century. The idea became firmly established in his head that he would not see her today. He moved in his chair, saying to himself that so long as he knew that, why should he sit in the coffeehouse now?

Mustafa forgot that he had always sat in the coffeehouse for no reason at all, that he had spent long hours there. He had never grown restless the way he had today, even though he had been sitting there less than an hour.

He felt increasingly uneasy and desperate as time passed. The waiting got on his nerves. He swore he would leave in five minutes if she did not appear. The five minutes elapsed but hope tempted him to renew the period and extend the deadline. She

did not appear. Desperate, he started to rise. Then he relented
and renewed the period, extending the deadline a third, fourth,
and fifth time.

He distracted himself for a while with the carbonated drink,
which he deliberately drank slowly, and then by reflecting
there was ample time. The clock at the coffeehouse had not yet
struck the half hour. When it struck half past he would rise to
go . . . where? At this hour he was always in the coffeehouse
and didn't go anywhere else. He did not know where to go.
The important thing was his need to leave, for he had waited
more than long enough. There was a limit to the suffering occasioned by waiting. Never before had he thought about leaving this soon, for he had never been waiting for anything. A
person who isn't waiting for something can sit for a whole lifetime in one place until he rots and the worms eat him. But desire can cause him to rise. It can make him energetic so that a
feeling of time and life pervades him.

A person who waits for nothing, who desires nothing is
dead. Mustafa for that reason did not hesitate. He thrust his
hand into his pocket to take out the money for the waiter. He
was coming to the rescue of his volition, which had lost patience. At that moment the sound of a window being vigorously opened reached his ears. Mustafa's ears had become like
those of a cat. They were on alert to pounce on every sound,
no matter how minute, especially sounds from windows and
balconies.

He raised his eyes to Dr. Hilmi's balcony in a reflex motion.
Then he saw her. It happened suddenly; it came in his hour of
despair and anxiety. He could not keep his heart from pounding. He smiled at her without meaning to. Perhaps a surge of
happiness caused by the relief of his doubt made him smile. It
was in fact a sincere and truthful smile. It spoke of honorable
pleasure, not vulgar flirtation. The proof for that was that it
occurred spontaneously. It seemed to have burst out to express
a powerful inner feeling. He wasn't aware of it or of himself
until the moment he saw the window closed in his face in response to it.

What bad luck! Was he crazy? By smiling he would lose

everything. What a fool he was! But he hadn't done it on purpose. It wasn't his fault. It was bad luck, nothing more or less.

Mustafa was very sorry and chided himself a lot. He was
afraid he had alienated her. He wished she had not appeared
today. All the same, Mustafa felt relieved in the depths of his
heart. A decisive end had been put to his doubt. He was certain she wasn't a visitor or a stranger. She was a permanent
resident of this house, of the house he saw before him, the one
next door to his. He had a small, uncovered balcony adjoining
one of its windows. This was happiness enough for him today.
If he had angered her with the smile, perhaps she would forgive it one day.

In any case he was delighted to know that she lived in this
house and that she opened the balcony windows most of the
time. She would open them again as usual. She naturally would
not deprive herself of light and air just because some fool
smiled at her from Hajj Shahhata's miserable coffeehouse. Was
it miserable? For the first time Mustafa thought of that coffeehouse with disdain. He opened his eyes to his surroundings. He took a critical, disapproving look at its old tables
and chairs, and the large vapor lamp that hung over the sign
that dirt and time had erased. All that was left of GREAT
COFFEEHOUSE OF SUCCESS, SHAHHATA MUHAMMAD,
PROPRIETOR were the words SHAHHATA and COFFEEHOUSE.

He threw a sweeping glance inside, past the glass door panels,
most of which were broken. He looked at the seated patrons.
They were noisy and so was the sound of the backgammon and
domino pieces. Astonishing! How had he been able all that time
to sit near this hodgepodge of effendis, turban wearers, and rustic felt-cap guys? They were all lower-class types. The voice of
Master Shahhata could be heard crying out from within, "A
light for the pipe, mate."

One of the waiters passed him then, wearing a traditional
vest with sleeves and a scarf around his skullcap. In order to
prove how up-to-date the coffeehouse was, he had added to
this attire an apron. He had placed a rose behind his left ear
with a sprig of fresh marjoram. Mustafa chanced to look at
what was on the table in front of him. The design of colored

flowers on the water glass set on the tin tray had been eroded by age and repeated washings. Then there was the alleged Spathis bottle. He perceived that this really was a sleazy coffeehouse.

Remembering how close it was to his residence, he realized why he had frequented it. At that second he remembered something he had seen. It was the image of that tall, broad-shouldered man with the black upturned mustache who had visited this same coffeehouse regularly, sitting in front of him. Puffed up like a cock, he had filled the world with a phony racket of commands and countermands all the time he was there. His gestures were arrogant and haughty in a ridiculous, affected way. He had kept lifting his eyes to the empty balcony until he despaired and left.

Mustafa laughed to himself at the memory of those scenes that had so frequently amused and entertained him. But it wasn't long before his face clouded over a little. Fear afflicted him now that he understood which girl had attracted this man. He had seen her once the way Mustafa saw her yesterday. This man lived in the same house he did. He had met him one day coming down the stairs from the upper floor. His own position was exactly comparable to this man's in every respect. The only difference was that the other man had gotten the jump on him in watching the balcony. Now this man had disappeared. It had been some time since he had been at the coffeehouse. Perhaps all he had achieved with her was disappointment and despair. If this predecessor had failed, why shouldn't he, the subsequent suitor, fail as well? This was clear! The harbingers of defeat had appeared less than forty-eight hours after his happiness. Hadn't the window been closed in his face today?

Despondency crept into Mustafa's heart. Mustafa, like any young man ignorant of women, wasn't able to see in what had happened anything but aversion and rebuke leading to dejection. He bowed his head a moment in distress as he wondered what to do. Should he give up all hope? What would become of him if he determined that he had no choice but to return to the empty life he had been living? Merely thinking of his past life terrified him. There seemed to be an abyss between him and it, even though he was separated from it now by only a day.

Was he to return to living as he had before, a dead man, not waiting for anything, not hoping for anything, without his heart pounding for anything? Could this be called life? Would he be able to return to it after he had learned that his excuse for putting up with it in the past was ignorance? Not when he had seen the light with his own eyes. . . . He raised his hand in a gesture of annoyance. He called the waiter and handed him the money for what he had drunk. Then he rose without a final glance at the balcony. He must have used all his will-power to prevent himself from looking. He went off in no particular direction, his head bowed and his hands in his pockets. Going through his mind repeatedly was: *My fate will be identical to that man's. One day I must disappear too and flee the coffeehouse.*

But hope budded again as his flattering soul began to create excuses to cheer and comfort him. He began reviewing in his imagination the ridiculous images of Salim. He enlarged and exaggerated all their silly and comic aspects, till it was clear to him that Salim wasn't a person suitable for the affections of a beautiful and delicate young woman. He began to compare himself with him, gauging what they had in common and how they differed. He concluded with a verdict in his own favor. This man did not resemble him in any way. Their fates would in no way be similar. They were neither alike nor comparable. If he actually were like that, he would have thrown himself in the river a long time ago. Yes, he would definitely have thrown himself in the river ages ago.

This phrase seemed to please and comfort him. He began repeating it to himself with conviction and clear articulation: *Right! I would have tossed myself in the Nile ages ago.*

So this anxious man was able to restore some composure and peace of mind to himself. He imagined the light had dawned before his eyes again.

CHAPTER 17

If Mustafa, at the moment he smiled at Saniya, had raised his eyes to the window of the neighbors who lived above him, he would have felt fiery rays piercing him from eyes behind the wooden shutters. Zanuba's eyes had never faltered in her surveillance of him and Saniya since the day of the quarrel. She may have been the first person to see and recognize the improvement in Mustafa's attire as well as the reason for it. She was likewise possibly the only person who caught that smile on Mustafa's lips directed toward Saniya.

This was enough for her: that Mustafa would smile at Saniya and she at him. "God! God!"

She waited till the folks—except for Muhsin, who was in Damanhur—gathered and then told them what she had seen, exaggerating the facts and adding everything she imagined would take place. After a smile, what was next if not a rendezvous and letters? Afterward she had seen Mustafa rise. Where would he be going if not to meet the one he had just been smiling at? It so happened that a little after Mustafa rose, Zanuba saw Saniya's maid go out in her wrap on some errand. Zanuba imagined that Saniya had sent her maid after Mustafa. She added that to her account of what she had seen. Then she asked the grim-faced Abduh and Salim, "Are you asleep? Fine, these are letters going back and forth, twenty-four-carat certain, openly in broad daylight."

It was in this way that the disaster fell on the two men. Hanafi and Mabruk were equally astonished. They were skeptical that all of this could happen with such speed, especially since Mustafa was a quiet young man and no one had been aware of his existence all the time he was there.

After Zanuba was sure her words had sunk in, she asked them to draft a letter to Saniya's father, who was legally responsible for her conduct, so he would pull her up short. This was the only correct course. This was their duty as sincere, responsible neighbors. The Prophet urged people to care for even the seventh neighbor. Salim agreed at first, moved by the anger that suddenly swept over him, to write the letter.

But Abduh was furious. He suppressed his nervous anger and burst out shouting, as though this was his relief valve, "No letter will be written! No letters will be sent! If you're really a man and a captain, go downstairs to the fellow. I swear by God Almighty no letter will be written. That's cowardly. I will never permit such cowardice. No letter . . . I know my job!"

Salim asked him, "What do you mean you know your job? What are you going to do? Beat him up?"

Zanuba's eyes were gleaming with vengeance as she said, "Do what you see fit, but there's got to be a letter too."

Abduh screamed at her, "Shut up!" Then he turned on Salim and said, "I tell you it's cowardice. It's base. It's what a woman would do."

At last Salim was convinced by Abduh's words. Zanuba's attempt to get them to write what she wanted failed. Then she thought of having the letter written secretly by a public scribe of the kind who are always on call, who set up their tents or offices outside the courthouse for Al-Sayyida. She would not be deterred. She put on her black wrap that afternoon and went secretly to a scribe. In order to conceal from him her actual goal, she began as if the reason for her coming was to ask him to write a normal letter to Muhsin. When Muhsin's letter was finished she pretended the idea had just occurred to her to ask him to write the anonymous letter.

Saniya opened her eyes the next morning with a smile for the day. She stayed in bed thinking about what she had done yesterday and about the happiness she was anticipating today. What else but happiness did she have to look forward to from now on? She had never known life could be this sweet. She had lived through seventeen springs, but the beauty of the world had never been disclosed to her the way it was today. Everything was beautiful this morning. Everything was smiling.

All this because Mustafa had smiled? She had seen many people smile at her in the street or on the tram when she was accompanying her maid, Bakhita, going back and forth to the clinic of a dentist who was putting fillings in her molars, which had been damaged by bonbons and sweets. Indeed, she had at the very least seen the smiles of Salim and Muhsin. But she hadn't felt what she did on seeing Mustafa's smile. It seemed this smile had turned her life upside down and changed the world in her sight. Everything before her and around her began to smile.

All the same, she had greeted it by shutting the window in his face. Saniya laughed, revealing her pearly teeth, when she thought of that scene.

She was chock-full of contentment, pleasure, and inner delight at treating him so roughly. She asked herself happily what he could possibly be saying about her now. Then she stopped laughing and said in a voice trembling with delight, "The poor dear."

All the same, another conflicting emotion had a share in her heart. It was a feeling of regret, compassion, and anxiety. She feared she might have hurt him more than she should have—that she might have severely wounded his feelings.

This emotion persisted, and she scolded herself, or pretended to scold herself. For in reality the feeling of pleasure at her rudeness and of delight in her roughness still fluttered around the edges of her heart. She found the solution at last, however. She was able to reconcile these two apparently conflicting emotions. She would compensate him for the mistreatment. Yes, she would show him some good treatment or at least not hurt his feelings after today . . . this poor, charming, young man.

She smiled.

The sun's rays reached her pillow, and her ebony hair gleamed in the light. She felt its warmth and put her pure white hand to her head to shield it from the sun's heat. But she remembered the time and realized she was later than usual getting up today. She rose at once and walked across the carpet with her bare white feet. She stood in front of the mirror in her silk nightgown. Her hair, which had not yet submitted to the morning comb, hung down, beautiful and black, covering her eyes. She shook her head to put it in place and to remove this thick veil from her eyes. She saw in the mirror an image she contemplated for a long time with admiration, as she turned slowly in every direction. How could it be? Was this marble neck hers? And these upraised breasts whose shadow showed clearly through her silk chemise! This waist that she encircled with her two hands to confirm how slender it was in the mirror? How amazing! She hadn't known she was this beautiful.

She smiled at her reflection too.

Then she took the comb. She drew it through her hair while gazing with satisfaction at her face and lips. She began to sing a short, cheerful song, a ditty, while changing from her nightgown to her housecoat.

When Saniya finished dressing and primping, today taking more time than usual, she gave a final look at her reflection in the mirror. Then she walked to the door of her room with the dainty steps of a beautiful bird. It seemed that everything about her today had become several times more charming and delicate than before. She was now in both her body and soul like an exquisite butterfly too fragile to be touched. Perhaps it was the radiant joy and luminous happiness that made her feel so light that she was today more a bird in flight than a solid body.

But as soon as she opened the door of her room and went out into the hall she stopped, dumbfounded. Fear gripped her without her knowing why. She heard a row between her father and her mother, revealing a high level of anger.

The sound came from the closed door of her father's room. She couldn't make out the words, although she clearly heard her name being repeated from time to time. Then her father used the expression "your daughter" in addressing her mother violently. Saniya froze where she was, aghast. It was clear that evil was ready to ambush her.

She had no time to reflect or gain control of herself. Her father's voice continued its frightening and thunderous explosions. Then the door was opened with such force that it almost came off its hinges. Her father appeared with a letter in his hand. When he saw her in front of him in the hall he shouted, "You're here?"

He paid no heed to his daughter's pale face, nor did he give her time to reply. Instead he pushed his hand toward her with the letter at once, screaming, "Take it! Take it and read! Read and tell me the meaning of the words written there."

Saniya did not move, nor did she take the letter. She wasn't strong enough to do anything. But her angry, raging father advanced on her as his fury increased. At that moment her mother appeared and shouted at him. She tried to pull him back without success. She wanted to get between him and his daughter to protect her. He pushed her away violently and approached Saniya. He yanked her arm, grabbing her hand roughly. He pressed her fingers around the letter, screaming, "I told you, read what's written here! Read these words! I'm a man who has always lived honorably. I've served in the Sudan and seen combat."

Saniya could not bear any more. She was at the breaking point and would have fallen to the floor had her mother not rushed to take her in her arms. She looked askance at her husband and said, "Won't you shut up, man! Can she stand talk like that, poor thing?"

But the father did not keep quiet. Instead, his rage increased. He took his daughter's limp arm and shook it violently while he demanded that she read the letter. The mother shoved his hand off her daughter and then took her to the nearest chair, holding her in her arms.

At that the father advanced and raised the letter to his eyes. He shouted, "You're not willing to read it? Then I'll read it. Listen."

The Eminent and Respected Dr. Hilmi,
    To begin:
    After greeting you, we inform you that there is a passionate love affair being freely conducted between Saniya Hanim, your daughter, and a man who is one of the customers of the coffeehouse facing your illustrious abode. Letters and signals

pass nonstop between the balcony and the coffeehouse. We have brought this to your attention because of our respect for you and because of our concern for your good reputation and our desire for the honor of your name.

Yours sincerely,

Signed:

A Sincere Friend

As soon as the father got to the end of the letter he shrieked at his daughter, "You have ruined my reputation. You have soiled my honor. My military honor! You ruin my name after I participated in the Battle of Omdurman!"

He did not finish, because Saniya, weak as she was, her eyes closed and her head on her mother's breast, began to shed tears that flowed silently in streaks over her face. When her mother suddenly noticed these silent tears, her compassion was moved to the bursting point within her.

She flared up in her husband's face, shouting, "Be quiet! Be quiet then, without any Omdurman or Om'umran. Man, you are going to kill my daughter, who is my life. Should I be happy with you then? God's name, this girl can't take this! Shame on you!"

She raised her eyes heavenward before turning them on her husband.

"By the Prophet, she's been falsely accused," she said. "May the one who slandered her be struck down along with his children! You who wrote this letter, may you be struck down, along with your children, your sight, and your health on account of this morning."

The father said sharply, "You mean your daughter has never stood on the balcony?"

The mother answered immediately, "Never . . . never! O deliverer! O omniscient God! On the balcony? May the tongue be cut out of anyone who says that."

She apparently had a flash of inspiration, for it occurred to

her just then that this anonymous letter must have come from
Zanuba. Yes . . . since the reason for the quarrel between her
and Saniya was precisely that. It hadn't been long enough for
that to have been erased from the heart. So it was Zanuba who
had done that, motivated by her anger at Saniya. The mother
seemed to have found an approach to defend her daughter and
a decisive argument of her innocence. Her face brightened,
and she sat up to deliver some telling words. But her husband
remembered at the same time the other letter that had fallen
into his grasp, the letter signed by Captain Salim, the letter
that his daughter hadn't known about and that he had subsequently returned to the sender. He no longer had any doubt
then as to the accuracy of this second letter, for the two confirmed each other.

At that he turned to his wife and said fiercely, "Fine . . . and
the captain's letter. Have you forgotten it?"

Poised on the verge of victory, the mother was taken by surprise. She looked at her husband and asked apprehensively,
"What letter from the captain?"

Then she remembered she had gone to Zanuba to complain
to her about her relative Salim, after her husband had told her
about the affair of the letter. So there was no way she could
deny it.

She reflected a little. Suddenly her eyes sparkled, for she had
found what she should say. "All the calamities have come from
Zanuba and her relatives. The first letter as much as the second came from the ill-omened direction of Zanuba. Has any
word or hint of information come from any other quarter but
Zanuba?

"Since the matter is confined to Zanuba and since Zanuba's
words cannot be trusted, because she is an enemy and relations with her have been severed, what value is there to this
anonymous letter, which doubtless is from her? No one but
Zanuba would have dared do this."

This is a summary of what the mother realized and she told
her husband, after she briefed him in detail about the relationship with Zanuba and the secret of their quarrel and that she
was the one who was looking at the coffeehouse from the

balcony whenever she came to visit until Saniya scolded her for that one day. Then Zanuba had gotten angry, sworn and cursed, and departed. And here she was finally having recourse to blaming everything she had done on Saniya.

The mother closed her decisive statement and defense by raising her arms toward the sky. She prayed fervently, "May God show you, Zanuba! May God repay Zanuba for what she has done, for the sake of this awful morning."

The father calmed down and his expression showed that he was receptive to this argument. He began to say of Zanuba, "My goodness . . . this must be an evil woman!"

The mother added immediately, "Very . . . very. That's well known! Can our Lord get any angrier at her than he is? Our Lord never condemns anyone unfairly. This woman lacks beauty, wealth, and a sweet tongue. She's over forty today, and the lady is still a spinster."

The parents' discussion of Zanuba lasted for some time. Then the father looked at his daughter. He saw that her eyes were closed. He gently took her hand to feel her pulse. He whispered to her mother to move her to her bed for a little rest. She was in excellent health but had suffered some psychological and physical stress. He punctuated these words by tearing the anonymous letter to shreds, while raining curses on Zanuba, that evil woman who had caused all this.

CHAPTER 18

How amazing! A whole week had passed and no trace had been seen of Saniya on the wooden balcony. What had happened to her? Was she sick? Had she definitely fled and left forever after that one accursed smile?

This was what the despairing Mustafa asked himself in the coffeehouse after persistently watching and waiting for a whole week to no avail. Saniya had actually avoided the balcony throughout this period, but not because she was ill. It was not because she had fled, never to return. It was rather because of what her father had said and the effect of the anonymous letter on her. She did not want to do anything to upset her father's tranquil retirement or to make this soldier emeritus at the end of his days think that his daughter had not protected his honor.

All this because of a man's smile?

She reflected on her situation a long time and remembered that this man was not bound to her by any tie. She knew nothing about his heart or character. Indeed, she didn't know who he was or what he did. He was totally foreign to her. Why should she suffer all this for his sake? What had he done for her? Except that smile. . . . Should an honorable girl be interested in a man like this? She sensed something inside her that she hadn't been aware of before. She was no longer that frivolous, playful girl who was tempted to flirt and toy with every man she encountered. Nor was she that girl whose nature made claims on her because of her passionate youth—whose developing heart wound her up so she ran every which way, looking at everything, inquisitive, anxious, and unsteady.

No, Saniya now had progressed beyond this stage. She had moved from anxiety to belief, the belief of a woman in life's purpose. She had grasped intuitively what a woman lives for and how she lives.

Saniya's education and culture did not exceed that of her classmates who had graduated with her from the same school for girls. Her reading of stories might have helped her further her mental development and her speculations, but belief cannot be acquired from reading alone without experimentation or direct observation. Saniya had read a great deal about honor and virtue, but it was only today that those terms meant anything to her. Her intuition was calling out to her this truth: Virtue in a woman does not mean she should never love. Virtue is for her to love with sublime emotion a man with a sublime heart and character.

But was Mustafa a man of sublime heart and character? This was the question. This was the subject of her present doubts. It caused her to separate herself from a man she was unsure of because all she knew of him was that he had smiled at her.

Thus she really did avoid the balcony. She was busy most of the time pondering and reflecting alone in her room. Crying made her feel better frequently and provided her one form of solace. She wept because she could not answer her doubt-inducing question. She did not want to show herself to him or to employ any stupid and flirtatious stratagems and silly signals. The part of her heart's truth that she had grasped today raised her above all this and made her think that nothing but isolation and tears matched her noble sentiments.

For the third time Mustafa swore that he would forsake the coffeehouse for good, since he had not seen Saniya. And here he was, starting another week. Would he keep his oath or break it like the previous one and postpone the deadline by another week? Yes . . . now the renewal period for deadlines and their extension was changed from hours and days to weeks. But this time he was resolutely determined that today would be his last in the coffeehouse.

Yes, there was to be no hesitation, weakness, or forbearance from now on, because he too had pondered his situation for some time. He had reflected that he was attaching childish importance and phantasmagoric hopes to nothing. What had come over him? What change had occurred in his life? Was just seeing a girl at her window, which she had immediately shut in his face, enough to make him devote all this time and thought to her? Who was she? What link tied him to her? Nothing! He didn't even know her name. Her feelings toward him were clear. She didn't look at him at all. She would see in him nothing but an impudent man who was one of the patrons of this sordid coffeehouse. If she had only shown some small sign or a single hint that she was aware of his existence, he could have considered it a tie and link between them. Indeed his knowledge would have amounted to a pact and a covenant. But what could he tell himself now? What could he use to reassure his anxious heart when every link, even that of the air, which he could imagine they both breathed, had been cut off after the wooden balcony was closed? On what then could he pin his hopes? Who could tell him? Perhaps, despite her beauty, she was one of those dull or flighty girls who knew nothing about deep emotion. How was he to know she had a heart and would be able to understand him and what he felt?

These ruminations and doubts brought him to the decision to desert the coffeehouse. Yes . . . he had to flee the coffeehouse, flee it just like that man with the broad shoulders and erect mustache. The image of the man, Salim, came back to him, but this time he felt some affection and pity for him. He imagined he had disappeared in despair after attempting to attract the attention of the goddess of the balcony with all the tricks and stratagems he was able to muster and with everything that his unemancipated mentality thought witty and elegant. Yes, he had been extremely ridiculous, but wasn't he a victim? Wasn't he also worthy of compassion? He had loved, anticipated, and hoped . . . then he had failed, become dejected, and had disappeared.

This image helped to reinforce Mustafa's determination. So he cast a last glance at the darkened balcony, which had not been opened for ten days. He called the waiter decisively, like a person preparing for serious action. He paid, rose, shaking himself off, and looked right and left, deciding which way to go, as though choosing a path of no return, but suddenly that idea occurred to him that always came to him when he rose this way. He went limp. Sweat flowed from his brow. His enthusiasm, drive, and determination seemed a mirage no less preposterous than the mirage he was fleeing. He would leave the coffeehouse. Fine! But to where? Where would he go? To the brothels and whores or the company of those friends who were no less fallen than the fallen women? But he had finally discovered nobility in his heart and uncovered inside himself unsuspected beauty and purity. Or should he go to another of the coffeehouses of Al-Sayyida district in an attempt to pluck this girl from his heart—to remove her from his heart, if that was possible. Fine . . . but what awaited him then, after that, since it was by the light of this woman that he had begun to understand the value of life? What was to be the destiny of his heart, which had been as dead as an antique clock that had stopped? Now it was pounding with life! Should he forget the pleasure of those new sensations this girl had inspired in him when she had shown herself to him? Certainly not! It was impossible for all that to go. How simpleminded he was to assume that by merely getting up or paying the waiter he could end everything. Indeed, why was he thinking of leaving? It was no doubt a revolt based on his disappointed hope—but why had he hoped and why should he be despondent? Why should doubts beset him? It should be enough for him that she had inspired him, even if unintentionally, with those beautiful and noble sentiments that nothing and no one had disclosed to him before. He would remain in the coffeehouse always, not to look at her or watch for her, but to nourish his heart by being near her. The mere thought that he was near her sufficed.

Mustafa returned and sat back down. His soul was relieved by this outcome, although he wondered how it was his habits had taken this poetic turn.

Mustafa kept coming to the coffeehouse as usual, not hoping for anything except the grace of God and a happy chance encounter. He saw that the window remained closed and he wasn't upset or disgruntled. One day when he was having a siesta as usual after lunch he wasn't able to sleep. So he got up, dressed, and went down to the coffeehouse early to kill some time and drink a cup of coffee. It was three o'clock. The waiter had scarcely brought him the drink and left when Mustafa saw two women coming out of Dr. Hilmi's house. One of them looked young and svelte in the latest fashion, while the other who followed her was a maid in a black wrap. Mustafa didn't doubt that she and her servant were coming out. His heart pounded rapidly. Different thoughts about what he ought to do jostled together in his head. He was confused and flustered. How should he act? He saw them walking along the street toward Al-Sayyida Zaynab Square. He began to ask himself apprehensively and anxiously what he should do. He was afraid they would go too far and disappear from sight before he decided. He was afraid too that an opportunity as auspicious as this would rarely return. He had been waiting for weeks for nothing more than a glimpse of her on the balcony. At last, although he had not reached a decision, his emotion alone propelled him. So he found himself leaping from his chair, leaving the drink he had ordered. He shot off after them without realizing what he was doing. The two women reached Al-Sayyida Square and got on the streetcar heading to Al-Ataba al-Khadra by way of Abd al-Aziz Street. Mustafa arrived after them, saw them climb into the section reserved for women, and stood there indecisively, until the conductor blew the whistle and the streetcar began to move. Again it was Mustafa's heart that decided suddenly. He jumped on the same tram. He didn't know where he was going, why he had done that, or what the consequences of this act would be. He purchased a ticket for Al-Ataba al-Khadra, although he asked himself: *How do I know she's getting off at Al-Ataba?*

Then he dropped this point to brood about her going out at such an hour. Where to? Where was she heading? Was she in the habit of going out at this time every day, while he was sleeping off his lunch in bed? Was it necessary for him to suffer insomnia today in order to learn that? What a blessing insomnia was!

But the important thing was for him to pay very close attention to where they got off so if they did get off before Al-Ataba

he wouldn't miss it like a fool. For this reason Mustafa glued
his eyes to the women's compartment. He looked at nothing but
that. When the streetcar reached Abd al-Aziz Street, she and
her maid got off. Mustafa hadn't been expecting that. He had
assumed they were heading for Al-Ataba al-Khadra. He didn't
notice they had gotten out until the streetcar had started to
move. So he rose as though crazed and took a mighty leap out.
He turned around to look for them fretfully and found himself face-to-face with Saniya. He blushed in embarrassment.
His heart was throbbing. He stepped back out of their path,
which he had blocked with his leap. Saniya was equally self-
conscious and blushed as deeply on seeing him confront them
suddenly. Her gauzy black veil, however, concealed the tint of
her face. She noticed his blush and proceeded on her way, followed by her maid. Mustafa stopped in his tracks, stunned by
the shock. He let them go off without being aware of it until
they had almost disappeared among the passersby. Then he
remembered them and remembered that he wanted to learn
where they were going. So he rushed off quickly to search for
them. When he caught up, he slowed his pace and trailed them
at a distance until he saw them enter a building halfway down
the block.

Mustafa stood apprehensively for a moment in front of the
door, asking himself what they could want in this building and
whether he ought to follow them in. His eyes fell on the assorted
brass plaques by the door of the building. They announced a
doctor, an attorney, and a merchant. Without further hesitation
he plunged through the door and bounded up the steps after
them. He found them in front of a suite on the third floor. The
maid was ringing an electric buzzer. The door opened right
away, and the two women entered. Mustafa saw the door about
to close behind them. He hastened to it and shoved it with his
hand to keep it from shutting. He went in with his heart
pounding . . . perhaps because of his rapid climb and leap. He
cast his eyes around the place. He was in a doctor's office. He
deduced this from the male nurse who opened the door and led
the ladies to a women's waiting room. Overcome by vexation
and sorrow, Mustafa watched them enter that room set aside for

them. The nurse returned to lead him to the men's waiting room. He followed without thinking.

Mustafa shortly found himself among several waiting men, some in modern dress, others in traditional attire. He took his seat politely after greeting everyone. He too began to wait quietly.

But what was he waiting for? It was only at this moment that Mustafa became aware of his situation. Why was he here in this room? He wasn't ill. What was he to do when his turn came now and he was shown in to the doctor? Moreover, what kind of doctor was this in whose clinic he was waiting? He didn't even know if he was in internal medicine, a surgeon, an ophthalmologist, or a specialist in ears and throat. He turned with anxious confusion right and left. Should he ask those around him about the specialty of this doctor? But his question would shock them. They would be amazed at this sick man who came not knowing what kind of doctor it was. He preferred to keep still. Perhaps between now and his appearance before the doctor God would grant him relief. Or when he entered the doctor's office and saw the type of tools and instruments there, his specialty might become clear. For that reason there was no harm in waiting.

But he remembered something else: He hadn't come here to see the doctor! Who cared about his office with its instruments and equipment? Where were she and her maid? Where were the two women? He suddenly rose to his feet in a way that attracted the stares of the sick men waiting there, but he paid no heed and went to the door and out into the hall. He looked around and saw where the women's waiting room was. Its door was open. He went that way and passed by the door quickly. Then he came back and stood by the door for a moment, looking over the faces as though he had a relative or in-law he was seeking among those present. Suddenly his eyes fell on those of Saniya. She was looking at him, but she lowered her black eyes to the floor at once with becoming modesty. Mustafa quickly fell back and returned to his place in the room for men. The blood had risen to his face. He bowed his head, staggered by the impact of that look.

There was no doubt that she recognized him, that she was aware of his existence. Otherwise, what was the meaning of this unusual look? Yes, she had begun to pay attention to him; he was sure of that. He felt now that there was indeed a tie between them. Her eyes' captivating rays, which had plunged into his heart just now, formed a stronger bond than iron chains. He had done the right thing by following her today. He would always follow her wherever she went. But was it possible this was her first visit here, or had she frequented it for some time unbeknownst to him? Was she ill, then? The poor dear . . . and with what malady, do you suppose? Was she in pain? Could he bear to find out about her pain and not be in pain himself? Impossible! He would feel pain as she did, be sick as she was. It would be sufficient happiness and comfort to him to be sick like her, with her very own illness. Yes, with her own disease! Nothing else . . . If only he knew what her illness was! That was the problem. But the matter was simple. All he had to learn was what kind of doctor's clinic this was.

While he was in the midst of these thoughts and emotions, a patient entered who had a handkerchief over his jaw and the lower part of his swollen cheek. When Mustafa saw him, he grasped the doctor's line of work. God had spared him the trouble of asking. He was in a dentist's office. Praise God, he had turned out to be a dentist. Mustafa's mind was at ease about her now, and about himself. Teeth? Everyone requires dental care. Some people who can afford it and have a delicate constitution keep a dentist on retainer to look after their teeth. What a happy opportunity it would be if he could always see her at the clinic. Why shouldn't he get his teeth treated too? He put a finger in his mouth at once to search and explore. Perhaps he would come upon a tooth or molar needing a filling. All he could find was a wisdom tooth that hurt him a little—according to his claim now—whenever he ate or drank something cold.

The time passed till only a moment remained before Mustafa's turn. The nurse came to notify him. He asked him to be patient, saying he would go in directly after the lady who was currently in the dentist's office.

Mustafa rose immediately and headed for the hallway. He threw a quick glance at Saniya's place in the women's room and did not find her there. He concluded she was in the dentist's office now, unless she had already left without his seeing her. Mustafa wasn't agitated or sad, because he knew he would encounter her frequently in this clinic. The nurse came then to ask him to enter. He was a little surprised, since he had not seen anyone leave the dentist's office. When Mustafa asked about that, the nurse told him the dentist's office had another door that opened directly to the stairway.

Mustafa finally went in. He was received by a man whose hair had gone gray and who was wearing something like a white linen overcoat. He realized that this was the dentist and greeted him. The dentist answered him quickly, motioning for him to sit in the examining chair. Mustafa tried to speak to show him the wisdom tooth he was going to complain about. The doctor, however, didn't give him time and had him open his mouth. Taking a dental probe, he began to dig away at all of his teeth. After a moment he quit probing. Straightening up, he told this new customer that no fewer than twelve teeth needed fillings.

How had he found these twelve? Who could say! Mustafa vainly attempted to convince him that all his teeth were sound, that he had eaten extremely well with them for years, and that his only complaint was the wisdom tooth. Even this tooth did not trouble him much. All this talk evaporated in the air. Mustafa was finally forced to yield to this dentist, who rolled up his sleeves and turned on the electric drill. He began to test Mustafa's teeth, both the sound ones and those with cavities.

When the doctor finished, he led his patient to his desk and began to write up a bill that specified the advance payment, the balance due, and future appointments. The appointments were what principally interested Mustafa. These appointments had to correspond to Saniya's; otherwise what was the use then? But how could he arrange that when he didn't know Saniya's precise schedule? Was it possible or appropriate to say to the dentist, "Make my appointments at the same time and on the same day as those of Miss ___"? So Mustafa was in a quandary and hesitated. The dentist continued proposing days and hours to him while he used work as an excuse to refuse, anxiously and hesitantly. Finally he thought of picking three o'clock, for it was at about this time that Saniya came today. Then he thought that Saniya's next appointment might be for the day after tomorrow, since you don't get treatment two days in a row. He asked the dentist at once to make his next appointment for that day, declaring it should be for three o'clock sharp. The dentist paused for a moment and leafed through the appointment book in front of him. Then he looked up at Mustafa and told him that was not possible the day after tomorrow, because the lady who left just before he came in would return then to terminate her treatment begun two months before. If Mustafa wanted, he could come at three thirty, in other words just after her, like today. After that he could come at exactly three and take the place of that lady, since her treatment was ending.

Her treatment was ending? Whose? How unfortunate! She had been coming here for two months? Had he come here today to take her place?

Mustafa's heart throbbed. He was startled by the thought that he would not be able to see her at the clinic and that her treatment was finished or would be finished in a couple of days. He had come in only at the end of the period. He couldn't keep himself from shouting in surprise, "The young lady who was accompanied by her maid?"

The dentist looked up at Mustafa with mild astonishment and replied in the affirmative. Mustafa added as though to himself, "Her treatment's over? How can it be over?"

The dentist corrected him with a smile. "Day after tomorrow will be the last day of treatment."

Mustafa paid the amount requested and accepted the appointment sheet, inattentively, glumly, and gravely. He departed, asking himself like a lunatic why he had agreed. Why would he come? How would he be able to come after she had stopped? What use was there to his coming?

He had scarcely reached the stairway before he heard the dentist behind him, warning him from the clinic door not to eat any hot foods, or cold or hard food, from now on. He should observe extreme care when he chewed so as not to disturb the roots. He should confine his food, so far as possible, to liquids like broth, milk, and so on. There would be no harm in morsels of fresh bread dipped in the liquids. . . .

Mustafa was furious. He descended the steps in a rage, saying to himself, "This is what I've accomplished today! All I've got to show for it is my broken teeth."

CHAPTER 19

Mustafa returned home, sad and dejected. He couldn't stop wondering how she had been going to the dentist for two months without his knowing. When he did find out, here she was completing her treatment and about to stop going. If only he had not learned about it. He always learned things too late!

Now what was he going to do in order to see her? What a fine opportunity he would have had to meet her at the dentist's and to follow her at a short distance going and coming. Now that this was no longer possible, what could he do? Seeing her on the balcony was a matter that could not be guaranteed.

Mustafa fell asleep. When he got up, these ideas were still in his mind. In the midst of his dejection and despair he remembered that she was going to the dentist for the last time the next day and that no matter how bitter that reality was, he did have before him an opportunity to see her there the next day.

He felt somewhat reassured by this thought, even though a voice called out to him at once asking what value there was to seeing her a single time when absence and separation for he knew not how long would follow.

Mustafa trembled a little. He felt a strange emotion arising within him, a desire born of despair. He resolved straightaway to undertake a daring deed. The dentist's appointment tomorrow was his last opportunity; he had to treat it with great care. Yes, when would circumstances arise again that would allow him to be near her under one roof? By God, if tomorrow did not work out, all his hopes would collapse. So he had better hold tight to this final day. He would strike with desperation and not think of the consequences.

He went at once to the table and took some paper and a pen. He began to write and write, with sweat pouring down. Whenever he spawned a word or sentence it seemed that a part of himself emerged with it. He spent a large portion of the night bent over the paper revising what he had written. It seemed to him it wasn't what he wanted to write. He would have liked something else or something more; there were things inside him that he knew, and he felt them overflowing and resounding, but none of them made it onto the page. He was forced, after fatigue and repeated revision had exhausted him, to retain what he had written, despite its defects, and put the letter in a clean white envelope. Then he went to bed. His eyes were bloodshot from staying up so late, from writing, and from his raging emotions.

When Mustafa rose in the morning, the first thing he did was to take the long letter he had drafted the day before and reread it. He paused a moment, brooding apprehensively. At last he seized it and tore it into pieces, which he threw in the kitchen wastebasket.

His mind was awake and refreshed this morning. It seemed to him that emotion had almost led him astray. Why was he writing such things to this girl? The pages were truthful. That was right. He was simply informing her of some of his sentiments for her. That was true. But what was all that to her? She might perhaps not be blamed if she said to herself after reading his letter: *What does this man want from me? Yes, what does he hope to get with his pages gushing with emotions?* He liked her! He couldn't imagine life without seeing her. So he said. Fine! Then he should marry her! Instead of a long letter like this, he should go to her father or send someone as his deputy to him or to her mother to arrange an engagement. Who? His maternal uncle's wife could substitute for his deceased mother and this uncle could stand in for his late father. Then his thoughts moved from all this to his financial situation and how he would live after getting married. Should he take a dwelling suitable for her in Cairo then? Should he liquidate his business holdings in Al-Mahalla al-Kubra? But what would he do if he didn't find employment in Cairo? What would be his social status? Would she be content with him if he had no occupation? But why should he concern his mind with all this? Was a man like him unable to procure a position? The important thing now was for him to follow the straight path and ask for her hand from her family. There was no place for vacuous letters. This was what his intellect dictated to him . . . his intellect of ten o'clock in the morning when the commotion of life and the activity of the material forces of renewal make all creatures subservient to materialist logic.

But at noon, with the heat of the sun alleviated only by wisps of breeze from the Nile, the commotion abated a little. People stretched out in the shade with their eyelids half-closed against the glaring light that sketched undulating and quivering shapes in the air. It was a time when the imagination began to awaken and everything once again fell under the sway of emotion. Then Mustafa began to regret that he had torn up the letter. He looked at his watch. Only a short time remained before Saniya was scheduled to go to the doctor. This was his last chance! This was the last day he could meet her there. What had he prepared for this auspicious moment? How could he be lazy, hesitant, and indecisive at a time like this?

Thus the other, emotional logic returned to him, and he unconsciously followed its dictates. He went immediately to the table and took paper and pen. But he came to a halt when he remembered what he had done that morning. Still he convinced himself by saying that he would not write numerous pages like yesterday. Instead he would make his feelings toward her clear in two words or two lines only. He remembered about asking for her hand from her family. There was nothing to be gained from the letter. He hesitated a little. But soon he felt the need to write his letter to her. Yes, he would ask for her hand and marry her if she accepted, God willing. But all that wouldn't rule out this letter, which she would surely read. He had a pressing need to tell her how he felt about her and to know what she thought about that. The question wasn't just one of attaining a material goal by a direct route as stipulated by the intellect. There was also an overriding question of emotion and of his heart, which wouldn't be at ease or at rest until it learned whether there was a mutuality of sentiment and emotion or not . . . or at least it would not be calm or settled until it explained how it felt and received a reply. Mustafa sensed this need of the heart. Even if the engagement and marriage were arranged, he would still be in a terrifying need of knowing what she thought of him. Thus Mustafa became fully convinced. He seemed to realize that the intellect's logic differs from that of the heart. Each of them is sound. Each of them is necessary. He bent over the paper to write a number of lines quickly and then placed his letter in an envelope. After that he called his servant and asked for his lunch, which he wolfed down. Then he went down to the coffeehouse to watch for the girl and her maid to emerge.

As soon as three o'clock sounded, the maid appeared at the door. Mustafa's heart was pounding. He prepared to rise. But the maid walked alone out to the street and stopped a passing vehicle. Only a moment later Saniya emerged. She headed for the carriage. Before she got in she turned toward the coffeehouse and looked at Mustafa. Then she climbed up. Her maid followed her, and the carriage drove them away.

Mustafa stood there for a time, almost dumbfounded. He had first of all assumed they would be going by streetcar like the previous time. He hadn't anticipated the carriage. Second, there was the impact of that look. If the niqab hadn't hidden her mouth, Mustafa would have seen a smile there. But amazingly enough, he had detected this smile in her eyes. It was an unusual smile. Many elements mixed together in it, if only Mustafa had realized: pleasure, flirtation, and deep emotion. He merely grasped that she was beginning to notice his existence and to remark his interest in her. Mustafa was delighted. The carriage disappeared from sight. He roused himself but was shaking. He ran off quickly to look for a carriage. He was agitated and afraid he wouldn't catch up with them. But then he remembered he knew where she was going and calmed down a little. All the same, he hailed a carriage so he wouldn't be late. En route, he kept thinking about her, about that look, and about her taking a carriage today.

Yes, why had she taken a carriage today? Because she knew he would follow her in the streetcar? Perhaps she got off to a late start today. Perhaps she had always gone in a carriage except the day before yesterday, when she had chanced to go by tram. Or perhaps she wanted to save time. In any case, this wasn't an important question and didn't require all this thought. There was absolutely nothing out of the ordinary in her conduct. What about a lady taking a carriage? Didn't he want her to ride in a carriage? He continued brooding about all this until his carriage arrived in front of the dentist's building, where he quickly climbed out and went upstairs. The first thing he did on entering the clinic was to cast a glance at the place where Saniya had been in the women's waiting room the day before yesterday . . . as though it was impossible for her to change places. He didn't find her there and trembled. He looked despondently at the other side of the room and saw her sitting beside her maid. She looked at him, and he blushed in embarrassment. He vanished at once from her sight, heading for the men's waiting room, where he cooled his heels, wondering how he could get the letter to her.

A beautiful idea finally came to him. It was to ask the nurse to call the maid accompanying the lady to step out of the women's waiting room. Then he would deliver the letter to the maid for her to give to her mistress, on the understanding that it was from the dentist, for example. But suppose Saniya asked the nurse who was asking for her maid? What would he reply? Moreover, what sense would there be for the dentist to send her a letter just before he saw her? If he gave the letter to the nurse himself to deliver to Saniya, he would awaken the man's suspicions and expose Saniya and himself to gossip. This uneducated maid was the best messenger, but how could he summon her?

Mustafa didn't arrive at a satisfactory solution and feared his opportunity would be lost in this hesitation over strategy. Saniya's turn would come and she and her maid would enter the dentist's office to exit afterward by the other door without his seeing her. The opportunity would be lost. He rose resolutely, determined to carry out the idea without regard to the consequences. He summoned the nurse in the hall and asked him to call the maid from the women's waiting room. He didn't say any more than that. The attendant went to the maid at once and motioned from a distance for her to come. She hesitated a little and looked at her mistress, who told her, "Get up, Dada Bakhita, and see what the nurse wants."

So Bakhita rose and went to him. He pulled her along by her hand in silence until he delivered her to Mustafa, who took a deep breath. He took her aside and removed the letter from his pocket to hand to her. He said, "Give this to your mistress at once."

He did not elaborate, convinced that fewer words were better in these circumstances than many. The maid took the letter and said, "Yes, sir." It didn't occur to her to ask who it was from.

As soon as Mustafa saw her take the letter to Saniya, his heart was transported with happiness. He felt he had achieved everything he wanted from this place and left the clinic immediately. He seemed not to be walking on his feet but instead felt transported aloft by imaginary wings. He went down Abd al-Aziz Street, forgetting that his appointment was waiting for him at the dentist's.

CHAPTER 20

Muhsin's condition grew progressively worse. His teachers, after scratching their heads for a long time, were unanimous that unless a miracle saved him, he would definitely flunk this year. He had grown pale and spoke little. His uncles felt sorry for him and began to force him out on excursions to try to revive him. They would walk beside him in silence, still not daring to be the first to speak. The contagion had possibly been passed on to Abduh, whose situation also began to resemble Muhsin's. He tolerated little talk in his presence and especially not any mention of Saniya. Zanuba had recently developed the habit, whenever she learned some news or observed something from her window relating to the neighbors, of rushing to spread the word among the folks when they gathered around the dining table. But Abduh categorically forbade her to do that and forced her to keep totally silent, at least in their presence. Thus the home became like a cemetery, and they were like ghosts, entering and exiting silently. At first this annoyed Hanafi Effendi and Mabruk. Yes, what had Hanafi done? The others had an excuse for keeping quiet. What excuse did he have to let them bury him with them? He tried to talk, joke, and banter with them, wanting to cheer them up, but couldn't get any of them to listen. They weren't willing to be amused. So he was obliged to fall silent.

Muhsin's grief was certainly so great it had such an effect on those around him. The moment this poor wretch heard from the street the sound of a piano being played in a house, he would turn yellow and then green. His heart would rise and fall. His steps would falter. He would attempt the impossible— to control himself and hide his sudden pain.

Days had passed, never to return, when he had listened to the sound of the piano with her beside him, teaching him how

to play, holding his hand in her delicate one. He had taught
her to sing. She had listened, watching him with admiration
while he sang:

> Your figure is amir of the boughs
> Without any rival,
> The rose of your cheeks is sultan
> Over the flowers;
> Love is all sorrows,
> O Heart, beware,
> Rejection and separation are
> The reward of the daring.

The specter of those days appeared before the youth. He
paused as a fit of weeping overcame him. Then he said to himself, erupting in his solitude:

> Love is all sorrows,
> O Heart, beware,
> Rejection and separation are
> The reward of the daring.

Yes . . . he used to smile when he taught her that, during
those happy days that had ended. He had smiled because he
thought the song was just a song and that the warning and ad-
monition it contained were merely words. How could he have
known that everything that had happened would be over so
quickly and that all this was waiting for him?

> O Heart, you loved and came to regret;
> You began to complain of what you endured;
> No one would have mercy on you.

The song said this too.

Yes, "You began to complain of what you endured!" He was
deprived even of a chance to complain. Would she come close
enough to hear a lament now? No. Impossible! And he would
not allow himself to complain to his comrades. That might
provide some relief, but what was the use?

Abduh and Salim frequently kept him company, sensing a bond between their hearts and his. He perceived intuitively Salim's burning desire to start a conversation with him and to seize some opportunity to talk about that topic, but Muhsin preferred silence. All the same, whenever they noticed a woman in a green dress or heard the sound of a piano or any mention of electric wiring, they all felt a shiver go through them. This was the sole language they found mutually intelligible.

Extraordinarily, Salim changed into another person. Muhsin's sensitive heart had enough of the sacred fire in it to fill Salim's heart and also to make up for the deficiencies of Abduh's heart. Salim was not naturally predisposed to sensitivities like these. His relationship with Saniya did not require all this. Without doubt, if he had been alone in a community like Port Said and the same thing had happened, he wouldn't have carried on this way. Was it then contagious? Or a question of imagination and suggestion? Is the heart not a frighteningly powerful source? A single powerful heart may suffice to inspire a wide variety of other hearts.

Thus Abduh's and Salim's feelings began as admiration and sympathy and ended as a shared participation. The deeper Muhsin penetrated into his pain and the more they shared it with him, the more they both felt elevated above their original stature.

With the passing days, as they lived with Muhsin and his beautiful grief, every evil or hateful feeling in them toward Saniya or Mustafa evaporated. Even stranger than that, Saniya had been transformed in Salim's eye. He had forgotten the material woman with her seductive body and upturned breasts like two oranges. All he remembered of her now was a spiritual name denoting none other than a Beloved for whose sake they suffered. They were witnesses and elegists for the torment of this young person who had given up so much for the sake of his Beloved.

Yes, when Muhsin remembered now the day he saw the farm laborers at the estate toiling and suffering while they sang for the sake of the harvest—their Beloved—raised high in pile on pile and how they had gathered like worshippers with their scythes, their bare feet and bodies scarred by cold and heat, work and oppression, when he too had thought of his Beloved, a question had shaken him: Would he be able to suffer as much for the sake of his Beloved? Or did he not share the same blood as these laborers?

Muhsin, despite what had happened, was just not able to expunge from his thoughts the letter he had received at the farm and had retained. Not even the truth could destroy the imaginings and fantasies he had constructed for such a long time about that letter. The imagination is at times stronger than reality.

For this reason Muhsin kept getting that letter out when he was alone to read and scrutinize it. He repeated those sentences, which he interpreted very freely as his imagination lent them meanings they had never had. He hadn't forgotten that Zanuba had said that this letter had been drafted by a public scribe in front of Al-Sayyida courthouse, but all the same he couldn't bring himself to tear it up. He clung to it and to its familiar phrases as though imagination, through its persistence, had lent it the force of truth, or fantasy had become belief. How can truth defeat belief unless the intellect defeats the heart?

One day Salim surprised Muhsin in his bed when he had carefully removed that letter from its envelope and begun to read it as usual, with slow deliberation, behind the curtain of a lowered mosquito net. Salim couldn't control himself. He broke his silence and shouted with apprehensive joy, "A letter? A letter from her?"

Muhsin raised his head in surprise. He tried instinctively to hide the letter. The honorary president, Hanafi, was stretched out on his bed near them, seeking relief in sleep from the sorrows he shared voluntarily. When he heard the shout of joy that Salim emitted, after not hearing him say anything for a long time, he felt sure that the hour of mercy and redemption had dawned. He brushed the covers away briskly and sat up in bed. He shouted warmly and zealously, "Tell me the good news, boys."

Salim at once left the room, searching the house and calling, "Abduh! . . . Oh, Abduh!"

Commotion reigned. If Zanuba had been present, she would have been astonished at this sudden turnabout in the silent residence to which a semblance of life had returned. But she had gone out accompanied by Mabruk for a visit, so she said. Perhaps she had in fact gone visiting, if only to share her latent hatred, which hadn't cooled, and to publish what she falsely invented about her adversary. Or perhaps she had fibbed and gone with Mabruk to search for the community's skilled sorcerers.

Abduh was in the living room at the drafting board, working and groaning to keep himself busy. He threw down the pen in distress with another groan of vexed and despairing anger at this state. When he heard Salim call, his expression changed at once and he hurried to see what the news was.

It wasn't long before Muhsin found himself surrounded by his comrades. They were looking at him expectantly. The smile of hope on their faces touched him.

He couldn't remain silent this time. The sight of their hope and joy moved him. He put his hand under the pillow and brought out the letter. Yet he hesitated a little and felt embarrassed, for he remembered that the letter dated back some time. They no doubt thought it was new. He would disappoint their hopes. But all the same he wasn't able to maintain his planned silence and isolation from them after this. He had to share with them this little bit he had left from Saniya. He stretched his hand out to them with the letter. Salim took it and spread it open for Abduh to see. They read it while Muhsin watched the expressions on their faces. At last they returned the letter to him silently. Their hopes were disappointed in a way that disturbed Muhsin. He heard Abduh grumble, "It's from Zanuba?"

Salim raised his head to look at Muhsin as though he were asking him in amazement what could bring him to read a letter like this.

The youth responded with a muffled voice, his head bowed, "She's the one who wrote it!"

Salim asked gently in a soft, polite voice, "She who? Saniya?"

Muhsin nodded in the affirmative. At that Salim took the letter a second time to reread it, and Abduh began to read it again too, over Salim's shoulder. Then Muhsin began to point out for them the letter's important phrases and to explain them. He glossed their hidden meanings in the way he understood them. Salim repeated these phases and compared them to what Muhsin claimed they meant.

He shook his head and said in a low, despairing voice, "No . . . not at all. That's not the meaning."

Poor Muhsin became pale. Abduh nudged Salim with his elbow and quickly said, "That's the meaning exactly. Read it again and you'll understand." Then he turned to Muhsin and said gently, "Haven't you seen her since you got back from your trip?"

Muhsin replied immediately, "No way!" Then Muhsin remembered that he actually hadn't gone to her after he returned. He hadn't seen her at all, even though she had urged him to come quickly. She was awaiting his return with impatience. Here was her letter and her expressions telling how great her anticipation was.

This thought brought him some hope and energy. Yes, he was the one at fault, because he hadn't gone to her right away. Indeed he had betrayed her trust. It was he who had mistreated her.

His joy increased with this thought. He burst out telling his comrades about it and about his experience with her before the trip, about the handkerchief that he had snatched but that she had awarded him, after drying his tears with it. Here was her handkerchief—still in his possession. He hastily brought out the silk handkerchief for them. Salim took it quickly and waved it at Hanafi, shouting with joy, "If you love the Prophet, pray for him."

President Hanafi, who was searching for his glasses to see what Salim was displaying, asked, "What's that?"

Salim held the handkerchief before Hanafi's eyes and replied, "Her handkerchief! Her handkerchief! We have her handkerchief!"

President Hanafi rose respectfully and said in a grave voice, "Her handkerchief! God is most great!" Then he raised his eyes to the heavens and kissed his hands front and back. He said, "Praise God! A blessing from God! This is enough for us! What better trophy could we want?"

After handing the handkerchief to Abduh to let him have a turn admiring it, Salim added with delight, "She told us to come but we didn't go."

Hanafi shouted immediately, "We're the ones at fault!" Then he pulled his skullcap down to his ears and put his hands on his hips. This honorary president began to dance as he sang, "We've got her handkerchief, her handkerchief. Mister, her handkerchief. Beautiful handkerchief, beautiful . . . beautiful!"

Abduh scolded him because he was afraid Hanafi would turn the situation into a comedy with this commotion. But the president in truth did not intend any mockery. It was simply joy that had been suppressed. It seemed that the lengthy silence and melancholy in this house and being obliged to keep pace with his comrades for a time and repress his merry temperament had affected him. When he understood that life in the house had returned to normal, he let himself go. For that reason he wouldn't stop the hubbub and commotion. Abduh shouted at him again, "Please, that's enough!"

He stopped singing, approached Abduh, and told him joyfully, "She asked us to come, but we didn't go."

At that Salim suddenly advanced on the group. A thought had occurred to him. "Hush . . . listen, all of you! Here's a suggestion."

They all looked at him, asking at the same time, "What?"

Salim said slowly, "I suggest that Muhsin should go. What do you think?" They signaled their approval.

Muhsin was watching what was transpiring before him with a smile. He was secretly pleased by the expressions: "We have her handkerchief" and "She told us to come" and so forth. He was touched that the word *we* had taken the place of *I*. He was comforted to have his personal property become communal. He had been able to give all of them hope and delight. From that moment, he felt he was responsible for the well-being of these folks and that he was now willing to do anything for their sake. He would never again deny them what was his. He agreed to go to meet Saniya. Perhaps he would achieve some result that would cheer up the folks.

CHAPTER 21

Saniya heard the afternoon call to prayers from the mosque of al-Sayyida while in her room. Since noon she hadn't slept a wink and hadn't stopped thinking about the letter she had received from her servant the day before at the dentist's office. From the moment she saw it in Bakhita's hand she had sensed who it was from. Her heart had started pounding at once. But she braced herself, took it, and tucked it in her dress. When night came she entered her room and locked the door before opening the letter with bated breath. Her breast rose and fell as she read it to the end. Then she raised the letter to her mouth, unconsciously, to kiss it. Tears flowed down her face to her mouth. She could not say whether she fell asleep or did not sleep at all that night. All she knew was that she was in a state she had never known before. The first thing she did in the morning was to read the letter again. After lunch, here she was once more, alone with her door locked and the letter open before her. She was gazing at its few lines, which had been able to provide her, both day and night, with the most beautiful happiness she had known throughout her life.

The letter was in this simple style:

My Lady:

Excuse my daring. I have been forced to act this way. For about a month the keys of my life have left my hand for that of another person. I no longer remain the only person holding the reins of my affairs. If I dare to write you, it is because I naturally want to know the opinion of that person who is now in charge of my happiness and sorrow, and perhaps my future. I attach importance to your opinion because I do not want to be selfish and because I love you to such a degree I

would prefer my own suffering to a marriage that your
feelings reject.

> Sincerely and respectfully
> yours,
>
> Mustafa Raji
>
> 35 Salama Street
> Second Floor

This man must be sincere in what he said, because she too
had experienced the same feeling—that her life no longer remained something that belonged to her alone. For her also, another person had gained control over the hours of happiness
and the hours of sorrow in life. The amazing thing was that
the expressions of this letter were a perfect match for her own
feelings, as though it had come to express the feelings preoc-
cupying her. What further indication of the truth of his emotion was needed after that? Couldn't heart speak to heart, as
they say?

She began to murmur with delight, "Yes! Heart speaks to
heart." One thing still troubled her: What was she to do? How
was she to act? Should she take a pen and reply? Or, despite
her confidence, certainty, conviction, despite her happiness
and joy with him, was it correct or appropriate for her as a
sheltered and honorable young woman to write to a man, who
was in any case not related to her?

She looked at the letter in her hand once more and proceeded to brood about this question, which had preoccupied
her since morning. Her glance fell on the expression "I attach
importance" to your opinion. Then she raised her eyes to the
line before it: "I want to know the opinion of that person
who is now in charge of my happiness . . ." and so forth and
so on. She bowed her head for a moment. Then, leaving the
letter on the chair, she went to the mirror and looked at the

reflection of her face, which was rosy to the point of being flushed from her continuous psychological agitation and uninterrupted thoughts. She smiled at herself with happy satisfaction. Then she said in a low voice, as though addressing her reflection with conviction, "Mustafa is waiting for my opinion. Mustafa has a right to know. That is one of his rights." The logic of the heart won another round. Then something else occurred to her: What if she were able to address him directly? Or at least to waste no time and send him a smile or a look that would constitute a complete answer? He was very close to her. Didn't he say he lived on the second story of the house next door? She was on the second story too! Yes! What good luck! His small, open balcony was opposite her window. She hadn't thought of that. What a fool she was!

She left the mirror and hastened to her window, which she opened to gauge how close his balcony was. Yes, it was very close. Only two meters separated them, because her room was at the end of the house on the side next to the neighbors'. What bliss! She didn't need the enclosed wooden balcony. There was no need to frequent the piano room and attract her parents' attention. How blind she was! Why hadn't she realized before how beautifully located her window was? It was true the wooden balcony looked directly out at the coffee-house, but what was the coffeehouse to her now? She would gesture to him from her window to go out on his small balcony, where he had not appeared a single time since he came. Then she would be able to converse with him from the privacy of her room during a tranquil night. The two meters between them wasn't much!

While she was lost in these beautiful thoughts someone knocked. She closed the window quickly and went to open the door. Her maid, Bakhita, informed her that young Muhsin was in the piano room. He had asked first for the senior mistress, but she was in her room performing the afternoon prayer along with other devotions. So he had asked to see the junior mistress.

Saniya, who was a little surprised, muttered, "Muhsin?"

She stood and hesitated for a moment. Then she looked up at Bakhita as though asking her why he had come. Finally she walked with heavy steps to the piano room.

Muhsin was there, sitting on an isolated chair. He had thought about Saniya's entry a thousand times. He would become pale and blush with her every movement as she drew closer. His heart rose and fell every time he thought of seeing her and uttering the momentous lines he had rehearsed in his head for days before he came today.

Suddenly he sensed the fluttering of her gown at the door. He sprang up, turned white, and stood in confusion, unable to speak. Saniya looked at him from the threshold with a severe, inquisitive glance. But she immediately approached him, as though touched by pity at the way he looked. She put her hand out to him and said in a kindly way, "How are you, Muhsin?"

Swallowing, he replied without lifting his head, "God be with you." Then he fell silent.

She was also silent, of course. Since she still thought it peculiar he had come, she was waiting to learn the reason. The silence lasted for a long time. She seemed to grasp, finally, that it was no use waiting for him to start. So she began, "Did you hear what your aunt did?"

Muhsin had anticipated this question and had prepared a reply. All he had to do now was to speak. He opened his mouth and uttered at first some trembling, agitated phrases. He said that he and all the household were angry with his aunt Zanuba because of the way she had treated Saniya. But how was that his fault? Why should Saniya hold him responsible for his aunt Zanuba's offense?

Saniya said immediately, "Who told you, Muhsin, I'm angry with you?"

This answer calmed Muhsin, and he relaxed a little. His embarrassment and fear dissipated somewhat. He seemed to have given this answer of hers a broader interpretation than it warranted. His understanding of it delighted him. He asked in a voice that trembled a little, "Is it true, you're not angry with me? Do you still feel the same way about me you used to? Like the day before I left?"

Saniya, who looked somewhat perturbed, said, "Of course! What have you done?"

But Muhsin did not pay any attention to her answer. He burst out with boyish enthusiasm, telling her about his trip, about waiting for her letter, about his return, about his desire to see her, about being afraid to visit her once he returned, and about the ill-omened thought that had overwhelmed him that she had totally forgotten him and didn't want to see him at all, and about those gloomy days he had spent remote from her. All that without daring to mention Mustafa or his role in what had taken place. . . . Saniya listened to him absentmindedly. She bowed her head frequently, especially when Muhsin talked of his pain at being far from her. Then he told her about her handkerchief, which was his consolation and his companion. He put his hand to his pocket. Here he felt a bundle of papers that contained poetry and prose he had composed and written since he and his uncles had decided he should visit Saniya. From that day till this visit he had been roaming about, wandering through public gardens and parks and along the banks of the Nile. His despair had been mixed with a small portion of delicious hope. Muhsin with his poetic temperament had previous experience composing poems, ballads, and lyrics for various occasions. So why not now, when his entire existence was in question? Today, shortly before he had come, it had occurred to him to present her everything he had written, so she would know the contents of his heart.

The youth finished his prepared statement. He was blushing, and his throat was dry. He looked at her, waiting to see what she would say, but she couldn't reply or found nothing to say.

She kept quiet for a while, feeling anxious. Then she rose in distress and said, "No, Muhsin, I'm not angry with you at all." This was the only response she had for everything he had said.

Muhsin was a bit bewildered but remained silent, waiting hopefully for her to say something more.

But she did not speak. She sat down again for a moment. Then she felt bored and looked at Muhsin, who had his head bowed expectantly. She rose halfway, as though suggesting he should leave, and said, "In any case, thanks, Muhsin. You can be sure I'm not at all angry with you."

Muhsin felt disappointed then. His eyes opened to the frightening reality, but like any desperate person, he closed them quickly and clutched at the impossible. He said in a pleading voice, "Do you remember the piano lessons?"

She fidgeted in her seat and said without much enthusiasm, "Of course I remember them."

The youth steeled himself and said, "But I've forgotten my lessons. I need you to go over everything we did again."

Saniya lowered her eyes and did not respond. She thought of Mustafa. She had no spare time. Her life was such that she couldn't spare a minute for anyone except Mustafa and thinking about him. She grew annoyed and said coldly, "I don't have time."

Muhsin braced himself again and entreated her, "Don't you want me to come?"

She did not answer at once. When she replied, she said, "Muhsin, I have a lot to do now."

Muhsin's confidence was waning. Sweat was dripping down his body. The world looked grim to his eyes. In a despairing voice he said, "You mean this is the last time I come? This is the last time I see you?"

He lost control of himself. His tears rolled down, and he started sobbing. Saniya observed this and heard the sounds of his sobs. She turned her head away, trying not to see. But she noticed that his voice was beginning to get louder. So she rose and hesitated a little. Then she turned toward him and said in a peevish, gruff voice, "What's the matter with you, Muhsin? Are you a crybaby? You're too old to cry."

But Muhsin was not able to restrain himself. He continued sobbing, moaning, and imploring her in choppy phrases. He told her that all he asked was just to see her. Yes, he had reached the point where all he desired was to be near her, that he should live nearby. So let her love Mustafa or someone else. He would never come between her and her happiness. Indeed her happiness was his happiness. If she would only not deprive

him of seeing her. Was this so much for her to grant? A look
would cost her nothing, while it would be his entire life.

In this fashion he continued to utter despondently and
only half-consciously words that mixed with his tears. Saniya saw there was no way to hush him up or stop him. So she
let him speak and rave. She went to the wooden balcony and
opened its window. She started to look out it, not hearing a
word he said.

Muhsin grew a little tired. He fell silent and looked up. He
found the woman he had thought was at least listening to him
retreating from the window with a red face after granting
someone an enchanting smile. He naturally knew who it was.

At that moment Muhsin grasped that the woman in front of
him was not Saniya. She closed the window and came back.
Her breast was heaving with delight. As soon as she saw Muhsin facing her with wet eyes, she frowned and asked peevishly,
"Are you still here, crying? Is that what you came for?"

Muhsin stood up. He felt it necessary to leave and now understood that the affair was over. She advanced toward him
and asked in a calm tone, "Are you going home?"

He pulled together all his strength to quiet his nerves and
say, "Yeah . . . I'm going home." But he kept standing there,
like a motionless statue.

Saniya seemed to fear he would start talking and weeping
again on the pretext of the farewell. So she suddenly drew
back from him and walked slowly toward the door as though
leading him there. But she was leading an imaginary person;
he hadn't budged from his spot.

She reached the threshold and stood there as though waiting. Muhsin came to his senses, grasping the situation. He saw
she was giving him a tacit invitation, indeed a fairly unambig-
uous one, to depart. He saw her expectant stance of visible annoyance, or at least of urgency and haste. So what, then, was
he waiting for? What was keeping him and stopping him from
leaving her at once, as she herself desired? The reality—which
he had sensed and suppressed, deceiving himself about it,
blinding himself so he wouldn't perceive it—was so obvious
to him now that there was no room to mask it or for self-

deception. It was so transparent it was naked. She not only did not love him but had never loved him. If she had been nice to him in the past to a degree that seduced and misled him, it was due to her heart being empty. She had a natural tendency, like any young person, to flirt and joke. Now that she was in love, she had quickly forgotten that past slack period. When a woman fell in love, she considered her life to have begun at the onset of that love. She no longer remembered what came before it.

Muhsin wasn't old enough to understand all this about women. This was, precisely, the first of his experiences. Despite his total conviction then that everything had ended and that the name Saniya must be erased from his memory for good, he kept standing there, not knowing what he was waiting for, just as she remained at the door while her weariness with standing was apparent. She didn't want to say anything, in order to avoid opening any new discussion. She needed to be alone in her room to gaze at Mustafa's letter. It was Muhsin's bad luck that he had come to her on her happiest day . . . on a day when there was no place in her mind or being for any person or thing other than Mustafa. A day like this can make a woman, even a tender woman—indeed a prophet or a saint— harsh and insensitive when she encounters something that interferes with that happiness. A happy woman in love can be selfish to the point of brutishness.

Finally Muhsin saw she had leaned her hand on the door and moved her leg to give it a rest. He knew he was annoying her by standing there, by being there. He walked to the door and silently shook her hand. He pulled her silk handkerchief out of his pocket and gave it back to her silently. She took it without a word. Then she said calmly, "Thanks for the visit. On behalf of Mama, I can tell you she thanks you a lot too."

Muhsin hesitated a little before departing. Finally, he didn't know why or with relation to what, he took from his pocket the sheaf of poems and prose and handed it to Saniya. She took it in astonishment. He departed quickly and speedily descended the steps. Only God knew the secret feelings of this youth's heart at that hour.

CHAPTER 22

It did not take long for the condition of Mustafa's small balcony to be transformed and for evidence of new life to appear on it, after it had been closed day and night and neglected, with dust piling up on its floor and railing. Mustafa hadn't been conscious of its existence, since he spent so little time in the house. His servant had not given it any consideration, because he was busy with other things. But it was now the place with top priority and was open day and night. Pots of flowers and fragrant herbs were lined up on it, and Mustafa began to spend there the time he used to pass at the coffeehouse.

Since this transformation, Mustafa, who had been happy just to glimpse Saniya, rarely passed a day when he did not gaze at her and converse with her. A veritable enchantment took hold of him the unforgettable day he heard her voice for the first time returning his greeting. She was smiling from her window in the middle of the night. Then there were those delightful, extemporaneous discussions during the following evenings. He hadn't known this girl was so bright. How delightful her conversation was, how fine her repartee, and how charming her gestures! After conversing with her, Mustafa was convinced he had discovered in her whole new kinds of beauty, over and above her beauty of form and body. Was it a beauty of spirit? He did not know. He only knew that he had come to love her a thousand times more intensely than before. He could not bear to have a day pass without hearing her voice. For that reason he waited impatiently for night to come, so darkness would shield them from the eyes of passersby.

But if the eyes of the two lovers were open, the eye of the jealous critic wasn't asleep either. Zanuba quickly uncovered the new developments on Mustafa's balcony. This was easy for her, since one of the living room windows was located directly above Mustafa's balcony and overlooked it. All Zanuba had to do was peer down to see and hear everything that took place.

For this reason, over the course of several days she slipped away from everyone else to go to the living room at night and stayed there until the conversation below her ended. It seemed that she couldn't bear to keep secret for long what she saw. She soon confided in Mabruk and made him her partner in the observation and surveillance. He was the only one who was unable to oppose her, accepting her invitation without argument or protest. Moreover, of late, the others and young Muhsin in particular had begun to seem strangely and frighteningly subdued. Yes, it frightened her; she didn't know why. All the same she felt it impossible for her to broach this with them.

So whenever the time for the rendezvous arrived, she gave Mabruk a wink, and they went to their positions at the window, where they began to follow developments. Zanuba would whisper in the servant's ear from time to time, while pointing out what was going on in the conversation, "Do you hear that, Mabruk?"

He would nod his head at her, looking like a moviegoer who didn't want anyone to interrupt his entertainment. But Zanuba would frequently nudge him and slap him on the shoulder, asking wrathfully, "Do you see the vile girl?"

Finally Zanuba's rage intensified, and the malice of this jealous woman boiled over. She would stop at nothing to disrupt their bliss. So she told Mabruk to fetch the duster and the broom. He was to pretend he was cleaning the window, and the dust and dirt would fall on Mustafa.

The servant retorted skeptically, "Does anyone dust their windows at night?"

She shouted at him, "That's what we do! Do we need a partner?"

The matter didn't stop there but escalated to their tossing down dirt, wastepaper, and fruit and vegetable peels from the living room window, letting them fall on Mustafa's balcony. Zanuba chose nighttime, first because that was when they met, and second so she could argue—if anyone objected—that she was only throwing these things into the street by night when it was deserted so the street sweeper could clean it up in the morning.

For that reason, as soon as she finished eating, she would remind Mabruk, "Don't forget! Collect the cucumber peelings."

The servant would answer her with a wink, "I won't forget, so we can throw them to the drake."

But naturally none of this kept Mustafa from going out on the balcony. He was enraged, however, that he was unable to protest. Saniya had categorically forbidden him to utter a word. Saniya understood this provocation and thought the best thing was to keep silent and pretend not to notice. She knew that Zanuba could not be beaten when it came to squabbling. She no doubt wanted to start a quarrel at any price. Why expose oneself to her and her filthy tongue? One had to put up with it, then, and say absolutely nothing.

Yes, Saniya comprehended right away that these acts were Zanuba's alone. None of Zanuba's relatives would think of doing something like this, not even Muhsin, to whom Saniya had been rude. She had mistreated him and more or less thrown him out that day. All the same, he would not be able to do this.

Strangely enough, this thought reminded Saniya at once of Muhsin and of the bundle he had handed her just before he departed. She had dropped it in her room, she knew not where. That prompted her to search for it so she could read these pages. For some time she had overlooked and forgotten them.

When she opened the bundle, sheets of poetry and prose fell out. She started to read and found her name linked with epithets of love and adoration. She was raised in the imagination of this poetic schoolboy and in the heart of this lad to divine rank. She read some memoir-like selections in which he confided to her his sorrows. Saniya was incredulous that she should have rewarded him for this with her brutal treatment. She remembered how he had wept in front of her. She had ignored him at the time to think of her own love. She had asked him to leave in a humiliating fashion. Had she done all that? She, who at least knew the right way to do things? Does a woman in love forget even that? Yes, she had wronged this boy. She did not deny that. She wished she could set right what had happened, to offer him some relief. Her conscience hurt her. She felt the burden of this injustice. But what could she do? She was a woman in love. She did not have even a small portion of her heart or thought available for anyone except . . .

At this point both the wrong and the person wronged began to fade away. Not a single trace was left in her soul of Muhsin or his poetry and prose. She went at once to the mirror. Then she looked at the sky and after that at her small alarm clock on the bedside table to see how much time was left before nightfall.

The moon was full that night. The clock struck ten. The members of the household had gone to sleep. All was still. Saniya rose from her chaise longue. In the darkness she put on over her silk chemise a dressing gown of rose muslin. She quickly patted her beautiful hair in place. Then she went to the window and opened it. The light of the moon burst upon her face. She was taken by surprise and retreated quickly back into the room. She smiled at once, however, for she saw that light from the silver sphere was illuminating even the corners of the dark room. She began again and proceeded fearlessly to the window. Mustafa was laughing. He must have seen and understood the secret of this delicious panic of hers. The young man was wearing ruby-colored pajamas trimmed with gold piping that shone in the light with the same gleam as his wavy chestnut hair. Everything about him on this beautiful night spoke of wealth and good looks. She was silent and smiled. She was gazing at the moon, which in all its roundness was looking down at them from the tranquil sky of Salama Street at that hour. An inner joy took hold of her. She laughed delicately, allowing her diamond teeth to flash in the moonlight, which seemed finally to have dazzled her. She raised her hands to rub her eyes gaily. Mustafa gazed at her, leaning his arm on the balcony railing, as though his heart were suddenly overflowing. He looked at her and said with a tone of censure softened by a quavering tremor of love, "You're half an hour late tonight."

She replied with a smile, "Right!"

"Why?"

She looked at him mischievously. Then, laughing, she said, "Why? Do you want me to interrupt your colloquy with the moon?"

He replied immediately, "Which moon?" Pointing to her window, which framed her, he said, "The only moon I know rises in this window."

She laughed and bowed her head modestly. She wanted to say something. Hastily, with a noticeable impetuousness, she said, "Mustafa, it's very warm tonight."

Mustafa did not answer her. He seemed annoyed that she had taken the conversation in another, pointless direction; although this sentence, coming from Saniya, like all her sentences, was invaluable to him. Mustafa began to look around him at the night. Yes, the air was still. It seemed to be holding its breath so as not to spoil their tranquility. Mustafa remembered that it was the beginning of March. He said, letting the light, which was dancing and floating in this still air, fall on his face, "Spring is here!"

There was a breath of air, and a delicate breeze playfully stirred Saniya's magnificent hair. A strand was blown over her temple, partially blocking an eye. Mustafa looked at her and was torn apart by desire. He wanted to kiss that curl over that eye.

Saniya surprised him while he was giving her that long look and trembled, lowering her eyes with secret delight. Then, with some confusion, she raised her head and rearranged her hair, which the breeze had disordered. She looked at the sky and said with a laugh, both coquettish and delicate, "In spring, according to novels, the sky rains not water or snow but roses and daisies."

Saniya had scarcely completed her sentence when cabbage leaves and cucumber peelings fell on Mustafa's head. He looked up and shouted, "Is it raining? And not roses and daisies but cabbage leaves and cucumber peels?"

Saniya was forced to turn her face away and burst out laughing. Mustafa wanted to have a word with the window from which the cabbage leaves had fallen but remembered Saniya's warning and prohibition. He turned to her and gestured with his hand to ask, "Shall I keep quiet this time too?"

Saniya answered him by putting a finger to her mouth for silence.

Mustafa muttered, "Whatever you say." But a sudden idea came to him. He motioned to Saniya to wait a moment where she was. Then he went inside and was gone briefly. He returned carrying an umbrella in his hand. He opened it and held it over his head to protect himself. When Saniya saw that, she burst into laughter, trying not to laugh too loud.

At this moment too, Zanuba nudged Mabruk, who was tired and yawning from staying awake and on his feet while conducting the surveillance. She directed his attention to Mustafa's umbrella. She whispered, "Mabruk! See, the wretch we're bombarding keeps coming up with something new."

Mabruk stared at the umbrella and then said, "This, all kidding aside, acts like a parasol."

"What is it but an umbrella? You disaster! Otherwise, what?"

Mabruk looked at the brilliant moon. Then he said, "He must be afraid of getting sunstroke."

Zanuba protested in a whisper, "Go to hell! That's the moon!"

Mabruk replied, "It's all the same. If you'll excuse my saying it, moon-stroke is even worse."

Zanuba, who was having heart palpitations, grasped a large colocasia peel to aim at Mustafa's head. She asked, "A stroke from which moon, Mabruk?"

She said this in a low, strained voice. Mabruk turned toward her at once and looked at the peel in her hand. Grasping what she meant, he said to himself, "O preserver!"

Zanuba pressed him, threatening to strike, "A stroke from which moon?"

Mabruk answered at once, flatteringly, "The colocasia moon."

Zanuba laughed, affecting delicacy. She liked what Mabruk had said and agreed with it. She said jestingly and in good humor, "Oh, liar!"

She tossed the colocasia peel on Mustafa's umbrella and asked, "Is this young man going to be affected by anyone's blow?" Then she thrust her hand into the garbage pail beside her. She nudged Mabruk and whispered, "Don't let up, Mabruk, or else. There's still plenty in the pail!"

The servant answered her, "Set your mind at ease, calm your soul, and go to bed. Why don't you, all kidding aside, go to bed?"

Zanuba looked at him skeptically and anxiously and asked, "I should put my faith in God and in you and go to sleep?"

Mabruk replied immediately, "Absolutely! Totally! A piece of cake! Lady, I won't move from here until I finish emptying the whole garbage pail on their heads."

Zanuba walked away; fatigue and prolonged standing had exhausted her too. Before she left the room, however, she turned back toward him and cautioned, "I'm afraid you'll dump it out all at once and depart. One peel at a time the way I taught you. Understand?"

"Certainly! Most willingly. One peel at a time. You go then, before you're shoved out."

Zanuba hesitated, pausing distrustfully. She asked herself who was to guarantee that the mission would be carried out as she desired. She wanted to curtail Mustafa and Saniya's conversation with this drizzle of cabbage leaves so their chat would never get anywhere and no word or agreement would be concluded between them.

She went back to Mabruk to tell him that. The servant couldn't take any more from her and shouted, "What's this all about? Isn't the point, no offense intended, to mess up their reunion tonight? By your life, I'll make it their last night on this balcony. You just go to sleep."

Zanuba was somewhat reassured by Mabruk's forcefulness. She repeated the part she liked best: "'Their last night.' . . . Fine, let me see how clever you are! By the Prophet, I'll make it worth your while."

She went slowly to the door, taking her time. Mabruk watched her encouragingly and said, "That's the way. Shake a leg."

Zanuba finally made it out of the room, leaving Mabruk breathing heavily. Looking in the direction she had gone he

said, "God willing, you'll be stung. My Lord, isn't all this forbidden?" He looked down cautiously from the window to admire this handsome pair of lovers. He felt the way a man does
when he sees two beautiful pigeons or sparrows, male and female, cooing to each other. Perhaps it's a feeling for the beautiful, a feeling for harmony.

It was no doubt this feeling that made Mabruk say, while
looking at them as the lovely moonlight spread its wings over
them, "By the life of the Prophet, they're good-looking. May
God grant them happiness with each other."

Then he left the room carrying the garbage pail. He walked
on tiptoe till he reached the window of the lavatory, which
overlooked a small alley behind the building. He threw the
scraps out there. Then he tranquilly went to bed on his table,
saying to himself, "The fellow would have been blinded when
he saw, all kidding aside, horse-faced Zanuba, who does not
even do much for me. The poor fellow."

In this way, the rain on Mustafa ended, although he kept the
umbrella spread anxiously over his head. How could he know
there was nothing to fear from now on? Saniya observed his
anxiety and said to him in a serious tone that disturbed and
annoyed him, "The best thing is for you to move out."

He confined himself to giving her a look of grief, anger, and
rebuke. She pretended not to notice and said mischievously,
"Unless your rent is cheap."

Mustafa rebelled and retorted, "Rent?"

Smiling, she said calmly and cunningly, "Fine, don't get angry.
Forget about the rent . . . so long as it's close to your work."

Mustafa did not reply. He bowed his head a little. Then he
looked up and said, "To the contrary!"

Affecting surprise, she asked, "Far from your work?"

Mustafa replied immediately, "Very, very, very."

Saniya inquired at once, "Why do you live far from your work?"

Mustafa replied without hesitation and in a kind of protest,
"Do you want me to live in Al-Mahalla? Impossible!"

"Al-Mahalla?"

"Yes, Al-Mahalla! Al-Mahalla al-Kubra!"

"Your work is in Al-Mahalla al-Kubra, and you live here? What's your profession?"

"My profession? . . . My profession?"

"If you're ashamed to say, never mind."

"My father owned the Raji Textiles firm in Al-Mahalla al-Kubra."

"And you?"

"I?"

"You're a bon vivant who sits at Shahhata's coffeehouse?"

She said this mischievously and with a pretense of harshness. She was hiding her mouth with her wide silk sleeve to conceal her smile. Surprised, Mustafa was silent for a time. He looked at her, at the black eyes visible above her sleeve, and thought at first she was making fun of him.

His blood boiled. He burst out telling her his whole life story, truthfully and sincerely. He informed her of his desire to liquidate the business or sell it to the foreigner Cassoli and his plan to obtain employment in a government agency so he could remain in Cairo. He had not stepped forward to ask for her hand from her family until now because he had not yet carried out his idea. When he got the job and settled in Cairo, the first thing he would do would be to search for another dwelling that would be appropriate, in a modern district. Then he would send the wife of his maternal uncle, who was a cotton merchant, to ask for Saniya's hand from her mother.

Saniya listened to his long speech. Most of it she already knew. She had previously deduced it but wanted to hear from his own mouth the facts of his case. She had plotted to draw him out this way.

When he finished speaking and fell into downcast silence, Saniya hid her head in her arms. She emptied herself of everything including her laughter and delight before she raised her head. Pretending to frown angrily, she said, "From what I've understood now, you're an idle heir like the ones we read about in books."

He turned toward her, offended. Saniya drew back a little from her window and said in a tone of anger and scorn, "You, sir, are seeking a career as a bureaucrat. On top of that you were wanting to ask for my hand?"

Mustafa trembled. He looked at her sullen face and her lips, on which derision was sketched. He felt he understood nothing and that Saniya had changed in a frightening way in a moment. He wanted to speak, to clarify, or to plead and beseech. But she didn't give him time. She grasped the two shutters of her window and declared, "I thought you were better than that!" She said no more and closed the window in his face.

Everything went black before Mustafa's eyes.

CHAPTER 23

The following night when Mustafa went out on his balcony to wait for Saniya, he was in the most intense state of anxiety. He was afraid she was serious about what she had done the evening before and that he would never see her again. Hours passed as he trained his eyes on her closed window with something like supplication. Whenever another portion of the night passed, he shook with despair and fervently beseeched God to grant him a glimpse of her tonight if only for a single minute, because he couldn't bear to be parted from her and because for her to be absent tonight after what happened the night before would have frightening implications.

So let her come out tonight to reassure him. Then she could disappear again if she wished. He was determined to purchase from her a moment of this evening at any price.

None of these pleadings, which did not escape the confines of his troubled breast, were to any avail. No one paid them any attention, not even the still night, which enveloped him and heard them, and most of it passed while he waited hopefully.

Three nights, which Mustafa considered three years, elapsed in this manner. What inferno was he in now? He had been in paradise without knowing it and had quit it, plummeting not just to earth but straight to hell.

How had he sinned? What forbidden tree was it? How had he rebelled against her so she should drive him out and expel him from the bliss he enjoyed? She had deprived him of her light, which had shone from the window.

Mustafa began to review all her last words. Perhaps he could figure out why she was angry. From the hour of her disappearance he had thought of nothing but his devastating desolation without her.

Did she scorn him because he was an idle heir? But he had told her he was looking for a career as a bureaucrat. Did she disdain him because he had left his place of business and work to come live in Cairo? He remembered she had said to him, "You're a bon vivant who sits at Shahhata's coffeehouse." He did not know exactly what she meant, but a hidden feeling called out in him that he truly was an idle heir and actually deserved her scorn. A person like him had a frightening job before him. His father had begun it and he ought to continue it, if he was to be anything other than a lazy, idle, ambitionless heir. For the first time he felt contempt for himself. Suddenly force and determination flowed through him. His eyes lit up, and a curtain of clouds seemed to have drifted away from his vision. He saw the facts clearly. He told himself, *I'm a fool. It's true! A job as a bureaucrat brings in ten pounds . . . whereas from the firm, if I look after it, I'll earn a monthly income of at least one hundred pounds.*

Then he remembered her saying, "You, sir, are seeking a career as a bureaucrat? On top of that you wanted to ask for my hand?"

Did she disdain him because he was looking for a demeaning career when he had work that was more important and useful? Yes, he understood now. Didn't she have every right to disdain him and accuse him of being a fool or at least of lacking in manliness and vigor? "I thought you were better than that" was the last thing she had told him.

At this Mustafa rose. Some force seemed to propel him. He shouted to his servant to pack his suitcase. Thoughts, plans, and projects crowded together in his head. He felt that forces within him had been revealed to him.

An idea flashed through his mind: Was her anger at him a deliberate ploy to stir him up and goad his dying energy? Who could say? She was extremely bright. He felt a terrific desire to see her. In any case he would not be able to quit that place without telling her what he had decided. He was ready to do amazing and impossible feats for her sake. He also had to learn something about their future from her, just as she had learned about his past and present. He would not shrink from living in Al-Mahalla al-Kubra, even in remotest Upper Egypt, if she was with him.

But how was he to see her?

All of a sudden it came to Mustafa that her closed window could not remain closed all night and all day. She would no doubt open it early in the morning when she got out of bed in order to let air and light into her room. Why not watch for her early in the morning?

Then he reflected further, and another idea came to him. It was a hot night. She could not spend the whole night in her room without fresh air. She would no doubt make a special point to close her window only during the hours they used to meet. Then after the first part of the night she would get up and open it. From all these deliberations Mustafa reached a conclusion. He would stay up the whole night to watch her window from the balcony. He now had enough willpower to do much more than that.

Night came, and the time for their rendezvous passed. Mustafa got out a thick coat to wrap himself in and a scarf to put around his neck. The night was still warm but would turn chilly by dawn. As an extra precaution, he brought his umbrella, which he had never abandoned since the day of the cabbage leaves and colocasia peels. He moved a large chair to the balcony and sat with his legs tucked up and the umbrella spread over his head to begin his watch.

If Mustafa had only known, he had nothing to fear from Zanuba's side. It had not taken her long to notice Saniya's absence. She was the first person to enjoy Mustafa's distress at this absence. Zanuba, however, attributed the secret of this split between the lovers to Mabruk and his personal cleverness. From that day on she had a heightened appreciation of his abilities. Wasn't he the one who told her, "Go sleep. By your life, this will be their last night together"?

He had promised her and fulfilled this promise. That actually had been their last night together. Zanuba questioned Mabruk in amazement about what he had done to achieve this dazzling result. "By the life of your father, Mabruk, just tell me what you did."

But Mabruk was even more greatly and intensely astonished than she was. "What did I do? Who, me?" He was forced to conceal his own astonishment, though, asking himself in anxiety and confusion, *What should I tell her? That, all kidding aside, I threw the pail out the window of the john?*

He remembered his feeling for these two lovers. He was surprised at what had happened to them and began to ask himself morosely what could have caused the rift between them, as though the matter concerned him.

Finally he looked at Zanuba out of the corner of his eye and said to himself, *It's all because of the evil eye. She envied them.*

Zanuba did not let up on him, attacking again. "But what did you do, Mabruk, after I left you? Won't you tell me and relieve my heart?"

Mabruk turned toward her. He thought for a moment to invent something. In the end he asked, "Shall I tell you the truth or its cousin?"

"No, the truth!"

"The truth: I kept taking either a colocasia peel or a cabbage leaf, and after reciting, all kidding aside, a number of yasin over it, I threw that between them."

She smiled and told him with admiration and enthusiasm, "My God, sight and strength to you always, Mabruk. You're a regular elder statesman, sharp and in the know. You're a comfort to me."

At that moment Saniya was at her mother's side, speaking to her and joking with her. She was pretending not to be concerned about anything, but in fact she wanted to set her mother talking on a topic that interested her.

Saniya took her mother's hand and asked her, "Do you love me, nina?" The mother raised her head to look at her daughter and said, "Does anyone hate her children?"

Saniya said mischievously, "That's why, Mother, when someone wanted to marry me last year you told his family: 'We don't have any girls who will travel and live far away.'"

The mother said, "That's well known, daughter. Do I have

anyone to rely on other than you? I want the happiness of having you near me."

Saniya said with a meaningful tone, "Is that true, Mother? You're still traditional!" She was silent for a moment. Then suddenly she asked gently, "Did you go with Papa to the Sudan?"

The mother answered, "Daughter, your father went there before he married me."

Saniya persisted. "Suppose he had gone after he married you. Would you have accompanied him to the Sudan?"

The mother answered her immediately, "What an awful idea! What woman wouldn't follow her husband? Where he goes, she goes."

Saniya asked mischievously, "Would your mother have allowed you to go?"

Her mother answered, "My mother? My mother died when I was young."

"Suppose she had been living."

The mother replied, "God rest her soul. She was a dignified and intelligent woman."

"Just like you. . . . Isn't that so?"

The girl was silent for a moment. Then she gracefully picked up the discussion. She proceeded with it from stage to stage until she was able to show her mother, indirectly, that she would be wrong to retain the condition for marriage that her daughter should remain in Cairo near her. She was only stipulating that because she wanted to hold on to her daughter, not for any sound reason. A mother shouldn't be selfish or egotistical when it was a question of her daughter's future and happiness. It was necessary for a woman to follow her husband wherever he settled—just as her mother herself had said a moment before—and to accompany him to the community where his interests and projects called him.

Saniya wasn't an old-fashioned girl. She wanted to take an interest in her husband's work and to encourage him in it. She had gotten a pretty good idea that a man like Mustafa had interests and projects in the countryside, if nothing else the fields and estates he had inherited from his father. For that reason, she didn't hesitate to think about going with him and living with him in the country, if need be.

Saniya opened her window the morning of the following day to find herself faced with a strange and comic sight on Mustafa's balcony—the sight of a man wrapped up like a cabbage in a large overcoat with a thick quilt draped over that. He had put behind his head, which was covered by a scarf, a small pillow propped against the wall. On top of all that was an open umbrella, which came down over his head and hid part of his face. He was asleep and snoring.

Saniya knew exactly who it was and laughed wholeheartedly. It was Mustafa, and all signs pointed to his having spent the night on the balcony in this fashion. Poor dear! He had no doubt stayed up all night waiting for her, but given the early morning hour and the dawn breezes to brush his eyelids, he had gone to sleep and started snoring, in spite of himself.

Saniya hesitated a little. Should she wake him or leave him? Her love of sport won out in her. She left the window open and hid behind the curtains to see how he would react. Day broke and the sun caught Mustafa's face. He opened his eyes. At once he remembered he had come to await the opening of the window. He turned toward it with the speed of lightning. There it was, open, with no one at it. He struck his head with his hand in despair and tugged at his hair in anger. He was saying, "She came, she opened, and she left—while I slept like an ass."

Saniya heard this from her hiding place and laughed merrily to herself. She considered showing herself to him but saw him collect all his effects, his clothes and umbrella, and leave the balcony in despair. She decided to keep still and see what he would do after that. She would observe him from a short distance while staying hidden.

Mustafa realized that accursed sleep must surely overcome him if he tried to stay up all night. Sleep's onslaught would be most intense at dawn. So what should he do about it? He thought a little and finally devised a plan.

The next evening, Mustafa went out to the balcony with his

customary props—his clothes, pillows, and umbrella—like the previous night, when he had fallen asleep, but also brought an alarm clock, which he set for the hour he wanted to awaken, should sleep overcome him. He squatted on the large chair after he had wrapped himself as usual and opened the umbrella. He placed the alarm clock on the balcony's low railing before him, swearing that the opportunity would not escape him again.

Saniya watched all of this from inside her window. The alarm clock standing on the balcony wall made her laugh. She wished she could be patient and wait till morning to watch it go off. What would passersby in the street at dawn say when they heard the clock's alarm sound over their heads and saw that effendi sleeping there with his gear and umbrella, looking so strange on the balcony?

But she remembered how Mustafa had slept the night before and the chill air to which he was exposed at dawn for her sake. She didn't want to make him spend another night on the balcony just so she could enjoy an amusing spectacle.

When it was almost midnight she opened the window, intentionally making some noise. Mustafa sprang to his feet like a sleeping sentry surprised by his duty officer. As soon as Mustafa caught sight of her and saw that it was Saniya who had opened the window, she and not her ghost, and that his despair over not seeing her was a nightmare that had vanished, his countenance shone with a rare gleam of hope and joy. He rushed toward her impetuously and collided with the railing. He had almost forgotten there was the barrier of empty space separating them.

Saniya, however, kept her feelings in check and pretended to be serious. She asked, "Haven't you left for Al-Mahalla yet?"

Mustafa exclaimed in surprise, "Al-Mahalla?"

"Right, Al-Mahalla!"

Mustafa replied in a voice filled with emotion, "Ask me if I have moved from this balcony since that night."

Saniya concealed a smile and said in an angry and threatening tone, "You mean you want me to close the window again?"

He implored her, "The next time I'll end up in the hospital."

Lightening her tone a little, she asked, "Wouldn't it be better if you ended up in Al-Mahalla? Aren't you concerned about your business, Mustafa?"

The youth's heart pounded intensely at this last sentence. He raised his head after a moment and gave her a long look. Then he declared with decisive determination, "Saniya!" only to fall silent. He spoke again suddenly: "I'm leaving for Al-Mahalla tomorrow."

"Leaving?" she echoed happily.

He replied immediately, "But on one condition." He stopped. Then he broke out, "I'm going to send my uncle's wife on the first train."

Saniya hung her head and blushed.

CHAPTER 24

Events bore out the French archaeologist's prediction: "A nation that at the dawn of humanity brought forth the miracle of the pyramids will be able to bring forth another miracle . . . or many. They claim this nation has been dead for centuries, but they haven't seen its mighty heart reaching toward the sky from the sands of Giza. Egypt has created her heart with her own hands in order to live eternally." Perhaps this archaeologist who lived in the past saw the future of Egypt more clearly than anyone else.

In the month of March, at the beginning of spring, the season of creation, resurrection, and life, the trees turned green with new leaves, and their branches were fertilized and bore fruit.

Egypt too, in the same manner, conceived and bore in her belly an awesome child. The Egypt that had slept for centuries rose to her feet in a single day. She had been waiting, as the Frenchman said, waiting for her beloved son, the symbol of her buried sorrows and hopes, to be born anew, and this beloved was born again from the loins of the peasant.

On the morning of the memorable day, Muhsin was with his classmates when a pupil rushed in, breathless. On his way, whenever he met a cluster of people, he said a few quick words in a grave tone and the faces of the listeners fell. Eventually the news reached Muhsin's ears. He had just begun to think about it and what it meant when he found the whole school around him, whispering, arguing, and questioning each other. The school bell rang, but no one paid any attention to it. It was an amazing moment in the history of the schools. The pupils rallied in this fashion and on all their faces was the same awe-inspiring expression.

They were summoned to lessons but did not respond. It seemed that the day of resurrection had dawned.

Everyone was talking about a man Muhsin had never heard of before, but he sensed in a moment that he would sacrifice his life for this man. His enthusiasm reached the point that he was shouting at his fellow pupils, "Leave the school! Go meet your comrades, the students at the other schools. The matter is too important for us to think about anything else now." His comrades must have felt the same way, for they were all hastening toward the school gate. It was only a matter of minutes before they were all marching down the street. Muhsin thought about meeting up with the engineering school to join with Abduh, whose school was nearby. But they had not gone very far when they saw a crowd of students coming toward them. They discovered that these were the engineering students, who had also come out. Muhsin to his amazement saw his uncle Abduh at the head of them. He was waving his arms and shouting. His face was flushed and his brows knit. There was a ring to his voice that indicated a tremendous nervous excitement. The two schools closed ranks and all proceeded on to meet the other schools. Muhsin went to Abduh and put his arm in his. They marched on together, shouting slogans. Amid the commotion and the thunder of voices, Abduh asked Muhsin, "How did you come out?"

Muhsin replied with the utmost simplicity, "The same way you did."

That question and answer must have been exchanged repeatedly between all those students from all the schools and between all classes of folks. Each group and band thought that it had initiated the uprising in response to a flaming new emotion. No one understood that this emotion had flared up in all their hearts at a single moment, because all of them were sons of Egypt, with a single heart.

By sunset that day Egypt had become a fiery mass. Fourteen million people were thinking of only one thing: the man who expressed their feelings, who arose to demand their rights to freedom and life. He had been arrested, imprisoned, and banished to an island in the middle of the seas.

Osiris, who had brought reconciliation to the land of Egypt, giving it life and light, was also arrested, imprisoned in a box, and banished, in scattered pieces, to the depths of the waters.

Cairo was turned head over heels. Stores, coffee shops, and residences were closed. Lines of communication were disrupted, and demonstrations were widespread. The same turmoil arose in all the regions and throughout the countryside. The fellahin were even more vigorous than the city dwellers in their protests and anger. They cut rail lines to prevent military trains from arriving and set fire to police stations.

Muhsin returned home and found President Hanafi telling Zanuba what had happened. He was explaining to her the causes and reasons. He was rubbing his knees, which were tired and exhausted. He had also walked in numerous demonstrations throughout the day. Salim returned soon as well. He had joined other groups. Everyone began to talk about what he had seen and heard and to predict what would happen. They repeated rumors, which become plentiful in such circumstances. Mabruk arrived. He too said that he had participated in a large demonstration in Al-Sayyida Square. He had been accompanied by the butcher and his assistant, the baker, and the orange vendor. They had smashed and destroyed the gas lamps and the hedges, after arming themselves with stones, heavy sticks, clubs, and knives. He related that trenches had been dug there. With the others, he had dug a trench two meters deep and three across!

This became the household topic of conversation. Most likely the same conversation was going on in all other households. Abduh appeared and demanded supper soon, because he was going that night to the Azhar district, where a big meeting was to be held in the mosque. People would be discussing the present situation.

All of them except President Hanafi, who was tired and wanted to sleep, agreed with Abduh and wanted to accompany him.

By the time of the meeting, the situation was becoming critical. Al-Azhar was sealed off. The demonstrators had erected barricades behind which they fortified themselves. This district and the one called Tulun became arenas for bloody battles. It was said that many Egyptians had bared their chests to the machine guns with astonishing heroism. It was said that a Sudanese Egyptian had daringly advanced on a machine gun aimed toward him. He had snatched it and begun to brandish it like a club against his enemies.

Abduh and his comrades did not retreat. Instead they maneuvered until they penetrated the blockade by passing through narrow and little-known alleys; they attended the meeting.

A person looking at Cairo and its streets during that time would have seen a strange scene. In the midst of the demonstrations and chants fluttered Egyptian flags that showed the crescent moon cradling the cross. Egypt had perceived in a moment that the crescent and the cross were two arms of a single body with one heart: Egypt!

The situation became increasingly unsettled. Amazingly Abduh, Muhsin, and Salim rushed and plunged into the revolution with abandon. Perhaps Zanuba was the only person who noticed this. She thought she understood the secret a little. Those three, who not long before had been as still and silent as the managers of a bank that had failed, who had been choked by despair and depression as though their souls were prisons from which they could not escape—these three had exploded with the revolution when it did. They were back and forth, all wrapped up in it and in events that renewed and stirred their senses. Their gloom and melancholy had departed and been replaced by concern, struggle, and zeal. Perhaps young Muhsin was the one who was most patently influenced by that historic event. All the bitterness of unrequited love had been transformed in his heart into fervent nationalist feelings. All his desire to sacrifice for the sake of his personal beloved had changed to a desire for daring sacrifice for the sake of his nation's Beloved. This was what happened to Abduh and Salim as well, to a lesser extent.

Amazing! Was it necessary to have this revolution to purge these victims of their emotions? Moreover, something else— was this the indispensable miracle needed so Muhsin would not fail his exam this year? In fact, the consensus of his teachers was that there was no hope for Muhsin. He himself had not been thinking about the examination or the competency diploma this year. But now the revolution had closed the schools and canceled the examinations. So he had been spared the stigma of failure by a miracle. Muhsin, however, did not attach much importance to this matter. He did not look at the revolution with the eye of self-interest. His powerful emotions had been transformed into a general patriotism that dominated his whole being and made him oblivious to everything else, even his personal safety in these dangerous circumstances.

As soon as Mustafa journeyed to Al-Mahalla al-Kubra, he carried out his promise and sent his aunt, escorted by his servant, to spend a day in Cairo and visit the residence of Dr. Hilmi. She was to ask for Saniya's hand from her mother.

The agreement was reached in a preliminary way. The aunt returned to Al-Mahalla to announce the good news to the fiancé and to inform him of what she had done and what he needed to do. She had liked Saniya and began to describe her charms to Mustafa. Mustafa listened with joy and delight. She informed him also that it was Saniya who had smoothed things out. Without her, nothing would have been concluded with such speed. In fact, as soon as Mustafa's aunt left, Saniya sighed with happy pleasure. She was counting the days on her fingers. She waited expectantly for Mustafa to appear from one day to the next so they could conclude the matter. But alas! The day after the aunt's trip came that fateful day, and by nightfall the rail line between Tanta and Al-Mahalla al-Kubra had been cut. Mustafa was unable to travel to Cairo. Indeed he wasn't even able to write to Saniya to reassure her. No one could describe Mustafa's anxiety and distress. How could it be that at a time when he was able to see her publicly and to correspond openly with her as much as he wished, the link between them should be severed? But Saniya's sorrow was even greater and

her anxiety and grief more terrifying. Muhsin's image came to
her mind suddenly. In the depths of her soul she heard a cry
asking her if this obstacle wasn't her punishment for humiliating poor Muhsin that way.

No one knew for sure whether the three, Abduh, Muhsin, and
Salim, had joined a secret society, or what. The room on the
roof had become a depository for huge bundles of revolution-
ary broadsides. Every evening a cart drawn by a donkey
stopped at the door of 35 Salama Street. It brought a large
wooden box that the driver would carry up, with the assistance of Mabruk and the supervision of Abduh, to the room
on the roof. After it was emptied of its bundles, it was returned
to the cart. No one knew exactly where this cart came from or
where the bundles went. The three would have died rather
than reveal this secret.

One day a rumor went through town that people were being
searched. Everyone on the streets and in the alleys and every
patron of a coffeehouse or bar would be subject to search at
any time. Any person found to have a weapon or suspect papers in his pocket would be taken to prison at once. Unfortunately the rumor came too late. At that hour Muhsin and
Abduh were in a coffee shop called the Great Hookah. Their
pockets were stuffed with pamphlets that they were distribut-
ing right and left. Before they knew it, two English officers had
stormed the place, brandishing pistols. They were backed up
by armed Egyptian soldiers. Abduh and Muhsin were searched.
The pamphlets were pulled from their pockets. Their residence
was searched after that. The room on the roof with its
heaped-up bundles was discovered. This of course sufficed for
them to arrest the entire household. That was the least that
was done in such circumstances. Even President Hanafi and
Servant Mabruk were arrested. Hanafi was taken from his
bed. He was rubbing his eyes and swearing that he knew nothing. In fact, Hanafi was unjustly accused, because he did not
know what was in the room on the roof. But he was always
being falsely accused, and that fact did not at all spare him

from bearing his share of the responsibility. Only Zanuba was exonerated. All the evidence indicated she was innocent. She didn't know how to read or write and had no knowledge of anything. So they left her alone in the house—just her. The others were transported to the Citadel prison. Mabruk kept poking Captain Salim all along the way. He whispered angrily to him, "This is all your fault, Mr. Salim. You wouldn't stop searching, until, in brief, they searched us, as the saying goes."

He didn't finish because the soldiers guarding them stopped him from chattering on by waving their rifles at him. He put his hand over his mouth. Trembling, he said, "Military Excellency, there's no need for rifles. I've silenced my tongue for good. Life shouldn't be squandered."

CHAPTER 25

The five were crammed into a single cell at the prison. They slept all night in their exhaustion. When day came, Mabruk got up before the others. He began to look around the place and check out all the angles. He found high up in a corner a window like a projecting tower and figured out how to hoist himself up there. He looked out between the bars and saw a courtyard. He gazed around it. There, in the center, a trapeze had been erected, with a set of wooden parallel bars beside it. Perhaps they had been placed there so the officers and soldiers could train at gymnastics. But Mabruk didn't know that. As soon as he saw these things, he dropped down and shouted, "They've put up the gallows!"

The honorary president Hanafi opened his eyes at once on hearing that. He shook himself in alarm. Then he sprang to his feet and exclaimed, "The gallows! It's got to be the gallows! They're going to hang us! No. That talk doesn't make sense!"

He looked at Abduh, Muhsin, and Salim, who were sleeping or pretending to sleep in complete tranquility. He shook them and shouted, "Get up! Get up, boys! We're in big trouble without even knowing it."

No one answered him. Enraged, he said, "You mean sleep is sweet at a time like this?"

He heard nothing but the echo of his voice from the asphalt. So he said, as though speaking to himself and bemoaning his luck, "Oh . . . you can tell what a day's going to be like from its dawn. By God, you hooligans, it's turned out that you've dragged me down with you, you've brought me to the gallows." Then he was silent for a little. It seemed that the word *gallows* when he said it made him realize that the situation might be serious and nothing to joke about. He trembled. "No. This isn't a laughing matter."

He was silent for a time, brooding with terror about what awaited them. Suddenly, as though he couldn't bear even thinking about it, he jumped at his sleeping comrades and began pleading in a frightened voice, "Find us a way, brethren! Do me a favor! God reward you! Get up, Salim. You're a captain and understand this topic. Don't you have a pal or fellow officer here, a good man who will find a way out for us? But no, then you'd really be discharged. You'd really be in the mud! So what can we do, Lord? Abduh! Abduh, get up. Devise some plan for us, some stratagem to get us out. Still sleeping! Shame on you. So that's how it is! You're no good at anything except fooling around."

He gave up on them and turned to Mabruk, whose head was lowered while he too thought of the afterlife. His body language suggested he was saying to himself, *Your death has arrived, you prayer skipper.*

President Hanafi quickly interrupted him and asked urgently, "Are you certain, Mabruk, it's really a gallows?"

The servant raised his head sorrowfully and replied, "Oh . . . a real gallows . . . what else?"

As though to himself, Hanafi said, "Here's a disaster for sure! But will they hang us before they hear our case? Even if only before a military tribunal, Muslims? What kind of gallows is it, Mabruk?"

Mabruk said with his head lowered, "A good one!"

President Hanafi fell silent and began to pace back and forth in the cell nervously. He was thinking, reflecting, and arguing with himself. He said from time to time, "It doesn't make sense! It doesn't make sense at all!"

Finally he stopped. He turned to Mabruk and asked him to climb up a second time and describe what he saw outside in detail.

The servant obeyed. He looked again at the tall trapeze that had been erected and then at the low parallel bars beside it. He said, "To put it bluntly, they've erected a large gallows with a small one beside it."

Hanafi asked with some doubt and agitation, feeling that Mabruk was kidding, "What do you mean small and large? A large gallows and a small one. . . . What kind of talk is that? Come down, shaykh, none of this foolishness."

Mabruk cast a final glance at the small parallel bars. Then he said to convince and explain, "By the life of the Prophet's beard, is that so? This small one must be, no offense intended, for Mr. Muhsin."

At that moment laughter reverberated through the cell. The three, who had been asleep or pretending to sleep, sat up on their haunches, each in his cot. They were laughing at what Mabruk had said and at Hanafi's fear. Salim turned to Muhsin and said to him, while laughing, "Hear that? They've set up a kiddie gallows for you, just your size."

The youth replied, smiling, "I thank them in any case, but I would prefer to be hanged with all of you on the big gallows."

President Hanafi snapped back, "Will you swap with me? By God, I'm content with the little one."

The first thing Zanuba did after the folks were arrested was put on her wrap and go to the telegraph office. She sent a message to Muhsin's father in Damanhur about what had happened. The communication links had been repaired, at least the Cairo-Alexandria line, and travel the length of this line was possible, but with conditions. Tickets were issued on a personal basis by the government. The news descended on Muhsin's father and mother like a thunderbolt. His mother began to bewail her calamity, which had begun the day she agreed to send him to Cairo with his uncles.

Yes, there was no secondary school in Damanhur, but she ought to have thought of some other way, instead of trusting his uncles. It was all his father's fault. He had a good opinion of his brothers in Cairo and imagined they would take care of his son. She began striking her face, giving her husband and his brothers at least their fair share of blame and censure. She was yelling, "Bring me my son! Bring me my son!"

Muhsin's father did not wait till morning. Instead he packed his suitcase and took the first train he could get to Cairo. There he went like a madman, meeting influential contacts, asking and imploring to no avail. Finally it occurred to him to go to the English irrigation inspector he knew. Perhaps he would assist him with the higher authorities. The idea met with success. The man received him in a way that inspired hope. He took a personal interest in the matter, because the inspector remembered seeing young Muhsin the day of the banquet at the farm. He had been impressed by him and the ease with which he spoke English. But after some inquiries it became clear to him that it was a delicate question, because it was in the hands of the military authorities. For that reason it could not be resolved in one stroke. Muhsin's father desperately entreated him to intervene, if only to release Muhsin and not the others, who could wait till things quieted down. The inspector agreed to look into it.

The father then got permission to visit the folks at the Citadel prison. When he saw them, and Muhsin among them, he was astonished at their calm and cheerful appearance. After he had questioned them about everything that had happened, when the visit was coming to a close, he took Muhsin aside and told him to be brave and patient for just a day or two, since efforts were being made now to get him released, by himself. As soon as the young boy heard this he backed away. His face was flushed with anger and rage. He shouted, "Do you think I would accept to be released and leave my uncles here?"

The father was bewildered and anxiously turned to the others in confusion. He informed them it was impossible to free them now and that all he might be able to arrange was possibly to get Muhsin out alone. He asked their help in convincing the young boy, since his age and health weren't suitable for prison life. They all gathered around Muhsin, asking him to allow himself to be freed, with warm and sincere voices. He should obey and consent to leave, because he was young and not their age . . . and . . . and . . .

But Muhsin at times, and especially with regard to this issue, could be very stubborn. The visit ended that way. The father left; an idea that had just occurred to him made him smile. When the order to release Muhsin came down, whether or not he agreed would not matter, for it would be carried out by military force.

Following that visit, Muhsin became depressed. He expected the door to open at any moment and to be separated by force from his companions. He waited anxiously in this manner and at times with secret embarrassment when he remembered he would be released as a result of his father's efforts, while his uncles and Mabruk were left with no one to assist them. What pleasure would there be to life by himself in Damanhur, or in any other place, when he had felt the joy of sharing with his colleagues, the folks, in all variety of circumstances and times?

Pain, no matter how great, diminished when they all shared it. Bearing it seemed easy when they bore it together. Indeed it was transformed at times into solace that delightfully refreshed them. What did his father and mother want for him except isolation and egotism? From his inner depths he prayed secretly to God that his father's efforts would fail.

God apparently answered this fervent prayer. The English investigator returned sad and regretful, because after making a genuine effort, he had only been able to accomplish one thing for now. The young prisoner, or he and those with him, would be transferred to the prison hospital, where treatment was milder and living conditions were better.

He told the distraught father, "Calm down. In the prison hospital it will be just as though they were in a hotel or at home. This is the best place for them to pass the time in comfort, far from the strife in the city, until the day comes when they can be released. Naturally the question is sensitive now since the situation in the country is still critical. But after a few more days, who knows? You can be sure they'll be the first to be released, just as soon as the situation is stabilized. They are only detained temporarily for a set period of time. I won't abandon them. You can be sure of that. You can return to your community with your mind at rest, satisfied that you can depend on me."

Muhsin's father quieted down a little in response to the inspector's noble sentiments. Then he said hesitantly, "You mean I should go home? What will I tell his mother?"

The inspector answered him decisively in a confident and assured tone, "Go! I'm here!"

The folks were transferred to the hospital. The same day, Muhsin's father, accompanied by the inspector, went to visit Muhsin and his comrades in their new abode. The father began to stare around him at how beautifully everything was arranged. The beds were clean and in a row. There was a garden where anyone who wanted could go for a stroll—that is, anyone convalescent. There was a library, which contained a handsome array of books, as well as waiting and visiting rooms with leather chairs and couches.

He felt relieved. The inspector noticed and put his hand lightly on his shoulder. He said, "It seems to me that we can feel more at ease about their being here than at home. Here at least they are far removed from the disturbances and danger. The hospital is responsible for them."

Hamid Bey, Muhsin's father, was totally reassured and decided to return to Damanhur in order to calm his anxious wife and to let her know that Muhsin was surrounded by security, comfort, and peace. After he thanked the English inspector for his gallantry, he left him to get his bag. He would take Zanuba with him to Damanhur, since there was no reason for her to stay on alone amid the turmoil of Cairo.

Zanuba wrapped up the parcels containing her possessions but didn't want to travel before seeing her brothers and Muhsin in the hospital. Hamid Bey consented and the next morning accompanied her there. They found them in the ward, where they slept with their five beds lined up one beside the other. She stopped for a moment in surprise at this sight. They looked the same, just as though they were in their communal bedroom in the house on Salama Street!

Her eyes fell on Mabruk, who was stretched out on the bed next to Hanafi's. He was lolling under his covers in new, spotlessly clean white sheets. Zanuba couldn't keep herself from exclaiming, "Mabruk, you've got it made now! You waited patiently and struck it rich. Finally you're sleeping in a real live bed."

Mabruk looked at her without rising from his prone position. He said with a smile, "You see?"

Then he rose halfway in bed, leaning on his elbow, and said, "I'm going to tell you something. My body's gotten used to sleeping on beds, and that's that. By your honor and that of my mother, I will never sleep on a wooden table again. You all, all kidding aside, made a fool of me and had me thinking it was a bed."

Meanwhile Hamid Bey, Muhsin's father, was in the corridor outside, where he stopped a physician he knew and began to converse with him. He had already directed Zanuba to the ward where her brothers were so she could go straight to them and not wait for him.

After talking with Mabruk, Zanuba began to converse with the others. She learned from speaking with President Hanafi that he was happy with the hospital and especially with sleeping in this ward. The quiet was total and all-encompassing. The folks did not dare make a row or raise a ruckus, because they were subject here to the orders of the head nurse, not to the honorary president.

Salim asked about goings-on in the district and especially for news of effects of the recent events on its inhabitants or their neighbors.

Zanuba understood what he was getting at and smiled pallidly. With a sigh, she said in an insidious tone, "May you have such a happy wedding! The betrothal has taken place for sure, and the festivities will come soon."

He kept silent and did not reply. Muhsin turned over on his left side to look toward Abduh's bed and exchange some pleasantry with him in order to conceal the sorrow of his heart. Abduh for his part responded to this pleasantry with feigned attention. The bitterness in his eyes was mixed with indignation, even anger. He did not want to remember.

Yes, the marriage contract of Mustafa Raji and Saniya Hilmi became a reality. Mustafa had come to Cairo the day that communications were reopened with Cairo, a day he had been awaiting impatiently. He met with Saniya's father, Dr. Ahmad Hilmi, and they agreed to conduct the wedding the day the situation calmed down, the day the mighty exile returned to an unsettled Egypt.

Thus, the day Muhsin and his comrades were released from

the prison hospital coincided with the day of Saniya's wedding to Mustafa.

By a curious coincidence, the doctor whom Hamid Bey stopped in the corridor and whom he had known since he had a practice in the rural areas around Damanhur al-Buhayra was the same doctor who had made a house call on the folks at Salama Street when they were all ill with influenza. At that time the physician had been amazed to see them all grouped together in one room, one bed beside the next, as though they were in a military barracks or a hospital ward. This physician had not been able to keep from shouting at them, "No . . . this isn't a house. It's a hospital!"

He had smiled with surprise to see they had Mabruk, the servant, with them on the dining table, which by night became a bed. He had asked himself in amazement what induced them to squeeze together this way into a single room: *Do you suppose they're peasants who grew up in the country and became accustomed to living together, along with their livestock, in one room?*

Muhsin's father, Hamid Bey, during his conversation with the doctor, asked why he was there and learned he was now a doctor in the hospital. He seized the opportunity to ask him to look out for his son and brothers.

The doctor entered the ward and cast his eyes on the folks, who were lying down, one next to the other. He looked at their expressions and faces and remembered them. He remembered the ward in their home. He stood there in astonishment for a moment. Then he shouted good-humoredly, "Is it you? And here again too, each beside the other; each next to his brother!"

Paris, Gambetta, 1927

Glossary

Abbas Bridge: The Roda-to-Giza bridge, built in AD 1907 for Khedive Abbas II.

Abduh al-Hamuli: Egyptian singer and composer, lived ca. AD 1845–1901.

abla: Older sister; a respectful way for a young person to address an older woman.

battaw: Rustic corn or sorghum bread.

Champollion, Jean-François (1790–1832): French archaeologist and Egyptologist who deciphered the Rosetta stone.

cottage cheese (gibna arish): Fat-free salted white cheese.

diwan: A poet's collected works.

farik: Green wheat that is roasted, cracked, and stewed.

Fatima: Daughter of the Prophet Muhammad.

Feast of the Sacrifice, Great Feast, Eid al-Adha, Id al-Adha, Id al-Kabir: Major Islamic holiday that takes place during the month of pilgrimage to Mecca.

fino: French-style white bread.

flu: 1918 flu pandemic, also known as Spanish flu or Spanish fever; worldwide health crisis between June 1918 and December 1920 that killed 50 million to 100 million people.

fuul midammis: Stewed broad beans and often lentils mashed with oil and lemon juice.

fuul nabit: Sprouted broad beans soaked in water before cooking.

ghurayba: Egyptian shortbread.

gibna arish: *See* cottage cheese.

Hanbali: Adjective or noun for one of the most conservative "schools" or traditions of Islamic law and theology.

Hanim: A female title, like Ms., but which appears after the first name.

Hijaz-kar: One of the melodic phrases or tetrachords used for improvisation in Arab music; said to have been popularized in Egypt by Abduh al-Hamuli.

Husayn: Martyred son of Ali and grandson of the Prophet Muhammad.

jilbab: Long tunic or ankle-length shirt.

kantar: An Egyptian unit of measurement that equals 44.928 kilograms.

Al-Khalij Street: Built on a filled-in waterway in Cairo, it was subsequently widened to become Port Said Street.

Khamsin: Springtime dust-laden wind in Egypt.

kofta: Spiced meatballs.

lentils in a cloak ('ads bi gibba matbukh): Brown lentils stewed with onions and garlic.

Mihyar al-Daylami: Abu al-Hasan Mihyar ibn Marzawayh al-Daylami, Buyid era poet, a convert to Islam, d. AD 1037.

minin: Thin rectangular flavored biscuit.

Moret, Alexandre (1868–1938): French Egyptologist.

nina: Respectful way of addressing an older female relative, grandmother, or mother.

Omdurman, Battle of: On September 2, 1898, Anglo-Egyptian forces defeated the Mahdists at Omdurman, killing and wounding thousands of people.

Pure Lady, Mighty Lady: *See* Sayyida Zaynab bint Ali.

riyal: Monetary unit that equals twenty piastres.

Sa'd Zaghlul (1857–1927): Egyptian nationalist leader whose exile was a catalyst for the 1919 revolution.

Sayyida Zaynab bint Ali: A granddaughter of the Prophet Muhammad and patron saint of the section of Cairo where much of the action transpires.

shabshaba spells: A woman's ritual that includes an incantation and rapping the genitals with a slipper.

sister: In Cairo dialect the expression *yakhti* can be a way for a woman to address a woman, an exclamation meaning "How cute," or merely a catchphrase, such as "like" in US teenager slang.

Suq al-Kanto: Flea market.

ta'miya: Falafil bean cakes; in Egypt they are made with dried broad beans.

Throne Verse: Qur'an, al-Baqara [The Cow], 2:255.

Thursday: In Arabic, the fifth day of the week; mentioning it with or without holding out a palm with five fingers outstretched may help ward off the hot, evil rays of envy.

tiza, teeza: Polite way to address an older woman.

Tubah: Fifth month of the Egyptian Coptic calendar, approximately January to early February.

Umda: A village headman or mayor.

Umm Hashim: *See* Sayyida Zaynab bint Ali.

ya-sin: The mysterious opening letters of sura 36 of the Qur'an that give the sura its name.

Ready to find
your next great classic?

Let us help.

Visit prh.com/penguinclassics

PENGUIN
CLASSICS